NO MAGIC MOMENT

SECRETS OF STONE: BOOK FOUR

ANGEL PAYNE & VICTORIA BLUE

NO MAGIC MOMENT

SECRETS OF STONE: BOOK FOUR

ANGEL PAYNE & VICTORIA BLUE

WATERHOUSE PRESS

As always, for the man of my world.

Thomas, you and our girl make it all worth it...and teach me something wondrous every day.

Special thanks to amazing Elisa:

For knowing just what to say, and how to say it with your special love and humor.

I value you so much!

—Angel

For Aunt Mary.

No, it's not Hemingway, but it is from my heart—the exact place where all of my thoughts and memories of you are from, and what can be better than that?

Peace, happiness, and pain-free days from now until eternity—wherever it is your angel wings have taken you. We love you.

—Victoria

CHAPTER ONE

Michael

If any moment proved I was hopelessly in love with Margaux Asher, this was it.

Dirty water dripped down my face—technically, up my face, toward my hair—as I watched a water beetle scurry along the wall of the drain sewer off 5th and G in downtown San Diego. Yeah, the sewer I'd dived down headfirst, in the full suit I'd worn to dinner, still half-buzzed from the martinis I'd enjoyed at said dinner.

Thank fuck for those martinis. In some strange way, they helped with my inverted equilibrium. They sure as hell didn't hurt.

This was about as low as I went.

Literally.

Laughing at my private joke wasn't an option. I settled for grunting. Good compromise between breathing and passing out from the stench. America's Finest City was a different world below the surface.

"What? What is it? Do you see it, Michael? Do you see it?"

In an instant, I forgot about the smell and the wet—and the fact that if Andre's hold on my ankles slipped at all, I'd be reenacting the *Star Wars* trash compactor scene, minus the blasters and the Dianoga. Or so I hoped. But even facing a giant sewer snake would be worth it to banish the dread in my woman's voice.

"Andre," I barked at the burly Jamaican, "don't let go."

"I got you, boss."

Now wasn't the time to tell him I hated that "boss" crap—and the laugh he surely intended as reassuring.

"Michael!"

Margaux's cry was shrill. She'd been in this panic for at least ten minutes now, when our after-dinner walk had gone from relaxing to horrifying in the space of five seconds. Instead of gunshots, our black moment had been delivered in five pings—the sound of a small gold ring falling to the pavement and then disappearing through the hole in the sewer cover.

"Do you see it?" She choked it out this time. Hell. My girl did not like bawling, despite how much she'd softened in the three months since our relationship began. She fought the tears with everything she had. Her conflict echoed down the sewer, shattering my heart and steeling my resolve. Find the damn ring. The jewelry represented a huge chunk of her past, the only part that had meant emotional safety for her. She wasn't strong enough to lose it yet.

I knew it. She knew it. I just prayed Andre knew it too.

"Michael. Talk to me!"

I grimaced. "Not in a position to chat right now, sugar."

"Just tell me if you see it." Her breath caught again. "Please. Please tell me you—" A car horn cut her off, something sporty by the tenor of it. "Hey! The translation of Maserati isn't *license to be an asshole!*"

Andre's grip tremored from the force of his chuckle. I grimaced and then swore. "Not funny, man."

Margaux backed it up with a gritty girl-growl, a sound curling straight to my cock, which apparently didn't care about its current setting. "Drop him, and your testicles are mine."

"Not until you've dealt with other testicles first," I muttered.

"What?" she shouted.

"You mentioned testicles," Andre explained.

"Oh, for—" She snorted. "You two want to focus with your big heads for once?"

Andre snickered again. I wanted to bark at him but was busy smirking myself. God damn it if my princess wasn't more irresistible with a pissy bee under her figurative crown. On top of that, envisioning her in the middle of the street above me, leaning over the manhole in the slinky dress and pumps she'd worn to dinner, still unsure whether to play out her stress with sass or penitence...

Yep, it was official. Even hanging upside down in a sewer, I had a hard-on for the woman.

The sooner I found the damn ring, the—

"Bingo."

"What?" she shouted.

"Bingo," I yelled back, curling fingers around the small gold circle that had, by a pure miracle, caught on a steel peg to my right. Miracle was putting it lightly. The band, not fancy, was sized for a child of nine—the age Margaux had been when she first received it. It never left her pinkie finger now—except, as we'd learned the hard way, on cold nights when her fingers contracted. It had become just as important to me once I knew the story about who had given it to her. I'd never forget the night she'd dug so deeply into her past and all its pain to give me the confession. It had been the start of our journey from friendship to passion...and finally love. The trust she'd handed over to me that night still blew me away at times. It was a gift I'd never take for granted and a responsibility I'd never diminish.

She meant so damn much to me.

More than I could screw up the courage to admit.

But somewhere, somehow, I was going to have to do just that.

She'd put the secrets of her past into my care. It was about damn time I gave the same to her.

I'd start with giving her something more pleasant.

"Dre," I shouted. "Let's roll it up, man."

"Oh, my God," Margaux exclaimed. As soon as I emerged, brandishing the gold band, she screamed, "Oh, my God!"

Before I could remind her I'd just been down a hole dripping with slime and runoff water, she mashed herself against me. As her body and lips molded to mine, the ecstasy of her yelp hummed through me. "I love you, Mr. Pearson," she declared against my mouth.

I chuckled, ordering myself to enjoy the moment—and for the time being, leave my morose thoughts from the sewer in the sewer. "I love you too, sugar."

"No shit!" As she slipped the ring back on, I literally watched her reconnect with that part of herself. Joy flowed from her, but it wasn't the only thing. She was grounded again. Solid.

I didn't know if that recognition was heartening or disconcerting.

She muted the conflict by kissing me once more. *Whoa.* This time, there was tongue—the kind of tongue I loved. Pulling at mine, as if needing my mouth deeper inside hers... usually her fun little way of asking to have other parts inside her too. She emitted a kittenish mewl and waited for me to give back the Captain America version, before dragging away with a lust-heavy gaze.

"The knight who saved me."

I smiled. "The princess who saved me."

"Take me home, stud. This princess aches to reward your bravery."

Andre had already pulled up in the BMW, waiting for us to finish the PDA as he yanked open the door to the back seat. With his other hand, he extended a small silo of baby wipes. "Not saying you smell worse than a baby's batty, but..."

I chuckled at his Jamaican slang. "But you're thinking it."

"Never said that, either." His lips twitched as he kept the hand extended, waiting to take the cloths I scraped from fingers to elbows.

"Thanks, man." I made sure our gazes met. "And not just for the cleanup."

As I expected, the big guy just rolled his eyes. "Not a worry, brother."

When he shut the door and sealed us in, I swept toward Margaux in one lunge, lowering for another kiss. Now that we weren't in the middle of the street, I attacked her with deeper passion and growing need.

"What if I don't want to wait for my reward?"

Her eyes flared at the husk in my tone. As she nudged her head up and bit into my bottom lip, she replied, "You still smell, Sir Knight."

"Exactly how you like me."

"We'll get the car dirty."

"Exactly how you like it."

I watched my edicts curl through her, making her writhe

with renewed arousal. Yeah, I was in love with a woman who reveled in orgasms on silk sheets, beneath gold showerheads, and in marble elevators—but my princess also craved being taken like a peasant, her passion just accepted and enjoyed, as raw and raunchy as she could get it. Getting her to admit that? Another thing entirely—which was why I yanked the decision from her sometimes. Told her exactly how hard she'd take it from me and love it as I did.

"You want me to get you dirty." I hovered my mouth over hers, tempting but not giving, while pushing a hand beneath her dress and bra. We both moaned as the bud inside stiffened. "You want me to put my naughty hands all over you...to make your body as filthy as your mind."

She cupped a hand to the back of my neck. Tried to drag me down for another kiss. I held fast where I was, pinching her nipple at the same time. "Say it, Margaux. Tell me you want it—and exactly how."

Her throat vibrated with a little snarl. She knew the sound drove me to sexual insanity. I resisted the temptation, steeling my jaw.

"Say. It."

I shoved her dress open wider, trailing my hand to her other breast. Her breath snagged as I rolled the erect nipple between my knuckles.

"I...want you," she rasped. "God damn it, I need you, Michael." Her fingernails dug into my neck. "Satisfied?"

A rumble prowled up my throat. "Not yet. And you know why."

She shot her free hand to the front of my slacks but only worked the loop of my belt free before I caught her intention and captured that hand. Slammed it to the cushion beside her head.

Her eyes flared. Her lips parted. Her hips bucked. "Oh, Christ!"

"You're getting warmer."

"Bastard."

"Say it."

"Fine. Fine. I want you to get me dirty. To put your grimy hands all over me. To defile me with your touch...make me hot for your nasty cock."

As I growled approval, I was conscious of another sound blending with it—Andre's low chuckle, fading as he disappeared behind the partition he'd activated. I grinned, knowing he'd return us to the El Cortez the long, long way. Margaux had all but ordered me to move into her condo in the swanky building after I'd terminated my lease in a heartbroken stupor three months ago, thinking I could forget her by accepting a job offer in Atlanta.

Idiot.

As if I'd ever forget this woman.

As if I ever wanted to.

I moved both hands to the front of her dress, opening it more. Let my smile widen as my stare fell to the front clasp on her bra. With a twist, I released it. With a snarl, I watched her breasts fall free.

"Holy fuck, how I love these tits."

She returned my smile, purposely lifting her chest. Little minx. She knew exactly what I'd want to do then. I dipped my head, transfixed by the sight of her gorgeous puckered nipples. I sucked one breast in, teething her flesh but licking her nipple. Margaux sighed, digging her hands into my hair and shooting a thousand points of heat down my spine, into my balls.

I should've known she wouldn't be happy with just that. The woman was like an electron, never satisfied keeping still, even when all but ordered to do so. With my attention focused on her incredible chest, she knew I wouldn't be minding the store inside my pants. Sure enough, before I knew it, she was unzipping my fly and reaching in. With eager surety, she palmed my throbbing dick through my briefs.

"Goddamn."

She blinked up at me, eyes glistening like huge emeralds, teeth sneaking over her lush bottom lip. "Is that a dirtball between your legs, or are you just happy to see me?"

I narrowed my gaze. "You sure you want to play it like that?"

Her smile deepened—as she scraped her nails lightly over my balls. "Maybe I do. I never liked playing in the dirt. The teeter-totter was more my thing. Up, down. Up, down..."

I laughed, though I didn't want to. The action sped up my heart rate, pulsing more blood into the arousal she played with such expertise. Jesus. She knew me so well. Knew exactly where to stroke, to push, to tease. "Why doesn't that surprise me?"

She licked her lips, all feigned innocence once more. "Was I missing out...not diving into the mud with the boys?"

I swallowed heavily. "The mud can be rough."

"Hmmm. I think I can handle rough."

"And brutal."

"Good."

I laughed again, this time on purpose—to distract her. Just as she tried to get a bigger handful of my sex, I dropped my grip to her waist and completely turned her over. With a gasp, she grabbed the top of the seat, her knees hiked on the cushion.

"How do you like the dirt so far, princess?"

The rise and fall of her shoulders gave me an immediate answer. Her breaths came faster as I shoved her skirt up and her panties down, fully exposing her to my gaze. Damn. And I'd thought her breasts were mesmerizing? I couldn't stop caressing the milky globes of her backside, astonished and humbled that this breathtaking body was all mine.

"Ohhhh..." It spilled from her as I slid my fingers between her thighs, encountering the cream that always made me think of nectar from some far-off land. Perhaps another planet. From the start, that was how I'd seen Margaux Asher. Right, wrong, or completely lunatic, she was like a gift in my life from another galaxy—and I wasn't sure I ever wanted to change the perspective.

"My treasure." I rasped it as I palmed her mound, splaying fingers over the cropped curls that shielded her most sensitive flesh. "I need more of this."

"Yes," she whispered. The lights from the road played over her neck and breasts as she arched back for me. "Yes, Michael. Oh, God. Touch me there...please."

I pressed myself over her, inhaling the spicy mix of her favorite perfume. "You mean right...here?" I slid the tender flesh back, releasing her trembling nub, making us both shudder. "You want me to get your little clit dirty? Make it shiver and shake so it opens you up to be fucked by my nasty cock?"

She kneaded the back cushion of the seat, muscles cording in her shoulders. Illicit and rumpled, her dress bunched around her waist, her nudity flashing in and out of shadows as Andre drove us through the night. We sped along the freeway now, the car nearly alive around us, rocking from the force of the acceleration.

"I'm—I'm already open. Damn it, Michael. Give it to me!"

She finished it on a gasp as I leaned back, spreading her cheeks so I could gaze at her pussy, open and wet and perfect. "Look at this cunt," I growled. "Even in the dark, I can see it glistening. So ready for me."

"Yes." She parted her thighs, stretching her lace panties to their limit between her knees. "Ready. Michael. Michael."

I could resist no longer.

"Hang on, princess."

With one push, I breached her entrance.

With the second, I lunged completely in.

She screamed. I groaned.

One long moment, savoring every clench and constriction around me—and the glimpse I surely had of heaven—before I began the steady, hard pace that matched the fast-lane thrum of the car. She didn't want the granny lane tonight. She wanted the rush, the adrenaline...the dirt. It was my supreme pleasure to give her all three.

"Oh, hell," she rasped. "So good. So good."

I couldn't have agreed more. She smelled so good. Felt so good. Fucked so good. I told her so by grabbing her nape with my teeth, digging in just enough to zap down to her clit. As that wet bundle quivered beneath my fingers, I knew it had worked.

"Rub yourself, sugar. Put your fingers right here and make yourself dirtier for me."

She complied without question. Her strokes pushed her folds against my shaft, tightening her body's grip on my erection, dragging a taut moan from the depths of my balls and out of my throat.

"Dear God, woman. I need to fuck you hard."

She abandoned her masturbation in order to grip the cushion with both hands again—bracing for my deeper, harder plunges. "Yes."

"And you need to take it."

"Yes."

I reared back, framing her hips with my hands. Slammed into her with the full force of my lust and need. Rejoiced as she squeezed around me, tighter and then tighter still, finally pulsing with the violence of her release. A string of profanity tumbled out of her, high and ragged and unthinking, filling my cock and stretching my control. Still, I wasn't done with her. No way. I needed more. Needed to drain everything from her, as she'd completely consumed me.

She'd barely come down from that wave when I reached in, massaging her clit all over again.

"Michael. Oh, my God. I can't. Not so fast—"

"You can." I pinched her stiff flesh, tearing a full scream from her. "You will."

"No."

"Yes."

"Ohhhh, fuck!"

"That's it." I ground into her, thrusting as deep as I could, reveling in the crush of her sex around mine. "My darling, dirty girl. Do it for me again, Margaux. Let me feel you come. Now. Now!"

Her whole body clenched. Her head fell back, a soundless shriek spilling from her parted lips. She pumped her hips back into mine, milking me with her orgasm, all but demanding that I follow her over into the ecstasy.

I sure as hell did.

Pressure surged. Exploded. The world careened so hard I almost questioned if Andre had rolled the car. I fell over her, sinking teeth into her shoulder as I emptied my essence into her hot, perfect channel. The shudders of her passion urged me on, dragging more and more come from me, bringing on a sarcastic wondering about having any swimmers left to give her, ever. Sure, we weren't concerned about condoms since Margaux had started on birth control pills, but that didn't mean I didn't entertain dreams of it being different one day— of coming inside her so our child would grow from that fire. A little girl with all the beauty and intensity of her mother...

I forced the thought back while ordering my body under control. But the dream was persistent, and it grew every day.

I wanted a family with this woman.

I wanted a life with this woman.

I needed to be with this woman every day for the rest of my life.

Springing the news on her? Different story. Much different.

One step at a time, man. It's not like you can just handcuff her down and make her listen.

Or could I?

CHAPTER TWO

Margaux

"Do I even want to know what this is for?"

My hulk of a driver—and now, undoubtedly, best go-to guy on the planet—lugged the midcentury schoolroom desk and attached chair into the middle of my condo's living room. It was perfect, the centerpiece of my grand scheme to help my man celebrate his first day of professional freedom from my mother. Coincidentally, it was also the fulfillment of a secret fantasy we'd confessed to each other after he'd toured me through the offices of the Aequitas firm last month, when he was still considering their obscenely generous offer to come on board their elite team, representing some of the biggest names in international business.

Aequitas occupied a building in the East Village that had been lovingly restored from its shoe factory beginnings—already a plus—but the firm's elegant take on exposed brick and wood had won me over. That, and the fact that after Michael explained that the desk in his future office was a refurbished piece from a girls' private school—the headmaster's himself, actually. Well, it hadn't taken much imagination—his or mine—to make the jump from there.

Andre's wry snicker brought me back to the present for the time being. "What?" I rejoined. "It's charming, isn't it?"

"Mmmm-hmmm. Charming."

"Shut up. I'm switching things up in here, décor wise, and this is my focal piece. Just set it there." I pointed to where he stood, wanting him to leave before he asked more questions. The man often knew I was lying with just a glance, so the sooner he got the hell out of there, the better.

Besides, I still had preparations to make.

"Did you pick up the dry cleaning?" I asked.

"Not yet. You had me on a scavenger hunt for a specific desk, remember?"

I sniffed delicately. "Well, you did a great job. I appreciate what you found. But now off you go. I also need you to finish the other things I texted to you while you're out doing errands." *Because you're sure as hell not hanging out downstairs, conjuring ideas of what Michael and I are doing with this desk.* "And don't come back until tomorrow, okay?"

"Because of the redecorating?"

I lifted one eyebrow in my should-be-patented death stare.

Andre's belly laugh filled my condo like the late-afternoon sunshine still streaming in the windows.

"Tomorrow."

"Yes, ma'am, Ms. Asher." With a ridiculously grand bow, he backed out the front door.

I had about thirty minutes to get ready. Michael had messaged to say what time he was leaving the office, and I'd added his brief commute time on top of that. I wanted to be fully dressed when he walked in the door.

I'd been pondering the details of this role play fantasy since last month, but after what he did yesterday, crawling in that filthy sewer to get the cherished pinkie ring Caroline had given me as a child? Yeah, above and beyond. Or was it below and beyond? Did it matter? One thing was glaringly clear. I owed him more than a quick fuck in the back of my car—even if said sex had been heart-stopping and amazing. Somehow, he just kept getting better and better at that end of things...

A stupid grin spread across my face as I halted completely, leaning against the wall. Damn. Just thinking of him...I'd literally stopped in my tracks.

Oh, yeah. It was official. I was in love. Me, Margaux Corina Asher, in love with a man who more than deserved to be loved. Not one of the typical, poor-excuse-for-a-man losers I'd always fallen for, but an actual, amazing, gorgeous, sexy-as-sin, smart, funny, caring—did I say sexy?—guy.

He was quickly becoming the center of my universe. My everything.

It was a little unnerving.

Maybe a lot.

Thoughts for another time, woman.

I hustled down the hall to our bedroom, ready to make the full transformation into naughty schoolgirl. I had a punishment coming—at least I hoped I did—and my headmaster was due home in exactly twenty minutes.

The outfit had been waiting in the back of my closet, far from the prying eyes of my assistant and fashion consultant, Sorrelle. Dear God, the boy would never let me hear the end of it if he saw the plaid skirt, white knee socks, and patent-leather Mary Janes. For the top, I had a starched white blouse—two sizes too small. I left the top three buttons open, exposing Michael's favorite red-lace bra beneath.

I rimmed my eyes with heavy black liner, added a thick coat of mascara, and finished off with some of the dark berry lip stain I wore every day of my adult life. It was the curse of being a blonde. If I didn't color my lips, I looked like a corpse. That was just all there was to it.

I contemplated my hair. Pigtails or braids? I settled on low pigtails so my instructor could pull them if he saw fit. And God, I hoped he saw fit.

Almost time.

I kept my fingers crossed, at least mentally. Michael definitely let my naughty side run wild, never turning away when I needed things rough. At other times, he could be the gentlest lover on the planet. It was such a puzzling dichotomy, making him all the sexier to me with every passing day. Often I wondered how so much complexity could be wrapped in one person. There was still so much to figure out about him—but we had time for it all. Neither of us could or should rush it. At just three months, our relationship was still in its infancy. We had so much to discover about each other, and I looked forward to all of it. It was so damn good to be running toward someone, not away.

I reached for my final prop. The hunk of bubble gum was going to help play up my naughty-student act, if I could get past the overwhelming sweetness. Why did I used to sneak this stuff behind Andrea's back as a kid?

I hurried to my desk in the middle of the living room, grabbing a cookbook from the kitchen to stand in as a textbook. I also pulled out a ruler but left it behind on the island. I had no idea how he'd react to all this. Men were strange sometimes. Talking about fantasies was sometimes their preference over making them come true. If Michael gaped like he'd just entered a freak show, it'd be better not to complicate things with a cavalcade of school supplies.

I did take a couple of sharpened pencils—brand-new number twos—and lay them end-to-end in the well on the desk's top. Like any good student, I sat up straight with my hands folded in front of me. The only thing out of place was my exaggerated gum chewing. It lent to the schoolgirl bit but also helped with my nervousness.

Keys jangled in the hall.

My heartbeat skidded in my chest.

Showtime.

I tried to call the circus in my stomach to rest. Would he play along with me? I was almost certain he would...but how far? In what direction?

Uncertainty assaulted me.

A simple question had never turned me on more.

The door swung open. I looked up, brandishing a cheeky grin. Blew a big pink bubble out of my mouth with a long hiss.

Pop.

I sucked the gum back in and kept chewing, adding a little wink. Getting deeper into character helped keep the circus under control—especially after I took in my man from head to toe. He'd worn one of his sharpest suits today, nearly black navy that was perfectly fitted to every lean, muscled inch of him. Finishing the look was a burgundy tie, a color he turned into a power look with the force of his presence alone.

I really loved that suit on him.

Within ten seconds, I squirmed in the seat. Wet for him. Wanting him.

"Well, what do we have here?" His sensual growl moved through me while he shucked his jacket and slid his briefcase onto the island in the kitchen, right next to the wooden ruler. Though I had a blind spot due to my lower level at the desk, I sensed he stashed the ruler in his back pocket. I'd find out for sure if I pushed him far enough...and earned a punishment.

Oh, it was on.

"Hi there." I blew another bubble. Smaller this time. Popped it with my teeth and sucked it back in. Michael watched every movement with darkening eyes—and, I observed as he walked out from the kitchen, a hardening crotch. *Oh, yes.* I grinned a little wider.

"Hello there." He started unbuttoning his sleeves. Rolled them both to his elbows. *Oh hell, yes.* "What's going on?"

"I've come for detention—just like the slip said, Headmaster." I chewed loudly but added in a mumble, "Although I didn't expect the proctor to be late."

He lifted both hands to his waist. "What did you just say, Miss Asher?"

His snarl was terrifying—and so fucking hot. He'd taken the bait and jumped right into character—as I'd known he would, deep in my heart. Never letting me down.

I loved this man so much.

"Nothing." I snapped it breezily, diving deeper into my own persona. "Nothing at all."

"Perhaps you meant 'nothing, Sir'?"

I gave him an exaggerated blink through my heavily coated lashes. "Of course. Nothing, Sir."

He prowled closer. I smiled bigger. Holy crap, he was good. So damn good.

"Miss Asher, I've been seeing a lot of you lately. Your behavior is getting out of hand. It's possible some corrective action is necessary at this point."

I gasped and worried my lips together. "No! Please, Headmaster. I promise, I promise I'll be good."

"That's what you said last time you were in my office, young lady."

"But I mean it this time. I do."

"So tell me, why were you sent to my office? Exactly?" He eyed me carefully. I picked up the vibe instantly. He was playing along while trying to understand what I wanted out of all this. While we'd talked about the fantasy, we hadn't exactly discussed a line-by-line. I could never let this man go. He was clever enough and brave enough to go toe-to-toe with me on every level.

I blew another bubble for dramatic effect. Michael sighed, giving it equal weight. "Give me the gum, Miss Asher. You know it's against school policy and it's unladylike to be chewing it in front of me."

I slid another glance up at him. "You gonna make me?"

He walked back to the counter, grabbed a tissue from the box on it, and then paced back over to cup it in front of my mouth.

"Spit it out."

"No."

"Do not defy me. It will only make things worse for you. It's a disgusting habit anyway." He pressed his other hand against the side of my face. "There are much better uses for that pretty little mouth."

I lifted my stare to him, eyes as wide as I could make them while depositing the gum into the waiting tissue. That certainly didn't give him the victory. I purposely left a long trail of saliva from the gum to my mouth, letting the edges of my lips turn up when Michael answered with a rumble of arousal. Our eyes met as he wadded the tissue around the gum. His gaze had gone dark as caramel. This new game, allowing us to be a combination of our real and pretend selves, was turning him on as deeply as it was me.

"Better." He dropped the tissue into the wastebasket and then returned to stand in front of me, legs braced like before. The bulge in his slacks was visible...and mouthwatering.

I licked my lips. I couldn't help it.

"Eyes up here, Miss Asher."

I raised my face, hitting him hard with my pout. "Yes, Headmaster."

He was so damn delectable. The power in his exposed forearms. The determination in his set jaw. The arousal in his stare, thickening by the second.

"Do you like seeing the effect you have on your teachers?"

"No, Sir. Not all of them." I winked again. "Just you."

He arched a brow. "You think pretty words will get you out of your punishment?"

"Is it working?" I tried batting my lashes, but he lunged, grabbing me by a pigtail and forcing my head back.

"You tell me if it's working."

I croaked out, "Errrr...no, Sir?" Moisture gushed between my legs. His brutal handling...it was heaven.

"That's right, young lady. It's not. So stop playing around. You're in serious trouble."

"Yes, Sir. Very, very serious." With my head cranked back, I had nowhere to look but at his furious, gorgeous face. Holy shit, what he did to me, looming over me like that. His lips formed into a hard, sensual line. The depths of his eyes glowed with mischief and promise.

It was so much.

Almost too much.

I flinched, instinctively trying to turn away, though I

forgot I was being held in place by my hair. Michael yanked on me again, sending more thrills down my spine, right into my core.

A low moan vibrated from my throat. My eyelids grew heavy as my brain turned the pain into endorphins, already bringing a sensual high.

The rustling of material brought my attention back to my headmaster. His jaw tightened as he opened his pants with his free hand, releasing his thick, erect cock. His shaft was so close to my cheek I could feel its mesmerizing heat on my skin. My eyelids threatened to slide closed again, dragged even harder by the sweet anticipation of what was about to happen.

He jerked on my head again. My eyes popped back open. So much for reveling in the moment.

"Your mouth gets you into trouble, doesn't it?" he drawled. "It would seem that you need something to occupy it. Is that about right, Miss Asher?"

His hand was woven so tightly in my hair I couldn't move anymore. I had to be still. Accept what he gave me. It was thrilling and frustrating at the same time.

"Answer me, girl." His voice turned as hard as his erection, deep with arousal.

"Y-Yes, Sir. That's what I need. But—"

I sighed as he rubbed his length along my cheek. His skin was soft as velvet, but his rod was hard as steel—once again, my perfectly dichotomous man. A whimper spilled out. I struggled, desperate to take any bit of him into my mouth, but he dug his grip tighter. My scalp stung with pleasure. My pussy vibrated with need.

"But what, baby girl?" He nearly barked it. Damn man knew he was torturing me, but the gruff undertone of his voice conveyed that it wasn't much better for him.

"I can't reach you. It's—you're—it's too tight. I need you." I was whining, and I knew it. Not that he hadn't heard me whine before. Now, it just felt like more. It was more. Getting to be his little schoolgirl was bringing out my brat, and I already sensed how he loved it. "I can't get to you. To what I want."

"And...what do you want?"

"You. Your cock. Your steely, hot dick in my mouth."

"You will get what I give you. Nothing more. Nothing less. Is that understood?"

I pushed out another pout. He couldn't take that from me. "Yes, Sir."

"Good. Now open your mouth."

Damn it. I guess he could.

With my breath slicing my chest in nervous spurts, I did what he said.

"Wider. I really have a lot to give you today."

Again, I complied. This time, more willingly.

"That's a good girl," he crooned. "See? I knew you could follow directions...if properly motivated." He finally released my hair, shifting that hand to my lower jaw. In a decisive sweep, he hooked a finger inside my mouth. "This gorgeous mouth is built for fucking, Miss Asher. Has anyone told you that?"

"They—they haven't, Sir."

"Then you need to be shown that I'm right." He stroked a finger along my tongue. "Now be still and let me do what I want to this pretty hole."

"Yes, Sir." I sighed again.

He added another finger to the first, thrusting them in and out a few times. I almost became a puddle there in the chair. Being treated this way, purely hot and sexual, was exactly what

I craved—and oh, how this man knew it. Was there any part of me he didn't see, didn't understand? The realization bound me to him more...body, senses, and soul.

I couldn't wait to learn what he had in store next.

Only the fulfillment of a thousand more fantasies.

He pulled his fingers out of my mouth, sliding them back under my jaw. With his other hand, he fed his cock into my mouth. Already, he was impossibly hard and huge. I nearly gagged, but he eased back out before that happened. He always knew just when to stop, right before it was unbearable.

He pulled on my head, working my mouth around him again.

We both groaned. I loved sucking him off. I loved focusing on his pleasure, especially when he guided me through ways to do it.

He angled my face back and pushed in farther. I sucked air through my nose and relaxed my throat, letting him in deeper with each stroke. With a couple of urgent actions, I shoved his pants and briefs below his backside, allowing me to sink my nails into his skin. He had the hottest ass on the planet. It was tight enough to tempt but full enough that I had something warm and solid and all Michael, instead of all Calvin Klein.

I set a hand free to cup him from the front. His balls swelled beneath my fingers. He hissed and gritted a low "Fuck!" as I built up a steady pressure and pace. He continued to fuck my mouth, thrusting harder and harder, his urgency building. I yearned to pull off in order to beg for his cock in other places, but that would earn me yet another punishment.

Ding.

Lightbulb of genius, meet Margaux's brain.

It took a little effort, but I finally broke free from

his grip. "Headmaster," I whimpered. "Oh, Headmaster, pleeeaaassse...I need you to fuck me. In my pussy. Please?"

Michael didn't shift his position. His dick bobbed in front of me, heavy and shiny and red. "What did I say, young lady? About your choice in any of this?" He pulled again on a pigtail. "I'm waiting."

"And *I'm* desperate." I lifted a defiant stare. "I'm not wearing panties under my skirt. My pussy is throbbing. If you don't fuck me, I'm going to use my fingers and do it myself."

His head tilted. His brows arched. "You absolutely will not." Deliberately, he pulled the ruler out from his pocket. "Not unless you want to feel my discipline on your ass...or anywhere else."

I didn't answer him. Instead, I leaned back in my seat. Slowly and deliberately, I inched up my skirt until I knew my proctor could view my exposed pussy. I hadn't lied to him. I was so frantic to be fucked I would accept the punishment of his ruler—not that it wasn't my intention to begin with.

Michael's nostrils flared. The idea of affecting him like this, much less the physical proof before my eyes, made my belly tighten and my channel clench. I knew he could see it too. Could see my pussy lips squeezing, needing his cock slamming between them.

"It's all for you, Sir."

He bared his teeth in a feral smile. "Damn right it is."

"I'm very, very naughty."

"Damn right you are."

"I deserve to be punished."

"Yes, you do."

"I'm ready to take what you can give me. Tell me what to do, and I'll do it." I stopped, waiting for his gaze to reconnect with mine. This was the part I really wanted him to hear. The part that made this stunt worth it. "You make everything I do worth doing. Every risk I take worth taking. There isn't another person on this earth that I have ever been able to say that about. I mean it, Sir. Each and every word."

For a long—very long—moment, he was utterly still. Finally, he rasped, "Margaux. Christ. Marg—"

I made him choke to a stop by sliding my index and middle fingers into my mouth. Air left him in an audible rush as I pumped them in and out, just as he had. He pulled in another long breath, this time in arousal, as I hiked one leg up on the desk. The other, I left on the floor...opening my entrance completely to his stare.

He growled. I raised one eyebrow. We were back in full, sexy character.

"Miss Asher."

"Hmmm?"

"Don't do it. I'm warning you. Don't do it."

"I can't help myself, Headmaster. I need to be fucked so badly. If you won't do it—"

"I didn't say that. You're simply too impatient, girl."

"Maybe I am. But...I just can't wait...any longer."

In one motion, he lunged forward—and slapped the inside of my thigh with that bitch of a ruler.

"Owww!"

"I said no. If anyone fucks that pussy, it will be me. No one else. Am I completely clear, Miss Asher?"

Tears welled in my eyes. That ruler stung like a motherfucker.

"Have I made myself clear?"

"Yes, Sir." I managed it in a whisper.

"Very good." As he issued the praise, he dropped to his knees, continuing to study my very exposed sex. He leaned in, pressing his mouth to the place he'd just struck on my thigh—before sucking hard on it. I shrieked from the renewed bite, but he gripped my knee and pulled me farther open. "Keep your legs where they are, girl. Understood?"

I nodded a shaky yes, not trusting my voice through the new tears. He was pushing me, of course—exactly what I'd asked for. He was becoming a bit of a sadist...and I think I liked it.

"Out loud," he demanded. "Answer me out loud."

"Yes. Yes. I understand." I wiggled in my seat, waving my pussy in front of him, hoping it incited him to bury his face in it. My clit began to ache. My thighs began to tremble. This was so good—and so bad. So perfect yet such torment.

"Be still. Did you just roll your eyes? Do you need another reminder from the ruler?"

"No!"

I quickly covered my mouth with my hands. I'd spewed it way too fast, betraying my abhorrence of that particular punishment. Now he would keep it in his arsenal for sure.

"Then what do you need, Miss Asher?"

I concentrated on staying still. It was agony, since my sex was a quivering, shaking ball of need. "Your mouth. Your cock. Anything. Anything. My pussy needs you so badly!"

He dug his fingers into my thighs, wrapping his big hands around to hold me in place while he dipped his head... and feasted on my soft flesh. My head lolled back, and I moaned out loud. Oh, God, it felt so good. Wet, slick slices of his expert tongue, making everything slip away as pleasure flooded, building a tidal wave of sensation like none other I'd experienced.

This was, undoubtedly, going to be the best orgasm of my life.

So close.

So close.

I was lost in all the sensations, piling higher atop each other, that I barely understood when he smacked the ruler down again. It was like watching it happen to someone else...a comparison I'd always thought ridiculous, until now. When the sting set in, I realized it was indeed me.

I glared at Michael. "What the—why? What'd I do?"

But as I blurted the words, he again started licking the place he'd struck. I flinched, thinking he had another sadistic hickey in mind, but this time, his tongue was warm and adoring. It felt like fire under my skin, moving right up to my pussy with the exact same effect as one of his spanks, except the beeline now zipped from my thigh to my core.

He matched his knowing chuckle to my startled outcry. "My little student finally begins to learn her lesson."

"Yes. Yes, I've learned. And, God, it feels so good."

"Mmmm. Yes."

"I just—I just—oh, shit, Michael!"

He switched from my thigh to my clit again, which was twenty times more sensitive. As he nibbled at my tender flesh, he pushed thick, skillful fingers into my entrance...one then two then three.

I shuddered.

Screamed.

I was seconds from exploding, my hands buried in his soft, perfect hair. I couldn't decide whether to push him off because the sensations were too much or hold him closer as I climbed to the edge.

"You're so close, little girl."

"Yes. Please don't stop! Please...don't..."

"I have no such intention." His voice was a low, knowing prowl. "You're going to come for me, sugar. Harder than you ever have. And just when you come down from this one, I'm going to bend you over this sweet little desk and fuck you so hard you're going to beg me to stop."

"I—I can't breathe. It's so much..."

"You can take it."

"No! Too much!"

"You can take it."

"I—"

"Get ready, baby. It's about to get better."

He slapped my thigh with the ruler again—in the same spot he'd impacted the other two times.

Everything stopped. There were no feelings at all. Until the hot flood came. Pain. Pleasure. Then more pain. It stung so much, until he licked the whole area with the flat of his tongue. His palm came next, spreading the sweet heat into my skin— until he hit the button on overload again by pinching the same spot. My skin was so red and tender, and it was amazing.

And not over.

His mouth settled back in on my clit, sucking it in, peppering me with bites and kisses in between. "Come for me, baby. Do it all over my tongue. Let me drink you in."

"Fuck!" I screamed. "God, yes! Like that!"

He pulled my clit in tighter, suctioning it exactly as I'd treated his dick with my mouth. He knew I loved it like that and took full advantage of the secret. Pressure built and then burst, sending me over the top. The orgasm drenched every nerve ending in my body. He was right. I'd never felt anything so damn good in my whole life.

Just as my body settled down, he again licked the bruised area of my thigh. I whimpered in appreciation of his tender kisses—until he sank his teeth in.

I yelled out. "Fucking hell!" And before I knew it, smacked him in the back of the head.

Ohhhhh, shit.

The look on his face was so hard to read. Not that I needed to when he spoke again.

"Miss Asher?"

"What?" I snapped. "It hurt!"

He cocked his head "And you're still being punished."

"I'm sorry."

"No, you're not."

"Okay, I'm not."

He stepped back. Stamped one last gaze on my spread pussy and then directed, "On your feet. Stand in front of your desk."

His quirking mouth told me were still playing—not that it reassured me much. I was in deep shit.

"I need to go to the nurse's office."

"Denied. Stand in front of your desk like you were told."

Now he really made me nervous. The twist disappeared from his lips. The rest of his face showed no emotion either. His cock, however, stood at a ninety-degree angle from his body. He kicked off his pants and briefs, giving me an even better view of its stiff beauty. Something—maybe a number of somethings—about all this had him aroused.

Arms folded across his broad chest, he took a step back, expectant of my obedience. I stood and straightened my skirt before stepping to the front of the desk. As soon as I stopped, Michael moved to stand in front of me, face-to-face. His chiseled features were still intense, but I didn't get a vibe of anger.

What, then? What was he thinking?

"Do you make a regular habit of hitting your teachers, Miss Asher?"

I tried to look extra contrite. "No, Sir."

"Look at me when you speak to me."

I stared up into his stunning hazel eyes. "No, Sir." I couldn't help but grin.

"Is this amusing, Miss Asher?"

"No, Sir." I was pretty sure the mirth in my eyes betrayed my lie.

"I'm going into the other room to get something for the last part of your discipline."

The ruler wasn't enough?

He placed his hands on my waist and turned me around with a commanding whoosh. "Face your seat. Bend over the desk. Put your hands on top of it, and don't let them up. Stand like that and think about what you did wrong until I get back."

"Y-Yes, Sir."

He bounded upstairs to our bedroom. I obeyed, admitting a twinge of real fear at what he'd attempt if I didn't. Nerves—hardcore ones this time—joined the feeling, no doubt stirred by the vulnerable position he'd ordered me to take. My ass was barely covered by the skirt, and my feet were braced at shoulder width. The air teased at my swollen, sensitive pussy.

I hoped he'd bring back some new toys—fun ones this time. No matter what, I vowed to be a patient student and not cause more trouble.

Minutes stretched like hours. Finally, he returned bearing what sounded like a plastic bag. I couldn't determine what he pulled from it but used every force of my will to keep my stare straight ahead and my body in place.

He lowered and started moving around by my feet. It didn't take long to determine that he'd brought leather cuffs, each bearing a large carabiner hook, which he used to secure my ankles to the desk legs.

Damn. Damn. Damn.

He quickly finished my ankles and then rose to yank my wrists forward. He looped one of my own scarves around them and then pulled them toward the back of the chair. I was officially bent over for him, in more ways than one.

Vulnerable. Using the word five minutes ago had been a vast understatement.

He stood back, grunting in satisfaction. I dared a quick glance up. The bastard looked very pleased with himself.

"Errrr...Headmaster?"

"I have a gag in here too, Miss Asher. Do I need to use it?"

"No, Sir. But I have a question."

"I'll allow one question."

"Why are you tying me up? Isn't it better for you and... things developing...if I can move around?"

"Apparently not, with you. I just got cracked in the head. For my own safety, I've decided you may need some extra help." He squatted down so our stares were even and flashed me a conspiratorial wink. "You know, sugar, you may like it."

I narrowed my eyes and released a little growl.

Michael chuckled. "Well, are you comfortable? You may be there awhile."

"Maybe a pillow under my stomach?"

He grabbed one off the sofa and slid it under my torso. "Better?"

"Much. Thank you, Headmaster."

He gave me a sweet kiss on the forehead before stepping back behind me and flipping my skirt up, exposing my ass.

"Damn it, Margaux."

"What?" I fought to swing my head around. "What's wrong?"

Just like that, the insecurity beast reared its ugly head. I wasn't surprised. Who wouldn't find themselves stumbling over a few emotional triggers when tied in four places to a piece of furniture in the middle of their living room, taking a bath in streams of autumn afternoon light?

"Nothing." His tone was a thick rope of meaning. "Nothing at all, sugar." He ran his rough hands up my thighs and over my ass cheeks, spreading them wide, sinking fingertips into my flesh. "You're the most stunning creature I've ever seen."

"Oh." I couldn't get out much more than that. The reverence in his voice... It affected me more than physically. Deep in my chest, strange sensations of warmth unfurled. Beautiful sensations...

"Baby...if you had any idea what you look like right now, with the sun on your skin and our passion on your pussy..." He interrupted himself, clearing his throat with a rugged cough. "It's completely unfair that one person should possess so much beauty. But I won't be the one complaining to the universe about it."

I had no response at that point. There weren't a lot of options after a man flipped one's heart over a hundred times, right? There was nothing I could do or say but let him adore me—easier said than done—no matter how brainless it seemed.

For a girl like me, it could be difficult. Perhaps impossible. In Andrea Asher's world, you weren't human if you weren't perfect. Even now, I worried about all the wrong Michael would see in my body, instead of the right.

No. I didn't have to believe that anymore. Despite how unnerving it was, I dipped my head, closed my eyes, and let his words of love surround me. This was Michael. My Michael. He'd never hurt me and would never knowingly let harm come to me. I trusted him with that surety and so much more. I'd let him lock me down without thinking twice. More significantly, I let him openly stare at me in this state.

I felt his heat against me. He rubbed my back with long, firm strokes, continuing his words of worship in such perfect whispers my mind gave over to my soul...and soared. His physical warmth and emotional bolstering had me glowing everywhere. Everywhere.

Soon, he drifted lower and gently petted my sex from behind. The steady pressure beckoned my senses like a light in the growing twilight of the room. I leaned deeper into his touch with each pass, moaning and purring, opening for him... craving him.

"Michael." I rasped it like a prayer. "Michael."

"What, sweetheart?" His voice was soft but urgent. The headmaster was gone. He was now the lover who knew every perfect way to touch me, every wonderful thing to say to me, every exquisite way to love me.

"Please!"

"Please what? Tell me what you need, Margaux. I'm all yours. I'd move a fucking mountain for you."

"No mountain," I cried. "Just you. Do it. I'm begging you! Fuck me, Michael!"

He slipped right in through my wetness, barely needing to push. Though we'd been making love night after night for months, he still stretched me to the fullest I'd ever been. It brought pain—but the purest kind. The kind that came with the most perfect ecstasy my body would ever know.

The desk lurched forward with his commanding, demanding thrusts. We started inching across the floor. Neither of us cared. All that mattered was the passion pounding from between my legs and then spreading through my lower half. My entire body was possessed by him. His body. His heat. His desire. But he consumed more than that. My spirit. My will. My heart. Everything I had, everything I was...belonged to him.

His fingers skated up my ribcage, reaching beneath my blouse to pluck at my nipples, granting no mercy even when I screamed. If I wasn't on sensory overload before, that sure as hell hit the max capacity button.

I wouldn't be able to hold out much longer. My body jumped back to where it had left off only minutes ago, on the brink of another mind-melting orgasm.

Michael leaned over me, breathing heavily into my neck. "You feel so good, princess. So damn good. So tight around my cock. Goddamn."

"Harder," I gritted. "Need it...harder."

He scraped his teeth against my neck. "Beg me."

I didn't think twice. I didn't think at all. "Please. Fuck me harder, Michael. Do it. Make me cry. Punish me!"

I had no idea where the words came from. Maybe, deep inside, I knew they'd tempt his beast again. And maybe I should've kept my mouth shut—because out of nowhere came the hell spawn ruler again. This time, he struck the fleshy globes of my ass. I shrieked, though I was thankful he hadn't gone again for my inner thighs.

He didn't break the rhythm of his cock while spanking me a few times on each side—enough to make sure I'd be standing through meetings tomorrow. Finally, he flung the stick aside to gain leverage for really pounding into me.

"I hate that thing," I muttered, as it clattered against the wall.

"I love that thing," he growled.

"You're a monster."

"And you're the sweet girl with the red ass that's driving me insane." He lunged even harder. "Let it go for me, Margaux. Come again, princess."

"I'm so close..."

Not a lie. One more naughty move and I'd be gone. As if Michael read my mind, he reached around, found my clit, and pinched my flesh so hard I saw stars. They blinded me, bringing a climax so fast and intense I couldn't even announce its arrival. I went mute as the explosion lashed my body. Michael kept pounding away, groaning hard as his completion came too.

Minutes or hours or days might have passed while we drifted back down to earth. "Jesus Christ, girl," he muttered, still slumped over my back. "You're going to be the death of me."

I laughed breathlessly while he fumbled with my bindings. A few moments passed before he was able to fully concentrate and set me free.

We tumbled to the floor in each other's arms, sweaty and satiated, grinning and sleepy like we always were after a satisfying romp—though I wondered if romp would have to be replaced by a new noun this time. Terms like best sex of my life instantly made that short list.

He pulled the throw off the back of the sofa, down to where we lay on the floor. Neither of us spoke. It wasn't necessary yet. It would happen eventually though. Michael analyzed everything. It was something I loved and hated about him.

He added a couple of the big couch pillows to our impromptu bed before asking, "Where did the desk come from?"

I laughed again, unable to hold back. "I sent Andre out to find it."

"Christ. I'm never going to hear the end of this one."

"I didn't tell him what it was for." I batted him playfully.

He grunted. "Sugar, he's a guy. And not as dumb as he may act at times." He hitched up, leaning his head against an elbow and tugging on one of my pigtails. "Well...the outfit's a keeper. That's an order, Miss Asher."

I played with my pinkie ring. "And the ruler?"

"You liked that, after all?"

"Took a little getting used to, but yeah."

Michael grabbed my hands in his much larger ones, stilling my nervous twisting. His warm skin surrounded mine, comforting me at once. His nearness always gave me security and confidence—two elements I struggled with daily, no matter what the world at large believed. I didn't care what they thought, anyway. The only person who mattered was the golden god of a man sprawled against me now.

I looked into his eyes, floored by the love I saw there. I wondered if he saw the same thing in mine.

"Do you have any idea how much I love you?" he whispered.

I smiled. "I hope I do."

A peculiar expression took over his face. This was normally the point where he started the postcoital analysis thing, but his expression was far from analytical. It was... pensive. No. Expectant. Not that, either. "Hmmm."

That sure cleared up...nothing. "Hmmm...what?"

"Funny that we're bringing up all this love stuff right now."

"Why?"

"Because after what happened yesterday with your ring, I really started thinking about us. Me. You. The lengths I would go to for you. The depth of how much I love you."

"I love you too." I lifted fingers to his face, caressing his jaw. "I meant what I said earlier, you know. Every word."

"Good. Now let me finish."

"Ohhh...kay." I almost made it a question.

"I know you wear that ring everywhere—because it means so much to you. That's why I did what I did yesterday. It wasn't because of the ring itself but because of you. Because of how much you mean to me. That could have just as easily been anything else you cherished."

"I know that." I leaned over, nuzzling the base of his neck. His tie was loose, but I unknotted it all the way and tossed it to the couch. "My Captain America."

He scooted a finger beneath my chin and tugged up. "It made me realize something, Margaux. Something significant."

"All right." I took advantage of the chance to kiss him. "What?"

He took a deep, long breath.

"I want to make a commitment to you. I want the world to know that I'm committed to you. I want you to marry me, Margaux. I want to be your husband, to take care of you every day In sickness and health, for richer and poorer, through the shining times and the shitty times—for the rest of our lives. I want to be the man you always turn to when you need someone to lift you up and even when you don't. I'm—this is— hell, it's not coming out at all like it should, but just make me the happiest fucker on earth, okay?" He lifted my hands and smashed fervent kisses on the knuckles. Then again. "Say yes. Say you will be my wife. Wear my ring, Margaux. Wear a ring that will come to mean as much, if not more, than the one I fished out of the sewer yesterday."

I answered him with dead silence. And didn't know if I had anything beyond it.

I sure as hell hadn't seen that coming.

CHAPTER THREE

Michael

"Michael."

It wasn't just how she whispered it.

It was the silence before it. The kind of silence that stretched beyond nervous, even uncomfortable.

Into gut-wrenching.

"Michael." She looked up. For two seconds. In the first, she yanked out my heart, stripping it of its hopeful joy. In the second, she rammed it back into my chest—full of defeat.

"Right." I mumbled it while breaking our gazes. "Got that message. Loud and clear."

"Hey." She yanked on my hair, pulling me back around. "I love you, okay? I do."

"But..." I uttered the word for her. Her answering wince shouldn't have been so encouraging, but misery loved company and all that depressing shit.

It wasn't like I'd planned for the words to spill out—though, I now realized they'd been pushing all day. While organizing my new office, I'd thought of doing the same in a new home, with Margaux. Over lunch with Carter and Grace, the fraternal twins who'd been charged with showing me the ropes at the firm, I'd considered what it would be like to tell them about my weekend plans with my wife. After that lunch,

I'd even paused at a jewelry store window to check out the engagement rings.

"But what?" Margaux sat up, pulling the blanket over her cleavage. The demure move was surprising, considering how I'd just had my wicked way with her breasts and nipples—which made it arousing as hell too. Great. "You don't see the dozen ways an engagement would be a shitty idea right now?"

So much for arousal.

I rose and refastened my pants. "So your idea's the highlight of the night, and mine's the shitty stuff."

"Excuse the hell out of me?"

"You heard me."

"Wait. Whoa. Hold on there, cowboy."

Hold on. That had been my plan, hadn't it? I'd wanted to hold on for the rest of my damn life. I'd never laid myself barer for a woman—which, apparently, had been a shitty idea.

I stomped across the room, looking for my keys. Another tangle of feeling rolled across my chest, tight but filthy, like a tumbleweed hitting a swamp. Clashing ecosystems aside, the ball collected what it had to off my soul—the acceptance of why she'd really turned me down.

"So, no harm, no foul," I muttered. "I get it, okay? Dressing up the guy from the apple farm doesn't make him any less the guy from the apple farm. If I'm Mr. Right Now instead of Mr. Right, then so be it."

My keys were on the floor, near the school desk, where they must have fallen from my pants when—

Of course.

Fuck.

I avoided looking at the cuffs still attached to the furniture, afraid of what I'd remember now...of what I'd feel now. All the ways she'd captured my heart, multiplied deeper. That she'd trusted me enough to give herself to me like that... It had gutted me and then filled me right back up. Humbled me but made me soar to the fucking stratosphere. But clicking sexually didn't mean matching in other areas. Not the important ones. And now, I had to be okay with that. She hadn't given me a choice.

"So be it?" She stood as she bit out each word, wearing an expression I couldn't decipher. On one hand, she'd never looked more an incensed princess, though her gaze bore the pain of a lost little girl. I blinked back, confused—until she shot out a fist, brutally clipping my shoulder.

"Hey. Ow! What the—"

"You are such an idiot."

"I'm an—" I rubbed my arm but froze as she let the blanket fall. Nothing like this woman, pissed off and nearly naked, to strip me of coherent thought. "I'm not the one who said no," I growled, shoving back the arousal.

"Did you hear me say no?" Margaux snapped. "Ever?" She stepped around me and marched to the kitchen, reaching for the bottle of wine we'd started last night after capping off our passion in the car with another round on the counter in here. She recorked the cabernet, reaching for the Scotch instead.

"Pardon me for splitting hairs. Where I come from, a shitty idea translates to the same thing."

"A shitty idea right now." She dumped the amber liquid into a highball and then shoved it at me. "Drink. That's not a request. You have to calm the hell down."

"I am calm."

"Not working, buddy. Not with me." She tossed back half the liquor in her own glass. Was anything more erotic than this woman, still spilling from her schoolgirl threads, downing

Scotch like a Highlander? "Just because you're not punching the wall doesn't mean you don't want to."

I shot out a huff and downed the damn Aberlour. At least it would take the edge off my growing fantasy to fuck her again—a fact my bedraggled suit would be shit for disguising in a minute.

"You ready to listen now?" she prompted.

I replied by nudging my empty glass forward, demanding another round. She obliged, though kept her stare locked on me as she tipped the bottle.

"Tell me something," she murmured. "Why do you think I'm such a freak about keeping this ring?"

I waited a second to respond. Was she serious? Did she think I didn't know that answer? No. That wasn't the case. But she wasn't playing around, either. Raised with little knowledge of the word play at all, Margaux was only comfortable with the word in the bedroom or the shoe store.

"It represents happier times," I finally responded. "And the woman you experienced them with."

Her lips inched up. Her eyes softened. Damn. Knowing I'd touched her heart... I felt as huge as a Sequoia.

"And what else?" she pressed.

A frown pushed my forehead. "It probably centers you too," I guessed. "Focuses you on a stronger version of yourself."

Long before I'd even kissed the woman, I'd figured that the sass she slung at the world was a sham, ordered there by an equal hoax of a mother. Andrea Asher had simply expected Margaux to be strong, without the necessary lessons for the integrity beneath it. Fast-food character building, doled out by a woman now on the International Wanted List for her caviar taste—and the white-collar crimes she'd committed to finance it.

"Hmm." Margaux inched her grin up a little more. "That's a good one. And true, as well."

"But there's more." I inserted the word willingly this time.

"A lot more." She set down her empty highball and made no move for a refill. Instead, she leaned against the counter, thoughtfulness taking over her face, twisting the ring with the fingers of her opposite hand.

"It's okay," I urged. "I'm here."

She pulled in a deep breath. Finally uttered, "Connection."

"Connection?"

"That's the more. The ring...it's connecting me. Back to... me." She shook her head, and I almost thought she was going to laugh off the introspection. Though it made no more sense to me than her, I was glad when she pushed on anyway. "For so long—too long—I've been living as an extension of Andrea Asher's world. Okay, so I was probably the best-dressed one in the garden, but it was still her garden. Yet now..."

"You don't know what your garden is supposed to be about."

Her shoulders lowered, releasing visible tension. The fact that I'd said it, not her, cleared a lot of the air between us. She reached for my hand and squeezed, despite the sadness of her next words.

"Damn. I don't even know how to start a garden."

"Of course you do." I grabbed her other hand. "You just don't know it yet."

Her eyes slid shut. When she opened them again, there was no mistaking the bright sheen across their emerald surfaces.

"I'm still missing pieces, Michael. Lots of them. How am

I supposed to promise myself to you when I don't even know what myself is?"

I lifted her hands to my lips. Pressed into them, acknowledging—and hating—the desperation of the move. To watch her struggle through moments like this, fighting to learn even the simplest truths about her heart, gutted me. I saw the enormous courage of that heart. I also saw the fucked-up wasteland of a childhood she'd had to drag it through—a wilderness that would've beaten her spirit even bloodier, if not for that ring.

"You think we all get to have all the pieces, sugar?" I released her fingers to stroke my knuckles down her cheeks. "News flash, Miss Asher. I fell in love with the pieces I already have."

She sighed and smiled. "And I love all the pieces you've given me too."

I dropped my hands. "Shit." Her resolute tone, added to the sigh, didn't require a rocket science degree to interpret. "There's another *but* coming here, isn't there?" Because this night hadn't gone downhill fast enough from the first two.

She notched her chin higher. "You deserve more than pieces, Michael." Then higher. "But so do I."

I rolled my stare toward the ceiling. "Yep. Here it comes."

"Don't." She stabbed a finger to my sternum. "I'm not your damn fishwife, nagging you about taking out the trash. I'm the woman who loves you—"

"Margaux—"

"And the woman you just proposed to." She pushed off and stepped back. "Unless you were only fucking around or something."

A hundred switches of fury flipped in my blood. "Did I

sound like I was fucking around?"

She folded her arms. "You want an honest answer to that?"

"Damn it." I muttered it while dipping my head, confirming I'd already figured that part out. I'd really turned this into a crap pile, hadn't I? Yeah, even knowing that the woman didn't let me keep calling her princess just because it was a pretty word. Sometimes—a lot of times—she yearned for petticoats and chivalry, for old-fashioned school desks and rules she could push...and for a marriage proposal from a Disney movie, my knee on the ground and her ring on a pillow.

"I thought we were talking about you."

"Which equates to you, dumb shit." Now she poured herself more Aberlour. "That's the way it still works, right? The two shall become one? Lookin' at the other half of me? Anywhere you go, let me go too?"

I sucked in air through my nose. Muttered back, "Yeah. That's how it still works."

"So maybe you have something to tell me?"

I ground my jaw. *Not without serving you a heaping plate of ugly, my love. Not without showing you my deepest pain, my worst shame—and my darkest fear. That you'll take one look and decide this prince was more than you bargained for.*

"Michael." Forget princess. She stamped both syllables with queenly command, setting aside her drink to stand before me. I'd conjured her as a Highlander just minutes ago—now she was a royal one. Her stance made me wonder if the schoolgirl shirt was about to spring an ermine cape. "We've already been through so much. You've helped me past so much..."

I pushed my gaze back into hers. All her fire, spirit, passion, and love waited for me. I swallowed past a tight throat. She was so beautiful—and deserved to live every day knowing that. "I'm glad," I murmured. "No. I'm delirious. What I said, earlier...it wasn't just words for the middle of a good screw. I'll be here for you, baby. Always."

Her lips tightened. "And I love you for it. But that's only half of what we are. I need to be your safe place too."

I lifted my hands toward her hips. She stepped out of reach again—damn it. She was keeping this shit real—free and clear of any pheromones, hormones. or chemistry that could get in the way.

"I'm not hallucinating this, okay?" she asserted. "Don't think I didn't learn anything useful from Andrea. The woman didn't know a lullaby from a rock ballad, but she sure as hell taught me how to spot a person holding back secrets." Her head cocked, emphasizing the muss of her hair, piling more arousal onto my tension. "You think I've simply written it off that you call the police substation in Julian every week to check on the farm—not Carlo, your mom, or anyone at the farm? Speaking of your mom, do you really think I don't see those strange glances you trade with her, when you assume I'm preoccupied with my phone? Are you assuming I've forgotten the bruises she disguised with makeup when we went to visit over the Fourth of July?"

A lot of times, silence was the best response. I banked on that now.

"For all your talk of wanting to help with my pieces, you're still holding back a shit pile of yours from me, Michael." She swallowed so hard, I heard the lump slam the bottom of her throat. *Note to self—rethink the silence-is-best thing.* "If you think I'm pissed off," she pushed on, "then think again. You're not pissing me off. You're breaking my heart."

Hell.

I reached for her again. She stumbled back again. Sometimes, being bigger and faster came in handy. I captured her after two steps, yanking her against me and growling into her hair. "Your heart is the most precious thing in my world."

Her frame remained rigid. "You have a shitty way of showing it."

She wasn't going to relent. Admitting it to myself didn't help the impression of being a lion in a corner. I couldn't exactly swing out with teeth bared and claws exposed, so I chose another counterattack—pulling her head back by her scalp and then crushing my lips to hers.

Sweet fuck.

Nothing like planning a little retaliation—and gaining some sweet perks.

I'd taken her by surprise, meaning she had no time to think of a defense. Everything she turned over in that kiss was her purest instinct, wild and open, sighing and free, brimming with all the fire and sensuality that had first hardened my cock, long before my idiotic brain caught on. Back in the days when she was just the boss's daughter, a headstrong blonde with an impressive sarcastic streak, and I was another cog in Andrea Asher's corporate wheel. I'd damn near gotten off to thoughts of kissing her like this and never understood why. Now, I comprehended every speck of it.

She was meant to be mine.

And always would be.

So why did I have to smear that with filth from my past? With degradation I'd never asked for? Why did I have to keep paying the price for what Declan had done?

It ends now.

Before I could stop it, my soul punched the same words

over my lips. I'd broken off a kiss like that for it too? What the hell?

"What the hell?" Margaux's echo was stabbed with equal confusion "What are you talking about?"

I kissed her again. She tasted doubly as good, the bite of the Scotch mixing with the sweet magic of her passion, plunging my mouth back over hers for more. Goddamn, if I could only ravage her like this for hours...

The thought made it hell to drag away, but if she was half as affected as I was, now was the time to do it.

"It ends now." The words dovetailed into my purpose, so why not? I punctuated by lifting her right hand off my chest and curling her pinkie finger toward my lips. As I brushed a kiss over the gold circle there, I delved my stare deep into hers—and realized my intention of mesmerizing her was a massive fail. Instead, I wondered where my lungs had stashed my air and where my brain had dumped my equilibrium. "You take my breath away."

Her features trembled too. Nevertheless, she prodded, "Michael?"

"This." I tugged on her hand as if it were the most obvious answer in the world. "This. The ring—and all the mystery about it—why don't we end it? For good?"

Her forehead furrowed. "Huh?"

"To accept my ring, you need to get pieces back from this one, right?"

She added a catlike head tilt. "Why do I smell a giant pile of distract-the-girlfriend?"

"Full disclosure?" I countered. "Maybe it is a distraction. But it's also a solid offer." I tucked her knuckles against my chest and let my forehead dip to hers. "Your happiness...it's everything to me, Margaux. You keep telling me how you sense Caroline has been near, how you even think you see her sometimes." With the slow track of one tear down her cheek, I knew her reply to that. "So why don't we learn the answer for sure? To find her, reconnect with her...to find more of those missing parts of you?"

"God damn it, Pearson." She angrily swiped the tear. "That's one hell of a distraction."

I grinned. "I like pulling out the stops for you, blondie."

She popped up on tiptoe and rammed a kiss to my lips, as if intending to punish as well as pleasure. Did I dare tell her that the only true punishment for me was a life without her? Hell, no. First, the tinge of salt on her lips turned her into a pure taste of heaven. Second, I vowed to make so many of her dreams come true, she'd never want to leave my arms. This dream was one of the biggest—the quest for Caroline Beecham, the woman who'd been more mother to her than Andrea Asher ever was and then paid the price for it by being banished from Margaux's world when Margaux was just a kid. After pulling that loser move, Andrea had ordered no tears be shed over the matter. Almost two decades had passed since then. Margaux still didn't know what had happened to Caroline.

My girl's single tear, even now, was a blaring broadcast of how meaningful a reunion with the woman would be—no matter how hard she tried disguising it with a snarky smirk.

"For the love of Gucci." Like every good princess, her favorite colloquialisms were a creative take on the Almighty. "I need to be more careful, don't I?" She wound her hands around my neck and tugged at the ends of my hair. "When you're up to something, you're really up to something."

I snaked my lips upward. "I like being up for you, sugar."

Her answering smile could cut miles through the emerging fog outside—not to mention my cock, now straining to prove my words as truth to her. "Incorrigible."

I flipped up her skirt. "Just the way you like me."

She hitched her legs around my waist. "Just the way I love you."

CHAPTER FOUR

Margaux

"What about the back?" I whirled around again, flattening the silk fabric of my gown to my figure.

"Just as amazing as the front." Michael pulled my hands into his, trying to calm my nerves. "What has you in such a fit? The School Arts Foundation is one of your favorite causes. You've done these things a million times. You'll be the belle of the ball, like you always are." He kissed the tip of my nose, careful not to smear the color on my lips.

I tried breathing deeply while studying my reflection again. Sorrelle had brought his A game to get me ready, but a million butterflies still duked it out in my stomach.

"I don't know. I guess—I don't know."

I knew exactly what it was, but I didn't want to tell him.

It was him.

He was special—more than that—and tonight, the whole world would officially know it. It was our first major function as a couple, meaning even Hollywood and New York would send teams to cover it. The photogs would be crawling all over the place looking for hot pictures and a hotter story, turning my nerves into a jangled mess.

Talking to him about it wasn't going to make anything better, especially because he'd been working so hard this whole week. His long days at Aequitas had been followed by nights of diving into research about how the last eighteen years had seemed to swallow Caroline Beecham whole. So far, his quest had turned up nothing but dead ends and frustration, making him more excited about getting to dress up and shine with me at the gala tonight.

He was right about the gown, though. It was amazing, fitting like a second skin. Black satin clung to my top in the form of a strapless bodice, gathered under my breasts into a rectangular rhinestone cluster. The material was fitted down to my knees, where wisps of chiffon, also in black, took over down to the floor. The chiffon added movement and depth even when I stood still, a plus when a lot of red carpet posing was in my near future.

Sorrelle had pulled my hair into a severe top bun and then tamed every stray piece with industrial-strength hairspray. My makeup was intense but feminine, and my jewelry, all diamonds, was selected to accent the rhinestones on the dress. Michael wore a classic Tom Ford tuxedo that complemented my dress perfectly.

To the regular onlooker, we had it nailed. If I could wrestle the inner chaos, I'd feel as perfect as I looked.

We loaded into a limousine for the event, wanting to make a splashier entrance than my 750i would. The travel time was only fifteen minutes from the El Cortez, so I leaned into Michael's side and tried to relax as we soared into the night, seeming to fly over the Coronado Bay Bridge, escaping to the Silver Strand for the evening.

The arrival line clogged Adella Avenue leading into the Hotel del Coronado, so Michael and I made small talk and little jokes as Andre inched the car toward the front of the line.

My nerves finally began to calm, soaking up the energy from my smart, sexy beau.

Michael was good for me. Damn good. His company made me happy, content...solid. I began to wonder why I'd been so damn nervous back at home—

Until cameras flashed through the tinted glass.

One last check of my hair and lipstick, just before the back doors were whisked open by the attendants. Andre's friendly face came into view as he extended a hand to help me onto the red carpet. Michael got out to help from the other side, ensuring there were no wardrobe malfunctions. The dress was pretty safe, so the car exit went smoothly. I accepted Michael's waiting arm and then gripped him a little tighter as we followed the carpet down the path into the magnificent Victorian icon known simply as the Hotel Del.

Having lived in San Diego my entire life, I'd been to so many events here I knew the property like the back of my hand. Regardless, the sight of the distinct red cupolas, sprawling white buildings, and scenic beach was never a disappointment. It was easy to see why event planners and filmmakers loved the place.

We smiled our brightest smiles—and entered the gauntlet of flashbulbs and questions.

"When's the big day?"

"Who are you two wearing?"

"Margaux, when are you going to make an honest man of Michael?"

Blah, blah, blah. "I need a cosmo," I mumbled into Michael's ear. "How's that for honest?"

"Good call." An enticing smirk curled his lush mouth. "Let's stick together. Looks like the sharks are swimming in packs tonight." He emphasized the invitation by leaning over and kissing my neck just below my ear, making me grin and then shiver. He knew every spot on my body that elicited tremors like that...every single way to liquefy me, no matter where we were or what we were doing.

I peered around for a broom closet to haul him off to. And hoped, by some off chance, there'd be a random ruler in it too.

Of course, the flash of a camera went off right at the same moment, reminding me of the zero privacy we'd have tonight.

"At least they don't know what I was thinking." I gave him a playful wink. "But I'll tell you later if you want."

"Oh, I want."

I gave him a saucy grin and waggled my brows. "Now, about that bar..."

Michael took my hand and tugged me away from the photographer. Not surprisingly, we found a bar in less than a minute, adjacent to the ballroom the event was being held in. I wasn't sure it was the bar we were supposed to be at, as these society things often had private bar set-ups inside the room itself, but it was already nice to be free from the crowd for a few minutes, so I didn't tell Michael.

After he purchased two bottles of beer and I ordered a cosmo, we gave a ridiculous tip to the adorable girl behind the bar and braced ourselves to reenter the main event room.

Until shock froze me completely.

"Oh, hell no." I barely noticed half my drink sloshing onto my wrist.

"What's wrong?" Michael demanded. "Is it too sweet? I don't know how you drink those things in the first place. Do you want me to get you something else?"

"No. It's not the drink. In fact—" I slammed back what was

left of the cosmo, finishing it in one gulp.

Michael's mouth dropped open. "Shit. The last time you did that, I ended up with my nuts in a vice."

"Yeah, it's not you this time either, stud."

"Then what's going on, princess?"

I pointed toward the easel just outside the ballroom door. "That."

The poster, a student-designed advertisement for the School Arts Foundation, depicted several details about the event—including, in huge red letters, the name of the evening's star speaker.

DOUG SIMCOX

Please, earth...open up and swallow me whole.

I closed my eyes for a long moment, hoping I'd just read the thing wrong. But reopening them dumped me right back into the *This is Your Life*, Margaux Asher lightning round—without the cool mushies to show for it.

Doug Simcox was a former second baseman for the New York Yankees—and the man who'd swept me off my feet for eight months until dropping me with the thud heard round the world. In the process, he tore my heart out, tap danced on it for everyone to see, and then handed back the remains in a banker box, along with everything else I'd left at his place—to which he promptly changed the locks. I'd handled my devastation and humiliation with the immaturity that fit my age, resorting to extreme tactics to win him back—including, but not limited to, a flashy attempt to take my own life.

Jump forward. *This isn't then, girlfriend. You're not that person anymore. You're healed and adjusted—and best of all, you've explained all this in full to Michael already.* There'd be no fireworks of the gasping, dramatic variety from our corner of the ballroom this evening.

So why did he stare like I had sprouted another head?

"What?" I snapped.

"What?" He repeated it like stating I had a nose on my face. "You just stopped like you saw a ghost and then gave yourself a cosmo bath." His sarcasm vanished as soon as he stepped a little closer, gazing into me with his hazel intensity. "Are you okay? With that?" He nodded at Doug's picture, splashed on a poster opposite the first, as if needing to give me more clarification. Seriously, people took the blonde thing too far sometimes—even him.

"Oh, come on." I scoffed in the same direction. Doug's press release photo was such a bad glamour job I wondered what mall he'd gone to for it. So cheesy, bee tee dubs. "I am super great with that."

"You're sure?"

I shrugged—one shoulder, to emphasize how much I didn't care. "My love, that is what they call ancient history." I lifted my sticky hand. "Now, buy me another drink while I get cleaned up, and then let's go have some fun. What do you say?"

Michael smiled and kissed me, though flecks of doubt lingered in his eyes, bronze against the rich gold. Okay, maybe I was pouring it on a little too thick, but I was not about to let Doug Simcox get to me—especially in front of Michael and especially after I had come so far.

I loved Michael Adam Pearson.

End. Of. Story.

Many more guests had arrived. Everyone milled around the room, socializing via the typical grip-and-grin. Michael and I checked out what was available in the silent auction area and even bid on a few of the items. Michael had his heart set on a signed *Terminator* movie poster. It was so not hanging in my condo, but we could worry about that if he actually won the hideous thing.

"Have I told you how stunning you look this evening, Miss Asher?"

I winked up at him. "Not in the last twenty minutes. You're slipping."

"Hmmm. I'd better think of a way to make it up. We have an entire limo to ourselves on the ride home. If your Bimmer's back seat was big enough, imagine what we could do in one of those bad boys." He enfolded me in his warm embrace, smelling woodsy yet expensive in his tux, teasing me with the playful words while trailing naughty kisses up my bare neck.

"Okay, stud...you'd better stop, or we won't last to enjoy the main course." I wasn't kidding and conveyed as much with another quick glance.

His eyes gleamed with mischief. "Is that so bad? These things are tedious, right? Admit it." He added extra bribery with more kisses against my nape.

"Duly admitted—but they're expecting our bright, shiny faces around here for a while longer. Plus, we dropped ten grand a plate, so let's stick around and at least see what they're serving." I leaned into him, feeling his erection growing and pressing into my belly. I couldn't help but giggle. He was always ready to go, and I loved having that effect on him.

"Fine. Play hard to get. It just makes you hotter, baby." He pushed away with a dirty grin. "I'm going to get us another round, to make sure we have enough anesthesia for the pain of old Dougie's speech. Why don't you find our seats?"

"Yes, Headmaster." I dropped it to a whisper for his ears only. It was worth the grin that spread across his gorgeous face as he headed toward the bar again.

The tables were lavishly set in an ivory and gold theme to match the ballroom's décor. Each place was marked with an engraved name card and the event program. Quickly enough, I found our spots smack in the middle of the room. After sitting, I resorted to an old but harmless habit—nonchalantly checking out the other place cards at the table.

I didn't get very far. An elderly couple took their seats directly across the round, so I smiled and introduced myself, explaining that my date would be coming along in a moment. Busying myself with the program was a safe choice after that, trying to find familiar names on the Arts Foundation Board—and pointedly ignoring anything that mentioned Doug.

In short, the program wasn't very exciting.

"Excuse me...miss? Do we know each other?"

I didn't recognize the voice, so I kept pretending to read. I was so not in the mood to be hit on, and Michael's jealous side, even in its mild form, wasn't pretty.

"Excuse me...miss? Aren't you Margaux Asher?"

The guy had the balls to touch my arm. I jerked from his reach and looked up.

"I am Margaux Asher." I stared at him with irked expectancy. I had no idea who he was, though I couldn't ignore the hint of familiarity now setting in. The refined angles of his face, beneath the world-weary creases. The distinct shade of his blond hair, though streaked liberally with gray. The intensity of his hazel gaze...

"Forgive me. You must think I'm rude, just approaching you like this."

"Rude wasn't the first word that came to mind." Arrogant, maybe. Pushy, definitely.

"Ah, yes. I know you and you don't know me. That is awkward, isn't it?" His smirk reminded me of grease on water. "But you do look lovely tonight, my dear. Where is that handsome boyfriend of yours? I saw the two of you arrive. It's not like him to let you out of his sight for very long, is it?"

I stood up, enabling me to address the stranger in a softer voice. "Listen, buddy. I'm not into making a scene. Whatever your play is, deal it. If you need to say something, say it. I'm feeling nice, so I'll tell you right now—if you're still lingering here in a few minutes, it's going to turn into a bad night for you."

There. Good deed accomplished and no photographer the wiser. I'd definitely warned him and been so quiet that only he and I had heard the exchange. That didn't diminish the full-scale creeps I got from him. If Michael didn't end up being his escort out, I'd be sure that security was. On the other hand, maybe I did want a camera nearby. The man's sinister smile sent chills up my spine. I looked around the room again for Michael, but still no sign of him.

"Oh, take it easy, Greta Garbo. You have a flair for dramatics, don't you? Just like your boyfriend. He's always been that way, even when he was a boy—making up tales taller than the trees he climbed around in. He was pretty damn cute, little Michael, finagling stories for his mother's attention. Oh, and did she give it to him. Di's sun rose and set on that boy's word."

For one crazy moment, his wistful tone pulled at weird parts of me. I was damn sure nobody spoke of my childhood like that, and I allowed myself to get caught up in the daydream he painted—

Until his tone turned into a snarl, as soon as he mentioned Diana Pearson.

"But, goddamnit, now those two are just stubborn peas in a pod—causing trouble where they don't even realize it."

My mind crashed back to the here and now—as logic connected the dots about why he looked so familiar. "Wait. Are you—" Data began to connect about why he looked so familiar. Oh, God. Was this Michael's come-and-go weirdo of an uncle? I glared at him harder, almost sure of it. Having spent more time at the farm since July, I'd heard bits and pieces about the man and his rocky past with both him and Diana. Neither of them ever, and I meant ever, said a good word about him. "Damn. You're Michael's—"

"Get away from her! Right now!"

Michael didn't issue the command. He bellowed it—from at least twenty feet away. Everyone seated in between now craned necks and exchanged murmurs, fascinated by what the commotion was about.

Crap.

Crap.

I popped my eyes wide toward Michael, silently begging him to tone it down before the photographers sniffed the testosterone on the air, but judging by the shade of red his face had gone, there was little hope for a reel-in.

"Declan!" he boomed. "So help me, if you so much as put a pinkie on her skin, I'll have you thrown out of here and into the goddamn ocean. Better yet, I'll do it myself."

"Michael." I gritted it while grabbing his arm and twisting as hard as I could. "You need to settle the hell down. We already have stares—we don't need a scene. All press isn't good press. We don't need the sharks scenting you in the water."

"You're right." He nodded and inhaled deeply. "I know. You're right." His lips thinned as he met his uncle's stare. "I don't know what the hell you're doing here or who you bribed to get in. I just want you gone. So help me, Declan, I want your sorry ass out of here, or I will make sure security does it for you."

What the hell?

Screw *This is Your Life*. I was living *Twilight Zone*. Some furious creature had taken over my boyfriend's body, and I didn't know who he was anymore.

Declan didn't make things any better. The older man straightened and chuckled, actions that antagonized Michael beyond their surface value. Michael clenched his fists repeatedly and breathed through his nose like a raging bull. I'd never seen him so physically agitated in my life, which only spiked the attention of everyone at the surrounding tables, morbidly curious about the spectacle unfolding at ours.

Security guards appeared in the doorway. Some partygoers joined them, pointing in our direction.

I tugged on Michael's arm. Desperation inspired boldness. "Please," I demanded. "Stop this—both of you. Security is here. Sit down or take it outside. Michael—we're about to be front page news again, and not for good reasons this time."

Declan unfurled another Crisco grin. "Listen to the lady, Mikey. She's got beauty and brains. How you ever landed a piece of ass so fuckable is a wonder, boy."

I almost—almost—went ahead and told Michael to flatten him.

"Don't talk about her like that, you worthless piece of shit! In fact, don't talk about her at all. Don't even look at her. Your ugly face doesn't deserve the pleasure of her beauty!"

Declan chortled. "Oh, hell, you are fire and brimstone. What my associates wouldn't pay to help channel some of that ambition—"

"Shut up," Michael seethed.

"Tsk. You're passing up a stellar opportunity."

"I said shut up." He wheeled around, tucking me behind him. "Last warning, you gutter-sucking asshole. Get out of my sight, or I will fucking kill you!"

Well, that did it.

Hotel security surged into motion. A verbal threat of that nature was apparently the icing on their red-alert cake. Two Andre-sized men bounded at Michael, each grabbing one of his arms and lifting. He had no option about the direction they pulled, toward a side exit used by the banquet servers. I grabbed my handbag and followed behind, heat crawling up my face. Just about everyone watched us leave the room.

"You've got the wrong guy! He's the asshole. He's the one you should be worried about!"

One of the guards chortled. "That's a new one—huh, Pete?"

"Sure thing," his partner volleyed. "We never heard that one before, buddy."

"Let me guess. You also haven't been drinking tonight, right?"

They kept up like that, at Michael's expense, while dragging him down the back corridor. Thankfully, we were now away from prying eyes—and camera lenses.

Finally, I ran to get ahead of them, forcing them to stop. "Officers—please. Can't you let him go?"

Michael flashed a glare and growled. "Margaux."

I pushed the invisible Mute button for him. Getting into

it with him wasn't going to help the immediate problem. "I promise we'll go right to the car," I told the bigger of the two, Pete. "Then we'll leave the property. I give you my word. I have a driver here waiting for us. Please, enough of this already. We don't need the bad press."

Useless. The pair tightened their grip on Michael and kept power-walking toward an exit door ahead.

"Please! Stop!"

I poured on the girly angst, always a sure-fire guy-freezer. Pete didn't look happy about it, though. "Ma'am, listen. It's the policy of the hotel. As its security professionals, we have to uphold that policy. He caused a scene and openly threatened another guest. I don't care if you're Minnie Mouse and he's Pluto. It doesn't matter. The rules are the rules, and we have to follow them or we lose our jobs. I would love to send you on your way out that door, but I can't. I have a wife and a baby on the way. I can't lose this job, okay?"

"I get it." I held out both hands, palms spread. "But for one thing, you don't need to be throwing him around like he just made a pass at your prom date. For another, who will know if we slip out the back door? No harm no foul, right?" I went for my big guns—the wide kitty-witty eyes. "I'm sorry we've caused you trouble, I am—but there are so many photographers here tonight, and we could use some privacy. Would that be too much to ask?" Annnd the even bigger guns. A flash of my wallet and a little yank on the cash inside. "I have a couple of friends here named Ben who can help make it worth your while."

Pete glanced at his buddy. Their silent communication wasn't long but told me everything I needed to know.

"All right," Pete finally muttered. "I'll see what I can do."

"Thank you." I rushed out a breath. "I'd appreciate it.

But...where are you taking us now? The parking lot is in that direction."

Yes, I was still anxious. We weren't out of this yet—and I couldn't help noticing how quiet Michael had gotten, without any help from my Mute button. And in this situation, a quiet Michael was a scary Michael. He was either planning or brooding. Neither was something I wanted to deal with at the moment.

"There's a back exit down here," Pete explained, "that opens to the beach. If you take the path around to the right, it will bring you out to a parking lot. You can tell your driver to meet you there."

I looked down at my phone, and I wasn't getting reception at all.

"Damn it. No bars."

"True that," he answered. "You'll have to go around the building a little farther, about a hundred yards that way." He pointed in the opposite direction of the parking lot he'd just told me about. *What the fuck?*

I narrowed my eyes. Kitty-witty became pissy wildcat. "Did I mention that this is all to keep the press away from this mess?" I charged.

"Yeah, yeah. We heard you, lady."

"Good—which means you also know not to jack me around, right? Petey, you don't want to fuck with me."

"Right, right." Though he groused about it, his face was properly somber while accepting the bills I pushed into his palm. I hoped to God it actually helped the situation.

We emerged from the building. As Pete had said, the beach was straight ahead to the left, the parking lot to the right. The sharp October air was, for once, a welcome sting on my face.

I caught Michael's stare. Correction—glare. He still struggled a little against the guards, body clenched and face tight. His hair hung in his eyes, thick and sweaty—and, damn him, on a purely physical level, pretty sexy.

Lust was not made for a moment like this.

"I'm going to go tell Andre where to pick us up, okay?" I told him. "I'll meet you right back here."

His expression didn't change. Not that I expected it to— or that it would've been just a tiny bit helpful.

Damn it.

I didn't have time for this bullshit. He was the one who'd decided to make a death threat to his uncle—in public—and had us thrown out of a charity dinner, with the threat of it being documented by a dozen leading gossip rags. Now he acted like some, if not all, of it was my fault.

I lifted the hem of my dress and stormed off in the direction of a cell phone signal.

Fuck him—and fuck the testosterone-fueled horse he rode in on.

CHAPTER FIVE

Michael

The pair of hotel thugs—pardon me, security professionals—didn't let up their hold until they'd escorted me all the way to the beach. There, the patient knightly thing they'd been pulling with Margaux was dropped like the act it was.

"Okay, asshole." The burlier of the two, a jackhole named Pete, jerked me away from his buddy, as if dislocating my shoulder would appease the dick growth gods. "Time for you to cool down."

His buddy grunted as he hurled me into the sand. "Well said, bro."

"Yeah." I rolled onto my elbows. Screw the tux—wasn't like I was going back inside. "He's a goddamn rocket scientist."

I dragged a hand through my hair, trailing sand over my face in the doing. Like I fucking cared. Wrath still pummeled my bloodstream, and I wasn't ready to flush it anytime soon. If I stayed enraged with Declan, I didn't have to think about still being afraid of him.

Yeah.

Even now.

The fear.

Every time I even thought of the man's face, it burst into my gut all over again, festering until it emerged as the emotion I could deal with—the fury. It lent me power over the helplessness...and the guilt. All those years of taking the brunt of his violence because I had no choice and then watching him do the same to Mom. Hating him more every time. Wanting to throw acid on the worm he really was. Dreaming of the day I'd be big enough to fight back, to bash his face in—

Before I could.

Because the coward left.

Between my fifteenth and sixteenth birthdays. Just like that. Not that he'd ever settled in with us at the house, thank fuck, but the week between his little check-in visits stretched to two. Three. Four. A month. A year. Then ten. Mom and I had been preparing to celebrate that milestone when Dec turned back up like the disease that he was.

Mom and I were older by then. Wiser. I'd filed the restraining order that day. Within a couple of days, the security system was upgraded on the house. I'd even installed a tracking device in Mom's truck—

But the fear returned. And with it, the anger.

The shit I refused to process, despite Mom's attempts to get herself aligned and move on. Part of that, I understood. Moving on, I could handle—but who the hell wanted to be reminded about memories of their mother being thrown against the wall, berated until she cringed into a heap, "disciplined" until there were welts? Bruises that had kept her in the house for days...

Marks that made me pray, with every fiber of my being, for Declan Pearson's painful death.

A death I'd pleaded even harder for once Margaux exploded into my world.

Because of her, I'd smiled again. Laughed again. Yeah, at

first it was at her expense, something I'd never be proud of—but soon, she had me smiling with her, for her. Didn't mean the little spitfire didn't piss me off, but this anger was the good kind. The kind love always conquered at the end of the day. Did I want the canker of Declan anywhere near it?

The answer to that had come tonight—in all its disgusting glory. The poison that hit my soul from the moment I walked into the ballroom and saw that cocksucker's hands all over Margaux...

The memory clung to my brain worse than the sand on my suit. Then the nausea. The terror. The rage.

Radio sets squawked. Pete and his pal punched their earpieces and yelled that they were on their way to the hotel's newest emergency. They left without a word, letting me struggle to my feet in a private bath of humiliation.

It'd be at least another ten minutes before Margaux and Andre connected and the car was ready. Before then, it was best for me to lie low. Very low.

I turned and trudged along the beach, grateful as hell for the empty sand and the wind brushing up from the water. Walking off the edge seemed a damn good choice right now. With my phone in my pocket, it'd be easy enough for Margaux to call me back. Only a few key things to focus on now. Breathing. Stepping. Calming.

The air was filled with fall smokiness and a charged chill. The wind carried faint laughter from one of the hotel's balconies, where a group had decided to take their party outside. I looked across the water, layers of cobalt and silver sliced by the brilliant beam from the Point Loma lighthouse, but called a silent bullshit on the light. If my brain were a ship, it'd be crashed on the rocks by now.

Sort of like the ones just up ahead now.

Sort of.

The boulders were more suited for children's pirate play and teenage make-out sessions than shattering ship hulls, but they suited my purpose just fine as well. Finding a perfect crevice, I sat my ass once more in the sand, rested elbows on my raised knees, and then dropped my head between them.

What the hell now?

Coming clean with Margaux was no longer an option I could ignore—but what would she say when I did? The shit with Dec... It wasn't only a few minor childhood memories. Getting back at him had guided so many decisions in my life. Training in martial arts and maintaining my fitness. Entering law school. Living no more than two hours from Mom, ever.

Would Margaux be furious that I'd kept all this in for so long? Worse, would she stare at me with sadness...pity?

"Christ," I muttered. Not the fucking pity.

I wasn't her mental charity case, now or ever. We might be living in her place until I banked enough for a real home, but I took care of things on other levels for us—including the emotional one. She got to lean on me, not the other way around. The woman had spent too much of her life being her own sanctuary. It was about damn time someone else was her safe harbor too.

Safe harbor. Yeah, that's you—the guy hiding out in the rocks on the beach.

My head shot up.

Pussy pouting time was over. I had to man up about this. That meant letting Margaux in—everywhere. Trusting her as deeply as I kept demanding she trust me. And, yeah, even walking away if Declan was still in there, infesting tonight's party—a strong possibility, considering he'd likely scored a few free sympathy drinks from the hotel alone.

Speak of the goddamn devil.

I'd no sooner gotten to my feet than the voice from my nightmares broke over the sand, growling a profanity. Instinctively, I tucked back against the rocks. Even if I wasn't shrouded in shadows, I knew Declan's bite wasn't directed at me. The man always swore at me as a casual conversation enhancer.

There was nothing casual about his tone now.

"—more fucking time!" It was the back end of a statement that hadn't had a favorable start. Wait. The man's face, twisted in a grimace I'd never seen before, revised my assessment. No way was that a statement. It was Declan's version of a plea.

As his expression screwed tighter, I felt mine widen. Beneath my breath, words tumbled out. "What the—"

"More...time." A second man stepped into view, accompanied by three others. All four were somewhere between Declan and me in age, with gym-honed muscles evident through their dark T-shirts. Their dress pants and luxury shoes were custom, male model vanity emphasized by the gallon of hair and beard product split between them. "They say it's a luxury, Mr. Pearson," the ringleader continued, lifting a practiced smirk, "in which case, you've had a steady diet of caviar for the last six months."

Every word was like a surgical incision on the air, refined and precise, increasing my confusion. Were these the associates Dec had referenced back in the ballroom? The urbane fab four weren't what I expected in the way of money-hungry moguls. Like I'd met a lot of those in my time.

One fact was crystal clear. Every move they made caused

Declan to jump like a kid about to get immunizations. I didn't want that to turn the Euro trash into my new heroes, but it did.

"Menger...listen—"

"Listen." Euro number one bit out the word. "The Principals have listened to you for nearly a year, Declan. Their generosity about such attention has been more than ample."

"You're right," Dec soothed. "Of course. You're right. They've been more than fair."

"Fair." The man spat that one too. The tension beneath Dec's jaw told me everything I needed to know about Menger's little hollah-back-as-emphasis habit—and how quickly it went from amusing to irritating. "Covering your losses at the tables into six figures? I would indeed call that fair."

Suddenly, the man's weirdness was more endurable, despite the clench of my own jaw. No wonder Declan had picked up his sniffing around the farm since summer—not to mention his assault on Mom right before Independence Day, carefully planned for when there wasn't a single eyewitness around.

Acts of a desperate man.

From the time I could understand something like a gambling problem, I'd suspected he had one. Nobody took business trips to Vegas that lasted for weeks on end, supplemented by jaunts to the California tribal casinos in between.

But six figures...

Dec was light years beyond a problem. He was addicted— and had been banking on the farm's underground spring as his ladder out of a very deep hole.

Mother. Fucker.

"Menger." Just like that, Dec switched to offense—or

at least tried to. But while he stomped forward, squared his shoulders, and growled both syllables, his fingertips shook. He was close to pissing his pants in fear, and the fab four clearly knew it. They curled small smirks as he struggled for a cavalier tone. "Your concern about all this is...touching, but the Principals are well-aware of why my payments have been delayed."

"Of course they are." Menger dipped his head. I didn't believe his gentleman's act any more than I bought the guards' politeness in the ballroom. "As they are aware of your condition, given that three months ago, all you needed was three more months."

"It was an estimation." Declan gritted every syllable. "They know that, damn it. There are variables that can't be predicted—"

"Estimations. Variables." Euro trash clucked his tongue. "More unpopular words, Declan—words that are beginning to sound like excuses."

His accusation was a hive of bees thrown at Dec's bear. He surged, hands curled like claws. "You know what, Menger? Fuck you! On second thought, I wouldn't waste a drop of jizz on your pathetic ass." He sneered at the man's backward glance. "Don't worry, honey. All your pretty boys are still back there. Must've had the brainwashing at a good lather this morning."

As Menger's wingmen pushed forward, the guy snorted to counter Dec's growl. "Your insolence is alarming, Pearson."

"And your presence is an offense, Menger."

"Is that really what you'd like me to relay to the Principals?"

He waved the pretty boys forward by another step. Dec stood his ground.

"You can relay exactly what I told them last week. If they want the rights to the underground spring on the Pearson Farm, the buy-in must come from Diana and Michael Pearson. They're devoted to each other, that farm, and all the hicks on that hill. As long as the state's in this drought, the water in the spring is prioritized to the farms in Julian."

My grip tightened on the rock wall. Wasn't a surprise that Dec uttered the words like Mom and I had Ebola. To him, loyalty and love were the same thing.

Menger's reaction was more unnerving. The man cocked his head the other direction, as if Declan had simply rattled numbers off a spreadsheet. "And you never tried to exploit the dynamic? Tell the boy his mother would be comfortable for the rest of her days with the money? Tell the woman her son's law education could be all taken care of?"

"If they worried about being taken care of, do you think we'd be having this conversation?"

Menger began a chuckle. When the expression never came to fruition, I tensed on Declan's behalf. Crazy what the human instinct was capable of, despite raging override attempts by one's heart and mind.

"Ohhhh, Declan. This was never intended to be a conversation."

Chalk a huge point for my instinct.

With one lift of Menger's finger, one of his apostles moved like Sea of Galilee lightning. Within a second, the guy had scooted behind Declan and had Dec's arms pinned back. Menger rolled the same hand, sending the other two hulks marching in. Didn't need instinct to call the follow-up shots to that. The pair wasted no time going to work on Dec, each landing three punches into his gut. As mob discipline went, it was light, but even casual martial arts training had taught me the importance of accuracy over force. If those two were as thorough about their combat skills as their T-shirt fit, Declan was already hurting. His buckled knees and harsh grunts proved the theory.

"I'd tell you to fuck off, Menger, but you'd have to have a dick first. But since you simply are one—"

Or maybe they didn't.

The henchmen went to work again, two blows each this time. Declan groaned hard. A deeper version spilled out as the third henchman released him, hurling him face-first into the sand. He lifted his head, beard dripping with dirt and eyes feral with fury, only to be doused in a round of laughter from Menger and the boys.

"Shit," I muttered, gut twisting. *Not a wise move, dickheads. Declan Pearson hated being laughed at. Hated it.*

Dec jolted to his feet and landed a jaw-cracker to the nearest goon's face. He was rewarded with the same from Menger himself.

My brows jumped in appreciation. As capable as the guy seemed, I hadn't figured him for a hands-on operator. He grimaced at the blood on his knuckles, probably the same red slobber at the corner of Dec's mouth.

Declan wiped the shit from his beard before seething, "You. Fucking. Guppy."

Menger rolled his eyes, notching him yet higher in my esteem. "Shut up, Declan. Please."

"Suck my cock, Menger. You don't mess with me, boy. Not like this. Do you know anything? The Principals can't stand having their messes spread in public. Discretion is everything to them. Which means—"

"They selected a perfect evening to suggest we accompany you." Menger smiled, as demure as James Bond about to shiv a villain. "Discreetly, of course," he added. "Perhaps after they learned you purchased a ticket for tonight's festivities, coupling it with the assumption that you'd try to influence your nephew, using his little blonde fluff as bait..." He shrugged with more movie screen finesse. "The rest, as they say, belongs to simple logic."

Dec fumed through a long silence, giving me a chance to think. No. Screw that. I fumed too. The props I'd given Menger were shattered as soon as he turned Margaux to fluff. Now I didn't know whose skull I craved to bash in more—Declan, for the brass of daring to touch Margaux to begin with, or Menger, for regarding her as nothing but a pawn in the power game between Dec and the Principals?

Who the fuck were they, anyway? Legitimate mafia or glorified thugs? Did I want to know?

No time to contemplate that answer—not when I'd been hauled into this mess. That meant memorizing everything that happened now, even when one of Menger's men pulled out a tube of hand sanitizer and offered it to the man. Menger used the stuff liberally, scrubbing his bloodied hands before speaking again.

"For the love of God, stop sulking. Michael's violence didn't surprise you any less than it did us. Do not feign that it did. The Principals merely thought ahead about exploiting it." The man moved back toward Dec, deliberately digging in his toes to spray sand with every step. "In short, darling Declan, I could let these boys beat you for another hour, and the Principals wouldn't be happier." He quirked a little smile. "Maybe I should let them do more...a little stress relief for everyone. Maybe that would make you happier too?"

Declan spat sand. "Fuck you!"

"Hmmm." Menger sighed, a direct clash to the fist he snapped out, clipping the unharmed side of Dec's face. "Sadly, you aren't my type. Now, trading places with your nephew, for the chance to get my dick near that lovely little Margaux Asher?" He hitched a hard knee up into Declan's groin. "Trashing you completely might be worth the mess after all. If Michael will be blamed for this all the way to a holding cell, then she'll need some special comforting—"

My vision turned red and then black. One second of imagination was all it took. One instant of envisioning that scum with his cheap sanitizer hands near Margaux...then on her...

I was galvanized.

"Careful what you ask for in comfort, asshole." I surged from the shadows, already aiming a fist for Menger's chest. Made it advantageous to go for his neck after that. Two of his boys reacted at once to intercept. I opened up a fierce grin. *Bring it on, dickheads.* It was pure bliss to feed my fury up my arm, catching the first henchmen between his ear and jaw. I got him hard, making him soften and then slump.

The second goon was so stunned, he froze.

I swung my attention to Menger. Grinned again.

Right before the chickenshit backed away—and then ran into the night. His two upright buddies followed, dragging the third between them.

Just before a woman's shriek cut through the night.

Declan and I peered toward the hotel, where two housekeepers stood on the walkway with their carts, gaping at us. One of the women snatched up a handheld radio.

"We need security on the beach in front of the towers. Now!"

In less than a minute, a couple of security guards appeared—followed by twice as many managers and at least a dozen photographers. The guy who'd snapped me in the ballroom clearly believed in mitosis. I had no idea this many members of the paparazzi existed in San Diego, let alone gave a damn about an apple farmer's kid standing up for his girlfriend at a society fundraiser.

"Hey!" one of the shutterbugs yelled. "It is him!"

"Yep. He's here," another chimed. "Genius move to listen to the security chatter, Jerry."

"Right?" An older guy, three cameras dangling from his neck, nodded. "I knew Mikey was too pissed to be done tonight."

I growled low in my throat. "Not you douches too."

"What a scoop," someone else interjected. "Let's hang tight for a few. I'll bet Margaux makes an appearance too."

"Prep for the fireworks."

Their laughter opened up a moment to round back on all of them. If Declan was just a rankled grizzly, then I was a full-bore dragon—about to fry their collective asses with fire and brimstone.

"Gentlemen." My locked teeth kept it to the correct side of composed—barely. "Back off. Right now."

Jerry lifted one of his three cameras and smirked. "Awww, come on, Mikey. We're only trying to do our job. If we were a barrel of apples, you'd be happy."

Especially if it came with a dicer. But they weren't getting even that out of me, since Pete and his team had reached Dec and radioed for a medical team. Not surprisingly, my uncle remained silent—slicing glares at me that, to anyone new on the scene, spoke volumes of accusation.

Fan-fucking-tastic.

Sure enough, one of the photographers jabbed his chin at me. "Guess you got your pound of flesh now, yeah?"

"No shit," drawled his buddy. "Man, I can't decide on which cut he got in better—the right or the left."

"Neither." It was one thing to water the weeds of their insolence. It was another to let them grow lies. "I didn't do this." Swerving back to the guards, I pointed down the beach. "There were four of them, all looking like European fashion boys. Black T-shirts, designer pants; tallest is six-two or three, and the head honcho is a few inches shorter. A gallon of hair product between them. If one of you takes off now, you can probably—"

"Catch them and their little dog Toto too?" Pete rejoined.

"God damn it." I dragged a hand through my hair. Would arguing with them even get me anywhere?

Like fate was going to let me entertain more than two seconds of an inner conflict tonight.

Especially if the enraged blonde at the edge of the sand had anything to say about it.

"What. The. Fuck?"

Like a rehearsed chorus line, every photographer swung their lenses at the gorgeous, glowering love of my life. The air exploded with light, the flashes illuminating the rage on Margaux's face. Damn it if the fury didn't multiply her beauty by a thousand, flushing her cheeks and flaring her lips. I would've been fantasizing about other ways to make her look that way, if not for the dread invading my gut—pounded in by the accusation in her eyes.

As if the nonstop schicks were just bug drones, she stepped out of her heels, onto the shore and straight to me. Only a few of the leeches were ballsy enough to follow her, gambling on the risk of carrying their cameras across the sand in exchange for a juicy scoop.

"So." She slid hands to her hips while casting her hundredth glance at Declan. Clearly, she didn't know whether to offer him sympathy, comfort, or disdain. The fact that she even debated the issue jacked my gall. "You...want to explain this?"

"Other than the fact that I didn't do it?"

Her gaze narrowed. "What? You were strolling on the beach to cool off and Declan just walked into your fist?"

"Beach—check. Cooling off—check. The rest of it? No." When her expression didn't falter, my jaw locked to the point of pain. I stepped away, struggling to process what the fuck that did to my gut now. And my heart. "You really don't believe me, do you?"

Margaux's shoulders sagged. "I don't know what to believe, Michael."

"Me, goddamnit." I retreated again as she moved forward. Her nearness, always my shelter, was like a stab. "You believe me."

"Michael—"

I didn't know how to interpret her tone either. Softer but sure as hell not empathetic. A dilemma you wouldn't find yourself in if she knew the full truth about Declan by now.

Wasn't like I could spit it all out now—or in the foreseeable future. Not when a security goon approached, apparently Pete's captain, to relay that they'd need to file a full report and would need me to follow him to their offices...and would need me to "stick around" in case it was necessary to notify the San Diego PD as well.

The bed I'd made—its mattress full of my secrets.

It was the shit pile I'd have to lie in now.

CHAPTER SIX

Margaux

Hello, bad. Meet your new best friend, worse. Get cozy, we're going to be here a while.

I listened to the banquet servers chatting in the hallway just beyond the hotel's stuffy security office. Dinner had been served and cleared away. The gala's attendees were dancing and laughing their way into the night, making memories they would bring up the next time they saw each other around town.

Not us.

I was starving and sick to my stomach at the same time. Michael looked five times as miserable, slumped in the chair across the room, his bowtie now a limp black worm. They wouldn't let me sit beside him. Maybe they thought he'd try to make me lie for him or something. Like that was going to happen, considering I could barely form a coherent sentence at this point. I doubted he could either. Neither of us could focus on much beyond the looming question of the night.

Would dear old Uncle Declan be pressing charges against Michael with the San Diego PD or not?

Since they'd determined Declan's injuries serious enough for an ambulance transfer to the hospital, things weren't looking so good for my boyfriend—though Michael still swore up and down, to everyone who'd interviewed him, that he hadn't laid a hand on the man.

There was the damn rub for me.

Did I believe him, or didn't I?

In principle, I should've stood by my man, right? Should've had his back, no matter what. If he did do it, I should go down swinging right beside him. *Take no prisoners, go down with the ship*, and—

And all those other sayings for desperate people.

I'd made it this far in my life by leading with my head, not my heart—no matter how strongly the latter wanted to be involved. That made it hard—very hard—to ignore the glaring evidence against Michael. Nonetheless, this whole scene was ridiculous. These night school-trained security guards were acting like Quantico-honed agents, throwing around so many acronyms and bits of legal jargon I was pretty sure they no longer understood each other.

I observed that Michael hadn't told them he was a lawyer. It was likely on purpose, stemming from hope that they'd slip up and violate his basic rights, clearing the way to have the case thrown out if and when the time came for court proceedings. Well, I wouldn't be the one to spill those beans. I could at least back him up on that.

I finally rose. It was hell to sit there and keep still, watching Michael's tension grow by the minute. I wasn't helping, and I sure as hell could guess why.

I longed to simply take his hand for a moment but wondered if the Keystone Cops would bash it in if I did. Instead, I murmured, "I'm not leaving, okay? I'm just going to go look for something to eat, maybe a cup of coffee. There must be some dessert left in the ballroom."

Lame, lame, lame—but it filled the air with something

other than the guards' stupid posturings. I turned, trying to smooth my dress out, but it was hopeless. I'd been sitting haphazardly for so long, the satin part was creased and the chiffon layers were a mess. Whatever. My appearance fit my mood, so I embraced it.

"Hey. Hey...Michael?"

He didn't even lift his head. "What?"

Be sweet. Be supportive. Be the keel in his ship. "Do you want me to bring you anything? Coffee?"

"No. I'll be fine."

"Okay."

Translation—got it, you dick.

I was trying. Really trying. This compassionate shit wasn't naturally in my wheelhouse, a weakness that'd been all but beaten out of me by Andrea. Moreover, this just wasn't the place to air our dirty laundry—like I could do anything about that, either. Clearly, he still stung from what had gone down at the beach, probably feeling like I'd not shown the proper support when first arriving on the scene and eyeing Declan with all those bruises and blood. But what would he have done in my shoes...if he'd seen what I had?

Yes, he was hurting. But he was also being unfair. Eventually, when all of this blew over, he'd see that.

With that thought as comfort, however thin, I left the room.

Wasn't tough to discern where the gala was located from here. I simply followed the typical DJ'd music back to the ballroom. To my good fortune, dessert was still being served. To my very good fortune, there were at least eight chocolate choices.

I was also able to grab a cup of coffee from the buffet. It

tasted like complete shit, but it was hot and it was caffeine. I had a bad feeling this night was far from over. My bad feelings were rarely wrong.

What a mess.

I pulled a chair into the shadows, all appetite for the sweets suddenly gone. Instead, I wrapped my hands around the small white cup of bad java, hoping it would chase away some of the damp chill from outside.

I tilted my head back against the wall and exhaled, trying to simply relax. A few minutes passed. Maybe it was an hour. I wanted to disconnect so badly, I didn't care—

Until realizing that someone was hovering nearby, attempting to get my attention.

Shoot me. Please, shoot me.

"Do you mind if I join you?"

A man's voice reached over the thump of the music. I peered up at him but couldn't make out his face from where I sat.

"I'd really prefer to be alone."

"Margaux...it's me. Doug."

Well...shit.

"Doug...Simcox?" He stepped closer. Same slightly goofy, all-American grin. Same PC blond crew cut and shoulders that had nudged him close to home run records during his career. Slicker suit this time, though. Much slicker schmooze-and-cruise game.

I sighed and wished the coffee would turn to vodka. "I remember your last name, Doug."

"How are you?" Another step. A disarming dip of his head. "You look great."

"Right." I rolled my eyes. "Thanks. That makes me feel so

much better. Sure, God. Why not? It's been one hell of a night already. Let's just go for broke."

He lowered into a chair next to me like a fireman approaching a wet cat in a tree. "Uhhh...yeah. I guess you've had a rough one, huh? I kind of heard your boyfriend was in a fight...?"

"He didn't do it." Why I was defending Michael now, I wasn't quite sure—but I sure as hell wasn't going to sit here and let Doug tear him down.

"Oh." He blinked, seeming puzzled. "I didn't know you were there too."

"I wasn't. But he says he didn't do it, and—"

"You believe him?"

"Of course I believe him." I stamped my best bitch stare to the end of it. He should remember it well.

"Of course you do. I didn't mean to offend you."

Old habits really did die hard. I'd gone bitch face, and now, right on cue, he went pouty boy. I pulled in a long breath. My Mercury was definitely in retrograde or some shit-tastic thing like that, because tonight was turning into a perfect storm of crap I so didn't need.

"Listen, Doug. I'm having a shitty night. This is awkward as fuck. I'm sure we can both agree on that. Unless you actually need something, can we just...I don't know..." I stood and parked my coffee on a table. "I should go."

He shot to his feet too. "No, no, it's okay. I moved in on your space, and—" He hitched a gee-whiz shrug, one of his signature moves. "I'll let you be. I only thought—well, you looked like you could use some company."

I felt his sincerity. Wasn't about to feel guilty about stomping on it, but I summoned enough civility to reply,

"Thanks. But company is the last thing I want right now."

"Okay, well. At least accept this." He reached in his pocket and pulled out a business card. I had no intention of keeping it, but if he'd leave that much quicker, I'd take a stack of the damn things. Anything to send him on his way. "Sounds like you may need some help figuring out what really happened tonight. Just so happens I'm in the business now. That's right. I'm a real-live private eye, baby."

The bastard had to be joking—but not very well, despite flipping on his strongest mega-watt smile. There was a time when that grin would've melted my panties off. Now I was plain annoyed.

"Uh...thanks. Don't be surprised if you don't hear from me, though. You can understand why, I'm sure."

He had the grace to drop the smile. "Listen, Margaux. I get it. We have a lot of water under our bridge, and some of it is pretty muddy. But I'm the best game in town when it comes to this shit, if you'll allow the horn tooting for one minute."

"Or two? Or three?" I chuckled. "Gee, Doug, don't hold back on my account." My sarcasm underlined the subtext. He'd always thought he was God's gift—to everyone and everything.

"Fair shot." He held up both hands. "But a lot has changed since we dated. People change, grow up. I made a lot of mistakes when we were together. I didn't treat you the way I should've. There are a lot of things I regret—and I can't do a damn thing about them now." He grew quiet, looking at his feet. "But seriously, if things get too huge to handle and you need some fast, thorough investigative work, give me a call. I can help."

I gave him a wry side-eye. "Gotcha, Miss Marple."

He didn't flinch. "You know that big case all over the news

last month, about the toddler who was abducted and taken across the border?"

My eyes narrowed. Only those living under rocks wouldn't have heard about the Christopher Landen story, at least in San Diego. It had been the lead local news story every morning, afternoon, and night. It had been the subject of arguments on social media and the beneficiary of many local fundraisers.

Last week, the child had been returned—through some miracle, totally unharmed—to his home in a city suburb. His parents had sobbed, thanking the angels who'd brought him home. Celebration parades had been held in his honor. There was even talk of renaming one of the local sports parks after him.

"Wait. That was..."

"Me." Doug beamed. "And my team."

"Wow." It was a little unbelievable. The self-absorbed asshole who I'd dated for eight months wouldn't have done anything altruistic, let alone put effort into finding a missing child.

"It was pretty grueling and took a coordinated effort, especially since his abductor went across the border. We worked day and night until we were able to bring that kid home. It was the single best day of my life so far." After a moment of staring at me because I couldn't stop staring at him, he muttered, "What?"

"Nothing," I replied. "But maybe everything. I'll admit, I'm a little impressed. I didn't think you had something like that in you."

"Like I said, Mags, people change."

Just like that, our little détente was officially over. "Don't call me that, Doug. Not ever again. Do you understand?"

"I—it was—I thought we were—"

"We weren't." I wrestled back the urge to throat punch him. "We can't. You, me, us, that whole time of my life is dead and buried. Got it?"

"Easy. I didn't mean to set you off. Only an old habit."

"Well, unlearn it. Fast. There are way too many demons down that road for me."

"Fine. Understood. It won't happen again."

A long silence passed between us. I lowered back into the chair. Now I really did need a drink, but my hands shook so badly, I doubted my ability to hold a glass to my lips.

Mother. Fucker. One stupid slip of a nickname, and I was right back in that hospital room, inches from a death I prayed for, all because of a broken heart from this asshole. We'd both played our part in the mess, but he knew—knew, even now—how shitty it had all been for me. Logically, I knew the room still had air, but I was nearly suffocating. Damn triggers.

I started twisting my ring. Calm, deep breaths followed. I took more and closed my eyes.

And pictured my Captain America's smile.

Michael. Of course. He would save me from this agony.

But where was he?

My eyes flashed open on the dawn of my stupidity. No. He needed me right now—only I'd behaved like an ass, flouncing out of that security room, paranoid about making him understand my comfort level on the supportive girlfriend gig.

What the hell was I thinking?

I shook my head in shame. Stood in a harsh rush. I shouldn't be here with my past. I needed to be with Michael—

My future.

A bright smile spread across my face as my plan cemented

in my mind. I'd go find Michael, tell those morons in security they couldn't keep him any longer, and then have Andre take us home. We'd have that good Scotch. Run a warm bath. Then we'd work it out, all of it, together—because that was what we'd promised each other. How we'd do it all from now on. We'd share our successes and our failures. Together.

I turned one more time to the man now leaning in again, eyeing me with abject curiosity. Go ahead and stare, buddy. As much as Doug's heart had grown, I doubted he could comprehend one-tenth of the connection I shared with Michael.

"Listen, Doug..." I grabbed his hand and gave it a fake politician squeeze. "I'm glad we ran into each other, okay? Sorry for the bitch-itude. I'm under a lot of pressure tonight. Things are really tense with Michael. We just don't know where it all stands."

"It's cool," he reassured. "But maybe that's something you should ask him in person—after he clears the seven hundred bees out of his jock strap."

"Huh?"

"Here he comes."

He disengaged our hands. It was too little, too late.

I groaned and spun toward the door—weathering the frantic echo of just one word through my brain.

Shit.

Shit.

Shit.

CHAPTER SEVEN

Michael

Fuck.
My.
Life.

Yeah, the universe could have supplied worse reasons for the sentiment. The fundraiser could've been sharing the hotel with a clown convention or one of those "furry" cons. Chad could be standing here, nagging about when we were escaping to the bar so I could watch his pick-up attempts on anything in a skirt. The Big One might have finally hit, and we'd all be sliding into the Pacific right now.

Instead, after the grilling from hotel security and the PD, I'd not been able to reach Margaux by text or phone so had stupidly returned to the ballroom—

To find her bringing one of my worst nightmares to life.

With Doug fucking Simcox.

It was the final nail in this screwed-up night. I led the pack on crazy, didn't I, actually thinking my girlfriend had taken this time to reconsider her shit? To, say, go somewhere and think about the man she'd been living with for three months, then recognize he was smart enough to see the idiot move of going publicly aggro on a guy—even a douche like Declan—and then turn around and go for more punching practice on the asshole?

She'd clearly misjudged a lot of things about me—like assuming I'd behave now to make up for the shit Declan had started earlier. Like how I'd just dive into being the good boyfriend, understanding and sweet, even when finding her with the shit jockey who'd shattered her heart. Why the hell should I invest in being that guy when she'd given up on him too?

At least she didn't hide her stress. Her face betrayed the dread of the screws popping off my moorings and flying into Doug. Couldn't say her fears were unfounded. Not yet. While approaching Doug and her, I jammed my hands into my pockets. Better hide the fact that they'd become fists again.

She took a few steps to meet me, flinging her arms around my neck. "Thank God you're here."

I didn't reciprocate the embrace. Her hands fell to her sides. She bit her lip, looking tense and unsure, not that she gave me more than two seconds to evaluate. That privilege belonged to Simcox, as soon as she swung her stare to him again.

I dragged in air through my nose, hoping for a calming influence, but was assaulted by a sour stench instead. Wasn't anything the hotel could be blamed for. That smell belonged to one thing only, and I was repulsed that I recognized it so easily. It was the sewage of jealous rage.

"Michael? Are you all right?" When she turned back around, she assessed me physically, dipping her gaze over all of me. "They only questioned you some more, right?"

I steeled my jaw. Forced the shield to cover my heart too. Didn't matter. The worry in her voice was like a blowtorch, threatening to sear it. She'd been distant and quiet in the security office. What the hell was this fresh concern all about?

"Do you even care?"

"Of course. I—" She pulled back, looking hurt at first, until green fire flared in her eyes. "Why the hell would you say that?"

I grunted, letting my gaze travel to Simcox. "Looked like you were filling your time just fine when I walked in."

Margaux shot her hands back to her hips. Her gown, even rumpled, swished so every line of her delectable figure was accented. "Michael Adam. Don't."

"'Michael Adam don't' what? Drag up the past? Looks like I'm a little late for that, baby. Did you two have a nice little trip down memory lane while I was playing a thousand and one questions with Andy Griffith and Barney Fife?"

"Wonderful," she muttered. "Way to prove it taught you a damn thing, Opie."

She wanted Opie? I'd give her fucking Opie. "Thanks, sweetheart. This is the perfect ending to a dream of an evening."

As if matters could get worse, Simcox loped forward with the exuberance—and social aptitude—of a Saint Bernard. "Hi there. Great to meet you. I'm—"

"I know who you are."

His grin faltered. "Uhhh, right. Well, then." He recovered within seconds, extending a hand. "It's Michael, right? Pearson? Like I said, good to meet you, man."

I let him hang for a good five seconds. Ten. His composure teetered in the silence. *Yo—point to Pearson. Boosh, Dougie-poo.* Totally childish? Yeah. Totally satisfying? Fuck yeah. And why the hell not? Ancient history or not, Margaux would carry scars because of this big mutt for the rest of her life. He'd cleaned up well with a shit ton of hair gel, a professionally close shave, and a tailored black suit, but he was still a goddamn mutt.

Did I wish they'd never broken up? Of course not. But there were ways you did things and ways you didn't. The golden rules of guy code. He'd snapped at least a couple by breaking up with a woman when she wasn't on solid emotional ground, jumping on a plane for his next away game, and never looking back. To the best of my knowledge, he'd never even checked in with Margaux again.

The asshole looked intent on making up for lost time now.

"Well," he said after we finally shook hands. "Guess I should really thank you. You got the party rolling with one hell of an ice breaker."

Touché, fucker. "Anything to help the cause. The arts are pitifully neglected in our schools these days."

"Much agreed, my man."

Without lowering my head, I smiled—with my mouth alone. "I'm not your man."

"Uhhh...pardon me?"

Through her teeth, Margaux seethed, "I said don't."

I grinned again. What the hell. Might as well enjoy my stint in the doghouse. "You heard me. I'm not your man, Simcox." I rocked back on my heels, glancing around as if we were just shooting the shit about the Chargers' chances for the upcoming season. "Don't even try to pretend we're friends or that you care one shit about this cause."

Margaux pushed forward again. She raised her hands as if to embrace me, but they froze in midair, stopping in front of my chest, as if there were an actual wall between us.

My gut turned over.

How had we gotten here?

This time last night, I was sprawled on her living room floor after the most incredible sex of my life. Now, I felt like the goddamn puppy who'd peed on the carpet.

"Michael." She finally wrapped her fingertips around my tuxedo's lapels. The tenderness in her tone unspooled me worse than her ire ever could. "Let's just go home, okay? Andre is waiting out front."

I debated how to respond to that. After all the venom I'd hurled at Simcox, it was Margaux's tenderness toward me that finally rankled the guy. I smirked, openly gloating. He tensed, openly fuming. I wasn't about to throw a punch at the Neanderthal, but if he wanted to rumble, I was more than ready.

The Del's security team had other plans. They appeared in two separate entryways before approaching cautiously.

"Mr. Pearson?"

I didn't stray my stare from Margaux. She was really the only one who mattered here. "Yeah?"

"Perhaps it's a good idea for you to call it a night."

Shit. Was the directive-by-diplomacy thing still a thing?

I didn't care. I slipped my hand into Margaux's, meshing our fingers. "Sure. I can think of some very nice excuses for going home early...can't you, sugar?"

Dougie-poo's face discernibly tightened. Too bad, so sad—you lose, bastard.

"Thanks for taking the time to catch up, Mags. It was nice."

Or not.

"Mags?"

She didn't see the glare I swung at her with it, already stabbing hers into him. "Damn it, Doug. I told you—"

"Sure you did," I growled.

She yanked her hand from mine. "Okay, you want to go

at it with me as well, Pearson?" She scooped both hands into the air between us, beckoning with her fingertips. "Come on. Let's just do it right now. Take your best swing and then let me put you down right after, because God fucking knows, that is seriously what I want to do to you right now!"

Like a sliced hot air balloon, everything inside deflated. Crashed. Then burst into flames. In their wake, my senses were a black mess I didn't even want to sift through.

Without another word, I turned and paced out through the lobby. As Margaux had said, Andre waited with the car. I stalked past him, climbing into the limo and slamming into the corner seat, nearest the driver's partition.

We traveled back across the bay, now haunted by fingers of mist, in silence.

No. Not complete silence.

As staunchly as she tried to hide them, Margaux's soft sniffles filled the air every couple of minutes. Every one of them stabbed my heart like a rusted dagger.

And my own damn hand was on that hilt.

We pulled up the wide drive in front of the El Cortez. The car had barely stopped before I let myself out, digging in my jacket for my car keys. Despite that, I turned to assist Margaux out of the car. Her fingers were cold against my palm.

For a moment, just one, I gripped them tighter. Yearned for her to meet my gaze...and see the words I couldn't speak yet.

I'm trying, princess. God damn it, I'm trying.

Instead, she worked her hand free once more, instantly twisting it into the depths of her skirt. Her head remained down as she regarded the keys in my grip. "I won't wait up."

I almost went after her. Maybe I should have. Was that

what she wanted? Fuck. I didn't know anymore. Back at the Del, I'd envisioned a wall between us—a barrier stacked higher with every one of her tears in the car. What had I done? Sat there like a mute asshole, not even offering to go to her. The memory of how she'd lashed out at me on the beach, instantly connecting me to Declan's bloody face, had been too fresh. It still stung like hell.

I was a mess. Plugs jammed into all the wrong sockets.

In order to figure it out, I had to disconnect and start over.

Once I got in the truck and pulled away from the Cortez, only one direction felt clear.

I headed for the mountains.

For home.

★ ★ ★ ★

The best-laid plans...

I didn't need the rest of it spelled out. It was the story of my life lately, so why did I expect different now?

I made it as far as Ramona before a crowd of cars, the aroma of coffee, and the siren call of Dudley's bear claws made me slow down. Frowning curiously, I pulled into the diner's parking lot. What the hell? The place was rarely open this time of night.

A group of kids in tuxes and formal gowns passed by, filling in the answer. Must have been fall formal night for the high schools.

Suddenly, blending into a crowd of teenagers felt better than a late-night greeting—and grilling—from Mom.

Too bad I was premature about the hallelujah on that freedom.

As I settled into a small booth in the back of the dining room, my cell vibrated. The name in the window drilled my jaw with tension.

Killian Stone.

For another two seconds, I wavered my thumb over the green button. Why I even considered the red one was a mystery. Fruitless cause, man. The man didn't carve time out of his Saturday night, especially at this hour, to ring up a buddy to shoot the shit. Whether he'd called on his own or at Margaux's request, I wasn't going to get out of this.

The green button it was. Damn it.

"Mr. Stone."

"Mr. Pearson."

"To what do I owe this pleasure?"

Killian chuckled. "You serious about that?"

I lifted a smile at the waitress as she brought my coffee. Dropped it as soon as she left. "I was hoping to be."

His heavy exhalation filled the line. "Claire and I were in bed. She was looking for a new book to read, but a swarm of celeb gossip alerts blew up her feed. You know what they say about the vultures."

"Yeah." I'd learned the back end of that one during my first week in corporate PR cleanup. "Can't dodge their shit if you don't know where they're circling."

"And some nights they like to circle longer."

I blew on my coffee, instantly recognizing the action as habit rather than practicality. No way would I be dumping the shit into the acid pond of my gut now. "So it's the Michael Pearson feeding frenzy for San Diego's rag sites tonight?"

"San Diego?" he countered. "Dude, your little fireworks show at the Del has already been picked up by the national feeds. I think TMZ's leading with you tomorrow."

I raked a hand through my hair. "Wonderful."

"That's one way of putting it."

"As long as I'm prettier than Kanye, right?"

"Oh, you're pretty, all right. Must be that combination of model perfection and animal rage. Last time I checked, a few thousand women were posting about how to get into your pants."

"Access to my pants is controlled by one hell of a gatekeeper, man."

Killian's pause was significant. "So Margaux's still speaking to you?"

"Define speaking." Sharing details beyond the initial drama in the ballroom with Dec seemed a bad decision right now.

"Damn. Claire was afraid of that. Honestly, so was I."

"It's fine," I insisted. "We're fine. We just need some space before we...talk some things through." When he threw back nothing but a snicker, I growled, "What?"

"Space? In order to talk things through, huh?"

I grimaced. "What the hell is wrong with that? You've never had anything to talk through with Claire?"

Another long pause. Too long.

Finally, Kil's snort filled the line. "You're not even at home, are you? Did you run off to a bar? Isn't going to help, my friend."

"Says the guy who ran off and played grunge Jesus for six months?"

"And almost lost the love of my life because of it," he asserted. "Pearson, learn a valuable lesson from my mistake. Go home and do your penance on the couch for a few nights.

Then she'll be ready to talk to you. Drinking yourself into a stupor only puts off the inevitable." He pushed out another telling breath. "By the way, Andre's driving, right?"

"I'm not drinking, goddamnit." Not even the coffee, which smelled pretty fucking good. "I'm just—"

"Not at home. Which is where you should be."

The waitress plunked down my bear claw. I stabbed a fork into the pastry and twisted hard, resigned to mutilating the thing instead of eating it. "There's nothing wrong with giving this some space."

As I spoke, rough rustlings crackled over the line. Only it wasn't Killian I heard next.

"Are you out of your damn mind?"

Claire's huffy bark would've made me laugh—except that she scared me in this state of rage. I held the phone back for a second, wondering when the raging bees would burst from it.

They didn't. But maybe honey was a good idea anyway. "Heeyy, Claire Bear—"

"Do not with the 'Claire Bear.'" More scratches on the line. When she spoke again, her voice was louder. "Why the hell are you out carousing, when—"

"I'm not carousing!"

"That's not the point. You're out, Michael Pearson. Do you know what that's doing to my best friend—the woman you claim to love?"

"Claim to love?" *You mean the woman I just proposed marriage to—who, incidentally, turned me down?*

"Don't piss defensive on me," she snapped, "when you repeatedly threatened to knock Killian's ass into the next century when he disappeared on me last year."

"What?" Killian punched it out from the background.

"He did?"

"This isn't the same."

"You think Margaux knows that? Margaux, who has deeper issues than I ever had about feeling accepted, acknowledged, loved? Margaux, who's been treated like a disposable toy by everyone in her life—who thinks maybe, for the first time, she's found a person who won't throw her away, even when times get rough?" She let out a little growl. "What the hell are you doing with that trust now, Pearson? Moping in some dark corner somewhere about how complicated your soul is, about how she won't get it? Opening all that baggage again, whatever the hell it is, and crying over the dirty underwear inside?"

I took a gulp of the coffee. If it rained acid on my stomach lining, so be it. Maybe I deserved the agony. "I'm not—"

"Save it." Both words were seething switchblades. "Stop sulking over your dirt and clean it up, Michael. Deal with it. You have a remarkable, beautiful, brave woman who wants to help you do just that. Get your ass back to her—and refuse to give up until you make it right!"

So. Silences really could be deafening. She'd gone so quiet, I wondered if the connection had been lost—until hearing Killian clear his throat in the background, communicating one clear message. Claire had just wowed the pants off her husband—if he was still wearing any. Better odds lay on him not—in which case, I guessed at how he craved to wow her in return.

"I'd better go," I finally mumbled.

"Great idea," Claire returned. "And hey...Michael?"

"Yeah?"

"I only get this pissed if the cause is worth fighting for."

A smile started in my heart and brimmed on my lips. "I

know, Claire. I know."

She didn't fight me on the nickname this time. Just like I didn't say a word once I got home—and found bedding waiting for me on the couch. A red blanket, a white blanket, a down pillow—items yanked off the bed from the guest room, driving it in that if she found my ass in there come morning, she might cuff me to the damn school desk.

"Penance on the couch." I echoed Killian's words beneath my breath while stripping off my tux and then settling against the massive orange cushions of the designer monstrosity. Though the thing was bigger than a lot of beds, it didn't relieve the clamps over my chest one damn inch—or make it easier to resist rushing upstairs, back to the place I belonged. Wrapped around Margaux Asher. Forever.

Tomorrow, man.

I could start forever...tomorrow.

By taking out my laundry and finally getting it clean with her. For her.

I was ready.

I had to be.

★ ★ ★ ★

Pound.

I flinched and moaned. Cracked open one eye, only to be stabbed by a glint of morning sun off the patio's steel rail. My legs tangled in the blankets as I reached for the pillow and thumped it atop my head.

Pound. Pound. Pound.

"No," I mumbled. "No. Uh-uh. Don't want any."

Pound. Pound. Pound.

"Damn it. No!"

Margaux's whine made me lift the pillow. I looked up in time to watch her clear the last few stairs into the room. Our gazes snagged, wrestling in lingering anger and brand-new awkward, before I succumbed to the temptation of gawking at the rest of her. Fuck, she was cute, all bed-head and sleep-lined face. Was that a little pajama set beneath her satin robe? With cupcakes on it? Wait. The woman owned pajamas?

Maybe I'd woken up in another dimension.

In which case, it should be no problem to fulfill my fantasy of peeling those cupcakes off her body and then launching a quest to taste her...frosting.

Reality thundered back in. More thumps shook the door.

Margaux glared at the locked panel and then back at me. Scraped her hair from her eyes. "It's Sunday, right?"

I nodded while yanking my tuxedo pants back on. Though the building didn't have a doorman, the condo was on the penthouse floor, meaning we still had to buzz people up...

Unless they were entities who didn't have to ask permission for that shit.

Dread fisted my chest. I forced one word past it, anyway. "Fuck."

"Huh?" Margaux sputtered. I hated the fear that crept into her eyes. "Michael? What—"

"Michael Pearson! Open up! This is the San Diego Police Department."

"—the hell?" She jerked her robe shut, switching to self-preservation mode without even knowing it. That was good. Very good.

"Stand back, sugar." I paced past her, toward the door. "Way back. This probably won't be pretty."

"Screw that."

So much for the reassurance she'd protect herself. She raced in front of me, twisted the deadbolt free, and whooshed open the door. Sure enough, a pair of San Diego's finest filled the space. They both examined her from head to toe before dutifully riveting their gazes back to her face. *That's good, fellas. Keep them there if you want to keep your gonads intact.*

"Officers." She braced a hand on the door frame and another on her hip. "Good morning. What can I do for you?"

Both cops were dark-haired and baby-faced, though one's face was etched by the subtle lines of experience. He was also the one who stepped forward and dipped his head. "Ma'am. Good morning. Can I ask you to step aside? We're here for Mr. Pearson."

Margaux clucked her tongue and tossed back her head. In her little lavender robe, hair tumbling down her back, she was one pair of stilettos shy of being a Maxim centerfold. I had to hand it to the guys in blue, who didn't waver their stares. They either had the fortitude of oxen or were secretly robots. I didn't care which. "Boys, you know I can't do that for you without a warrant."

The lead cop pulled out a piece of paper that looked all too official. "Well, good thing we brought one."

My gut surrendered to full-fledged dread. And disgust. And rage. Margaux reached for me. Again, her hands were icy—and trembling. Instinctively, I clamped them tighter. I hated this bullshit—but most of all, I despised how it affected her.

"I don't...understand." She barely kept it above a choke.

"I do." My statement was the polar opposite, entirely too certain of itself—just like my desire to spit on the fucking warrant. "Let me guess. Mr. Pearson's 'come to his senses' about the events of last night, right? Turns out I was the one who fucked him up after all, and now he's pressing charges?"

Margaux's fingers slipped from mine. The emptiness she left behind was as bleak as her mutter. "What?"

I nodded respectfully to the cops. "Can you give me a minute?" I requested. As soon as they assented, I pivoted back to Margaux, pulling her toward the kitchen with both hands on her shoulders. "Princess—"

"Don't." She pushed at my grip but didn't step totally free. "Not now. Don't you dare, Michael."

"Fine. But know that I'm sorry. I'm sorry. This is a mess now, and—"

Her teary huff cut me short. "A mess. Gee, you think?"

"There's a lot I haven't told you. That I need to tell you."

"Thanks for that update. I'd alert the press, but now I'm wondering how to keep their noses out of this fun tidbit."

"Damn it." I pushed my fingers in a little harder. "I didn't do it. Look at me. Tell me you believe me."

She raised her head. "Does it matter if I do?"

"It matters to me."

She swallowed hard. Raised on tiptoe to press her lips to mine. "I still believe you."

I didn't let her go far. As I kissed her again, I let every drop of gratitude in my heart pour into our connection—hoping that she could feel what her faith meant, what it would mean in the ordeal to come.

One of the cops cleared his throat. "Sorry, Mr. Pearson. We need to hustle this."

Margaux had a comeback for that. I watched it spark in her eyes and fight for release from her lips. She clenched it back, letting her frustration brim over in her eyes. It was a thick sheen right now, on the brink of tears—as if my soul knew the fucking difference.

I fought flinging a few shit biscuits of my own. No way in hell could I let any more anger taint this moment. It was too important to cram my brain with all the beauty instead. The proud set of her head. The morning sun rimming her hair. The blush in her lips from my kiss. I sucked it all into my mind, savoring the splendor before turning to face a lot of ugliness. Corporate lawyer or not, I held no illusions about the day ahead of me.

About the ordeal of facing charges for a crime I'd never committed.

Even worse, the confrontation of the reality behind it.

Declan had conveniently changed his recollection of things because he'd woken up and smelled the damn coffee— or, in this case, his desperation. Twisting the situation to his advantage had been an effortless hop from there. It was what the prick did best, after all.

As many times as that reality drummed my head, it was shitty as hell to think of voicing it aloud when given my obligatory phone call from the police station. I didn't punch in Margaux's number. Knowing my little spitfire, she'd already ordered a small army of lawyers into action and would drink my milkshake for using the call on her instead of Mom. She'd likely taken some initiative of her own already, alerting Mom that I'd be calling—and from exactly where.

Pegged that one right.

Mom picked up after half a ring.

"Michael? Michael?"

"Yeah, Mom. It's me."

"What the hell is going on?"

"Mom...breathe."

"Shut up. Are you okay? Margaux said they arrested you."

"Yeah." I took a breath deep enough for us both. "They did. But I didn't do it. I didn't fuck Dec up on the beach. Hell. Now I wished I had."

"Me too, baby. Me too." I heard her deep gulp. She was terrified, and I felt like shit about it. "And the scumsucker's pressed charges anyway."

"You sound as stunned about that as I am." I chuckled, more for her benefit than mine. Her answering snort wrapped my soul like a hug.

"Shylock wants his pound of flesh."

"My freedom in exchange for his way on the farm's water rights."

"Don't you dare do it, young man. I know that's easier for me to say than you. I'm not the one behind bars—"

"Bullshit." The word was rough, my tone tender.

Still she rebutted, "Bullshit?"

"That wasn't easy for you, and we both know it. You were a basket case when I got thrown into the hoosegow by Mary Beth Turner at the Sadie Hawkins dance."

No laughs this time—hers or mine. Silence descended, the heaviness unique to melancholy. Mom's tension was a tangible presence on the line, the threat of her tears pushing me to search for more words. Like my goodbye to Margaux, I didn't want to muddy the moment with sadness.

"The right thing to do isn't always the easiest, Mom."

"Damn it." Her snuffle clenched my heart. So much for banishing sadness. "You learned that one from me, didn't you?"

"Hmmm. Probably."

She laughed. Well, tried to. All too fast, it turned into a hiccup. Summoning fortitude by letting Margaux's face fill my mind, I pushed past the heartache. Leaned forward, closing my hand as if grasping for Mom's—ignoring the steel cuff around my wrist.

"Mom. Listen to me. Dec is going for the extreme zone about the water rights—more than we originally thought. He's in some deep shit with some nasty people, and this won't be the only play he runs."

Her breath audibly hitched. "Why does this not shock me in the least?"

"Because you're my smart, amazing *madre*."

"Oh, baby boy." Her voice quaked. "I love you!"

"I can't say more than that right now." I was saved from answering emotion by the guard at the door, circling his finger to signal I needed to wrap it up. "Just trust me on this. You need to be safe. Even safer than you have been. I wouldn't put it past him to be paying you a visit, whether it's by proxy or in person. Maybe you should have Carlo come stay in the house for a week or so."

There was a discernible pause before her careful reply. "Sure. Carlo. Up here. That might be...a good idea."

"Mom?" I actually felt myself grinning. "Is Carlo already staying in the house with you?"

She hmmphed. "That's none of your business, young man."

I laughed. "You may be right about that. Though I definitely approve. He's a good man."

"Stop fixating on him, and worry about yourself."

"Who says I'm fixating?" The idea of Carlo making Mom

happy was nice. Thoughts of the exact logistics of how...oh, hell no.

"Margaux's working on things as we speak, son. Don't worry. You'll be out of that shithole in no time."

"Thanks, Mom. I know."

I really did. If goddesses actually existed, they'd haul Margaux up Mount Olympus this second, inducting her as the patroness of determination. I'd be out of here as soon as she could move heaven and earth to do it.

That wasn't what worried me.

What Declan would try from here...

That worried me.

CHAPTER EIGHT

Margaux

"Okay, sign where I've highlighted the word 'signature,' date and time next to it, and then initial here, here, here and here. Two more on this page and then a signature, date, and time at the bottom. We'll bring your detainee out of holding, and you'll be free to go."

The woman was professional and pleasant but never bridged into warm or friendly. I didn't blame her. She'd probably supervised this procedure eighteen times today alone.

I looked up after signing in all the places she'd indicated, wanting to say thank you, but she was already gone. Another thankless task awaited her behind the thick glass.

I pushed the papers through the cutout in the window and then replaced the pen in the holder attached to the laminated wood counter. Finding a seat wouldn't be so easy. The rows of blue plastic chairs were mostly occupied, even at this hour.

I found a spot in the corner and leaned against the wall. Discreetly fished out some hand sanitizer, put a dollop in my palm, and then dropped it back in my bag. Within a few seconds, nothing remained of the gel but the strong, familiar scent.

If only Michael and I could wash away the weekend as

easily.

Not happening anytime soon. Concentrate on something new.

Looking around the room, I tried imagining the story behind each face. In the first row, a young blond girl sat with an infant carrier between her legs, rocking the baby in time with a soft lullaby. She was significantly younger than me. I wondered if she was picking up the father of the baby or even one of her own parents. Directly behind her, another woman looked tired and anxious, a feeling I knew too well by now. Funny, that commonality, though she and I were worlds apart. She wore a uniform from a local restaurant and twirled a pen through her fingers. I couldn't begin to imagine whom she was posting bail for. Husband or boyfriend? Brother or sister? Son or daughter?

I wondered what people thought when they looked at me. I was dressed simply enough in a white T-shirt, patterned maxi skirt, and flat suede boots, but even so, for me, it was all designer names. I hadn't dressed for show; it was just what I wore. The logos weren't emblazoned on the front, except for the small insignia on the front of my handbag. When I wasn't in the office or at an event, I wore little to no jewelry, so at least I didn't stick out because of that. I couldn't claim the same message about my grooming. My skin, hair, and nails were kept to my normal meticulous standards, so they likely gave me away as the one who didn't exactly know her way around a police station.

I pulled my cell phone out of my bag, trying to deal with my nervous energy. What the fuck was taking so long? Ms. Surface Pleasantry said she'd have my detainee brought right out. Didn't that mean now? Maybe jail-speak was different from regular world-speak.

I scrolled through emails, making sure I wasn't missing anything too vital at the office. I forwarded a few messages to Claire, apologizing about dumping things in her lap, giving a cursory update, and then promising to explain later in the afternoon—when, hopefully, I'd have answers myself. Since Michael had come in late and then crashed on the sofa, we hadn't spoken. Not civilly, at least. In general, he was damn lucky I'd come to post bail for his sorry, sexy ass.

That was when my heart stepped in with its little reminder about my decision from Saturday night. The little promise I'd made to myself and him before he'd gotten all hot and bothered—and not in the good ways—in front of Doug. I'd vowed to be supportive. Swore that we'd get through our shit together.

Groan.

I truly did want to help him, even with this clusterfuck. I wanted to hear his side of things and stand by him as it all was cleared up. But before I could do that, he had to give me some real answers. There was no other way around it.

Just as I firmed my resolve, his messy blond curls appeared through the window in a door across the room.

My chest tightened. I swallowed hard against the lump in my throat. Somehow, I managed to peel myself off the wall.

The deputy on our side opened the heavy entrance. Another policeman ushered Michael through by his elbow. Michael raised his head and instantly locked his weary hazel gaze on my face. I yearned to run to him. He looked haggard and defeated, and I wondered if he'd slept at all. God knew I hadn't.

"Pearson?" the first guard bellowed, loud enough for

everyone in the waiting area to hear without the PA system.

I stepped over as quickly as I could, anxious that he might shout again and wake the baby.

"I'm here." I used a regular voice to show the jerk it could really be done. The deputy, creepier up close than he was from twenty feet back, had the nerve to give me the head-to-toe as if we were in a nightclub. I felt Michael stiffen, despite being at least five feet away.

"I'll need to see your bail paperwork, miss."

I handed over the yellow copies of the forms I'd just signed. The officer quickly scanned them and then returned them to me.

"There you go, Miss Asher. Thank you." He caught my eyes with a smarmy smile. "I'm truly sorry you had to come down here today."

Without saying a word, I reached for Michael's hand. Thankfully, he took it. We turned our backs on the leering deputy and walked out into the fresh, crisp air of an autumn day in San Diego. I really wished I could've enjoyed it all more—the clear gold sunshine, the slight sting in the morning wind—but I only wanted to get the hell into the car. Andre and the BMW waited just a few spaces down, thank God.

Michael and I slid into the back seat in silence. But that game was about to be up. I refused to be kept in the dark any longer.

"We need to talk."

Michael scraped a hand through his hair. "It's nice to see you too."

"Cut the shit. Seriously."

"All right. If I knew exactly what shit that would be, maybe I—"

"Cut. It. Do you think I'm in the mood to be fucked with, Michael?"

"Right. And I am?"

"Good. So we're on the same page."

"Thanks. That told me a lot."

"Well, it should have."

I all but dismissed his answering glower. At this point, I didn't give a rat's ass about how tired he was. How could he have spent the night behind bars because of assumptions, confusions, and incorrect perceptions but still refuse to address the mud we were calling communication? How could he toss aside all the shit he wasn't confiding in me, the missing pieces behind all the drama with Declan to begin with?

Step right up, folks. It's the Michael Pearson show—the greatest illusion of okay you'll ever behold. Just ignore the hunk behind the curtain. He's real cute but a complete idiot.

Even now, he wasn't in the mood to listen or share in return. As we pulled into traffic, he made with the stoic shit like the walled-off pro that he was, staring out of the window and tapping a finger on the armrest.

From the front, Andre cautiously inserted a hum. "Miss Margaux, sorry to interrupt—"

"Ha!" It was harsh, and I didn't care. "Interrupting? Andre, there's not a thing back here to interrupt—is there, babe?"

My sneer met Michael's glare. Andre coughed, underlining the unnerving moment. "Well, uh...where to?" the Jamaican asked.

"Home," Michael barked.

I leaned forward—away from him. "Take us to Seaport Village, please."

"Right away." Not a note of sarcasm tinged it. Unlike the other grown man in the car, Andre knew better than to fuck with me once the frosty manners came out.

"Damn it. I don't want to be around people right now, Margaux."

I twisted around bracing stiff arms atop the cushion. "Too damn bad. I need some answers from you, hot stuff, and you're not going to escape from me this time in your big, bad truck. We're going public, where neither of us can run and hide. We'll walk along the waterfront, breathe some nice clean air, and you'll tell me everything this time. *Everything*, Michael."

He shuttered his gaze. I wasn't sure if it denoted agreement or dissent, as if I cared. I'd just signed his ass out of county lockup, so it was mine for a while.

I settled into the contour of the seat and stared out of my own side of the car as Andre maneuvered through downtown and then onto Harbor Drive, toward the popular tourist destination with its eclectic mix of architectural styles. The Village wasn't the intimate spot for a heart-to-heart, but sometimes being exposed was exactly what a couple needed— or so my gut told me. I was winging it a little right now.

"Here we are." Andre pulled into a coveted parking spot near the first row of shops. How the man always got so ridiculously fortunate with shit like that, I'd never know. He'd barely turned off the motor before Michael got out from his side, swinging the door behind him. Good thing I decided not to follow him. My legs would've been bloody stumps on the ground, remainders of a horrible accident.

At least I had my own excuse for a good, angry slam. "Michael," I called after him. "Michael!"

He slowed but didn't stop.

"Wow. This is new, ass-of-the-century ground for you, Pearson. I hope it lets up soon before you cross into unforgivable territory. Just throwing that out there. I know it's been a shit-tastic twenty-four hours and all, but letting it negate your general feelings for me—oh, wait, can I be bold and still call them feelings? Because right now, you're treating me worse than your goddamn family dog. After one night in jail, have you forgotten manners and respect of any kind?"

There. Getting it off my chest made it possible to breathe a little. And yes, he had the good sense to stop in his pouty tracks and turn and look at me, at least seeming apologetic.

He doubled back to where I stood, hands now braced on my hips, aptly representing my solid case of super pissed.

He stepped a little closer. When I didn't deck him, he leaned in—and for the first time since we'd arrived at the Del on Saturday, wrapped his arms around me. He dipped his head, kissing me on the lips, again very careful about it, as if testing that he was still welcome to do so.

"You're absolutely right," he murmured. "I've been a first-rate dickwad, and I apologize. You deserve better than this. You always deserve the very best of me."

I leaned back, looking up into his eyes. He still looked so wary, a tic pounding in his jaw, a pulse throbbing in his throat.

In an instant, I forgave him.

Not that he had to know that yet.

I pulled him close and buried my face in his chest. He clutched me tighter, kissing into my hair. We stood there for a while, exactly like that, simply savoring the nearness of each other.

I didn't want to let him go. Ever.

With the same air of reluctance, he pulled back. "Let's

find some coffee. There's a Starbucks across the way."

"Perfect."

Armed with liquid courage of the non-mind-altering variety, we headed along one of the Village's scenic stone pathways toward the waterfront.

The coast had become my solace, as it was to so many Californians. I didn't fully understand the pull until recently— and admittedly, I wasn't as Zen-deep into the ocean as Killian—but being on the water was definitely therapeutic and easier on my bank account than all the shrinks of my past. Right now, I looked out over the sparkling bay and sucked air in through my nose. I did it a few more times as we strolled slowly next to the water. My eyes slid closed as my shoulders gradually sank from where they'd been hovering near my ears. A similar energy drenched the rest of me too. Warm. Calm. Not completely stress-free yet...but better than I'd been thirty minutes ago.

I opened my eyes again. Michael had just done the same. "This was a good call." He leaned over, pressing his lips to my forehead. "Thanks for forcing it on me."

"I wasn't about to let you to drive off again." I looked down at my toes. I couldn't face him while voicing the rest. "You— that—tore my heart out."

"Margaux." The sound was strangled in his throat. "I... I needed space. I didn't mean to hurt you."

"But you did. We said we would face our problems together. And the first big one that showed up? You bolted."

"And I was wrong. It was wrong. What more do you want me to say?"

I stopped cold. "How about that you won't do it again? How about the reason why it happened to begin with? How about justifying the huge fucking trigger that Declan pulls for you? Why not start with any of that, Michael?" I refused to feel bad for a millimeter of the new tension in his jaw. "Not even a month has passed since the day you asked me to marry you, to spend the rest of my life with you—but I can't even guess why the sight of that man, your own uncle, unhinged you like that. Do you see why I hesitated about answering your proposal? We have some serious shit we need to deal with. Now, it feels even bigger than the night you first brought up marriage."

He didn't move. I tugged on his hand and pulled, making him walk with me again so people stopped veering around us. It was a Monday in October, so the Village wasn't packed, but the place did brisk business no matter what day or season.

"Well? Are you going to say anything?"

Michael sipped quietly at his coffee. Stared across the bay.

I wanted to slap him.

Finally, he murmured, "It's hard to determine where to start."

"What about at the beginning?"

He grunted. "Right. I'll get on that. Trying to organize a lifetime of memories and hate into one conversation... There's not really a beginning to that. Give me a few minutes, okay?"

"I'm sorry. I didn't know."

He squeezed my hand, reassuring. "Of course you didn't."

No. I didn't. But why was I filled with shame about it? There was another black hole I didn't understand, and that pissed me off all over again. Why did I feel so bad for demanding to know what was going on with the man I loved—the man who wanted me to share every detail of my life with him but wasn't willing to do the same in return?

I battled to keep myself wrapped in that ire, but one look

at Michael, and all the torment twisting his features, started to answer so many of those questions—in wrenching ways.

He was in pain. Deep inside. Not "oh, ow, that hurt" pain. It was "please, God, make it stop" pain.

I froze in my tracks. Reached for his free hand. "Just tell me what it is. What's going on, baby? Please. I want to help you. I want to be here for you, like you're always here for me, but you have to talk to me. You can't always save the world, Captain America." I tugged him over to the concrete ledge that lined the stacked rock break wall. We both sat. "You have to talk to me. It has to start right here...right now."

Michael dragged in a long breath. I pulled my feet up under me before yanking his hand into my lap, pressing it between my own, silently urging him with as much patience as I could force. In return, he toyed with his coffee cup, looked over the water again, kicked at the ground, picked at something that wasn't really on his thumb...

And finally, finally, looked me in the eye.

"This is so fucking hard," he grated. "Harder than I thought it would be."

"Why?" I cupped his face, peering into the hazel eyes that still flipped my heart on itself. "What are you so afraid of? It's just me. It's just me."

"I know." Nevertheless, he looked lost. "I know."

"Well...maybe the beginning is a good place. How's that? Declan is your..." He didn't say anything, so I continued. "Your uncle? Right? He doesn't look like Diana, so he must be your father's brother."

He rubbed the back of his neck and huffed. "Yes. My dad's brother. When my dad passed, he left the farm to all three of us. Apparently, Dec took that as a signed permission slip to become 'king caretaker' for Mom and me."

The air quotes he used didn't go unnoticed. "But caretaking wasn't what happened."

"Loosely interpreted?" he returned. "Actually, scratch that. Just consider it my little joke of the day. Declan really only wanted to get his hands all over the business. No, scratch that too. Not the business—his share of the profits. He came around every month acting like the doting guy, but when Mom refused to extend him credit on his share, he started getting—"

"What?" I tilted my head, forcing him to maintain our eye contact.

"Aggressive," he muttered, like a kid rasping his first swear word. "I...uh...I was still real young, so I don't remember it all from the very beginning, but yeah, aggressive is a good word. And angry. He was always angry. And he would say things, to me especially, but never when Mom was around." He blinked hard. Shoved his lower lip against the upper. Sniffed in hard. "They were—mean things, Margaux. Things my dad never said to me. I was just a fucking kid—so, yeah, I lost it sometimes." He shrugged. "Maybe I lost it all the time."

My breath stopped in my throat for a long second. "But—your dad died!"

"You think that mattered?" He pulled his hand free. Curled it into a fist and tucked it against his side...as if shielding himself. "Well, the tears really made him mad. Then he'd totally lose it..."

He trailed off, shaking his head, seemingly lost to memory. I watched, mortified and silent, as his Adam's apple bobbed in his throat, swallowing the pain. Without thinking, I grabbed his hand again, squeezing until I shook, battling to bring him back to where we actually were.

Back to me.

His eyes snapped to my face. Refocused. He actually smiled for a second, as if waking up from a nightmare.

"Hey."

"Hey."

"What just happened?" I modulated to quiet and soothing. I didn't trust his brief smile. Something was still going on in that head of his—confirmed by the new shake he gave it, shutting down his thoughts...shoving me away.

"No. Please don't shut me out, Michael!"

He jerked his head all the way back. For a long moment, he studied a trio of seagulls cavorting on the wind. I watched their reflections in the amber depths of his gaze, dark twists dancing against the light...like his memories had been all these years?

"Do you remember when we were in Julian, back in July?" he finally uttered. "When you first met my mom?"

I nodded, not wanting to interrupt.

"You were onto the right trail then already." He looked back down at me, lips lifting once more—but his smile was the kind that broke my heart, not melted it. "Mom and I have been hiding a lot of shit from the world for years...but you saw through it on your first visit to the farm." He grimaced and gulped again. "Fuck. Even I didn't see it at first."

"And you're supposed to know about makeup tricks like that?" I countered. "Stop beating yourself up for that, damn it...or you're just letting Declan win on the inside too."

He struggled to take that in, sniffing hard once more. "That scum-eating shit gave her a black eye!"

"I know. I kn—"

"There was a restraining order. We filed the goddamned

126

restraining order. But the bastard—he's clever. Caught her in town. Followed her like the fucking rat he is. Lurked and lurked until he got her at one of the few times she went somewhere alone...and then..."

I jerked hard on his hand. He was getting agitated again. It was clearly a living hell to relive the memories of his mom's suffering—but it illuminated so much for me. His need to protect everyone he loved...it made so much more sense.

But who'd been there to guard him?

The answer didn't matter, because that person was now me.

I reached out to soothe him. "Hey, listen. It's okay."

Michael jerked away as if I'd just spewed flames. Jolted all the way to his feet. "God damn it. It's not okay! Stop saying it's okay—because it's not! It never has been—and as long as that piece of shit walks the earth, it never will be. He wants everything we have, Margaux. Do you get that? He wants it all. He'll stoop to any level to get it!"

I cringed back, now pretty damn happy he stood away. With the force of my glare, I reminded him that he was shouting like I was the guilty party here—a huge discrepancy from the truth. Huge.

My silence pierced reality back in on him. "I'm sorry." He rubbed his neck again. "This is all so fucked up, princess. Now you can see why I didn't drag you into this mess—why I still don't want you anywhere near it."

I uncurled my body but hung on to my glare. "Well, that's total bullshit."

"The hell it is. Damn it—why can't you understand?"

"Because we're supposed to be in this together!" I barely got out the words coherently. "It's what we promised each other, remember?" I looked him in the eye, despite being terrified of the next question. "Or have you changed your mind now? Is this going to take you away from me?"

"I don't want that to happen. I swear I don't. But Saturday night, when I saw him talking to you...touching you? I thought I was going to explode."

"Well, you looked like it too."

"Don't you see? My worst nightmare has come true. He knows who you are, Margaux. He knows my biggest weakness. He's going to use it—use you—to his advantage. It used to be only Mom. Now he has one more weapon in his arsenal."

"So, we'll go to the police."

"Don't be so naïve."

"And don't be such a dick. Why is that naïve? Aren't the police supposed to help people? Protect them from people like your uncle?"

His face grew shadowed as his tension jacked to a whole new level. "My uncle isn't the only problem."

I looked on as his shoulders took on the stress too. His chest. Down his arms, into his fisted hands. "I—I really don't understand."

"There's more to the story."

"More?" As he nodded in strange little jerks, I asked, "Am I going to need a drink stronger than this latte?"

"Likely."

"Shit."

"That'll make two of us." The agonized smile spread across his lips again. "You know, I should've killed him when I had the chance."

"Stop it." I marched at him and punched him in the shoulder, even as he sat back down on the wall. "You need to stop saying things like that, damn it! That's how we ended up on Broadway this morning—where I bailed you out of jail. Remember?"

Michael was quiet for a minute. Two. He stretched his long legs out and crossed them at the ankles. I wanted so badly to crawl into his lap and just hold him, to make his pain go away for a while.

The yearning gave me an idea. "I'll be right back," I said with a little smile. "I need to run to the car."

He uncrossed his legs. "I'll come with you."

"No, no. It's fine. Save our spot. I'm going there and coming right—"

"No!" He surged up again, his fierce stance matching his tone. "From now on, until this shit works itself out, you go nowhere alone. I'm serious, Margaux. You take Andre everywhere—even to piss."

I raised a brow.

"Okay, take Sorrelle when you do that, but nowhere else alone. We're in some serious shit. You'll understand when I tell you the rest."

I let him take my hand and lead the way to the car. Andre was surprised to see us but understood better when I asked him to open the trunk, where I now stored some beach essentials—heavy wool blanket, baggy boyfriend sweater, flip-flops, sun screen, a couple of paperbacks, the latest issue of Vogue, a bag of almonds, a bigger bag of Skittles.

I grabbed the blanket and my sweater in case it got cool and informed Andre of where we'd be. I knew the perfect spot Michael and I could have some privacy and finish our talk.

When we got to the secluded alcove along the shore, I spread out the blanket and kicked off my shoes. I sat down, grinned up at Michael, and then patted the spot next to me.

"How did you find this spot?"

"I've become a beach bum." I giggled a little. "Actually, Kil told me he brings Claire here sometimes for romantic dates, and I wanted to snuggle with you a little bit. Now I think we both could use it."

"I think I agree." He smiled and kissed my temple as I scooted over, fitting my body against his. His warmth was perfect, sinking into me, filling the fissures in my soul, which had split so much wider the last two days.

I was so addicted to this man. I needed him like the air I breathed.

I swung my hair down over my shoulder so it didn't hang in his face and stared at him with intensity I'd been bottling up for days. This was exactly what I'd needed. One moment of looking into his eyes, as brilliant as flames through amber glass, and I knew his cracks had opened just as deep.

"I love you." I ran a finger along his lip. "I will do whatever it takes to make sure I don't lose you. I want you to know that, to believe that. You are the most important thing in my world, Michael Pearson. I can't be without you. I simply can't."

He swallowed hard and then licked at my finger. "I love you too, princess. And I'm so damn happy to hear you say that. I acted like an ass on Saturday...but I can't bear to lose you either, especially not to the clutches of my uncle."

I giggled again. Couldn't help it. "The clutches?"

"Don't laugh this off, Margaux. I've seen what that man will do to a woman. It—it killed me as a kid, having to watch him beat on my mom. When he hit me, it was fine. I preferred it, even goaded him into doing it, because there was hope he wouldn't go after Mom...but most of the time, I was wrong. He'd already warmed up on her and came to me next, or vice versa." He averted his gaze upward, glaring at the rock formations in the ceiling. "When I was old enough to fight back, I tried fighting for both of us. It was pretty useless. Sometimes it just made shit worse. We'd nurse our bruises together."

I brushed my hand up, struggling to smooth the tension from his brow. His words echoed with such sorrow and helplessness. "What kind of loser beats on a woman? And a little kid?"

"Domestic abuse happens more often than you think."

As he spoke, I rolled over so we could spoon. Maybe his response to my next question would come more easily if he didn't have to look me in the eye. "Tell me now, honestly, what happened on Saturday—after security took you outside." If he really had beat on Declan, I now fully understood where the rage came from. We'd deal with it after he told me the story himself.

He settled in a little closer, arm around my waist, before starting. His gruff snort tickled my ear. "Well, to no surprise, as soon as you were out of sight, those goons dropped me in the sand like the day's trash. One of them took a shot at me, which was how I ended up looking like I'd gotten into it with Dec."

I added a snort too. "Not that the Acme Guard School asshole will ever cop to that."

"Not even worth the effort, sweetheart."

"What saved your bacon with Porky Pig?"

"They got another call and had to leave. By then, I just let it go and walked down the beach a little. Tried to cool down and get my shit together before coming back in to you. I wasn't down far, only past an outcropping of rocks."

He paused, whether to let me digest his account so far or

to recall more, I wasn't sure. I rubbed his forearm, urging him to go on.

"I heard some men approach. Took three seconds to recognize one of them as the bastard from my nightmares."

"Declan."

"I prefer Fucking Declan, but yes. He was out there on the beach with a group of—shit, I don't know what to call them—goons? Guards? Henchmen?"

"Henchmen?"

"Hello, Al Capone, right? But that was what I thought. Modern-day mafia. *Esquire* meets the Corleones. Dressed in all black, greaseball smirks, slicked-back hair, and built like fucking brick houses, all of them. I wouldn't think of taking one of them on myself, let alone the four they had me outnumbered at—five if I counted Dec. So, I stayed in the shadows and listened."

I turned over and then sat up. He was right. This was getting serious. "What did they say?"

"I only heard Dec use one real name for anyone. Their leader's name is Menger."

"Their leader?" My heartbeat thudded in my throat. "What do you mean? Like, they were really some kind of a hit squad?"

"That's exactly what I mean." Michael scooped up one of my hands. "He owes them money. Lots of it."

"Them...who?"

"A group called the Principals. I don't know exactly who they are, but he's into them deep. Best I can tell, it's gambling debt. He always did like to play. Whether he racked it up locally at the rez casinos or out in Vegas, he has a weakness for it. And apparently, he's in some trouble now, at least six figures. Those men came to collect."

"Okay, so Uncle Dec is a loser to the third degree now. But what does that have to do with you?"

Michael let me go and scooted upright too—though the next moment, his head dropped between his bunched shoulders. As crazy as this ride had been so far, I sensed we were rolling to the worst part now. He growled, also broadcasting that he didn't want to tell me the rest.

"Baby." I dived a hand through his thick curls. "Just tell me. We've come this far. Get it out. There's no point in keeping any part of it from me now, especially if it's now going to involve me—which you've implied already."

He gave in to my tug, raising his head again. Expelled a decisive breath. "You're a damn smart woman, Margaux Asher."

I raised my brows along with my grin. "Are you trying to flatter your way out of this?"

"No," he sighed again. "Just stated it as the lead-in. These pieces are going to be easy for you to slide together."

"Okay..." I drew it out, purposely leaving the end open.

"California is suffering a major drought, right?"

What the state's water crisis had to do with Declan was a mystery, but I nodded. "Right."

"Who's suffering the most from the drought? Farmers, right?"

"Yes." The smart one was following so far. Good thing, since he took another huge breath and reset his shoulders before going on.

"The farm—my family's land in Julian—sits on a massive natural underground well. It's big enough to provide water for us and all of Julian and could likely be piped to San Diego as a substantial water source for the city."

My eyes popped wide—before threatening to jump out of my head. "And Declan..."

"Knows about it too." He grunted. "For years, the asshole's been trying to pressure Mom and me into auctioning off the rights to the well to the highest bidder. Oil company, gas company, the City of San Diego, the fucking Republic of Mars... The bastard will talk to anyone offering the highest bid for the water."

"Holy shit."

"Yeah. Holy shit." His glower matched my fury. "Sometimes I can't believe he comes from the same gene pool as my dad."

I stared out at the waves, focusing on the liquid layers of gray and blue to calm my thoughts. "Okay, just as devil's advocate and because I don't completely understand the situation, why wouldn't you simply deal with him by sharing the water?"

"Because our land would be destroyed. The methods of tapping into the well would devastate our farm, uprooting most of the orchard."

"Wow."

"Those trees have been growing for decades, some for close to a hundred years. Most of our employees would have to be let go. Families would be without incomes. Livelihoods would be decimated. The list of cons is a mile long. We use the water for everything in the orchard, making us one less worry for the San Diego Water District. We've been off their grid for close to thirty years."

"But would that stop the city from claiming eminent domain now and taking your land?" I sounded oppositional, but it seemed like Di and Michael had considered every reality. As long as he was sharing, I was asking.

"They don't want to go there any more than we do. It would be a public relations nightmare, the big bad politicians destroying the livelihood of local farmers. Right now, Mom and I couldn't agree more. We want to remain self-sufficient and lie low, business as usual. Pearson's has been a part of Julian since I was a kid, and if Julian is anything, it's easy and uncomplicated—the way the locals demand it. We don't want to be the ones dragging big city government problems to town, destroying the natural charm everyone's worked for."

I absorbed all of that through a contemplative pause. The rush of the waves and the murmur of the wind served as perfect filler.

"I hear everything you're saying, and it all makes perfect sense—but I still don't see where I figure into all this. Why are you so concerned about my safety? None of this feels dangerous to me personally, Michael."

He scrubbed a hand across his face and then hit me with a wary stare. "The conversation I overheard with Dec and those guys, on the beach...there was more to it."

"More?" My skin prickled. I didn't like the harsh glint in his eyes. Not one bit.

"You thought I was mad when I came upon him talking to you in the ballroom. That I'd reached my limit. Right?"

I nodded. With the whole story in place, it didn't surprise me how the man pressed every button Michael had.

"So this Menger loser started talking about how it'd be so convenient to make it look like I'd pounded on Declan instead of them. My own temper had just given him the perfect alibi."

I squeezed my eyes shut. "Oh shit."

"Damn right, oh shit," he growled. "But it gets better." He didn't let up with the fear-filled stare. "They know who you are too, sugar—and Menger was making dirtball comments about 'comforting' you if I was thrown in jail. It made me see red. I mean, a real red haze slammed over my eyes. I went on autopilot. Outnumbered or not, I didn't care. I jumped at the bastards from the rocks and was able to take out one of the goons before the others ran off—but before I realized what the hell was going on, the photographers swarmed in again, along with security. And you."

"So you really never hit Declan?"

"Not once."

"What did the photographers take pictures of?"

"Shit if I know. It was all a blur, especially after you got there. I was so furious that you didn't believe me." His jaw turned to steel again. "Do you have any idea what that felt like?"

"Michael—"

He waved me off. "It doesn't matter now."

"It does matter. Hear me out. And damn it, look at me."

He stared at the blanket for another thirty seconds. Finally, slowly, lifted his gaze back up.

"Do you realize the difference between then and right now?" I demanded. "How much all of what you just said means? Do you understand that if I'd had all this information on Saturday night, I would've known, with every fiber of my instinct, that you were telling me the truth?"

His lips parted on the start of a retort, but I stopped him with a sharp wave.

"Instead, I was totally crippled. Fighting blind. I was ordered into battle without a sword. I won't have to now. Thank you. I'm grateful that you've finally opened up and given me the whole story. Your past with this awful man, unfortunately or fortunately, depending on how you look at it, has contributed in a big way to the person you are right now. Our pasts shape our futures—and now that you've let me in on your past, we can build our future together. We've been working for this, Michael. Now, we just have some really bad people to clear out of the way first."

His long, unblinking silence would have stretched into unnerving—if not for the soft smile on his lips and the golden fire in his gaze.

Finally, he murmured, "How are you so amazing?"

I shrugged a little, smiling in return—and loving the fresh heat in my heart.

He reached over. Threaded a hand in my hair. Pulled me to him and then pressed a long kiss to my lips. It felt like we hadn't kissed in months, not just one day. His mouth was warm but tender, a physical plea for forgiveness.

I watched his face while he kissed me, something I didn't often do. With his eyes closed, I could marvel at his long lashes, the exact honey color of his hair. He breathed air in through his nose, absorbing me through all of his senses. I wanted to do the same...to drown in him completely.

When his mouth parted to deepen our contact, I let my eyes fall closed too...as my heart and my spirit opened. Finally, I enjoyed it for what it was—the end of a nasty fight and the beginning of new steps into the future.

Together.

CHAPTER NINE

Michael

Open heat. Soft surrender. Perfect passion. I could've added a thousand words to the string, all of them right and real, but none more fitting than the one resounding louder than all others.

Home.

I'd never appreciated the word more.

Never felt it more for anyone in my life.

Never ached more strongly for the chance to show her.

I let a moan vibrate through myself and then her, reveling in her immediate, intense response. She arched into me as if lit on fire, fisting my hair, pressing our bodies tighter. In that connection, she gave me the sweetest gift of all. The door to her soul was flung back open, and I knew her thoughts with the clarity of my own. I knew the depth beneath every tremulous shiver, every shuddering sigh, every harsh breath. I knew her again, in every recess of my exploding heart.

A cry escaped her, half breath and half plea, echoing everywhere in our little cove—and all the corners of my senses. "Michael!"

"Margaux." I grated it into her neck with matching need. "Oh God, sweetheart." I suckled her skin, trailing my tongue into the crevice between her neck and collarbone. When I added a tiny bite, she issued a full cry, her head falling back.

"Ahhh!" She drove a hand into my hair. "Mmmm..."

"I need you, princess. I need to know we're okay again. To be a part of you again."

She didn't answer in words. Just swiveled her head up and down and, as she clutched me tighter, compelling me closer.

"Say it." I pressed the words into her skin. Added a hard bite into the valley beneath her ear. At the same time, I slid a hand along the sleek line of her hip and the perfect indent of her waist, gliding my touch higher, higher... "Say it to me. Tell me you want it too."

"Yes." She lifted higher, pushing at me like a flower into the sun, opening more with every moment. She was so real about what she wanted...and needed to give in return. "Oh yes, Michael."

I swallowed hard, humbled in ways I never imagined. I had no right to claim her like this, no right to expect anything from her after the hell of the last two days, followed by the story I'd just dropped on her like a three-ton brick. But here she was, writhing and pulling and biting and kissing as if our passion was her sustenance and she'd been fasting for two days.

I pushed my hand up, toward the perfect promise of her breast. She sighed and shivered as her nipples hardened, visible through her bra and T-shirt.

I bypassed it.

Instead, I reached for the windblown hair across her face. The strands, soft as the lavender they smelled like, were the beginning of the balm I badly needed. Touching her, breathing her, loving her... I suddenly couldn't get enough. She alone could erase the last twenty-four hours of concrete, steel, and iron bars.

"I do love you." I uttered it only for her, for she was the only thing that mattered. The purest light in my world. The beautiful blade who'd been brought to cut my life wide open... and then heal it. "And I promise, I promise, there will never be secrets between us again."

She grabbed my hand. Pressed it against her cheek. Stared up at me with the smile of an angel but the gaze of a temptress. "I'm going to hold you to that, motherfucker."

A laugh erupted—the kind of sound only she could pull from me—filling every inch of my body and every fissure in my soul. Only now, the feeling was...more. So much more. Where I'd basked in it before, I drowned now and never wanted to come back up for air. The truth glared so brightly now. The secrets, my secrets, had barred me from this...walled me off from this tidal wave of joy and freedom and fearlessness.

Why the hell hadn't I come clean with her sooner?

I curled my fingers against her scalp and lifted her face, kissing her with hunger and desire that climbed by the second. When we dragged apart, our stares were heavier, our breaths harder. "I'm sorry," I finally uttered. "For everything."

I didn't need to elaborate. The fresh light in her eyes told me she'd already been through the list. "Shut up and touch me, stud."

With my hand still cradling her head, I gently lowered her to the rock floor beneath us. "My princess commands..."

The corners of her lips inched up at the fervent promise in my voice. I kissed them both while skimming my hand beneath her shirt and working my way up to her bra.

Front clasp. Fuck, yes.

After twisting the closure free, I thumbed one of her nipples and then the other. Both stiffened at once for me—

well, harder than they'd been before. They formed the lushest fruit I'd ever seen, begging to be unwrapped from her delicate white tee, the erect stems nested in areolas the shade of fresh apricots.

I groaned. Margaux whined. Her head snapped back as she lifted her chest higher. "Yessss. Ohhhhh!"

Her needy cry was a siren's song. My head dipped in its thrall, driving my mouth to one of her breasts. I sucked on her right through the cotton, only adding to the feeling that we were a pair of hormone-crazed kids playing hooky in the middle of a Monday morning. Her nipple strained against the fabric, tempting me to take more. I didn't hesitate. Her mound consumed my mouth. Her arousal dominated my will.

She was, in every sense of the word, my princess. My goddess. My savior. My strength. I rejoiced in the scent of her desire. Craved her pulse on my tongue. Existed, in this moment, for one sole purpose—to give her the best pleasure of her life.

Lust fed my blood and powered my movements, including the slide of my hand under her skirt. With silken strokes and fervent squeezes, I tracked up her thigh and over her lush hip, where my fingers hit the edge of her panties.

"Fuck—"

"Yes!" she finished for me.

I traced the top edge of the lace. "I need what's in here."

"Then take it."

Normally, that'd be my cue to tear away the lingerie—but if there was any time for leashing the caveman, it had arrived. She came first. Now and always. I'd proved it once by spilling my guts an hour ago. Proving it in this way was going to be a hell of a lot more fun—no matter how vigorously my cock battled the decision.

"Soon, princess."

The luscious peaks of her breasts instantly betrayed the effect of my hated promise...and how her body had hated our separation as much as mine. I didn't cloak any of my own arousal while gazing at her erect nipples, parted lips, and strained neck, throbbing with the wild cadence of her pulse. She was already a taut, sizzling wire, and I couldn't wait to electrify her even more.

With slow deliberation, I trailed my hand inward, caressing more of that soft French lace until I was hovering over the silk triangle covering her sex. I grazed the fabric with my fingertips. Margaux gasped and grabbed my shoulders with astonishing force. She almost derailed my aim of a steady, sultry seduction. Almost. I recovered composure by digging both knees against the stone and focusing on the pain from it.

A very temporary fix.

As soon as I pressed my thumb to her pussy, my blood turned to fire. My erection surged with agony. My lungs pumped with exertion, fighting the need to lay her flat and bury myself to the balls inside her.

"Michael! Shit!"

I rolled my thumb harder, still using just the pad. "So wet," I drawled, approving and low. "So succulent."

Her hips bucked, positioning for deeper contact. "Need... you," she panted. "Please. Your cock..."

"Not long now, baby. I promise." I leaned on my free elbow, curving my hand to her forehead, stroking off the dots of sweat. "But first, one for me to watch. Let me see it, Margaux. All of it."

The skin beneath my hand furrowed. "So good," she

whispered. "So close."

With her gaze still braced to mine, I pushed her panties aside. Her eyes flared. Her mouth fell open. I surrendered to a groan as my fingers met her soft, slick lips. "You really are my sugar, aren't you? Spun so sweet for me. So fucking sexy."

She dug harder into my shoulders. Her lungs pumped faster, pushing husky little sounds up her throat that might as well have been fists around my dick. Goddamn. Purgatory existed after all, and this was it. I was enthralled but tormented, ecstatic at her ascent to heaven but burning in a very singular hell.

"I love you," she rasped.

"I worship you."

"I'm going to come apart."

"And I'm going to catch all the pieces."

The flesh beneath my thumb began to tremble. The center of her desire, at last. I growled, deep and exultant, rolling my touch on the hot little bundle. Margaux panted faster. Writhed harder.

I pressed in once. She hissed.

Twice. She swore.

On the third, she screamed. Pushed up against my hand, all quivering thighs and glistening skin, before her sex clenched in a rhythm as primal and perfect as the beat of the sea on the rocks outside.

I kept stroking, helping her ride out the climax, greedily soaking in the electricity of every convulsion. In the world outside our grotto, gulls danced on the breeze and sunlight dappled on calm waters, but in here, I was the guy who'd belted a home run into the lights, the immortal who'd short-circuited a city with his broadsword. There can be only one.

This woman was my one.

I didn't let up the pressure. She tremored again, shrieking louder.

"Yeah, sweetheart," I encouraged. "That's it." I dropped my forehead to hers. "You're so beautiful."

"Michael." She sighed and then gasped. "Michael."

"Oh, yeah. So good. Give me another."

I was so absorbed in watching her face, I never noticed the little minx reaching for my pants. As she tugged down the zipper, a groan erupted from my gut—my cock's way of thanking her for the jailbreak. She gave me two seconds to enjoy the bliss before caging me all over again, sprawling her fingers around my shaft, scraping my balls with her nails. In the space of ten seconds, she'd given sweet torture a new definition.

"Damn," I gritted. "Oh...damn."

Let me go.

Squeeze me harder.

Did it matter? Nothing would ease the throb in my cock now—except the clutch of her core.

"You want another one?" She lifted her brows, mixing mischief and promise in one look, firing every cell of arousal in my body—and oh, how she knew it. "Not until you're with me, stud."

"Hmmm. That can probably be arranged." I finished it with a smirk, but the woman knew exactly how to wipe the look away, gripping me tighter and then backing off. Fresh blood surged between my thighs, making me unleash a hard moan. How the strain didn't rip my dick open right now, I had no idea. The milky drops I spilled on her fingers were little ease from the pressure. The deeper I pushed into her hold, the stronger I craved her.

"I need this." Her lips parted, exposing her gritted teeth. "I need you."

That did it. I'd been battling for the noble thing in keeping her panties intact, but that shit just wasn't happening. A twist, a jerk, and another twist, and I'd expelled the damn lace. Her pussy, trembling and glistening, practically called to me. "As I need you." I rolled my fingers into her folds, "I need this. Yes. Goddamn, sweetheart. So beautiful."

She dropped her legs open, letting me tease the erect pearl at her center. At the same time, she hitched one leg up, hooked a toe into the back waist of my pants, and pushed them halfway down my thighs. Silently, I thanked the Creator for those toes. Mentally, I made a note to send a fan letter to Tom Ford. These pants had survived a dust-up on the beach, an overnight in county lockup, and now an amazing hour in a little coastal cove that we'd remember until our nineties. And beyond...

Yeah. And beyond.

I wanted everything from this woman—even that naughty little smile of hers, bracketed by all the beautiful lines she'd earn by ninety. I wanted to share a whole life of this fire, this fever, this honesty, this love. Nobody had ever consumed this much of me. Nobody ever would.

I let the thought storm my mind as I fitted my erection to her entrance and turned our bodies into one. The line of her jaw tensed for a moment, as it always did... I selfishly reveled in the sight, as I always did. Knowing I stretched her, pushed her, filled her... It made me nothing short of giddy—and very ready to flood her from the inside out.

It was an even trade. Though my sex dominated hers, her soul commanded mine. Power for power. Control for control. A heart for a heart.

I loved watching the moment she recognized it too. Her lips curled in a wider smile. Her chest pumped, signaling the rise of her arousal. Her arms strained as she cupped my ass, urging me to take her deeper, harder, faster.

We ground in perfect sync, bodies formed flawlessly, hearts twined seamlessly. Wind swept around us. Sea salt mixed with the tang of our sweat. As waves gave in to the friction of the air, our bodies succumbed to the force of our passion, fusing and melding, pulsing and pounding, and then finally exploding...completing.

Together.

As it always needed to be.

As, so help me God, it always would be.

★ ★ ★ ★

We picked up a pizza on the way home, inhaling two slices each before Andre stopped the car at the Cortez's front door. Though the Jamaican didn't say as much, I read the happiness in his eyes when he opened the back door and caught Margaux and me closing the gap to each other by chomping at opposite ends of a string of cheese.

Margaux giggled as I cheated my way in, sucking the mozzarella and then kissing her in victory. Her laughter dissolved when Andre added a soft snicker. "Make any jokes about animated Disney dogs, and I'll make you eat this pizza box for dinner," she declared.

"Wouldn't dream of it, ma'am."

"Bullshit," she muttered.

"He'd be within rights," I asserted. "I feel like a damn tramp. Must smell like one too."

"It's not bad." She nuzzled my neck. "Kind of earthy. Interesting."

"Now you're full of shit."

She scowled.

Andre chortled. "It is, nonetheless, very good to have you home, sir."

"Damn great to be home, Dre."

I meant the fuck out of those words—but more so about fifteen minutes later, when stepping into the cavernous designer shower. When first moving in here, I'd joked to Margaux about the white-tiled stall, comparing it to a girlie version of a superhero incubation tank. Right now, I didn't care if she called it a magical-mystical mermaid cave. I'd never been so happy to be standing here, surrounded by all her female potions, sparkling beneath the torrent from the rainforest showerhead.

"Hey!"

I jerked my head around at her summons. She stood on the other side of the glass, bearing a pair of fresh shorts and my favorite soft T-shirt, featuring a silhouette of Bruce Lee on faded gray cotton. Shucked already were her own street clothes, switched for a pair of form-fitting yoga pants and a red tank top. Her hair was in a poofy bun, her breasts freed of her bra.

Where did I begin to thank God for this part?

"Michael?"

I let another beat go by before growling, "Best. Girlfriend. Ever."

One side of her mouth lifted. "Is that why you're sniffing my bath gels?"

I glanced at the bottle in my hand—with its label consumed

by white flowers and French words. "After smelling nothing but eau de wino? That would be a huge yes."

Her smirk grew. "So which scent is your favorite?"

I returned a knowing grin. After all these months, it still charmed the crap out of me when she tried to learn a new way to please me, however thinly disguised the effort. Her expression reminded me of the time she'd come home early to fix some of my favorite dinner dishes, only to make the sour cream mashed potatoes with cream cheese. Despite her horror, it had been surprisingly good.

I had a damn strong feeling we could do better with this one.

"I'm really not sure." I cocked my head. "Maybe I need to run some hands-on tests."

"Hmmm. You think?"

The comeback was barely off her lips before I slammed the bottle on a ledge, leaned out of the stall, and then pulled her back in with me. Beneath the warm spray, I smashed her body against mine, giving instant homage to the suck-face gods. Her eager mewl drove me to push her mouth open wider, commanding her tongue in long, selfish strokes. I made no secret of what that did to my cock. Though I'd pounded her like a teenager an hour ago, it didn't know the difference. From the feel of things, neither did she.

Yesssss.

I yanked at her hips, smashing her belly against my bulging length, raising one hand to start peeling back her top. With a frantic little growl, she peeled the whole thing off for me.

"Pants too," I snarled. "I want you totally naked and totally wet, sugar."

As she flicked the soaked pants against the glass wall, she

flashed an impish grin. "Wet was taken care of as soon as I walked in here and saw you."

I let my eyes return the smile but not my lips. "Cheeky girl." One who liked getting that way when she wanted Mr. Headmaster to come out and play. I could sure as hell do that. I'd role play the damn Emperor of China if this woman needed that.

"Perhaps." She nipped her lip in coy invitation, pressing back against the wall. "But you like my...cheek."

I stepped in, consuming her personal space and trapping her against the tiles with a hand planted next to her head and a rough touch sliding up her body. Water and goosebumps flowed beneath my fingers...silken thighs, hips, waist, breasts...a mesmerizing ocean I yearned to drown in forever. She was my tide. My current. My soaked little sea siren. If she dragged me under and never let me go, I'd die of happiness.

My hand ended its exploration at her jaw. With a slight push, I parted her mouth. The recesses beyond were pink and lush, compelling my thumb inside. She sucked the digit in, keeping her wide green gaze fixed on me, a naughty mermaid come to life—especially as she bit the web of flesh leading to my forefinger.

I hissed.

She grinned.

"You know what cheek earns you around here, Miss Asher?" Encouraged by the aroused flecks in her eyes, I dug my fingers into her hairline. "Specifically with the headmaster?"

My thumb fell free as her jaw popped open. "No, Sir. I—I meant no disrespect, Sir."

"Nevertheless, you're a naughty little thing." I worked my thigh into the space between hers, pushing until I felt her tremble. She handled the rest, unable to keep from rocking. "Are you riding my thigh with your dirty slit, young lady?"

She grabbed my neck, using it for support as she boldly returned my gaze. "Damn right I am, Sir."

I smirked. Just a little. "You know what happens to cheeky brats who ride their headmaster's thigh in the shower, don't you?"

She returned my smile. So damn gorgeous...and perfect. The playful turn on our role play was what we both needed right now. "Please tell me they get fucked, Headmaster."

"Oh, yes, they do, little girl. Thoroughly."

"Now, Headmaster? Please?" Her voice was a high, needy rasp.

I pulled my leg away, hardening my stare. "We're in the shower, missy. I only fuck clean cunts in here." It was the work of seconds to grab the bottle of foofy French gel and shove it into her hand. "Clean yourself. I'm going to watch, to make sure you get every inch."

I took a step back, crossing my arms. A pause stretched, full of as much sexual impact as the plank of my cock straining toward her. Margaux's longing gaze only made my flesh stiffer. Little temptress. I couldn't help but growl as she sneaked her tongue over her lips and innocently eyed the floor.

"Don't even think it," I drawled.

She looked back up, again all Tinkerbell innocence. "Think what?"

"Deterring me with a blow job." I leaned over, lightly swatting the insides of her thighs. "Spread these." Cupped her trimmed mound. "Then wash this."

Surprise, surprise. She kept her tongue inside her mouth this time. With her lips pressed together, she pushed back to the wall for balance—before pushing her legs apart.

I had to be the luckiest bastard alive.

I swallowed hard, unable to tear my stare from her sex. She was like a fantasy, with water descending and glistening on her short tawny curls...and the slick layers beyond. When she drizzled the pearly liquid down over them, my body bellowed a question at my brain.

"Goddamn," I grated. My cock seeped with so much precome, I wondered if there'd be any juice left for fucking her. My balls, throbbing and heavy, answered that query fast enough. They granted no mercy as Margaux spread the soap, working the suds across her pussy lips, into her folds. With breath seized in my throat, I fisted my shaft. Worked myself from balls to crown with the same sensual rhythm she'd established. More liquid spilled from my head as she leaned back to wash the soap away, exposing the entrance of her velvety tunnel to me.

She lifted the bottle again. I ripped it from her and threw it against the wall—before slamming her flat and smashing our lips together.

She opened at once, letting her mouth become a maddening preview of how her channel would feel—wet, welcoming, and slick. I ravaged her tongue with mine, giving her a taste of more things as well. This would be her fate, inside the magic of our glass escape. Ultimate surrender. Perfect desire. The highest peaks of pleasure I could possibly bring her.

Only when she moaned, signaling she'd accepted that recognition, did I pull away to let us both get air. She didn't move, except to gaze up at me through heavy-lidded eyes. "Am I clean enough, Headmaster?"

"You're perfect, princess." I kissed and bit my way from one corner of her mouth to the other. "And now I'm going to defile you again. All of you."

She nodded, clearly trying to form her mouth around words, but it wasn't time for words anymore. It was time to shove up and in, invading her with my cock, filling her with my passion. Her sheath was torrid, gripping me with velvet walls, clenching every inch of my swollen, stiff erection.

She latched a leg around my waist, gaining traction to drive her pussy down as I lunged up. Within minutes, the extra friction on her clit turned her into a quaking dervish. She cried out, driving our rhythm faster and faster. I watched her in profile, amazed all over again by the brilliant, passionate miracle of her.

Yeah. My miracle. It fit...so fucking perfectly.

And yet it didn't.

Of all the men on earth, why had the Almighty gifted her to me?

And maybe it's just best not to question the Big Guy. Ever think of that, asshole? Right. Maybe gratitude was really the smart thing here—along with giving her a climax that'd roll her eyes back in her head.

"Shit," she cried out. "Oh shit...Michael...it's so—"

"Good," I finished. "Yeah. Yeah, sweetheart. So good."

Her head fell back. I tunneled a hand into her hair, forcing her to look at me. She bared her teeth and did the same, nails biting into my scalp.

I pumped into her harder. Grabbed her tighter. "Come for me."

"You come for me."

Remarkably, I grinned. Smashed her with another

punishing kiss. Against her lips, I grated two words.

"Yes, ma'am."

Before my world detonated.

My vision went silver, then gold, and then back again as my cock flooded my essence across her fluttering walls. Margaux's mouth fell open on a silent scream as she rode me like a woman possessed.

Many minutes later, she slid from me, crumpling to the shower floor. I lowered with her, though I managed to twist the knob and shut off the water first.

Flat on our backs, soaked and exhausted, we gazed at the ceiling while our lungs returned to normal. When we finally tilted our sights back to each other, laughter burst out. We were ludicrous from exhaustion.

"As amazing as that was," she finally muttered, "don't you dare think of getting yourself tossed in the clink again."

I chuckled and lifted her hand, pressing a soft kiss into her moist palm. Her skin smelled like French flowers and satisfied woman. Perfect.

"Don't worry, my love. That's definitely on the priority list."

★ ★ ★ ★

I barely remembered the journey from the shower to the bed, only to thank God for Margaux's love of expensive linen as my head sank into the pillow.

When I opened my eyes again, it was to learn I'd just slept four hours of the day away. I groaned and sat up, palming the grit from my eyes, the sleep from my senses, and the disgust from my brain. The first two were easy erases. The last wasn't so simple. Rudderless wasn't a condition I enjoyed, one fucking bit. Ambition and productivity had been my ways of proving I was everything like Dad and nothing like the leech brother he'd left behind. The traits were largely responsible for why Quade McIntosh and Rin Samura had taken me on at Aequitas, despite the massive scandal that had taken my former employer down. The men were open-minded enough to see that Andrea and Trey's crime and flight from the country were because of their greed and deceit and no one else's.

It hadn't been so easy to call Quade and Rin about the bullshit from this weekend.

Actually, it had been pure hell.

Even leaning against the cushions of the 750i, sitting next to the woman I loved, it had sucked complete ass to call the men who'd put such faith in me and admit to the outburst against Dec. It was even harder to ask that they believe I hadn't done anything beyond the blowup in the ballroom, especially with my whopper of a finale that I'd just been sprung on bail from county lockup. There was no use in keeping it conveniently out of the conversation, since the court would be calling them to verify my employment for my official response to Declan's allegations. There was a good chance they knew every member of the top-notch legal team Margaux had gathered as well.

None of this shit had been a cheery week-starter for my bosses—I heard that much alone in their voices—but Rin and Quade confirmed that they stood by me. My gratitude had been met with the usual clichés—innocent until proven guilty, a clear conscience fears nothing, trial by media means shit—and I didn't care. They'd earned themselves a loyal barrister for life.

With that, I was back to the stress of the moment. My ass.

This bed. Four in the afternoon. Something was wrong. Off. Not aligned.

Margaux's absence didn't help things. Even after our morning of reconnection, things were off without her near. It had nothing to do with sex—though the sloth comparisons were easier to stomach when contemplating more hours of servicing her delectable body—but more an inner imbalance. I needed to know, one more time, we were back in sync.

Shit. Call a spade a spade, man. You need to make sure you didn't fuck things up that badly.

I kicked the covers back, rolled out of bed, and then trudged through ribbons of autumn gold to the dresser, hunting for track pants. After hitching a pair on, I made my way out to the landing and followed the sound of my girl's voice, determining she was downstairs in the office.

I lingered in the living room for a second, enjoying the chance to stare without her awareness. She stood at the desk, phone in one hand, scribbling on a pad with the other. The cupcake pajamas had been ditched in favor of a better outfit— one of my faded Julian Hard Cider T-shirts and nothing else. The cotton teased up and down her ass as she wrote, turning my secret vantage point into a lucky one, indeed.

Maybe I'd get lucky about that servicing-her-for-hours thing, after all. We'd had a great time on one desk already this week...

Or maybe my luck had run out.

As soon as I stepped into the office, she started like I'd cocked a shotgun. "I gotta go." She dropped the pen and sucked a lip between her teeth. "Right. Five o'clock. I have to go."

As she hurriedly ended the call and then plopped the phone down, I approached her with a couple of careful steps.

"Five o'clock for what, sugar?"

She turned and leaned against the desk. The position lent itself to more of my fantasies, but every inch of her demeanor confirmed her head didn't share that airspace. "Dinner," she replied, almost defiant about it. "We have reservations at the Brockton Villa."

I grinned in spite of her spooked cat vibe. "I love that place."

"I know."

"We'll be there just in time for sunset too."

"Yep."

I tugged on her elbows and kissed her nose. "You truly are the best girlfriend ever."

She didn't let me pull back. With her hand around my biceps, she stated, "Remember you said it and meant it."

Spooky mach-fived into strange. "Why?"

"Because Doug's meeting us there." She kicked her head backward. "That was him on the phone."

"Doug?" Screw strange. I moved things right into incensed. "Why the hell was he calling you?"

"Michael—"

"And why the hell did you pick up?" Comprehension slammed my brain—then deflated my dick. "Princess, I'm not into sharing. Especially not you. If Mr. Baseball, Hot Dogs, and Apple Pie thinks he can call you for some kinky reunion thing and—"

She shoved me away. "Damn it, listen to me." She raised her head, face calm in spite of her anger. Took a deep breath. Really deep. "I called him."

Her confession struck like a punch. I blinked as my jaw clenched, fighting the monster gnashing across my gut. "Why?"

"Because we need him."

"Why?"

"Because he's not just doing the whole ex-baseball guy speaking circuit thing anymore. He's trying to do some good in the world. He opened his own private investigation firm, and—"

"So now he's a private dick as well as a public one?"

Her hands hit my chest so hard I stumbled back again. "The only dick here is you, goddamnit. I'm trying to get you some help!"

"And the guy who landed you in a lockdown unit is the one you call for that?"

A bright sheen formed over her eyes. "I'd call hell itself for you, Pearson. Gladly pay them a visit in person, if it meant keeping you out of jail."

I grimaced. Scrubbed a hand over my face. "I know. I know. I just—"

"What?" she demanded into my weighted silence.

"I don't understand. You've hired half the lawyers in the city."

"Who are all bound by laws," she countered. "And it doesn't sound like Declan's friends care too much about shit like that."

"So we find a PI. It's sound wisdom. But Doug—"

"Is going to care more than the others." She practically punctuated the words with her wince, it came so fast. Still too late. "I don't mean *care* care," she revised. "I mean that he sincerely wants to help. Maybe he's even got residual guilt from...things...and feels this will even out his debt."

On a logical plane, it made sense. Across the tundra of my instinct, it sent another storm of apprehension. "And maybe he sees a great opportunity to be your shining star again."

She snorted. "Because that went so well the first time?"

"Because that's going so well with the guy you've got?"

"Shut up."

"It could be the truth, princess. We both know it." I spun for the door. Stopped myself from leaving by reaching for the doorframe, gripping it tighter than I wanted to admit. "I'm not giving in to Declan on the rights to the spring, especially now."

"Nor would I let you," she declared.

"Even if I go to prison for it?"

"You're not going to prison." While her comeback was drenched in all the determined fire of the Margaux I loved, there was no way to miss its charred edges of desperation. "Now go get dressed for dinner, damn it."

I did it without any more argument, seizing the chance to make her happy.

God only knew how few of those I had left.

★ ★ ★ ★

There was no such thing as a bad California sunset—but the sky got especially amazing over the Pacific in the fall, supported by the view we had while drinks and appetizers arrived at the table. As a few coastal clouds threaded the sky's fabric of brilliant purple, orange, and gold, Margaux helped herself to some lobster rolls while Doug and I dived straight for our alcohol. He'd gone for a porter ale from Hawaii. I opted for the Stone Arrogant Bastard, a local microbrew. Might as well broadcast my mood loud and clear from the start.

The drinks didn't make the silence any more unnerving.

It extended for at least another minute, thick as the

descending night, making the waves on the cliffs sound like blows to a punching bag.

To his credit, Dougie had the grace to look as uneasy as me. Though he was all business with his small keyboard and screen along with a paper notepad and pen, he jiggled a knee like a six-year-old in church. My nerves didn't manifest any better. My back teeth would be nubs in an hour. My right foot tapped the balcony rail, synced to the beat of the groovy jazz playing over the speakers in the eaves.

"If you guys don't eat some of this lobster roll, I'm going to scarf it all," Margaux grumbled at us, "and I won't be happy about the price my ass pays for it."

I chuckled and didn't have to fake it. My sassy, gorgeous girl, looking elegant but casual in a cream sweater and jeans, was trying so hard to smooth the air. I pulled her hand up and kissed her palm, openly appreciating the effort. "Lay some on me, baby—says the guy with a vested interest in your happiness and your ass."

As I'd hoped, she giggled.

As I'd expected—and was none too happy about that—Doug's face tightened.

Maybe his interest in her ass wasn't as platonic as she assumed.

"So, let's clarify Saturday night's timeline first." He tapped a few notes into his pad and then looked up. He'd arrived in jeans too but finished things off with a white button-front and a navy sports coat. The look earned him plenty of flirty feminine gawks, but the bastard only turned on the charm once he had Margaux's attention. Since she'd decided the lobster roll needed her full focus again, he turned the Dick Tracy stare on me. "After you went off on your uncle the first time—"

"You mean the only time?"

Margaux smacked my knee. "Be nice."

Simcox ran his napkin across his lips. I narrowed the corners of my eyes. *Nice cover for the smirk, slick.*

He asserted, "Well, according to Declan Pearson's statement—the account filed with the court—it was the first of two times."

"They also took Michael's statement." Margaux arched a brow. "Did you read that part too?"

"Of course." Dougie's tone gentled for her. I wasn't the only one who noticed. As Margaux stiffened, I reached for her hand again. Squeezed in blatant possessiveness.

She yanked free.

Dougie wiped his mouth again.

Ass basket.

"Let's talk about the organization that Menger referenced," he pressed on.

For once, we were on the same page. "Yeah," I agreed. "The Principals. What the hell?"

Doug leaned back in his chair. "About them..."

Margaux clanked her fork to the plate. "You know about them?"

"A little." He swung a look toward the faint glow over the sea. "But none of it is pretty, honey."

Margaux's stare whipped toward me. Shock took over her eyes when watching me take a lazy drag on my beer. "I'm good," I assured. "It's all good. Only the idiot fish chomp on the obvious bait." I flicked my glance back across the table. "Dougie knows that too, doesn't he?"

Simcox shrugged. The move was well-rehearsed, probably something women had creamed over when he was batting three-fifty with those shoulders. "No harm meant. Just...old habits, buddy."

"Old habits." I tilted another swig. "Just remember that part. Old, as in ancient history. Got it?"

"Stop." Margaux went for my knee again—with fingernails like daggers this time. "And cut the fucking caveman. And you"—she stabbed Doug's forearm with his fork—"cut the fucking Lancelot."

"The—huh?" he moped. "Lancelot?"

"I'm not made of hairspray and fairy dust anymore." She slammed the cutlery back down. "I can take not pretty now. Give this shit to me straight."

Doug swiveled his stare to me. I gave him my own version of a shrug. One shoulder, both brows. "You heard the woman. She can take it."

He canted his grin at Margaux. "You still floor me, Ms. Asher."

"As she does me every day."

His lips thinned. "So you've said."

"No harm meant." I deliberately glanced around the balcony, living up to the label on my beer. It felt fucking great. "Habits, as you said."

Doug sniffed, deep and noisy and pissed. I couldn't help a grunting laugh. That couldn't have been pleasant, considering the aroma from the cove's hundred sea lions, now riding firmly on the night's breeze. "You know, Pearson, I'm trying to keep this civil."

I cocked up one side of my mouth. Screw hiding it with a napkin. I actually still possessed a dick. "Sure, Lancelot. Sure."

"Is keeping your ass out of jail any kind of a priority for you?"

"Is it for you?"

He hurled the napkin to the table. "What the hell are you implying?"

"You tell me, Simcox. What am I implying?"

"Fuck."

The word ripped the air with its raw fury—and its brutal tears. Doug's sights bounced to Margaux as swiftly as mine, though I doubted the bastard's intestines were more knotted about making her cry.

Damn it.

I couldn't reach her fast enough. Literally, not fast enough. By the time my hand neared hers, she'd bolted from her chair, grabbed her purse, and detonated her glare at both of us.

"I give up." She jabbed a finger at me. "You can go to jail, okay?" Swung it at Doug. "And you can go to hell."

As she headed for the stairway leading down to the street, she pulled our waitress and the hostess to a stop. She pushed money into their hands.

"If anyone comes in here looking like a fan or photographer, even with a pretend kid's phone, stop them from getting to that table. Speaking of juveniles, you can get those two a pair of kids' menus. They can't be trusted with anything above chicken fingers and applesauce."

Doug and I sulked through three minutes of silence before lifting our beers in tandem. We eyed each other over our bottles as we chugged the rest of the contents.

I barely felt the impact of the alcohol over the roar of my senses—made by an animal I'd gotten too fucking familiar with lately. The swine of self-disgust.

Doug stifled a belch before muttering, "Well. Another round, or should we order up the chicken nuggets?"

I hated that I understood the subtext in his question. If either or both of us went after Margaux now, it'd only be asking for her boot in our balls and her snarl in our faces. She wouldn't go far, but it was wise to let her have every inch of that space, for as long as she demanded.

"Next round's on me," I said by way of response.

"Bullshit," Simcox countermanded.

"I'm not a goddamn charity case, Dougie." I waved at the waitress, indicating we wanted two fresh bottles.

Simcox closed his smart pad, set aside his notes, and leaned back in his chair so far the front legs lifted. "Tell you what. Stop calling me Dougie, and you can pay for anything you want tonight."

I snorted a laugh. "Well, shit."

"We have a deal?"

"Guess we do."

We reached across the table and shook hands.

Doug took his turn at the laugh. "Damn. We should snap this and then text it to Margaux."

I shook my head. "Yanking the wildcat's tail, man."

Doug chortled softly. "Some things never change."

CHAPTER TEN

Margaux

For the love of fucking Chanel.

What the hell was that?

I didn't have any more an answer now, standing on the street below the restaurant, than I had two minutes ago. For a second, I wondered if I was truly dealing with grown men. Those two were no better than four-year-olds in a sandbox, fighting over who got to play with the backhoe first. If we hadn't been in the middle of a damn nice restaurant, I would've knocked their rock-hard skulls before dumping their ice waters into their laps.

Even without that, half the restaurant had gawked.

Again.

And even though I'd paid off the help, we were likely to be splashed all over the tabloid covers.

Again.

I worked in the damn public relations business, and I couldn't keep my own face out of the rags, especially at the moment. The thought churned a laugh up in my throat, one of those hysterical kinds that made people glance sideways, betraying their worry about being shanked if they looked too long.

The giggle never made it all the way out.

Instead, tears welled in my eyes. My throat surrendered to a stranglehold.

Again.

Goddamn feelings.

Goddamn boyfriend.

I couldn't even screw up the girl balls to blame Michael. Not completely. Before I got involved with him, I'd been the one in charge of this shit. I'd stowed these things neatly away, tucked where I'd never have to deal with them again—ever. I plowed through the days and filled the nights with empty dates, parties, shopping sprees. Whenever emotions got stirred, I really did laugh. I'd throw down my big giant mixing paddle and walk on with my bad self to the next sandbox, never looking back at the scorched earth I'd left behind.

Not now.

No. Now I dealt with tears and sniveling. And the worst part of it all? They were all my own.

I shook my head in disgust, turned from where I knew Andre had parked, and headed in the opposite direction. I needed some air and a few minutes to pull myself together— away from my driver. Apparently, the Jamaican had become a part-time shrink. Not only did he know the fastest route to every venue in San Diego, he also knew the fastest course through my bullshit. And right now, I couldn't face his all-knowing dark-brown stare and approving little nod, letting me know it was fine to fall apart if I needed to, because he'd be right there to catch me. I loved him like the dear friend he'd become, but right now, I just needed some head time.

Head time?

What the fuck?

Suddenly, I wanted to cry even more. Throttle someone

harder. When had I become the fragile girl everyone watched so carefully, awaiting the little tells that she was about to go down in flames? Did that mean I was also the subject of their concerned, condescending conversations, whispered in corners when I wasn't around? *Poor Margaux. She's losing it, but if we stay close, we can see her through. We'll save her this time, before it gets too ugly...*

No way. I'd done this ride before, courtesy of Doug Simcox. Bought the ticket and then washed the T-shirt so much it was falling apart. I was done. Really, really done.

Rage boiled, steamrolling my self-pity. I smiled, recognizing its arrival. Balled fists, gritted teeth, twitching eyes. Rage was my old friend. I welcomed the bitch more than sadness or—gasp, God help me—helplessness.

By now, I'd stomped all the way to Prospect Street. I strolled past a few favorite shops, peering into their window displays. Nothing spoke calm to me like shopping. I could always do a little damage to my plastic and then reevaluate how I felt after. Best idea of the night.

I waited for the little tickle in my belly that came when I verged on buying something totally unnecessary. When it didn't crash in, I frowned. Shit. I was in deeper than even I realized. No sense buying something simply for the sake of it if it meant no contact high from my black card.

Maybe...I needed to go to the gym? Laugh-out-loud time now. Had I really just channeled that Michael Pearson thought? I would never understand the gym rat mindset, no matter how hard I tried, even for his sake. I hated exercising and always would—except for sex, which was so off the table right now. Pissed and horny were like socks and sandals. Mixing them was against nature's plan.

That led me back to where I'd started.

Fabulous.

Square one totally sucked.

My phone rang in my bag. With a sigh, I fished it out, curious who was bothering my perfect sulk.

Speak of the devil. A text. From Michael.

Where are you?

I stabbed angry thumbs at the pad.

Leave me alone. Go have some more fun with Doug. You two can't be done with your pissing tournament yet.

Is that why you left?

Gold star for the hot guy.

Come back. Please.

I thought begging was my bit.

Will doing it again bring you back?

Have Andre take you home. I'll find my own way.

I'll wait.

I wanted to cry again. Then laugh. The impulses were

tangled even more by the giddy ache in my stomach. The man truly made me crazy, especially when he turned back into his sweet, considerate self. I couldn't stay mad at him for long. My heart softened, inspiring a resigned sigh in my throat—

Until I thought of returning to the restaurant.

Where those two jackasses had embarrassed the crap out of me and nearly propelled us all back onto the tabloids' front pages.

I glared at my phone, so engrossed in composing my next smart-mouthed reply that I slammed right into another pedestrian. "Crap," I muttered. "I'm really sorry. I—"

I choked during my double-take.

The woman. That face.

I'd never forget it. I never had.

Over the years, she'd made sure of that. Every few months, never in the same place, she'd show up when I least expected it. Once at the outskirts of a fancy fundraiser. Next in the lobby at work. One time at the airport, when I'd been leaving for a business trip. The only time she'd made a repeat appearance was at the hospital, in those dark days after the break-up with Doug. She'd come every day, just for a few seconds, lingering in the hall outside my room. Most recently, she'd turned up again at the airport, on the day Michael and I publicly announced we were seeing each other.

Caroline.

It was her. I knew it now. I was close enough. She was real enough.

I was so shocked, I jostled my phone back and forth between hands, dropping it to the pavement and nearly shattering the screen. I caught it on the first bounce, but when I recovered from my clumsiness, she was gone.

"No. Wait! Please!"

Everyone on the sidewalk stared like I'd lost my mind. Maybe I had. At the moment, I was nothing but a woman clutching her cell phone for dear life, shouting to someone who wasn't there.

"Damn it!"

I turned to the closest bystander, a stylish elderly woman who'd definitely been giving her own credit card a workout.

"Did you see that woman? I bumped into her—she was just here—and then she ran off—right? Did you see her?"

The woman adjusted her dozen shopping bags in order to cup my shoulder. "Dear, are you okay? Did you fall? Did you hit your head?"

A man walked up, cosmopolitan enough to be her young son. "Maybe we should get you medical help. Is there anyone we should call?"

"No." I pushed free of their holds, smiling away my brusqueness. "It's fine. I'm fine. Honestly."

I needed to stop sounding like a crazy street person— granted, a crazy street person decked in the latest Manolo Blahniks—or Michael and Andre would be responding to a code 5150 at the closest county hospital.

How was this happening?

This time, I'd seen her up close. I'd touched her.

I needed to tell Michael. The need burned like a branding iron. I scrambled for my cell but stopped dead in my tracks again. I was still pissed off at him.

"Fuck! Damn it! Fuck!"

The couple who'd just stopped for me paused next to their Jag, looking freshly alarmed. I was acting like a lunatic, to anyone's observation. I had to leave. I needed air but was already outside. I needed to get away, but there was nowhere to run. Was this a panic attack? The one person I wanted to reach out to, I was furious with.

Fuck!

I sank to a bench, staring at my phone—then did what any normal woman would do. Or at least what I thought any normal woman would do. Normal and I hadn't had a lifetime to become besties. I was shooting a little blind here.

"Hello?"

"Sister mine." I let it out in a desperate breath, almost falling apart at simply hearing Claire's sweet voice. That bitch would know what to say. She always did.

"Hey. Hey." Her voice changed as soon as the reality of my tone sank in. "What's wrong? I've been sick with worry since getting your emails this morning. What's going on? Is it Michael? I swear, if he's upset you again, I'm going to kick his ever-loving butt. Tell me. Now."

Despite my misery, I laughed. "Are you knocked up again? You sound like a hormone-replacement ad." I couldn't help it. Her speech was hilarious. Claire Montgomery-Stone was five feet, three inches tall and maybe a hundred and five pounds after a holiday feast. Still, my girl knew the meaning of family and all the happy horseshit that went with it. If you messed with her tribe, she was coming for you—with both guns blazing.

"It is Michael, isn't it?"

I tossed back a knowing hum. "Is it?"

"Well, I know he has a dick. That automatically makes him a dick."

"Aha. So this is actually about my brother. Maybe I should be the one asking some questions. What did the amazing egomaniac Killian Stone do to get his little bear so wooly today?"

"I am not wooly." She giggled now too. Or growled. They kind of sounded the same with her.

"Can you meet up?"

"Grrrr. Wish I could, Mare. I have a doctor's appointment in thirty. My overbearing ass of a husband won't let me drive there myself, so I can talk while Alfred drives me."

"Won't let you drive? Why?" As the words came out, the answer started auto-populating my mind. "Wait. Ohhhh...so that's what this is about..."

"Don't start."

Her huff gave away even more.

"What did you do to lose your driving privileges?"

"I don't want to talk about it."

I barely held in my laughter. As awful as it sounded, my mood was lifted just hearing about their issues. It made me feel better, knowing other couples bickered over stupid stuff too.

"Out with it," I commanded.

"I got another speeding ticket. And if you laugh...I swear, Margaux, I will hang up this phone. You know how they set those speed traps on the Five? I didn't even see the bastard until it was too late. By then, he'd already flipped on the lights and climbed up my ass."

I busted into giggles, though muffled them with my free hand. My sister's third speeding ticket in the past year was doubly ironic because she hadn't even wanted her Audi, a gift from Killian, in the first place. Now she burned rubber like Danica Patrick in the thing.

Maybe life had a sense of humor after all.

"Are you laughing?"

"No. I'm coughing. Yeah...sure...coughing. I'm in La Jolla.

My allergies are a wreck. The sea lions smell gross."

"You're so full of shit, Mary Stone."

I sobered. "Oh. No. You. Did. Not." I allowed few people to use my real birth name and live to tell about it. Even then, the occasion had to be drastic. I'd let Claire survive. This time.

The little wench wasn't a speck apologetic about it either—not that I expected her to be. "I did," she declared, "and I'll do it again if you utter one word about this to that cocky hunk of a boyfriend of yours."

"I can't be responsible for what I say to him sometimes." Most of the time. "He has ways of making me talk, Claire. Dirty, filthy ways."

"Stop. I do not want to hear this!"

"You totally do. Don't be a prude. I'm not buying that anymore."

She cleared her throat—making mine tighten. The woman always found a way to steer back to the point "Okay, all kidding aside—"

"But the kidding was fun."

"—what's going on? Tell me, sissy. You're better now, but five minutes ago you were falling apart."

I curled my knees to my chest. While the night breeze off the ocean smelled infinitely better than the sea lions, it carried a chilled bite. "Declan Pearson has decided to pursue legal charges...about the drama from Saturday night."

Claire gasped. "Is that even possible? Did Michael touch Declan?"

I bit my lip. "Depends on who you ask."

"What?"

"It's complicated, okay?"

"Well, shit."

I was too exhausted to go into details and knew she'd forgive me the edit. "Well, I convinced him to hire Doug to help us with this whole mess. Doug has branched out into PI work, and he's good at it—and we are definitely going to need some outside help with this bullshit. We met him over at the Brockton Villa, to go over preliminaries about the case, and—"

"Wait. Whoa. Hold the phones. You hired Doug. Doug who? Are you talking about Doug Simcox? Mare...seriously?"

I borrowed a page from Kil's book, pinching the bridge of my nose. "Whose side are you on, anyway?"

"Yours. But nobody is going to be okay with that scumbag back in your life. No wonder Michael is coming unglued."

"The shit between Doug and me is water under the bridge."

"And Michael believes you?"

"I'm long over it, Claire."

She snorted. "If you say so."

"Okay, let me put it this way. If Killian were in trouble like this and Nick showed up offering skills that could help, wouldn't you put whatever reservations you had behind you? For Kil?"

"First, let's be clear. Killian would never need help from anyone because he is, after all, Killian. That being said, I would drill through a damn mountain to help that man—as I think I've proved in the past."

"Exactly!" Before she could formulate more of an objection, I plowed on. "Don't forget the thousands I've already spent on therapy about this too...right? Tons of therapy. Tons. That makes me so healed about this shit. So normal. I'm normal." *Say it enough times and even you'll believe it, babe.*

"Seriously?"

"Seriously."

A low rumble vibrated over the line. "Sister mine, you couldn't pass for normal right now if someone handed you a sweater set and June Cleaver's pearls."

"What's that supposed to—?"

"Hush. Just hush. What the fuck, Margaux? What kind of thread are you really hanging on to? And who the hell do you think you're fooling? What's the real problem here?"

"Christ, Claire. I—"

"I'm guessing it was your idea to bring Doug into the fold."

"So?"

"So...what's the deal? Do you still have feelings for him?"

"No!"

"Though you answered that a little too quickly, I still believe you." Her voice gentled. "I know how much you love Michael and how much he loves you. So this has to be about something else."

"It is. I had to leave the restaurant...leave them both there. They started going at each other like pissy schoolboys. I didn't know how much more of it I could take—or can take."

She let a long beat go by. Another. "Well, what would you be doing in Michael's position?"

I dropped my head to the top of a knee. Traced a contemplative finger along the edge of the bench. "I didn't think of it that way."

"Of course you didn't." The statement was more a sympathetic fact than an accusation. "You know you aren't into Doug, so you expected Michael to simply believe you and deal with it. But guess what, babe? They're men. Their brains fit inside the heads of their dicks. Doug was the cause of a lot of pain and drama in your life. Imagine if there was a female equivalent in Michael's past and she just showed up one day—and then he asked you to work peacefully with her. Could you do it?"

"I...don't know." I worked my chin up over my knee, rolling it around the cap as I inwardly debated. "If it meant getting his name cleared, like this could?" I lifted my head, newly resolute. "Doug is one of the top private investigators in the state, Bear. You know the Christopher Landen case, the one all over the news? That was Doug's team."

"Those are impressive credentials," she conceded. "And I know you only want the best for Michael...but you need to look at it from his perspective too. Emotions are new to you. I realize that."

"Watch it, you saucy little witch."

"Or what, fairy ice queen?"

My laugh echoed hers. "Fuck, you drive me nuts."

"I love you too." She sighed. "Just remember to take his side into consideration."

"Fine, fine," I grumbled. "I know you're right."

"Of course I am."

"Hey."

"Hmmm?"

"Why the doctor? Everything okay? Am I going to be an auntie?" I sing-songed the last part.

"You'll have to wait and see." She chanted it back at me.

"Ahhhh! Evil!"

"Speaking of evil, my jailer is already here. I'd better get off the phone before Kil disconnects this privilege too."

She finished it in a giggle. It was clear, even over the phone, that she adored my brother and all his overprotective ways. It helped that everyone knew that Killian Aidan Jamison

Klarke Stone would capture the moon, wrestle it to earth, and lay it before her feet if she even mentioned the desire to dance in moon dust.

They made me want to puke.

"All right, Bear. Kiss the man for me too. I appreciate the talk."

"Margaux?"

"Hmmm?"

"You know I really do love you."

"Bleccchh."

Things were suddenly so much better.

Eventually—hopefully—it would become second nature for me to turn to my family. My real family, the people I truly cared about, the ones I actually loved. My mother—well, Andrea—had my mind and instincts so warped, I still shied away from them...from needing anyone.

I didn't like it anymore.

Maybe, when life settled back down again, I'd do something I swore against ever trying again in my life.

Maybe it was time to go back to therapy.

★ ★ ★ ★

"Declan Pearson isn't taking a piss without us knowing about it."

I grinned gamely at Doug across my dining room table. "Well, you have my attention now."

"I have one man on him pretty much around the clock in Julian. My office girl-slash-media guru, Tiffany, is tracking every mouse click he makes online, including gambling sites, credit card charges, and social media. Another one of my guys is standing by here in town, in case he decides another San Diego field trip is in order." He broke into the update with a tight scowl, directing his attention to an equally somber Michael. "The connection to the goons, or whatever you called them from the night at the Del, is proving to be our sticky challenge."

Michael's mien didn't change. This was the third of our weekly check-in meetings with Doug, though the first that took place at the condo. Michael wasn't any more pleased about it than Doug was comfortable.

Leaving tonight's giant helping of awkward all for me. Goody.

I was damn glad Michael had already gotten home when Doug arrived—though I also didn't miss that sometime during the day, the school desk had been pulled away from the wall, farther than normal. The everyday clutter had been cleared from it too. The remodel definitely wasn't Sorrelle's doing, since he was assisting me at the office more and more lately, proving invaluable to the ramp-up team of Stone Global's beauty products division.

I wasn't sure if Michael's territory marker was adorable or annoying. I didn't want to flaunt our sexual shenanigans in Doug's face, and I sure as hell didn't want to be distracted with thoughts of that night, when we needed to focus fully on Doug's latest news. Right now, nothing was more important than clearing Michael of the ridiculous assault and battery charges. Our entire life was in a holding pattern, waiting to get over this hurdle.

Still, since he'd taken the time to clear the desk off, I wondered what saucy little act of defiance might earn me a punishment later. Hmmm.

"I don't know what you're insinuating...Dougie."

Shit.

Punishment tabled—unless it turned into Michael's instead of mine. This wasn't the most ideal situation for anyone, but tonight it was the most convenient. Michael seemed hell-bent on forgetting that part, jumping right into poking Doug with the alpha caveman stick.

To his credit, Doug actually grinned. "Excuse me, man?"

Michael chuffed and then growled. "Oh, come on, man. The way you just said that—like you don't believe me—that wasn't a slip."

"Stop." I grabbed his forearm and curled my nails in. "Stop."

"Stop what?" he flung. "Calling him on his truth, when he won't believe mine?"

Doug stood. "I believe you, okay? It's just that—"

"The fuck you do." Michael twisted his arm free and shoved to his own feet. "The fuck anyone does." With hands clasped behind his neck, he stomped toward the patio. "What are we even doing this for?"

"Michael." This was getting painful—in the worst translations of the word.

He spun around, spearing a stare into Doug. "Ohhh, wait. I forgot what a convenient opportunity this is for you, man. Yeah...great idea. Bilk your old girlfriend out of her money and have the chance to spend some nice, cozy free time with her."

Doug shook his head. "You're letting the stress talk, buddy."

"The stress—or the truth? Come on, it is a great idea, man. Getting rich while getting back in her panties. Real smooth."

Doug rammed his chair back under the table. "I don't have to take this."

Michael spun. "Neither do I. That's English, Dougie-poo, for get the fuck out of our house."

"Michael! Stop!" Now this was beyond painful. He was making an ass out of himself.

"Oh? So it's Michael, stop. Not Doug stop. Just Michael." He bared his teeth in a vicious smile. "Fucking. Perfect."

"Oh, my God." Against my control, my volume rose to match his. "Are we really doing this again?"

One end of his mouth tugged up, lifting those full lips in a sneer. "I don't recall ever doing this a first time." He threw his glare back to Doug. "Do you, buddy? Have we done this before?"

Doug held up both hands. "I'll just leave." Remarkably, he'd recalibrated his tone. The statement went along with his pose, an attempt at keeping the peace without placing blame. "I thought this would be easier for you guys, but we can reschedule something for my office."

I exhaled gratefully.

Michael let out a predatory snarl. "I get it. Now you're the hero too, right? I'm the hotheaded idiot boyfriend, and you're the sweeping knight, making everything all better."

Doug started shutting down his laptop. "Pearson, I'm not talking to you like this."

"Of course you're not. Why should you, Mr. I'm-Above-This?" He pushed behind Doug, puffing out his chest as Doug scooped up files. Yes, puffing out his chest. "I have it just about right, don't I, Simcox?"

I couldn't believe what I was watching. What the hell had the universe done with the understanding, levelheaded, I'm-a-patient-man-Margaux person that I loved?

"Michael!" I grabbed at his arm. My fingers smacked each

other as he wrenched away. "This has to stop!"

Doug slung his leather satchel over his shoulder. "It's okay. I'm going to go." Dipped his head a little toward me. "Will you be all right?"

"Great idea, Dougie." Michael squared off, shoulders tense and fists curled. "She'll be fine here—with me."

I stepped around Michael, shaking my head. "I'll see you out, Doug." As I passed, I flashed a backward glower that conveyed a two-pronged message. Michael had some explaining to do—and a mega-sized apology to issue.

While leaving with Doug, I grabbed my key off the hook in the foyer in order to get back into the condo. As I walked Doug to the elevator, color rushed my cheeks. Words seemed a hopeless concept.

Luckily, they did come. "I don't even know what to say. I'm mortified."

"It's okay," Doug murmured. "He's under a lot of stress."

"It's not okay," I seethed. "We're all under a lot of stress!"

"Stop," Doug protested. "Get back to him. Have a drink together. Maybe ten."

I battled for a smile. Wasn't happening. "I'm not sure what's going on in his head, but I promise this is the last time he'll treat you that way. I'll make sure of it."

The elevator arrived. Doug gave me a quick, friendly hug. I really wasn't comfortable with that either, but given the bomb Michael had just dropped in the condo, I didn't know if I was coming or going. I didn't even remember my steps back inside.

When I got there, Michael was pacing the living room like a caged animal. If I had carpet, I'd be concerned for the pile. I watched him make three laps before I finally spoke.

"What the fuck was that all about?"

"What?"

"What? Are you serious?"

"If you're referring to my frustration about being gawked at like I'm making up pretend bad guys, then—"

"Frustration? Is that what you're calling it? That wasn't frustration. That was being an immature ass. For God's sake, Michael. You're a professional attorney. Instead, you're acting like a child!" I stormed across the room, making my way to the mantel. I had to grip something other than his neck. "I expected more. Much more."

"Well." In the reflection created by the window, he'd slammed his hands to his hips. "Sorry I let you down, sweetheart—again. Guess there's a lot of that going on around here lately, huh?"

I whirled, the action causing my hand to catch a piece of blown-glass art that looked like a constipated seagull. It crashed to the floor, and I didn't care. "Is that what this is about? Is this some weird martyr bullshit, Michael? Some 'poor you for picking a loser like me' bit? That bullshit goes nowhere with me faster than anything I can think of." I crunched through the glass, sweeping out my arms. "Are you forgetting who you're dealing with? Compassion is an emotion I barely comprehend, let alone am in touch with, buddy."

He spread his arms wide, almost to plead with me. "Damn. You're right. How could I possibly forget who I'm dealing with? In case you haven't noticed, it's everywhere I fucking look!"

Rise in San Diego, a local tabloid, was lying on the coffee table. The two of us were splashed across the cover beneath the disgusting headline *Trouble in Paradise?* I'd meant to throw the rag out when Sorrelle brought it into the house after a trip to the grocery store. Now, I scooped up the piece of shit and winged it at him. It bounced off his chest and landed face up on the floor. Fucker didn't even try to defend himself.

"You. Prideful. Prick. Who's the one carrying us into the public mud bath? Look at the picture, damn it. It's you! You, making a fool of yourself in public...again. Don't stand there making insinuations that I'm the media whore who's enjoying this!"

I was suffocated by a furious fog as I stormed over to the stairs. Doug was right. I needed a drink—but first a long, hot, rage-melting bath in the master bathtub. Alone.

"Where do you think you're going?"

I stopped in my tracks. First, his tone. Second, the question itself.

I cocked my head to the side, still facing the stairs. "What did you just say?"

His steps were hard and measured. I kept one foot frozen on the second step.

"Where. Are. You. Going?" He growled it at my ramrod-straight back. "We're not done talking, damn it."

"We weren't talking. We were yelling." I let out an exhausted sigh. "And, yes. I'm most definitely done."

I lifted my other foot. He reached out for me, wrapping arms around my waist and then pressing his cheek to my... cheeks.

His face, hot from our argument, felt wonderful against my ass, even through my jeans. It felt good to have his arms around me, but nothing else. No, nothing else. I wasn't ready to make up by a long shot.

"Margaux."

"Don't. Michael...don't."

"I need you."

"And I need you. But not like this. I can't do—this." I pulled out of his grip and ascended the rest of the stairs. When I was safe behind our bedroom door, I flopped down on the bed, not sure what I wanted next. To scream? To cry? To hit something?

No.

Someone.

Damn it.

I dragged myself into the bathroom and started the tub. A big pile of bubbles was in order tonight, so I added an extra scoop of bath salts and cranked the handle all the way over to the etched *H* on the modern steel fixture. I locked the door, stripped, and sank into the tub up to my eyeballs.

Perfection.

At least the bath was.

I enjoyed the respite while I could. Eventually, my mind started churning again. I swallowed hard and forced myself to steam rather than cry.

Why did this feel like our first fight? God knew, it wasn't. Sometimes our relationship seemed built on one giant battle—which was sad and scary in its own right. But for some reason, this felt different. Because we lived together now? Implied meaningful commitment along with the dual toothbrush holder and his weights set on the patio?

No. The answer was right in front of me. I was just too terrified to confront it.

I'd never loved someone more than this. Michael Pearson was the man I wanted to spend the rest of my life with. My heart and brain were on the same page on that one.

He had to stop acting like a jealous teenager.

The conversation I'd had with Claire three weeks ago

replayed in my mind—as it had several times since. I'd been fighting to heed her wisdom. How would I feel in his shoes, if all this were turned around? I wouldn't like it, but I sure as hell hoped I wouldn't behave how he had either.

There was a soft tap on the door.

"Go away," I called out.

Michael's pause spoke a volume. He was struggling with this too. "Just...wanted to make sure you're okay. You've been in there a long time."

"I'm fine. I simply want to be left alone."

"Can I get you anything?"

Damn it. Why was he being so sweet now? Ohhhh, right. Because he'd fucked up and recognized the big penance coming his way.

"Just...please...stop." I couldn't grant him any slack. Not now. Maybe not for a long time.

"I don't want to stop. I want to fix this. Fuck...princess...I hate it when we fight."

"Then why do you keep acting like an ass?"

"Good question."

"Let me know when you have a good answer."

I took my time getting out of the tub and rinsing under the shower to clean off the bubbles before washing my hair. I was also deliberate about combing through the conditioner, giving myself time for each step of the routine. No more confrontations tonight. I couldn't handle them. Every minute brought a greater need to just collapse into bed and let sleep claim me.

When lingering in the bathroom was no longer viable, I quietly opened the door, shuffled into my dressing room, and slipped into some pajamas. I hated wearing the damn things but needed the physical shield tonight, adding as many walls as possible in literal and figurative form.

Just as quietly, I climbed into our empty bed. Normally, I'd search for Michael and we would climb in together. Not tonight.

I pulled the covers around my ears and drifted off to sleep quicker than I thought possible. The bath had done its job. I didn't fight the relaxation. The morning would bring the talk we both needed, when we were both strong enough for it.

This problem wasn't going to go away on its own.

There was no way I'd get that lucky.

CHAPTER ELEVEN

Michael

Once again, I slept on the couch.

Sure, Margaux was out cold when I went back upstairs to check on her, but getting into bed and stretching out next to her would've been as comfortable as sleeping next to a wall. Correction, a wall with the sexiest fucking curves in the universe—a wall who was barely acknowledging my presence at the moment.

The old axiom needed an overhaul. Don't go to bed angry— or when you've got a pounding erection for your woman.

Funny how that particular thought stuck like glue—yeah, the same stuff that coated every inch of my cock, keeping it stiff and sensitive all night. The shit received a refresh just before I opened my eyes, helped by a pair of my favorite smells—fresh coffee and Margaux's eucalyptus body lotion. Even for a hard-up guy in the doghouse, it wasn't a bad way start to the day.

Cautiously, I opened my eyes.

Tallied another slash in the good day column.

She wasn't standing over me with a box cutter or even the we-need-to-talk glower. I'd almost hoped for the latter. At least that'd mean she wanted to talk. Instead, she stood in front of the window, where she watched the burgeoning dawn in silence.

I rolled to my side as quietly as I could, relishing the chance to gaze at her. She only moved to sip her coffee, as serene as the golden fingers of light caressing their way over her, sifting through the sexy mess of her hair. The sky's deeper tones, some grays still hiding in the haze over the bay, were like the shadows that lingered in her eyes...and gripped my chest. Her robe hung open, exposing a new pair of pajamas. The black shorts and matching tank top, with a little gold crown embroidered over her left breast, covered enough but not enough at the same time—dunking my dick in more of that magic hard-on glue.

I tightened my grip on a couch pillow. This battle, craving her but fighting it, wasn't one I'd had to wage in months. So much had changed since those days when I'd pined for her from the corner of Andrea's office—though I certainly remembered similar expressions on her face as she'd stared out the window of that glamorous environment. I'd indulged long, selfish stares at her back then, wondering what thoughts had brought that dark blue-green to her eyes. We'd come so far since then. The answer to that dilemma wasn't hazy for me anymore.

It sure as hell wasn't right now.

The shadows across her face were because of me.

I released a hard breath. It meant the end of spying on her, but I also hoped it would relieve the claws of self-disgust tearing across my chest. No change. The fuckers were as tenacious as feral cats.

Margaux pivoted. Her face didn't change, but her stare lingered, trailing over the blanket slung over my hips. Thank God for that too. Nothing like greeting the woman who was barely speaking to you with the woody that had been your best friend all night.

"Hey," she finally said.

"Hey."

"I started coffee."

"It smells great. Thank you."

"You're welcome."

So far, so good. We were at friendly coffee house chatter—better than last night's closed bathroom door and her demand that I go away. Baby steps.

"Looks like it'll be a nice day."

"Mmm-hmm." A step forward or back? Her tone was pleasant, but tension still bracketed her face. "Won't be out much to enjoy it," she murmured. "The team's up to our eyeballs in the beauty line's premarketing shit. I'll probably just eat at my desk, though that'll be taking my life into my own hands. HR can't find a single temp who can listen to simple directions. The other day, my office smelled like mayonnaise all afternoon because—"

I silenced her with a wet, tender kiss on her neck. The moment she'd started the rant, I'd seized the chance to rescue her from it. With the blanket wrapped around my hips, I'd moved behind her before she could recognize the move. Worst case? I'd get slapped for trying. Best case?

Was this.

Her body pressing back against me. Her head falling back, fitting into my shoulder. Her determined ditch of the coffee cup, nestling it in the potted fern near the door before wrapping her hands around my arm.

When she exhaled too, the sound long and high, I needed no other inspiration. My head dropped, my jaw notching above her collarbone, my breath fanning her luscious cleavage—though remarkably, at this instant, I didn't give a shit about her cleavage. I yearned more to reclaim the heart inside her chest...the soul inside her sighs.

"I'm sorry," I whispered, holding her tighter to me. "I'm sorry. So sorry."

As she turned in my arms, she slipped a hand around my neck. It was torture to let her stare at me, especially because the shadows were still so tenacious in her eyes, but I didn't glance off. This was part of the deal. The opening up she'd been imploring me so much for. Doing more of this likely wouldn't have stopped me from confronting Declan at the Del—but we would've been better equipped to handle the aftermath.

"None of this is easy for you." She stroked up the back of my head, pulling my hair gently. "I do know that, Michael. You've done so much for yourself for so long that accepting help is hell, especially in this form."

A smile grabbed my lips and didn't let go. It was just as rough for her to give the empathy as it was for me to trust Doug—but her gift was like a boulder of gold. "Thank you." I tugged her closer. "You really do get it."

"Because I get you." She lifted her other hand, scraping through my stubble. "We came from different kingdoms, but our walls were cut from the same stones, built by the same kinds of fears. Tearing them down means we can see the sky, but neither of us knows how to fly...and it's scary sometimes." She kissed me softly. "It's scary a lot of times."

I nodded my way into repeating the kiss. Kept my mouth sealed to hers longer now, melding her to me with desperate, passionate need. "And sometimes, I can't even do the flying thing." I grimaced. "The cave is all I'm capable of, sugar."

"I know," she soothed. "And last night, Doug strutted into your cave."

"You mean took over the whole fucking cave?"

"He visited the cave."

"Well, I didn't like it."

"Well, you need to get over it." She stepped back, twisting her lips and clawing back her hair. "He believes you, damn it, even about Menger and the goons—and he's trying to help."

"All right, all right." I spread my hands as if trying to smooth ripples from water. Easing her ire was as just as unfeasible. The blanket slid an inch lower on my hips, and I didn't care. "And I believe you, so I'll try harder."

As she nodded, her features relaxed. "You know, maybe Declan will drop the charges altogether, once he realizes you're not backing down. Doug's team will unearth something about these Principals, whoever the hell they are. Wouldn't exposing them be worse for his position than owing them money?"

I braced my ass against the dining room table. "Logic might say so."

She cocked her head. "But...?"

"But what would be his next step be?" I pushed it out between tight teeth—and lungs that pumped with the frost of fear.

"Next step?"

I laughed without humor. "Oh, there'd be a next step, sweetheart, have no doubt. You want to talk about eminent domain? The man's adopted it as a personal credo. Dec has no trouble hurting people to get what he wants. Maybe worse."

Margaux began rolling her eyes but stopped when I grabbed my own shoulders, actually shivering. "Hey...hey." She marched back over and squirmed until I opened my embrace, letting her push all the way against me. "You're getting dramatic again, Caveman Joe."

I clutched her tighter. "Because I'm terrified, princess."

She angled back, grabbing my face with both hands. "I know. But you're also not fighting T-Rex on your own anymore."

I ran my hands along her back, letting the satin slide around, teasing at the exposed parts of her skin. "No, I'm not."

She pumped an arm up, looking every inch a golden blonde cheerleader fantasy—if one ever existed in a short little robe and sexy satin pajamas. "Hurray! Progress!"

I chuckled but sobered into a pout. "Does that mean I have to retire the caveman club now?"

She lowered her hand, only to go straight for my blanket. With a saucy little jerk, she released the whole thing. The cotton fell away, exposing my bare waist, hips, and thighs—and everything between—to her freshly heated gaze.

"Oh, Joe...don't you dare put away that club."

She moved in with a sexy sigh, gazing at me as she stroked a hand down, down, down, until—

Fuck.

She wrapped her fingers around my crown first, teasing the bulging flesh until I gritted out a groan. That didn't mean I had mercy. She focused on my whole shaft next, testing the limits of my cock with every long, knowing caress.

"I can think of some damn good uses for this...club." Her breath warmed the base of my throat but fanned from there, spreading across my chest as her fingers stretched around my cock. My hips, compelled by the magic of her touch, rolled with more urgent rhythm, craving the friction of our flesh.

"Caveman Joe approves of that message," I grated.

"See? Caveman Joe's a smart guy."

"Not that smart." I deliberately tugged back when she

rose up for another kiss. "If Caveman Joe was really smart, Jungle Jane would be naked by now."

She needed no other stimulus. In three clean moves, my little jungle girl tossed the robe, shoved down the shorts, and then flicked away the tank top. As she straightened, the room grew brilliant with the dawn, amber and peach rays turning her nudity into a living work of art. I stared with no more grace than a dork in an art gallery, afraid to move my hands for fear of smearing the paint.

She cocked her head and inched a tiny smile. "All better?"

I still couldn't speak. She was beauty that defied words...a perfection I seriously didn't deserve.

I gave up on constructing a sentence, let alone speaking one. At least movement returned. Slow slides. Reverent touches. Taking the time to remember every part of this, knowing it would be one of the things that brought a smile to my face when I prepared to meet my maker. I glided over the cream perfection of her thighs, into the adorable dip of her navel, across the curves of her rib cage, up to the stiff peaks of her breasts. With every inch I covered, Margaux inhaled with pleasure, transforming from jungle girl to dawn goddess...my own Aurora of light and desire.

"You take my breath away." My voice was rough with need, born in a part of me so deep, I couldn't identify it—nor wanted to. The words consumed the sublime tension before I dipped my lips to her nipples. The erect tips tasted as good as their cinnamon-sugar color, her taste bursting on my tongue. The warmth of her body spread into mine, inundating me... hardening me.

"You take my breath away too." She squeezed my dick even tighter, rolling her thumb through the hot moisture that pulsed there, far beyond my control...almost beyond my knowledge.

"Christ," I grated. "You make me lose my mind, woman."

As her eyelids dipped, heavy with arousal, sunlight glinted on the tips of her lashes. "That's the general idea."

"Not yet, it isn't."

Her gaze widened again. I was ready with a stare of pure intent. The lip service of my apology wasn't going to be enough. I needed to show her, in vivid detail, how precious a treasure she was to me...how I'd spend the rest of my life adoring her, pleasuring her.

She had time for a short, giddy yelp as I swung her around and then swooped her down, across the dining room table. "Michael! What the—"

"Ssshhh." I positioned her ass at the edge, with her legs dangling over. They didn't hang for long. With commanding yanks, I hooked her thighs over my shoulders—before my knees hit the floor. "Let me worship my sweet Tarzan girl."

A laugh sprang out of her, more brilliant than the entire sky beyond the windows. "Am I supposed to give one of those wild yells, then?"

"Not yet." I burrowed my nose between her trimmed ginger curls, inhaling her intimate scent. "Not until I find your magic forest jewel."

A startled cry burst from her as I started exploring, using the tip of my tongue. "F-Forest...j-jewel?" She tried to laugh. It was a cute little gurgle instead. "You did not just s-say that!"

"What? You want me to quit my...quest?" I nipped at the sweet pink layers that led the way to her deepest core. Took another deep breath. She smelled so fucking good, a mixture of eucalyptus and musk and woman. And wet... She was already so wet, her cleft dripping with rivulets of the smoothest, sexiest cream. Was there any bigger turn-on than knowing I'd done this to her?

"I—I didn't say to quit." Her hips jerked off the table. "Ohhhh...damn! Michael."

"Mmmmm." The more I sampled of her pussy, the deeper I craved to feast, to lick, to bite. Her body was a fruit that never ceased amazing me, seducing me, fulfilling me. At moments like this, I had to wonder if the fruit Eve had offered to Adam had truly been an apple. If that temptation had been anything like this, I didn't blame the guy for giving in, eternal damnation be screwed. "You're so perfect, sweetheart...such a delicious pussy...all for me."

"Yes." Her heels dug into my back. Her hands tangled in my hair. "All for you. All...for...ahhhh!"

Her shriek took over as I pushed past her hood with my tongue, swiping fully at the nub beneath. I eagerly sucked her throbbing clit, detonating another scream and vibrating her whole body. I took her to the precipice but let her hover in weightless wonder, like a diver on a cliff, waiting for gravity to take over the plunge. While the rest of her body froze, her sex kept trembling, almost reaching for me...

From the outside in, I wrapped both hands around her thighs. Gripped her hard...and then slid my tongue into her tunnel.

She orgasmed around me like a perfect jungle princess. Her screams filled the room. Her hips lunged up. She pounded the table in a crucial cadence, a golden wild woman, frantic with lust.

I rose up while the tremors still consumed her, spearing my cock straight into her. We groaned together at the violent bliss. Her head fell back. She flung her arms in the same direction, seizing the edge of the table to brace for my next thrusts...

But this morning wasn't about fucking her.

It was about giving to her. Connecting with her.

I went completely still. Let her feel my cock expanding, flesh to flesh, heartbeat to heartbeat, inside her. Only then did I start to move again, rolling into her like the waves into which the diver had plunged, deep and slow and hard.

She rolled her head back up and squeezed her hands, still locked behind my skull, even tighter. Her eyes, so brilliant and pure and green, threw open the depths of her soul for me. For the first time in my life, I opened mine the same way. As our bodies locked and twined, our hearts meshed and grew...a force that slammed me like a punch. My senses reeled, making me lean over, my body seeking the only stability that made sense.

Margaux. Getting deeper into her. Clinging harder onto her.

"Don't look away." It was an open plea, and I didn't care.

"Never." As the vow left her, she lifted her hips higher. I let my head dip between my shoulders, taking her mouth and her tongue, drawing in as much of her as I could. Her body gripped mine tighter, pulled me down farther, but it still wasn't enough. Would it ever be enough?

"Fuck," I gritted.

"I know, baby," she rasped back. "I know."

"I need to crawl inside you."

"I need to wrap around you."

"Take it from me, Margaux."

"Give it to me, Michael."

Her whisper told me everything—that she knew I'd surpassed referencing my body and now petitioned her with the fabric of my spirit, my heart, my seed. Her eyes gave me her understanding as her body gave me her surrender, taking me in, taking me higher...taking me to completion. With my stare fastened to hers, I came in a burst of light and fire and need— and for a brief flash, of fantasy. Just the thought of my liquid life forming a life inside her...I reeled all over again. Never had I wanted a truth to be more real.

Never had I known, with more clarity or conviction, that I'd met the woman I'd love for the rest of my life.

★ ★ ★ ★

"Oh, my God, Michael!"

Though I chuckled externally, my mojo did a touchdown dance. I loved making this woman feel good. I loved it even better when I made her groan like that—even with her clothes on.

I kneaded my thumbs harder into the arch of her foot. Her head fell back, over the couch's arm. "So the cramp is better?"

She flashed a contemplative glance. "If I say yes, are you going to stop?"

I leaned over to nibble the top of her foot. "I have a hard time stopping anything when it comes to touching you, sugar."

"Just the way I like it." She sneaked her teeth over her bottom lip. I watched, heating from the inside out, flowing the frustration of my cock into my rubs on her foot.

"You keep that up, and there won't be any way to keep me down."

Her chest heaved a little, as if contemplating a bite of the sinful fruit I offered. "I could call in late..."

"And Claire wouldn't guess why?"

She huffed. "Like she hasn't done the same thing a thousand times?" Using the line to distract me, she slipped her other foot in place of her first. "But, ugh, you're right. Talia and I have a meeting with the special-events company handling the cosmetics launch in Vegas, and then we have to decide on color names for the lipstick line."

I stroked into the valley beneath her toes. "Color names?"

"Yeah, like Rocket Me Red or Scarlet Charisma, only multiply that by a couple hundred. We have to whittle it down to ten."

I forced a serious façade. "How about Come-Fuck-Me Crimson?"

"Beast." She rolled off the couch as I gave in to a snicker.

"Your beast."

"Truth." She pulled me up and then stood on tiptoe to peck me on the lips. "I'm sure you have a busy day to start, as well."

"Hmmph. Yeah. A very busy day. It's going to be a jam-packed bundle of thrills."

She sighed and twisted her ring. "I'm sure this isn't any easier for Quade and Rin—but you can't blame them for asking you to lie low until this shit is ancient history."

I scowled as I slipped her shoes onto her feet—a pair of glossy black stilettos that turned her legs into pure sex and her toes into lethal weapons. "You're right. And I should be damn grateful they still believe in me." I caught her eye again, forcing a quick smile. "But a man of leisure I am not, sugar, unless those hours are spent servicing you."

Margaux allowed her gaze to travel off my face and over my bare torso. I hadn't hit the shower yet, so my track pants were the foot massage therapist wear for the morning. "If this is your idea of man of leisure, you need to reconsider that offer of being my official boy toy."

My grin turned genuine. If there was an upside to the Declan mess, it was the extra hours I'd spent having my ass kicked on Pacific Beach by Keir Healey, a buddy from college who ran his own personal training company. Admittedly, the extra fitness kept me from going stir-crazy. Now if I could only do something as worthwhile with my mind.

Today, I decided, I would.

"Sorry, sweetheart. The boy-toy fantasy will have to wait." I rose and held out a hand, helping her do the same. "I'm going to call Doug today. Arrange a time to meet at his office for those updates."

She looked up at me with distinctly shiny eyes. "For that, I'll gladly back-burner your harem pants and monkey vest."

I lifted a brow. "Show me a monkey vest, and we'll be visiting the school desk again."

"Promise?"

I yanked her into a kiss, deep and wet and languorous, while I still could. Once the berry stain hit those full lips, I had to share them with the world at large. "Off with you, wench," I teased. "The Stone empire awaits the jewel in its crown."

She gave a sassy smirk. "I think my brother may have something to say about that."

"Well, your brother isn't here, is he?"

She giggled, the sound swelling my heart. "Incorrigible."

I pulled her close again, hoping to sneak one more peck before the stain came out, but somebody knocked on the front door.

Correction. Pounded on the front door.

"What the hell?" I muttered.

Margaux's brows pushed together. "It's too early for deliveries. Even if it wasn't, I'm not expecting anything."

"Maybe it's priority from the office?"

"Or Doug?"

She issued that while reaching for the doorknob. I snatched her elbow, yanking her back. Her hopeful mention of Doug turned into my sinister suspicion of other parties involved in this tangle—actually, only one party.

"Wait," I gritted.

"What?"

"It won't be Doug."

The apprehension in my voice sharpened her gaze. "Then who?"

I tucked her behind me as I peered through the peep hole. Puzzlement eclipsed my alarm. "There's nobody there."

"Huh? But—" She fell silent as I unlocked the door and then cracked it an inch. "What...the..."

I was right. There was no one standing there.

But there had been. The ding and swoosh of the elevator doors were proof that a strange Santa Claus had arrived at our place a few weeks early.

Strange, indeed—for Santa had forgotten his sack, seemingly hauled all the way down from the Cayamaca Mountains.

Its exact origin was emblazoned in huge red letters across the heavy brown burlap—three words I'd seen so many times, they were part of my blood.

PEARSON'S APPLE FARM

"Well." Margaux cocked her head and looped a lopsided

smile. "I guess you were the one with the surprise shipment."

"Surprise is right," I replied, dragging the bag in.

"Care package from the hill. That's so cute. Maybe Di's worried I'm not feeding you enough."

"My mother loves you, and you know it. Besides, this doesn't feel like produce—unless they've started growing coconuts and didn't tell me."

She kicked off her heels and braced her hands to her hips. "What do you mean?"

"I mean it's fucking heavy, especially for a postseason haul. If it's apples, I'd be really surp—"

I was cut off by a long, taut moan.

A moan from the inside the bag.

A moan...I already knew.

With boldness only possible because of denial and stupidity, I plummeted to my knees. Margaux followed, helping me wrench at the sack. I yanked at the ties with focus born of panic, watching my hands as if through a tunnel. The distance didn't help the dread, confirmed in all the darkest reaches of my gut, via bile that ate my body and raged through my soul— forcing me to heed instincts that had, long ago, reaffirmed my uncle's evil for all it really was.

Margaux shoved the burlap aside—

Revealing a woman.

Hair that was the shade of mine—sort of. In the places it wasn't matted with blood.

A face that had laughed with me, smiled for me—barely recognizable through a maze of cuts and bruises.

Arms that had always been my shelter, my strength—now twisted, limp...lifeless.

No.

"Mom." I reached for her. "Mom!"

No.

I gripped harder. Harder.

You shouldn't. Don't disturb her. Get help. Call for help.

But I'd always been the help. I'd always been her help. We'd always been there for each other, shelter and comfort and strength for each other.

Not this time.

Where had I been when she'd needed me this time?

"Mom. Mom. Mom. Mom!"

Please.

Please.

Please.

Wake up.

Wake up.

Wake up.

"Mom!"

It was the bellow of an animal. The howl of a creature lost to the worst kind of rage and despair—because it was directed at the stubborn monster inside as much as the fucking beast who'd ordered this done to her. Perhaps had done it himself.

That answer didn't matter anymore. Who had delivered this damage—it wasn't important.

My mother was half-dead. Perhaps more than half.

And I was just as guilty of the violence as Declan.

CHAPTER TWELVE

Margaux

"She's alive."

It rushed out of me nearly as one word, a burst of triumph after pressing a finger to her neck and feeling the sketchy flutter of her pulse inside her clammy skin.

Not clammy. Wet. Di was taking a bath in her own blood.

But she was alive.

Barely.

I looked to Michael. Every cell of my body wanted to crawl into his lap and hold him. He looked like he'd just stared death in the eyes, lost the contest, and then retreated into himself, shoving back against the sofa. With knees clutched to his chest, he started mumbling to himself—fast, furious words I couldn't make out.

But one of us needed to think. To move into action.

"Michael? Michael!"

He didn't rip his gaze from his mother. Shock, disbelief, grief—probably a mix of all three—had already taken him hostage.

This shit was on me.

I answered that charge with a steeled murmur. "Do this, girl. You know you can."

I scrambled to the foyer credenza and then whipped out

my phone. Dialing emergency professionals should've been my first instinct, but it wasn't. I needed calming courage. Now.

My thumb jabbed the speed dial for Andre. I didn't wait for him to finish his greeting.

"Can you come up to the condo? Are you nearby?"

"Yeah. I'm on my way over now. Everything okay?"

"No." I fought to ignore the tremble in my voice. "Just hurry. Please."

I hung up with him and then frantically punched in three more numbers. It seemed like forever until the line connected.

"Nine-one-one. What is your emergency?"

"Y-Yes. H-Hello. There is a…well, a woman—my boyfriend's mother—here. On the floor. She's been badly beaten." I almost laughed. "Badly beaten" was a fucking joke compared to the carnage across Di Pearson's body. "Sh-She's unconscious. Can you help me? Please?"

"Yes. Can you confirm you are at seven-zero-two Ash Street?"

"Yes."

"That's the El Cortez."

"Does that fucking matter?"

"Can you give me your unit number, Miss?"

Oh. Right. It did matter. *Breathe. Breathe. Think. Think.* "I'm on the fifteenth floor. I'll have my assistant meet them in the lobby. They can't get up without a key card."

"Emergency services can, ma'am."

And apparently, Declan Pearson—or whoever had carried out his dirty work.

"Oh." Every word I stammered felt like pushing out a boulder. "Okay."

"Stay on the line with me until they arrive. Is the woman

breathing?"

"Y-Yes. I think so."

"Can you check? Take the phone with you, if you can."

I leaned over Di. Took a second to brush a hand over her forehead, cheeks, and neck. She was even clammier—and so damn cold. "She's breathing, but it's not right. It's soft and shallow, not regular...like in a regular pattern. God, I'm not making any sense."

"You're doing a great job. Can you hear gurgling? Does it sound like there might be fluid in her mouth or throat? Blood, maybe?"

"I—I can't tell."

"It's okay. Do you have something you can cover her with? A blanket, maybe? Is anyone else there with you?"

"I can get a blanket. Yes, my boyfriend's here, but I think he's in shock. He's—he's freaking out. I think."

I looked at Michael again. Freaking out? Was that his deal? Working at Andrea's heels for so many years, I'd witnessed crisis reactions of all kinds—but always from a distance, never as close as this. Never caring like this. He hadn't moved at all. Had he even taken a breath? He stared straight ahead, no longer at Diana, his lips still working on incoherent mumblings. I yearned to stop and be with him. I couldn't. Di needed me more. Didn't stop my heart from breaking in half at watching my strong, capable, protective man reduced to a catatonic mess.

"Do you know who did this?" The operator's voice snapped me back into action.

"No, goddamnit." Recognizing her question had to be a formality didn't ease my defensiveness. "There was a knock on the door. When we answered it, she was just lying there."

"Okay. Easy." She soothed it as I ran upstairs to get a blanket from the linen closet, taking the phone with me. "A few more minutes. Dispatch shows them pulling up in front of your building. You can probably hear the sirens."

At the same time, Andre barreled through the front door. "What the fuck?"

Under other circumstances, I would've gaped. I couldn't remember the last time I heard profanity come from Andre's gentle, kind soul.

"Who's there?" The nine-one-one operator hadn't missed it either.

"It's my assistant. My driver."

"That's—this—it's Mrs. Pearson." Andre gawked from Diana to me. "Who did this to her?" He knelt on the floor, stroking Diana's bruised cheek, until Michael's rapid murmuring caught his attention. "Shit. He's in shock." He yanked the blanket from the back of the sofa and settled it around Michael's shoulders. I blinked, calling myself five kinds of an idiot. Why hadn't I grabbed that blanket for Di, instead of running all the way upstairs?

You're not thinking clearly at the moment. And nobody's going to fault you for it.

More poundings came at the door. My heart punched my ribs just as violently.

"That's the police and the paramedics," the operator told me.

I groaned. "The police. Fucking wonderful."

"For everyone's protection," she clarified.

"Of course," I replied, apology lacing the tone. If I was being honest, I was glad of the cops' presence now. I wouldn't put it past Declan or his men to linger nearby, looking for more chances to spill blood for water—literally.

I gave a shaky "Thank you" to the operator before hanging up. As soon as the police declared the area clear for the paramedics, I pointed to Diana. The guys dived into action, calling out vital signs and other statistics to each other. They also barked out questions relating to Di's health, which I struggled to answer to the best of my ability, but they needed answers I just didn't have. I curled my arms against my body, fighting the encroaching helplessness and dread.

She's going to be okay. She's going to be okay.
She has to be okay. She has to be okay.

The mantra pulled a mantle of strength around me. I couldn't rely on Andre for the stuff right now. Both his arms were braced to Michael's shoulders, his entire face stamped with worry.

"Michael? Michael, my man?"

His firm but gentle voice seemed to reach where I couldn't. Michael looked up and turned a little, lips vibrating with an out-of-place smile. "Hey, Dre. What brings you here this morning?" He looked down and laughed. "And, dude, why are you all octopus arms around me?"

His face changed as soon as he took in the whole scene again. Andre, face locked in sympathy, wrapping the blanket around his shoulders. Next to them, a paramedic with a metal clipboard, writing feverishly as his partner continued to call stats. The medic on the floor, still roll-calling Diana's injuries—

Which yanked Michael's gaze back to his mother. "Oh, my God!"

"Michael." I reached to reassure him, but he lurched away.

"Mom? What the fuck happened?" He looked up, searching for me in the small throng now crowding our living room. "Margaux? What the fuck?" As forcefully as he'd just rejected me, he reached out for me. "Tell me!" His words were as painful and desperate as his expression.

I returned the force of his grip, as much for me as him. "Baby, do you remember opening the front door...about twenty minutes ago? And the burlap bag...from the orchard?"

His handsome features twisted with an agony that made my heart explode. "I'm going to kill him," he seethed. "I'm going to kill that motherfucker for this."

I dropped to my knees to make us eye level—and then leaned in and whispered for his hearing alone. "Damn it, Michael. Listen to me. You need to shut your mouth, right now. This place is crawling with police, and it's not going to change anytime soon." I clawed my fingernails into his wrists, forcing his attention. "Are you getting this? Do you understand me? We have no concrete evidence about who did this or what happened, so before you land back in jail while your mother is fighting for her life, you need to stay very, very quiet."

He looked away, disgust racking his face. I was right, an acknowledgment that clearly burned him to the core. He needed to be here for Diana, but his temper pushed him to the brink of losing that freedom. While we both had a good idea of who was responsible for this sick message, we had no physical way of linking the deed back to Declan—as if it were even a priority right now. Getting Diana to the hospital was the only goal we could or should focus on. If she had any chance of survival, the next hour of action was key.

But once she was out of the woods, Declan and his goon squad would get their payback. I silently vowed my allegiance to Michael on that.

There was another knock on the door, making everyone

but the paramedics jump out of their skin. The medical guys were oblivious to anything but Di, moving around her to start an IV line and clean up her wounds. "That's the ambulance, for transport to the hospital," one of them explained. He glanced up at Michael. "We'll be taking her up to UCSD, since they're the closest trauma center."

"Okay." Michael's answer, level and tough, indicated his head had finally gotten back in the game. I breathed easier, knowing he was getting his shit together. "Let me grab my shoes," he said as I opened the door for the guys with the gurney, "and I'll be ready."

The paramedic shook his head. "Sorry, man. We're going to need all the room we can get in the ambulance to keep working on her. But you can meet us in the UCSD emergency department." The guy continued informing Michael of how things would go after their arrival at the hospital. I listened carefully too, just in case Michael wasn't as together as he looked.

Everyone stood back while they loaded Diana onto the stretcher and prepared to depart. As soon as everyone left, Michael and I sprinted upstairs to gather necessary shit like Michael's wallet, my purse, and cell phone chargers.

When we came back down, the condo was eerily quiet, especially in the wake of the chaos and violence that had just reigned. Only Andre remained, standing in the middle of the living room, staring at his shoes like they were the most interesting things he'd ever seen.

He spoke calmly into the stillness. "Do you want me to drive?"

"Yes," Michael answered at once. "You can take her. I'll be in the truck."

"No," I protested. "Michael, I'm not sure that's—"

But he'd already stomped out the front door, slamming it hard enough to whack the foyer wall before it bounced back and closed in the frame.

I swallowed hard, wondering for a second if I'd simply blink and wake up from this morbid dream. When I turned around slowly, reality confirmed by the blood smears remaining on the floor, I choked against a sob.

Andre held out his arms. Folded me into them, letting me sob against his chest like the emotional little girl I'd become. It was pathetic, but I couldn't help myself. I indulged a minute and then two, but finally pulled back, swiping angrily at my tears.

"This bullshit needs to stop." I poked his wall of a chest.

True to form, he rumbled a deep laugh before guiding me toward the door. "It's our little secret, Miss Margaux."

"Damn straight it is."

"How about getting you to the hospital to see what's going on, yeah?"

"Yeah."

★ ★ ★ ★

Hours passed. Literally, hours. I waited with Andre in the outer waiting room of the emergency department at UCSD Medical Center, hoping for word on Diana's condition. Eventually, I marched to the nurses' station, demanding to know about her treatment and possible location, thinking we might have gone to the wrong hospital.

"I'm sorry, ma'am," the sweet-faced brunette at the desk said. "If you aren't next of kin, I can't give you any information.

I'm sure you understand."

I nodded, trying to look like I did—and shoving aside the admission that if I'd accepted Michael's proposal six weeks ago, I'd probably qualify as next of kin. Spilled milk now. Not worth stressing over.

I leaned over the counter. "Please. Please. Can you just tell me if she's here? Diana Pearson. P-E-A-R-S-O-N. You can check that, right? My boyfriend should be here with her. Since cell phones aren't allowed back there, he isn't even answering my texts. Can you just give a yes or no if she's here?" When she surrendered a hesitant glance, I went in for desperation and guilt-imposing. "That really isn't too much to ask, is it?"

When cutie pie realized I wasn't retreating without an answer, her sympathy turned into a glare. She wiggled her mouse, stabbed at the computer keys, and stated, "Yes. Diana Pearson was brought in via ambulance five hours ago. She was taken to the operating room and is still there. It's likely your boyfriend is upstairs in the waiting area outside the operating suites."

She pulled out a hospital map from a Plexiglas holder alongside the window we were talking through, unfolded it, and gave me directions using the back of her pen.

"We are here, in the emergency department." She exaggerated an X over the same words on the map. "Go down this hall, take the elevators on your right to the fourth floor, and follow the corridor to the ORs." More exaggeration, this time with a big circle around the words Operating Rooms. "The waiting area is just outside the suite. You can look for him there."

With that, she pushed the map through the cut out at the bottom of the divider, turned her back, and walked deeper into the nursing pod. Despite her words, I didn't pick up anger from her. She was just protecting herself from getting in trouble—or at least that was my rationalization for stifling the litany of swear words on my tongue.

Hell, maybe she was angry. My human barometer was out to lunch, and guess how many fucks I gave about getting it back at the moment?

I was only sure of one thing right now. Somebody was going to catch hell soon. I was nearing the end of my rope.

When I got back to where Andre sat with his head lolled against the wall, I nudged him in the shoulder.

"Hey, big guy, wake up."

"I'm not sleeping, you little shrew."

"No kidding? You should hear the sound that comes out of you when you're 'not sleeping.' It sounds remarkably like snoring."

"Do you want me to start telling people about the waterworks?"

"Aw, that's low."

"Some things just need to be done."

"I hate you."

"So why did you *not* wake me?"

"Mary Sunshine at the desk told me Di was taken to surgery and is still there. We have a good chance of finding Michael upstairs in the waiting area outside of the operating rooms."

"Then I guess we're going upstairs."

We headed for the elevator, soon stepping off at the fourth floor. It was easier to follow the overhead signs than rely on my addled brain, so we made our way through the maze of corridors until we came to the OR's waiting area.

Sure enough, Michael stood in the corner of the big room, clutching a paper cup of coffee. He stared out of the window into the courtyard of the hospital complex.

When I walked in, he looked right through me, as if I were a ghost. Out of habit, I grabbed for Andre, but he wasn't there. The traitor waited in the hallway.

"Hey."

I wrapped my arms around his waist, pulling him close. At once, he sagged into me with his full weight, forcing me to brace myself to avoid being knocked off balance. I welcomed every pound. It felt damn good to be near him again, letting his heartbeat fill my ear. He was physically exhausted, and I had a terrible feeling we'd just begun this awful journey. I held him, silently vowing to be there for every step with him.

"Give me an update?" I finally asked.

He drew in a long breath. "They've taken her into surgery."

"Right. Have they come out with any word?"

"No. There are internal injuries... They said they wouldn't know how bad any were until they got inside. She's lost a lot of blood, but they were able to give her a transfusion. The head surgeon doesn't think there is brain damage. She doesn't look like she had a lot of head trauma. I don't remember exactly how he said it. Something like...surface damage to her face. Fuck."

His voice cracked. I hugged him again, showing I understood. It was a cruel joke, if the doctors told him to be grateful it was just surface damage.

"Apparently, most of the bad stuff happened to her ribs," he went on. "The bastards also punctured one of her lungs and possibly lacerated her spleen. The docs speculated that she was probably kicked quite a bit. If—if her spleen has to be removed, her immune system will be compromised for the rest of her life. Fuck!"

"Okay. Sshhh. It'll all be okay. People live like that all the time. They have treatments for that." I returned his incredulous look with a firm frown. "I'm not saying that it isn't bad, Michael. Don't freak, but I'm trying to be positive. It'll be the key for her recovery. We have to stay positive."

He actually nodded—though he stepped back from me so decisively, it canceled my confidence. "I've been thinking about that too."

My stomach flipped strangely. "About...what?"

"I've had some time to myself this afternoon. To really think." He stared back out the window. "I've come to some... hard decisions. Ones you won't be happy with—but I must ask you to respect."

I agreed. I already didn't like the direction he'd just steered, simply by the new set of his shoulders—and not helped when he stepped back over, took both my hands, and guided me into the seats nearby.

He turned to face me, still clutching my hands, and took another long breath.

"Damn it, Michael. You're—you're scaring me."

He lifted his head. His gaze was rimmed in red and covered in torment—and still one of the most beautiful things I'd ever seen.

"Margaux...we need to break up."

I shoved his hands away. "Fuck that." Lurched to my feet, despite my liquid knees and swimming vision. "No. Wait. Fuck you."

"Sugar, I've given it a lot of thought, and—"

"I'm sure you think you have. But you can go fuck yourself and your thoughts, *sugar*." Screw the patience, the understanding, the positive thoughts, and the sweet little girlfriend. I unlocked the door for fighter bitch Margaux, and she barreled in, taking over, facing off at him, full glare blazing. "We've come this far. We've come so far, damn it. I love you!"

"And I love you. But—"

"No. Just no. If you think I'm going to walk away when you need support the most, you have no idea who you really fell in love with."

He rose, infuriatingly composed. "It's not just up to you. I get a say in this too."

I whirled, needing to not look at him. To not feel the pull of his presence, even now when I yearned to beat on him, tear at him...cling to him.

Finally, I could summon words again. "You—you once told me that your mom and I are the two people who matter the most in your life."

"You are."

"So...one is lying in there fighting for her life, but now you're letting the other one die—of a broken heart. Why, Michael? Why are you doing that?"

He pushed a hard breath through his nose. "You're not making sense right now."

"No. You're not making sense." I couldn't breathe, unable to escape this fight for my sheer existence. "What the hell?" I fell back into a chair. "How did we get to this? Why are we even talking about this?" Panic set in all over again. Back to suffocation. I shot to my feet. Michael followed right behind me.

"Damn it," he growled. "Margaux...baby...I need to protect you, okay? After this—after what happened today—do you even understand what it all means?"

"Yeah." I stopped. Let him collide into me. I hung on to his shoulders before he could get away. "I do. I understand perfectly, okay?"

He yanked free, face contorting. "Then why would you fight me on this?"

"Because I'm not afraid of him! Of any of them! Of Declan, Menger, those stupid goons, or any of their puppet masters. If we run, they win!"

"Then maybe it's time to let them."

I grabbed his hands. "Stop it! You've never surrendered before, and you're not doing it now. If your mother was standing here—"

"But she's not." He didn't let me go, but his tone was violent enough to cut me off at the knees. "Because she's in there—in her sixth hour of surgery. What's next, Margaux? You want to tell me that? What the fuck is next? Do I come home and find you in a bag on our front step?" He spun away to drop into a seat, hanging his head in his hands. "Do you know what that did to me today to see my mother like that? Do you have any goddamn idea?"

His head descended lower, as if the weight of the memories was too much to bear. I stayed standing. I understood his pain, but I was angry and ready to fight—to battle for us, for what we'd built. I was not going to walk away just because he said it was time or thought it would be too dangerous to stay.

"I do know," I rasped. "I was right there too, remember?"

He didn't look up. "But it was my mother, Margaux."

That stung, but I clenched for composure. "And that makes a difference...why?"

"You don't even like your mother. In fact, you hate the bitch."

"Michael, I never knew my mother. Are you referring to the woman who liked keeping me around as her show pony?"

"You know what I meant. So, what would you even know about what I'm going through right now?"

It sucked the anger right out of me. Or perhaps punched it out, with the force of pure shock. It was a cheap shot, taking me so completely off guard that I plopped down in the seat beside him. He'd really gone there. As the realization took hold, a mixture of hurt and anger welled tears into my eyes, stingy shitheads that had me rolling my eyes back, fighting them from tracking down my cheeks.

"Though that was completely unnecessary and a low blow, it's also true. I don't know exactly what it must have been like. But you know what, Michael? I've come to care about Diana... very much. And more than that, I love you." I lifted a hand to his hunched shoulder. Even now, I wasn't able to help myself. I needed the contact. I needed him. "I love you. And watching you suffer and not being able to help? That's breaking my heart more than enduring all this myself."

His muscles coiled as the words left me. Through one silent moment, they remained that way. Another. Finally, he gave me a word. One.

"No."

"No," I echoed. "No...what?"

"No." He stood, but didn't look back. "I'm sticking to my decision." I'd never heard such steel in his tone before. "It's over—for us. For...all of it. I'm calling Doug and ending his investigation immediately. I want all of his team off the case. I'll pay them whatever is owed outside of the retainer. You shouldn't be stuck with the bill on that. It wouldn't be right."

"It wouldn't be—" I couldn't move beyond sputtering it.

Not right? Because doing this to me—to us—was?

"Then I'm moving my stuff out of the condo." He rolled on through his speech as if I hadn't spoken. Time for being ghost Margaux again. "I need to get away from you as soon as possible so the target gets lifted off your back. It's the only way you'll be safe."

"Safe? What the hell? Michael, you're being ridiculous!"

"Mom is going to need me out at the farm for a while as she's recovering anyway—maybe longer. A nurse can stay with her during the days when I'm gone. I'll commute to downtown on the days Aequitas absolutely needs me." He spread his arms, bracing hands up against the window frame, never looking more breathtaking—or alone. "Now that Dec knows he can get to me in more private ways than court, maybe now he'll drop the charges so I can get back to work."

I found the fortitude—perhaps just the fury—to stand again. "How the hell can you be so matter of fact about all of this? So...so heartless?"

His shoulders rippled with more tension. "I'm just doing what I have to—what I need to—to keep you safe. It's the most important thing. It's the only thing."

"Damn it!" It was pitiful and full of loose, ugly tears. I still didn't care. Plenty of people cried in hospitals. For once, I actually looked like everyone else. "God damn it! I love you, Michael! Doesn't that matter? I thought...I thought you loved me."

"I—" He stopped himself with a vicious growl. "It just can't matter anymore, princess. Our time...it was beautiful. But it's run out."

"It's—" I whirled, beginning to pace. "You think I'm going to accept that, asshole? 'It was beautiful'? Are you kidding me?

Fuck you, Michael. Fuck you."

He swept a hand up, harsh and dismissive. "Don't come back here after you leave today. I'll keep Andre updated about Mom, and he can tell you if you need to know, but we need to stop all communication at once. It's not safe for you. They probably have the phones tapped."

"The phones—" I choked and even laughed, unable to finish. "Do you hear yourself? You sound completely paranoid!"

"No. I sound completely practical. I sound realistic. I'm not putting anything past him now, Margaux. A woman is fighting for her life right now because of that monster. I won't watch it happen to you too. I...can't. Please. Just please don't argue with me anymore."

I stared at him, tears running freely, leaving hot tracks in their wake down my cheeks. "You're breaking...my heart."

"There's nothing more I can do. I need to know you are safe. I will sacrifice a thousand lifetimes of my own happiness for that, baby. My own heart and soul."

For a moment, I confronted exactly that in his gaze, darkened to gold fire. His heart, his soul, his pain...reached out and connected with mine once more.

The last time.

No. No.

"This isn't over, Pearson."

"I'm afraid it is."

I pushed past him as I stormed from the waiting room, not making contact with anyone else—even Andre—who'd waited in the hallway. He fell into silent step beside me, knowing better than to request a play-by-play of what had just happened.

I had my cell out before we left the building. It powered

up as I waited for Andre to get the car, and I glared at it with growing impatience. After one speed dial push, it started to ring through. With every passing second, the awful lump built again in my throat. I hated calling Claire again like this—hated it—but I'd vowed only weeks ago to reach out to my family when there was a crisis.

This was a crisis if ever there was one.

"Hey, sweetie. What's going on?"

"I need you."

"Oooohhh kaaayyy."

"I'm serious." I held the phone away for a second to get a grip on my sob. "I'm about to lose my shit, and I didn't know who else to call."

"Oh, hell," Claire muttered. "You really are about to— What's wrong?"

I ordered my lungs to take in air. If I blurted everything now, there'd be no end to my breakdown. All the tabloids needed was one observant, loose-lipped hospital employee— or worse—to tip them off about an overwrought Margaux Asher in the carport. "Can you meet me at my house? Can you just get there? I'll come get you if I have to."

"It's fine. I got my keys back after a few promises and favors were paid forward."

"Oh, God," I groaned. "Not now. Please. For the sake of my sanity, Claire, not now."

"Take it easy, girl. I'll be there in thirty minutes. Will you be all right until then?"

Define all right.

"Yeah," I replied anyway. "But Claire? If you're into praying and shit? You might want to throw one up for Michael's mom."

She let out a gasp. "Diana? Why?"

"She's had an...accident—of sorts."

"What? How? Where?"

"She's—she's in really bad shape. I'll explain more when I see you. Drive carefully, please."

Andre pulled the BMW up. I slid into the back seat while hitting End on the call. After that, I didn't want to even look at my phone, knowing it wouldn't contain a single call or text from Michael. I threw it down on the leather seat and let out a big huff.

Andre turned a knob in the front console. My favorite Mozart filled the car.

I gave him a soft smile in the mirror. "Thanks."

"No problem. You need anything else?"

"Shit." It was the best answer I had. "Is there any liquor in here?"

"No, but I can stop somewhere."

"It's okay. Claire's on her way to the Cortez. Can you just take me home?"

"We'll be there in no time."

I laid my head back and tried to evaluate what had happened in the past ten hours. My life had changed irrevocably, and I felt like a bystander. Me, Margaux Asher, the woman who held life firmly by the balls and called all the shots, was watching it all circle the drain—helpless to do anything but absently hum along to Elvira Madigan, as its swelling sadness turned into the song of my shattering heart.

CHAPTER THIRTEEN

Michael

"Michael Adam Pearson! Stop this goddamn nonsense immediately!"

I grinned. What a difference three weeks could make.

"Did you hear me, you little shit?"

My smirk flourished into a chuckle, but I didn't relent my hold, continuing to carry Mom up the front steps before settling her into the porch swing. "Potty mouth, young lady," I chastised.

"Shut. Up." Mom fumed and tugged her jacket tighter. The weather had whipped from late fall to early winter over the last few days, biting a distinct chill into the afternoon. If the clouds hovering over the ridge moved in overnight, we'd even get a snow dusting.

I unlocked the door and then latched the screen open with the top slider. "You know that stuff doesn't strike the fear of God into me anymore." Not since the crack of Declan's belt had taken its place as the herald of horror in my life.

She flashed a smirk of victory. I let it slide, knowing it would transform back into a glower the second I picked her up again—not that she intended to make the task easier. "Stop it. Stop it. I can walk ten steps into my own house, Michael Adam!"

"Still not working." I half sang it, unable to resist a wider grin. If Mom was this feisty, she was starting to feel better. Joy washed in like I'd chugged a twelve-pack in twenty minutes. The difference between the Diana Pearson I'd watched over in the hospital three weeks ago and the spitfire who batted at my chest right now was black and white.

No. Not black and white—yet. We weren't completely in the white. Things were a pleasant tone of gray, like the mist in the orchard just before the morning sun finally burned through. The light was coming, just not yet. Mom's lung was recovering well, though her ribs still ached by dinnertime each day. While her face wasn't so swollen, many of her bruises were taking a while to heal.

Emotionally, we took each day by the minute—sometimes, when memories got rough, in smaller increments. There were bright spots, though. Many came for Mom courtesy of Carlo. The man was clearly smitten with my mother, and I was psyched as hell. He'd visited her nearly every day in the hospital, despite his responsibilities here. Now that she was home, he stopped by three or four times a day. She lit up like a Christmas tree when he was around, serving as a good balance for the glowers she reserved for me—at least when it came to the subject of Margaux.

Her reaction to my decision was an eerie replay of what Margaux had dished in the hospital waiting room, including the barrage of profanity and the angry crying. The cussing, I could take—but her tears, beyond unexpected, were another torture. Talk about an equilibrium burner.

My reaction had become that of any guy dealing with guilt, bafflement, fury, and fear at once—by sulking in the orchard for a couple of long hours, despite storming out of the house with no jacket at four in the afternoon.

I'd slunk back in with balls frozen and temper chilled, greeted by Mom's hug and a cup of hot cider. It was her version of a tenuous truce, and I'd readily accepted. The shot of brandy she'd sneaked into the drink wasn't a bad touch—and helped with confronting the new facts of my life after the time machine dumped me back in reality.

Number one, I had to set Margaux free. No more knightly lip service—I had to suck it up, grieve for what was lost, and then move the hell on, even if it gave me a damn ulcer. Not like I wouldn't be destroying my stomach on bachelor food for the rest of my life. I was done with considering the big show, commitment-wise. Margaux Corina Asher had been it. My one. It'd be unfair to subject any woman to the comparisons I'd inevitably make to her, and the sliver of my heart, if that, they'd earn for their effort. My soul was already officially off-limits.

Number two, it was time to figure out a real plan for the water rights on the spring. Even if Declan had a bullet in his brain tomorrow—and that was a huge, hopeful-as-hell if— there was a good chance that someone else in that nouveau-mafia group knew about the spring by now too. We had to confront the disgusting idea that the water was too valuable to be ignored now. Getting ahead of the curve and controlling the process by which the drilling happened might save most of the jobs on the farm. Those employees whose jobs we couldn't preserve could be retrained for the new project. Nobody knew this land and its capabilities better than the people who'd been devoted to it their whole lives.

Number three, it was time to play a few rounds of Where's Declan? Unbelievably, I was the one pushing to figure out where he'd run off to. Correction—disappeared off the face of the map to. As I suspected, the asshole dropped the charges from the night at the Del Coronado before Mom was even discharged—though the friendly visit I expected from the guy after that never happened. Almost three weeks later, I was still walking around like an idiot in a horror movie, afraid of my own shadow, wondering when he would slither back in like the worm he was.

Because of that, I'd thrown myself another curve ball and actually called Doug Simcox again. The first time had been as I'd promised Margaux, to terminate his services and call off his team, but this time, my motive was different. I re-hired them for long-distance observation—and not-so-long-distance protection, if the situation called for it—of the woman I loved.

A recipe for my own heartbreak? Maybe. Probably. As sick as it made me to think it, I'd probably pushed the two of them closer together. But a more important certainty gripped me. Andre couldn't watch over her all the time. During the rare times he wasn't around, nobody would take her safety more seriously than Doug.

I need to know you are safe. I will sacrifice a thousand lifetimes of my own happiness for that, baby. My own heart and soul.

I grimaced.

Nothing like being a man of one's word.

Thump.

The sound wrenched my thoughts back to the moment— and the sight that deepened my scowl.

"What the hell do you think you're doing?" I rushed to Mom, scooping an arm under her waist. She grabbed my shoulder with the force of a drowning woman, betraying how much my action must've hurt, though she made no sound except a tight grunt.

"Getting my ass back into the house." She accepted my support for the dozen steps it took to get inside and onto the couch. "Since someone was clearly checked out of the picture."

Irritation tightened my jaw. "I wasn't checked anywhere."

She spurted a laugh. "Baby, you were so checked out."

"You want chicken pot pie or pasta for dinner? I'll steam some of that broccoli I picked up this morning too." A change of subject was my only way off her cart this time.

Or maybe not.

"Michael." She grabbed my hand and pulled me down next to her. "We need to talk."

Attempting to yank away was useless. The grip she'd just applied to my shoulder now trapped my hand. "About steaming broccoli? Because right now, that's all I want to discuss, Mom."

She huffed and tugged, forcing my gaze to hers. It wasn't easy. The left side of her face was still a marble of purple and yellow, the deeper bruises taking longer to heal. "Margaux—"

"Isn't a subject open for discussion."

She scowled. "Damn it, I've been good about this."

"Good?" I scoffed. "Glaring at me a dozen times a day like one of my hands is a hook and I made the Lost Boys walk the plank?"

"Better that than breaking that girl's heart."

"At least her heart's alive."

"Pssshh."

She released me to wave her hand. I knew a good advantage when it came. In two seconds, I was back on my feet, finding a convenient excuse to move away and ripping her velvet blanket off the rocking chair.

"You know how paranoid you sound, right?"

I threw a glower over my shoulder. "Are you comparing notes with her or something?"

Her head dropped. She started twisting the ring on her left ring finger, never removed since the day Dad had put it there. Had she always done that? My speculation was cut short by her fresh snort and angry side-eye. "Common logic doesn't need bedfellows, honey. Neither does the truth. You're being Chicken Little—that's a plain-faced fact."

"Says the sky herself?"

"What's that supposed to—"

"Have you looked in the mirror lately, Mother?" I spread open the blanket with a sharp snap. "Or even tried to take a deep breath?" Wrapped it around her with determined tucks. "You were beaten to within an inch of your life. That's a fact."

"And we haven't heard word one from Declan since," she argued. "If he was even the one behind it."

"If he was—" Incredulity turned the rest into a stunned but humorless laugh. "Okay, Chicken Little officially calls Pollyanna on her shit. No, wait. You're not Pollyanna. You're that airhead princess, the one who trusts the old hag in the forest and then bites the apple and kills herself." I threw up my hands. "News alert, Mom. Carlo won't be able to wake you up with a kiss."

A blush assaulted her face. "Carlo and I are none of your business."

I chuckled. Her mortification was actually endearing. "You're right. Just like Margaux and I are none of yours."

She grumbled, loosening all the places I'd just tucked in. "Big stubborn shit."

I bussed her forehead. "Little stubborn shit."

"Get me my e-reader," she snapped. "I need to rinse this

anger off with a little Carly Phillips."

As I handed over her device, I stated, "If you need me, I'll be in the office." During her physical therapy appointment, work had e-mailed over some briefs that needed my attention.

Unsurprisingly, I didn't hear a peep out of her after that. When Mom dived her imagination into a book, it was common for hours of silence to go by. I only let one hour pass before ducking back out to check on her and to get the final vote on dinner.

"Mom?"

A soft snore answered from the couch.

I smiled quietly while pulling the reader from her hands. Between starting PT and getting miffed with me, she was exhausted, even without the help of her pain meds. I took that as a good sign.

It also meant I'd have to guess on her preference for dinner. I decided on the pasta and set dishes on the table for when the food was ready.

While waiting, I stepped quietly out to the porch. The air was even frostier now, though the clouds over the next ridge looked like they'd be staying put for the night. The sun's last rays stole across the valley, making the mist glow like Christmas lights were strung beneath it.

The poeticism was appropriate. Just this week, Carlo had brought in his seasonal crew to transform the orchard into a holiday wonderland with lights, piped music, and moving character vignettes. They'd been hard at it today, proved by the weary smiles they flashed on their way to their cars. I waved back and bowed my head in thanks. The holiday displays, to be opened right before Thanksgiving, were popular with tourists and locals alike. More than that, Mom loved them. I was grateful for anything that spurred her recovery.

After the men left, the air was hushed and still.

Until a small chime sounded, somewhere behind me.

I swiveled around, forehead furrowing. Not the stove yet, and it sounded nearer than that—like a phone notification of some kind. But I'd left mine on the desk in the office.

Another chime. A repeat of the first.

I dropped off the rail and walked to the swing, peering through the shadows. Sure enough, the cushion glowed from the light of Mom's overturned phone. She must have forgotten it while getting impatient with me this afternoon.

The phone glowed with an incoming text. I grimaced and hurried to close the screen before seeing a message from Carlo that wouldn't allow me to view the man in a wholesome light again. Mother definitely knew best where some matters were concerned. Whatever she and Carlo were up to was none of my damn business, and as long as he made her hap—

The thought vanished from my head.

Along with every other thought behind it, except for the one shoving three distinct words to my lips.

"What. The. Fuck?"

I hadn't closed the screen fast enough to miss the originating number of the text.

Not Carlo's cell number.

Margaux's.

Like a Mohican on a Mohawk, I focused my stare on the words.

*So glad to hear your PT went well—and that
the bear behaved himself. Rest easy. I'll check
in tomorrow.*

For at least a minute, I stared. The message implied that Mom had already texted first, probably after the PT appointment today. I'd caught a glimpse of her out in the waiting room while I confirmed her next appointment. She'd never looked up, intent on the message she tapped into her phone. Had she been sending a little update to Margaux then—literally behind my back—also talking about the bear in her message? Didn't take a rocket scientist to figure out who that little endearment was code for.

Just like it didn't take a second of hesitation for me to swipe my thumb down the screen instead—loading more texts between them. Then again. And again. And—

There were nearly ten days' worth of messages. I didn't read them all word for word. I didn't have to. Their main themes were clear.

Saturday

My son is an idiot.

No, Di. He's just scared.

Scared and stupid.

You can't blame him. It was bad when they brought you to our door that morning.

And it's over. And he needs you now.

He doesn't want me.

He doesn't know his own mind right now. Please don't give up on him, Margaux.

Monday

No word from the bear yet?

His mind is made up, Di.

No, damn it. It's not!

I miss him.

And honey, he misses you. Every time I look in his eyes, I'm reminded of it all over again.

Tuesday

The bear is on the prowl again.

Uh-oh. What now?

He heard some song on the radio, a sappy thing about moments and magic and forever, and turned feral on everyone.

Hell. I know that one.

Bet you do. He's not pretty when he's feral.

No. The song. I know the one you're talking

about. I'll be back in a bit.

Shit. I upset you.

It's okay. A lot of things still do that right now.

Thursday

I can't do this anymore.

Di? Are you okay?

I'm fine. He's driving me crazy.

LOL. I think. Breathe.

Call him, Margaux. Please. He's miserable.

That makes two of us.

"Michael?"

I jerked my head up. Barked out, "Yeah." Once I took a step back inside, the fucking Gettysburg battle of emotions flared across my chest again. There was my mom, laid up on the couch with a re-inflated lung, healing ribs, and a half-mottled face because of my bullheadedness, but I couldn't let go of the indignation and frustration now firing off round after round at my damn senses.

"What's going on? Why were you on the porch, growling to yourself?"

I hauled in a deep breath. Held up her phone. "Isn't that

what bears do?"

Her eyes slammed shut. "Well, shit."

"Yeah. Shit."

The next second, she one-eightied her bearing, staring back up at me like I'd merely told her the petting zoo goats ate my homework. "Give me my phone, son. You have no right to be spying on my texts."

I slid the phone behind my back. "And you have no right to be filling Margaux's head with unrealistic expectations."

She huffed. "We need to talk about this, Michael Adam."

I stomped to the coffee table. Parked my ass on it. Squared both feet to the floor and then braced my elbows to my knees. "You're damn right we do."

CHAPTER FOURTEEN

Margaux

"Lydia!"

My new secretary scurried into my office, looking like a bomb had gone off next to her desk. Her glasses were crooked on her beak of a nose, her hair tumbled from her once-tidy bun, and her shirt was untucked from her one-size-too-large pleated skirt. What grown woman wore pleats in this era?

Ones who had school desks as living room décor and liked saying "Yes, Headmaster"?

So not the thought I needed today. Hadn't needed any other day over the last three weeks either.

"Yes, Ms. Asher?"

I rolled both shoulders, battling the tension of banishing Michael's headmaster face to the back of my brain. After a deep breath, I shoved my coffee cup toward her like it was a snake with two heads.

"What the fuck is this?"

She pushed her glasses back up her nose. "That's... ummmm...the latte you asked me to get for you on my way back from lunch."

I took a brief look at the liquid in the cup. "Lydia?"

"Yes, ma'am?"

"Is this soy?"

"No, ma'am. You didn't ask for soy."

"I most certainly did."

"But—"

"Did you write down my order like I told you to?"

"Yes, on my phone."

Another rough breath. Christ help me, I was trying to be a kinder, gentler version of myself, if only to give the karma police a little help in getting me off this shit hill of heartbreak—but damn it, how instantly those pleats had reminded me of Michael.

Who the hell was I kidding?

Everything reminded me of Michael. Then gutted me again, just like this. And kept going until my soul was in shreds, just like this.

Which meant, at the moment, karma be damned. "Okay," I spat, folding my arms, "perfect. I'm going to wait here, wasting more of my valuable time, while you go find your note and see that I wanted soy milk in my latte—just like I've had in every latte my entire adult life."

She blinked. Then just stared.

"Lydia."

"Ma'am?"

"Go! I'm aging here, for fuck's sake."

She whirled, tripped over something that wasn't there, and bumped a shoulder into the door before making it past the portal. A few minutes later, she returned looking even worse than after the first bomb's detonation.

"Well?"

"It—it should've been soy, Ms. Asher. I'm very sorry."

"Well, hallelujah." I was elbows-deep into a partnership contract by then so didn't look up as I muttered it. Too bad—

for her—that the contract was a complete piece of shit and would have to be rewritten from word one. "You can both take notes and read, Lydia. See? This day wasn't a complete waste."

"Of—of course, ma'am."

"But guess what? Now I've had to call Andre to go get me the right coffee, because if that pile of paperwork on your desk is any indication, you can't leave again, can you?"

"N-No, ma'am. Ummmm...Andre?"

"My driver. You can deal with him when he gets here. Have you met him yet?"

"No. I haven't."

"Perfect. Let me know when he gets here. I don't want to miss a minute of it."

"Yes, ma'am."

Once more, she simply stood in place.

Growling out a huff, I rose and actually chased her out the door, slamming it behind her. At her distinct yeep on the other side, I was tempted to smirk.

I winced instead.

"What the hell is wrong with you?" I demanded it of my reflection in the mirror behind the door, which I always used to make sure everything was in place before I left the room. Three seconds of perusal revealed nothing had been physically disturbed—but nothing felt in place anymore.

Nothing.

I jerked up my chin. This bullshit with Lydia was the crap icing on the shit-tastic cake. She was the fourth receptionist the agency had sent over in the past three weeks. Really, how hard was it to answer the phones and fetch a girl some coffee?

Best to focus on the things I did have answers for.

The pile on my desk was just as high as Lydia's, but I

couldn't seem to concentrate. Wasn't like I'd been sleeping or eating well for nearly twenty-one days.

At least Diana was out of the woods and recovering nicely—as I'd gone ahead and learned straight from the source. Michael was dreaming if he thought I'd wait for updates from him, relayed through Andre like we were in eighth grade passing notes down the hall. Di and I were grown women, for Christ's sake. We'd been texting on a regular basis, and I was comforted to know her mood was good—most of the time. Michael had her under close watch, a cliché but an appropriate one, and was driving her a little crazy. Maybe more than a little. He was determined to keep her safe, translated as rarely out of his sight.

My desk phone rang, cutting into my thoughts. Perfect. A blind transfer from super-receptionist. I wondered how many glares I'd get from HR if I put in a requisition for candidate number five today.

"Margaux Asher," I barked into the receiver.

"Uh-oh. Is this a bad time?"

"Di." I sank back. "Sorry for snapping. It's been a shitty day."

"I know." Her tone, sympathetic but not sappy, grabbed my heart. She already knew how shitty most of my days were lately. "It's okay."

I blew off the melancholy with a little snort. "So, hey, you. How are you feeling today?"

"I'd be better if everyone stopped asking me that."

"I know." I used her exact tone for the echo. "But honestly, you have no idea what it was like that morning."

"Well, if I'm reminded one more time, I may go batshit."

I sighed. Just pulling up that scene at the condo made me

ANGEL PAYNE & VICTORIA BLUE

shudder again. In some ways, I didn't begrudge Michael his edginess. "So he's still hovering?"

"Hovering?" Di laughed. "Honey, hovering I could handle. Suffocating is more like it."

Yikes. "I wish I could do something to help you. Do you want me to send Andre to bring you into town for a few days?"

"I'd never be able to get out unnoticed. God, listen to me. I'm a prisoner in my own home. This is ridiculous."

I smiled ruefully. "It is, isn't it?"

The pause before her next words was significant. "Well... I'm afraid we have an even bigger problem."

"Oh?"

"Yeah."

"This sounds bad."

She filled the line with a throaty huff. "It's all my fault. I just don't know how to fix it."

Strangely, my pulse beat at the base of my throat. "Repairs are usually best when done with teamwork. Tell me what happened. Maybe we'll think of something with our heads together."

"I was hoping you'd say that."

"Come on. You knew I'd say that."

"Well, great minds, you know."

I let out a full laugh. Damn, I adored this woman.

"Okay. Yesterday, after we got home from physical therapy, I fell asleep on the couch. It was a pretty tough session, and with these damn pain pills too, I got really groggy."

"Whoa. Hold on. What do you mean, a tough session? How are you going to heal if you're already pushing yourself too hard?"

"Oh, God. Not you too." She sighed heavily. "Look, if

you're going to be mad at me, save it for the bad part. I haven't even come to that yet."

"I just care about you."

"I know, honey."

"Wait. What? The bad part?"

"Well, while I was on the sofa, you texted me. My cell was outside on the porch swing."

My throat constricted. "And so was Michael."

"And so was Michael."

"Oh, shit."

"Hmmmm, yeeaah."

"So...how much of our text conversations did he see?"

"Pretty much all of them. I'm not really in the habit of deleting things. I've never had to hide anything from anyone before." She filled the line with a tight huff. "I'm so sorry."

"Okay," I cut in. "Stop right there. You have nothing to apologize for."

"The hell I don't." Another break, longer this time, ending in her more sheepish confession. "I should've been more careful. He's not brushing this off. You didn't see how mad he was." She added in a mutter, "And thank God for that."

I took a turn at the huff. "Please. I've seen the bear mad before. He doesn't scare me."

"Yet another reason why I love you, dear—and why he needs you in his life!" Her laugh was a sweet jingle. "We just need to convince him of that."

As if compelled, my gaze fell—to the framed photo of him and me, still atop my desk, taken the day of Kil and Claire's wedding. We were in our formal finery, smiling and a little flirty. Like an idiotic sap, I couldn't stow it away. Not yet. Not while there was a sliver of hope that the man would wake up to sanity again.

Like I had any control over that alarm clock.

"I shouldn't have to convince him of anything," I stated. "The bonehead needs to realize it all on his own. Otherwise, it's not worth having. I learned that a long time ago—the hard way."

"You're absolutely right about that too," Di countered. "Sadly."

"So what now?"

"I'm not sure. He's been storming around the farm like he did when he was a boy and things didn't go his way."

"Must be fun for Carlo and the others."

"Well, he gave us all a break today, thank God. He was out the door as soon as the gal from the nursing agency got here. He might have gone to the office. Long drives clear his head."

That gave me a melancholy smile. "I know." I'd turned him onto long-drive therapy—he'd turned me on to the fun of hiking. Sort of.

Right now, I'd agree to scale Mount Whitney itself if it meant turning back time by just a month. An impossible dream.

"Diana...I'm sorry too."

"Oh, God. Whatever for?"

"It's me who's made things harder on you. It was selfish to sneak around and ask you to keep in contact with me after Michael forbade it."

"Now you stop right there, young lady. I'm a woman of a certain age—and a successful business owner, at that. I can make my own decisions. That stubborn-ass son of mine may think he knows what's best for everyone, but his head's jammed so far up his butt crack..."

As she let her heavy humph finish that, I giggled—and resisted the urge to inform Di that the subject of her son's backside, in any form, was a sure-as-shit way to brighten my day.

"You think I'm kidding? That mule doesn't know the gift he has in you, though it's right at his feet. So not another word of apology from your mouth, do you understand?"

"Yes, ma'am." I managed a solemn tone.

"In fact, I think it's high time you turn up the heat on this situation."

My heart skipped a beat. Another. "Really?"

"Yes, damn it. Really."

I grinned, declaring myself officially in love with her. This woman's mind worked so wonderfully—just like my own. For days, I'd been debating just getting into the car and heading up the damn mountain, back to Julian, forcing the bear to at least acknowledge me again. He owed me that. No, he actually owed me more, a debt not satisfied by hiring Doug and his beef heads for my babysitting detail—though in a way, I had them to thank for this new resolve. Once I figured out the new form of tabs he was keeping on me, the decision solidified. It was time for a conversation with the man who truly thought he could save the world. With Di's encouragement, my mind was made up.

"You know what? I think that sounds like a great idea. A little mountain air might do me some good."

"Hurray! Something to look forward to now. Just be careful driving up. Michael would never forgive me if something happened to you on the way, especially if he learned I'd encouraged it."

She didn't need to elaborate. By careful, she meant more than watching the road and ignoring texts. I'd have to be extra diligent, looking for any unwanted guests on my bumper or elsewhere.

"Well, then," I returned, coloring it with mischief, "this conversation will have to stay between us, won't it?"

I hung up with Diana and then finished the few things on my desk needing immediate attention. Since I'd had trouble digging in this morning, there were a few loose ends to tie up. After that, it was time to search for my boss—though, in this situation, that was defined as brother dearest.

I didn't have to travel far. When Killian had relocated to Stone Global's western office last year, he'd insisted his office be built out on the middle floor of the bayside building, claiming the water view was better from the lower floor. The dork hadn't fooled anyone. The marketing and PR department, headed by the redhead who held the key to his heart and his balls, was just one floor below.

I buzzed ahead, asking Kil's assistant if he was free. Britta confirmed that he was and greeted me warmly as I stepped off the elevator. Kil, who believed in keeping good people, had offered the woman an ungodly sum to move west with him—though the Golden State had yet to rub off on the classic Icelandic beauty.

"Good afternoon, Ms. Asher."

"Britta, please. Margaux, okay?" Though I couldn't blame the woman for still being a little skittish around me. When we'd all first met, nearly two years ago, I was a different person. A really scary, bitchy one.

"Of course," she replied demurely. "Have a seat. Mr. Stone won't be long."

Right. I didn't think so. Sitting was so not an option, considering the level of my impatient energy at the moment.

Instead, I paced around his lobby. Damn. Kil might not have been a Stone by birth, but he sure shared our posh taste. The polished bamboo floors were offset by bold blue sofas, designer marble tables, and a two-story slate waterfall embraced by a pair of cobalt fairies custom-sculpted by some artist he'd flown in from New Zealand.

Yeah, I needed to come up here more often and hang out—or even push for a suite like this myself. If I could get my personal life in order, I vowed to concentrate more on work, proving I was worth a setup like this. I used to make everyone at the office quake in fear—but now I was the one quaking. Hard.

I shook my head in disgust. When had I changed? And how? I wasn't sure I liked the woman—the wimp?—I was becoming. There were days I was totally fine with the transformation, but on days like today, when I caved in to needy girl? Not so much.

"Mary Stone!"

Killian's bellow came from deep within his office. Britta emerged, barely tamping a smile. I rolled my eyes just for her, making the smirk bloom. Tossing her a wink, I strutted into Kil's inner sanctum and closed the door, adopting the best death stare I could muster.

He looked up from the stack of work on his desk and snorted. "You going fluffy kitty on me already, little girl?"

No, he didn't.

Fluffy kitty. It had always been one of Michael's favorite bedroom looks for me.

Not now.

I hid my wince by plunking down my LV Speedy on the glass conference table and then checking my reflection in the glass. "Fuck you, brother."

He smirked. He'd been luring me into these sparring matches more and more since the day that had ripped my world apart, seeming to know what a good tension release they were for me. He was probably right.

"What brings you to my lair?"

"Lair?" One good eye roll deserved another. "You're sure full of yourself this afternoon."

"Sister, when am I not full of myself?"

"Hmmm. True."

He looked up, not limiting it to a glance this time. With his thick hair tamed for his CEO look, the hunker of his eyebrows was more pronounced. "You okay?"

"Sure," I answered, perhaps too hastily. "Yeah. Uh-huh."

"Oh?" He rose and strode around the desk. Damn. There was only one person on earth more intuitive about unspoken signals than me—and it was him. "Well, I'm guessing this isn't a business call, or I would've simply gotten an email." He cocked a hip to one of the plush chairs in front of the desk. "What's going on?"

"I—well, I need to take a few days off, if that's okay with you—and Claire, of course. I'm between big clients, and she's handling the Muller project. The cosmetics launch is solid for now—we're just waiting for final LEED approval on the plant, as well as creatives from graphics. Drake and Fletcher are scheduled for a research trip to Vegas to scout venues for the launch party, but Talia's got both of them in her back pocket... literally." I threw in the last part as a weighted aside but didn't miss Killian's chuckle. So the chemistry between those three hadn't gone unnoticed by him either—a subject for later exploration.

After the chuckle, Killian's expression sobered. He crossed his arms and then hiked one dark eyebrow, his way of commanding me to continue.

"Fine," I huffed, sinking into the other chair. "I need to go to Julian."

He scrutinized me for another moment. When I was on the verge of spitting out something regarding lab rats yearning to eat out the eyes of their scientists, he murmured, "Do you want to talk about it?"

"Not really. I've talked all I can. I think it's time to do something about it."

He lowered his head and pinched his nose. "How many times will you go chasing after him, Mare? Have you asked yourself that? And do you remember the last time you let a guy do this to you?"

I swiveled a glare. "Below the belt, Kil."

He held up both hands. "Duly noted. Sorry. But Christ, does this guy have you in a vampire trance?" He peered hard again. "He must be something pretty amazing to have you chasing up and down a damn mountain after him. Twice."

I smiled softly. "That's the perfect word. He is amazing. He makes me feel amazing—at least, he did."

"Did? Operative word here, perhaps?"

"I can't just give up, not yet. This isn't one for my normal cut and run. I believe, in my heart...he's the one worth fighting for." I swallowed hard before adding, "Despite everything."

He drew in a long breath, his eyes black as two pokers—that stabbed into my brain. "You mean despite his asshole uncle, the gambling debt, the nouveau-mafia thugs, and the gold mine of water his farm is sitting on?"

I almost laughed. "Claire told you, eh?"

"Some," he conceded.

"Some?" I grabbed the chair's arms, whirling fully toward him—and the inscrutability so thick he proved the Enigma of Magnificent Mile was still alive and well on the West Coast. "What the hell does that—?"

"Just doing my homework, sister."

"Homework." I tilted my head. "You know that I speak control freak, don't you? That I'm just hurling that into the Kil's Micromanagement file?"

He pushed out his bottom lip. "If you say so."

"Uggghhh." I let my head fall back in exasperation.

"But while we're on the subject...has anyone strange been around? Following you? Calling and hanging up? Any of that shit? Stepping up security isn't a tough thing to arrange."

"Pretty sure Michael's already handled it."

He scowled. "Then what's his fucking issue?"

"Haven't been in that loop lately." I went at my pinkie ring in angry twists. "He didn't give me a chance to even talk about it, just made the decision for both of us and took off. That's why I'm going back up the mountain. Yes, again. I have to try to talk some sense into him."

Kil lowered into his chair before wrapping his long fingers around mine. "Then you have my full support—and my wish that the idiot will see the goddamn light this time."

I squeezed back before declaring, "If he doesn't, I can't make him see it any other way." A hard breath rattled through me. "It'll break my heart...probably turn me into a zombie for a while. But I've learned from my past, believe it or not. Some scars are deeper than others, but eventually wounds heal."

At that, I stood with new resolution. Killian did too. Instantly, he wrapped me in a warm, tight hug. Gratitude joined my determination. We'd come so far. I couldn't imagine my life without him and Claire. I smiled without restraint, thinking how lucky I was now, surrounded by people who really cared about me.

Maybe wimp-woman wasn't such a bad thing to be.

"Uh-oh," Kil drawled. "What is that devious mind cooking up now?"

"Not a thing." I chuckled. "Just thinking...about how my life was supposed to have been so different from this."

"Regrets?"

"Not one," I countered. "At least not yet." A louder snicker erupted. "Thank God Claire has the best timing in the world."

He joined in my laughter. One fateful night, very long ago, I'd tried breaking them up by openly seducing Killian—long before learning he was my brother and weeks before Claire's dad married Andrea, making us all related in one bizarre way or another.

"Indeed," he concurred. "I thank God for my fairy queen every single night before closing my eyes to dreams of her. She is by far the best gift I've ever been given."

I gave in to a groan. "Before you make me want to vomit, I'm going to shove off."

He smirked. "Uh-uh. No hurling before chasing after bastard boyfriends."

I whacked his shoulder. "For that, I may just keep mum about the memo you're about to get from HR."

His groan was a uniquely satisfying sound. "Hell, sister. Not again."

"Hey! It's been a bad couple of weeks." I gave him a wink and a grin before grabbing my Speedy and heading back out. He gave chase, whipping the door back open behind me.

"Margaux!"

I answered without turning back. "What?"

"How many this time?"

"Four. I think. Maybe five?"

"Fu—" He stopped short. Britta must've stared his profanity into submission. "Dial down to HR," he growled instead. "Tell them we need a new receptionist for Miss Asher."

"Of course, Mr. Stone."

I stepped into the elevator, beaming out a sweet-as-Godiva smile. "You're a doll, Britta. You"—I pointed a graceful finger at Kil—"are not a doll. But I love you anyway, asshole."

Ding. Whoosh. The elevator doors closed behind me.

★ ★ ★ ★

By the time I returned to the condo and got everything packed, two more hours had passed, giving Alfred time to show up with the keys to a loaner car from Killian. It was his control freak suggestion, but I'd readily agreed, thinking it best that Andre didn't take me to Julian. Beside the fact that I didn't know how long I'd be staying, I couldn't ignore the real possibility that Declan, or anyone he'd hired to follow me, would be looking for the 750i. Lucky for me, that also meant the chance for a joy ride in my favorite of Kil's older cars—a Maserati Coupe. Though it was ten years old, it was in cherry condition with barely any miles on the engine. *Yesssss.*

It had been a while since I'd driven myself anywhere. I relished the freedom of being behind the wheel. This machine was, after all, the baby sister of the one and only Ferrari, and I was in the mood to really romp it up the mountainside.

There wasn't a lot of traffic on the road once I cleared

the city. Turning the radio off and listening to the engine purr allowed my mind to drift—but also to focus.

I expected Michael to be furious when he saw me. Any other reaction would actually be surprising—but as I told Di, I wasn't afraid of his anger. Above all things, it was never directed at me but because of me. That should've been weirder than it was. It even made me smile. I reflected on his gallant ways, always ready to slay the dragons that posed a threat to me. On top of that, he had a wit that went on forever and a sex drive that persisted—well, further than that.

Thinking of him without interruption made my nerves electric, my breasts all girly tingly, and my sex a damp puddle. Yeah. Michael Adam Pearson really could be a girl's dream guy—present time frame the one huge exception, of course.

The next focus of my navel gaze wasn't so pleasant—but why the hell not? I hadn't ruminated about Andrea in a long time. And love her or hate her, the woman had taught me to go after what I wanted in life. *See something you want, darling? Then march up and take it. Nobody gets the silver platter the easy way.* In essence, that was exactly my goal now—only I wouldn't qualify Michael as a thing I wanted. He was a piece of me. A need. My glue.

Would Andrea be proud anyway? Probably not. I'd given up on seeking that rare validation, wherever it was hidden. Now, with her criminal intentions coming to the forefront of all her lifelong manipulations, her approval was no longer something I even wanted.

By the time I pulled into Pearson's Apple Farm, the sun had nearly set and all was sleepy and quiet. A few chickens and a pair of squirrels scampered aside as I drove slowly down the dirt road to the house. The front porch light was on, illuminating Diana on the wide swing, rocking gently back and forth. A ceramic carafe of my favorite spiced cider waited on the side table, along with two mugs. My mouth was already watering, since I could smell it from a hundred yards away. Thank God I'd called after clearing the turnoff so she knew I wasn't far.

As soon as I put the car into park, I jumped out, happy and excited—welcoming the vision over the last time I'd seen her. Those memories would haunt me for the rest of my life, but to see her now, standing and smiling and opening her arms to embrace me...tears. Of course, damn it. The stinging heat filled my eyes and spilled onto my cheeks, and I didn't try to hide or wipe them. Happy tears deserved to be shed for what this woman had been through.

"Margaux!"

I laughed. "You, my lady, are a sight for my very sore eyes. No. Stay there, I'm coming!" I hurried up the porch steps so she wouldn't walk any farther than she needed to.

"Damn it. Don't you start now too." She put up a brave front, but it was easy to see the ginger care in her movements.

"Shut it," I rebounded. "You don't have to be the hero for me. Don't push yourself, especially if you know who is around. He'll yell at me for that as well."

We both giggled while sitting down. Di winced as she settled back into the swing. She'd strategically placed two cushions to make the wooden bench more comfortable.

"Would you be more comfortable inside, Di? It's already getting a bit cold." Massive understatement. I zipped up my leather jacket and did my best to downplay a shiver.

She waved me off. "Gosh, no. This fresh air feels fantastic. The doctor said I should get up and move around. I really want to sit out here, if you don't mind. Just for a bit longer."

"Then that's what we'll do. Your wish is my command. I don't say that to many people, so you should take advantage of it." I tilted my head thoughtfully. "In fact, I don't think I've ever said it to anyone."

Di laughed, bringing a smile to my lips. I poured us each some cider and then closed my eyes, damn near orgasmic, as I took a sip.

"The best," I murmured.

She bit her lip like a delighted little girl. "I also brewed up a batch of sun tea. We can have a glass later tonight, after we go in. I'll even put some bourbon into yours. I don't dare indulge, considering the drug cocktail I'm already on."

"No way," I countered. "I can't imagine anything making your iced tea better. You have to divulge your secrets. Second to lattes, I'm addicted to iced tea, and I just can't nail down your lemon/sugar combo."

"I'd be happy to show you how I mix it up. Not tough."

"Good!" I folded my hands around the warmth of my mug. "So what did you do today? Did you have therapy?"

She shook her head. "Had a reprieve. Those boys at Alpine PT are the meanest bastards in town."

I patted her knee. "They just want you to recover, like we all do."

"I know, I know. I hear it every day. And I get it...I do. Every day I'm stronger is another day of beating back Declan." Defiant gold glints appeared in her eyes. "The second I can move better, Michael and Carlo promised to take me down to the shooting range too. I'm going to get real skillful with that handgun."

"That's a perfect idea."

She angled a nod toward me. "You should do the same, honey."

"Damn straight." I sighed in resignation "I've really been meaning to, but then I get busy doing something else and forget. I know, I know—not a great excuse."

"Couldn't agree more." She took a purposeful drag on her cider, glancing in approval as I pulled out my cell and made an event on my calendar for the following Monday. *Look into firearms training.*

After stowing the phone again, I pushed out a deep breath. "And as for the giant elephant on the porch with us?"

Di snorted. "He isn't back from work yet. Some nights he won't return until seven or eight, depending on when he leaves the office. He usually calls at the turnoff, just like you did."

Another smile broke over my lips. "Who do you think taught me that trick?"

"Figured as much. And that goofy grin you have right now? I had one just like it, thinking the same thing when you called." She grabbed one of my hands. "He's a good man, Margaux. He loves you...and he misses you something bad right now too. I see it tearing him apart."

"You—you do?" Hope glimmered a little brighter in the center of my chest.

"Of course. I know, with all of his heart, he thinks he's doing the right thing."

"Has he come out and talked to you about any of this? About the way he feels being apart from me?"

Her features, as tender as a medieval Madonna already, softened in compassion. "Not in so many words...but I'm his mother. I know. I just know."

I tempered my reaction. Lines like the mama-knows-all

thing always struck me as a lot of hooey, but I wasn't going to trash her rights to the feeling. "I don't want to put you in the middle of this. If it's uncomfortable, we can just talk about your PT and iced tea and the farm and shit. I love it here, Di. I love you, and I want you to get well—but I love your son more than anything I've loved my entire life. I really don't want to leave here without him this time."

"Honey." She stroked a couple of fresh tears off my cheekbone. "I know. I know."

I firmed my jaw, needing her to see I had more to force out. "But if he tells me to go, I will. I can no longer make him look at something he's not willing to see."

"He thinks he's doing right by you." She lowered her hand to my knee, patting in emphasis. "He truly does. He's making you safe by keeping you away from us. And, Margaux, I won't lie, some of his anxiety is well-founded. Until this Declan situation is settled, the man is a viable threat to our world. Michael just can't face the idea of going through all of it again... of finding you in the same condition I was in." Her lower lip trembled. "He said...that he thought I was dead."

I pulled in a rickety breath. "Yeah. He did."

"He also told me that he thought he was dying too."

I dropped my head. "Shit."

"Then afterward, having to sit there and do nothing, unable to tell the doctors or police that he knew who did it, when they asked over and over and over. Hell, they all still probe me about it now. 'So you didn't see who did this?' they ask. 'Not one time? You didn't see what they were wearing, a tattoo, a scar, anything?'" She grunted and poured herself more cider. "They make you feel like you're stupid, a victim. Do you know how bad it makes me feel?"

I pushed out my haughtiest sniff. "I know how pissed it would make me feel."

"Oh, there are plenty of those moments too. When they command me to push a little harder in my workout...you know, just one more set, a few more reps? But that crap kills me more than physically. It guts my insides every time. Declan Pearson has terrorized us for the better part of my life and for all of Michael's. I want him to die, Margaux. If I could kill him right now, I would do it—with my own hands." She held out her hands, palms up, as if they were frightening organisms from another planet. "And what the hell does that say about me now? One man has completely changed my moral fiber—and it disgusts me. I was a good person. A kind, loving person. Now I'm no less of a monster than he is."

I raised my arm around her shoulder. It was like she hadn't drunk the cider. Her skin was cold, her limbs trembling. "Listen to me, Di Pearson. You are brave, strong, and one of the most tender, loving people I've ever met. You are good and kind, and that evil piece of shit Declan doesn't deserve the air and space he takes up. Don't you dare compare yourself to him again."

Her body shuddered beneath my touch. Her voice was just as unsteady. "I'm just filled with such...rage."

"I'd think that's completely normal after what you've been through. Damn it, you have every single right to feel what you are feeling! Give yourself some slack. You've survived a traumatic experience, and you're lucky to be alive."

She lifted teary eyes. "Which is what I should be focusing on, right?"

"Oh, hell no!" I humphed, perfectly emulating her feistier moments. "The fact that you want to kill that motherfucker?

Well, I'd be consumed with the concept. Shit, I'll even help you do it. Where can we buy the bullets? No, wait. You have horses, right? Let's draw and quarter him!"

She burst into giggles, making me grin with silly pride. I gave her shoulders another gentle squeeze and sneaked a glance at her pretty features, now noticing the stress that attacked the corners of her eyes and mouth. If she wasn't already in counseling, maybe that needed to be part of her healing process too. I couldn't know for sure and didn't feel right asking such a personal question.

Ugh. It sucked that Michael had cut me out of the loop. Some female-to-female bonding time would likely help her right now as well. We'd been sneaking the text messages and occasional phone calls, but Di needed someone to lean on. It was definitely something he and I were going to have to address when we spoke...

If we spoke.

No. I refused to let the doubts back in. Optimism was the course I'd picked, and I was going to stay true to it. Surely Michael would allow at least a civil conversation.

"If you don't mind, I'm going to go inside and freshen up."

Di cupped my cheek and smiled softly. "Make yourself comfortable, honey. My home is your home, you know that."

I hugged her once more. Oh, yes, I truly loved this woman.

After grabbing my purse, I made my way inside to the guest bathroom on the first floor. I was suddenly nervous about Michael's imminent arrival, and primping always calmed me down a bit.

My look was natural and casual after changing from the office this afternoon, a pair of skinny jeans and a red turtleneck, so I just ran a brush through my hair and put on some lip gloss over my berry stain.

I froze with my finger still at my lips.

Someone else had joined Di on the porch. I could make out conversation but not exact words, since all the windows still had their screens in, not changed to the winter storm windows yet. The front door was open, meaning only the screen door stood between me and the outside once I cracked open the bathroom door.

Shit. Shit.

It was him. My trembling knees told me even before his deep, resonating voice made my heart skip a beat. His baritone would always have that effect on me, no matter where I was when I heard it.

It was showtime.

I stepped into the living room on quiet feet, trying to hear what he and Di were talking about before he saw me. Not eavesdropping...merely a creative entrance.

"Holy crap. That's a sweet Maserati. Do you have company, Mom?"

"We do. But how was your day? The drive home?"

"Who stopped by?"

"She's in the bathroom, baby. Sit down and visit with me. It's so lovely out tonight."

"Uh-uh. It's too cold out here for you. Let's get you inside before you catch a chill. And why are you avoiding my questions?"

"Because you're paranoid and suspicious about everything?"

"Yeah. Someone else said that to me once."

"Oh? Sounds like a very wise person."

"Something like that."

"So tell me about your day."

"It was fine. Seriously, Mom. Just tell me who's here. I'm not in the mood for surprises. You know I don't like that shit."

"Michael Adam. Really, again with the potty mouth?"

I could see a smile break out across his lips. Oh, God... those lips. I wanted to kiss them hello more than take another breath right now. I knew they'd be soft and warm, demanding but yielding to my own needs too.

Love and longing welled in my throat. This was better and worse than I'd imagined. I'd missed him so damn much...so much more than I'd ever admitted to. Watching him from my secret spot made my pulse speed up. I wanted to stay in hiding just a few minutes more, capturing mini memories to call up in the future if this reunion turned out to be a disaster.

It wouldn't be.

It won't be.

"Bah," he scoffed good-naturedly. "Tell me if you haven't heard anything before. I'll be happy to stop and explain."

"Oh, yeah? Tell me if you remember the old bar of Ivory. I'm certain it tastes just as good today as it did when you were eight."

Well, hell. That did it. The mental picture of him rocking a bar of soap like one of his favorite bagels made me giggle where I stood, just inside the screen door.

As soon as he heard the sound, Michael's head snapped up.

I was busted.

And he was livid.

"Oh, hell no." He glared back at Di. "No-no-no-no-no! I swear, if you called her and told her—"

"Michael Adam!"

He didn't listen. He was too busy charging toward the screen door. Just before he could grab the handle and yank it, I stepped out—into his path.

"Surprise?"

Silence. Dead silence was more like it. Even the crickets and owls way off in the trees seemed to take a moment to gather their thoughts before launching into the next verse of their nightly songs.

"What are you doing here?" He looked me over from head to toe, tense as Lot expecting his wife to become salt any second. "You shouldn't be here."

"It's great to see you too. I've missed you too. Okay, your turn now."

He fumed.

I squirmed.

God. Seeing him up close? Smelling him? Taking him in from head to toe in his perfectly fitted mister lawyer man suit? Karma just bit me in the ass, big-time—and I had a lot coming to me in the karma department, so I couldn't really complain.

Involuntarily, I swayed toward him. The fates were truly fucking with me tonight.

"Margaux..."

"Well, you remember my name. That's a start." I shook my head a bit, battling to regain control of my senses. Clearly I was having a hormonal meltdown and he was having...just a meltdown.

I looked at him, trying not to be hurt. Or furious. I knew going into this that he wouldn't be happy to see me, but a little part had clung to the hope that it would all be different once he actually saw me.

Fool.

This is what happens when your heart does the guide work, girlfriend.

"I'm going to give you two some privacy." Di lurched to her feet. We both rushed to help her.

"That's not necessary," Michael gritted. "She's not staying."

"Don't be rude, Michael." Diana smacked his shoulder on her way into the house.

He glowered at her fading back. "Well, she's not!"

I let out a growl to match his. "She is standing right here, damn it."

"But you shouldn't be. You should be in San Diego, where it's safe." He gave me the Lot-and-salt glare again, stabbing a hand into his hair. "For the love of God, Margaux. What were you thinking, coming here? Do you have a demented death wish or something?"

I waited for him to look at me.

And waited.

A full minute later, he actually met my gaze. Instantly, I stumbled back. The pain I saw in his eyes... It sucked my breath away. I shook my head, confused. Where did all that agony stem from? Was it from seeing me? Missing me? Or was it true anger, simply from me being here? And if so...why?

My arms itched to reach for him. I wanted to feel him close to me, to have his warmth surround me, to make me whole again. But I couldn't ask for that. Could I?

"Please." It barely made a sound as it escaped unchecked.

"Please?" His eyes flared, illuminating their wild mix of silver moon and raging gold. "Please what? What the hell more do you want from me, woman? I'm in pieces, Margaux. Do you understand? I can't think. I can barely eat. Fuck, I definitely don't sleep. And you say please. You say please like I have the answers to make it right again!"

"You do! You're the one imposing these ridiculous conditions on us!" I stomped down the steps right after him—Christ, I was chasing him!—unable to control or contain myself. "Just—just hold me, okay? Is that too much to fucking ask? Just kiss me, even once, before you decide to send me away again!"

He stopped but didn't turn, hands on his hips. I swallowed repeatedly, determined my tears wouldn't clog a damn syllable I uttered next.

"But know this, Michael. If that's what you choose—if you do send me away—I won't come back up here again. This is the last time I chase your gorgeous, goddamned ass—so be really, really sure of what the hell you want."

He pivoted around, scuffing the packed dirt. "Are you... threatening me? Is that what you came here to do?" He had the nerve to laugh. But it was a cocky, "I'm protecting myself" type of laugh. He was in as much pain as I was.

I bit back my anger to quietly answer, "No. This isn't a threat. I need to function, to exist. You swore you'd be a part of that existence, yet you ran away—twice. I've only come to collect what's mine—what was promised to me. To prove to you that I still believe in us, that I believe we're worth fighting for. But I won't do it again, Michael. And I certainly can't do it alone."

He stepped closer. Then again. A narrow alley of night breeze was all that separated us.

I longed to leap into his arms and cover his face with kisses but somehow held back. He needed to make the move—to make up even that small space, because it represented so much more. The gap he'd put between us. Whichever way it went now, he was the one driving our destiny.

I watched his internal war, displayed through the chaos in his eyes.

He took one more step closer.

I trembled. And rooted my feet to the spot.

"You're in danger here."

He seethed each word like an animal warning off a foe. I gulped hard but jabbed my chin up.

"I'm in danger no matter where I am. Being without you—this ridiculous, stupid exile—is the worst thing I've ever had to endure."

He leaned in. I could feel his warmth now. The heat of his torment and rage.

"Get back in that car and drive back to San Diego, Margaux."

"Not until you tell me that we're over. Forever, Michael. Make sure it's what you want."

He took one more step.

I unleashed one desperate sob.

He moved so quickly, I stumbled back.

He was right there, catching me effortlessly and then sweeping me up—as his lips crashed down. He took my mouth in a furious sweep of passion, bruising me and caressing me at the same time. When we pulled back and I gasped, he moved in to suck on my tongue, possessing me from the inside as thoroughly as the outside.

I was breathless, helpless, and dizzy when he pulled back, staring down relentlessly into my face.

"I will love you until the day I die, princess."

Against every force of my will, another sob blurted out.

He'd uttered the words like a man going to the gallows. *No. Please. I love you!*

"That's why I want you to leave this mountain and never come back. Please, please...I don't know how many different ways you need to hear it, you stubborn, beautiful woman. I won't watch you suffer because of your association with me. Now take your things, say goodbye to my mother, and leave."

He released me in a series of awkward jerks, as if our bodies had been sewn together and he'd ripped the seams open. After pressing a kiss to the top of my head, he stepped away, his harsh choke barely audible, before he turned toward the barn. The barn...where we'd made so many memories just a few months back.

Gone.

The memories. And him.

I watched him go until I couldn't discern his shape from the rest of the shadows. Somehow I stumbled back to the porch, sinking to the creaky steps and listening to the sounds of the night as it called out, answered by the various farm creatures.

The only thing out of place was the sniffle and drip of my tears because I couldn't hold them back now if I tried.

CHAPTER FIFTEEN

Michael

I stalked into the barn and then right through it. All the doors were still open, since the display crew was working into the night to test out the lighting they'd rigged so far. Damn good thing. No way was the chaos of my mind and the turmoil barreling through my body going to confine itself to four walls and a bunch of hay bales.

The crew, working throughout the orchard, read the subtext in my stomps and wisely gave me a wide berth. No social hour right now for anyone but my fury and me—made even worse because it was all directed at me.

The images flashing to mind weren't exactly helpful little elves. Though my feet crunched across dry leaves and through thick mulch, other floors of other times took dominance now. The swirled carpet of the Hotel Del's ballroom, resembling a sea of vomit that supported Declan's move on Margaux. The dirty concrete of the county holding cell, doubling as a bed for three passed-out drunks. Finally, the marble floor of the condo's foyer, stained from the blood in Mom's hair as her head tumbled from the burlap sack.

The bag those bastards had stolen from us. From this goddamn orchard.

And I was the one being called a paranoid nutcase.

Regarded like a monster with no heart.

I had a heart, goddamnit. It was still here in my chest, struggling through every day as best it could. I cobbled it together every morning with threads of determination and packing tape of hope, bound by prayers that the day would end with Doug's check-in call, relaying that all was well and Margaux was still alive. Every night I let it fell apart again, my grief hidden by the shadows of midnight. If all the pieces made it to morning, I'd start the whole fucking process all over again.

Right now, midnight couldn't come soon enough.

I looked up, concluding it might be closer than I thought. The crew had gotten up more lights than I'd thought they would, illuminating the orchard significantly. Beyond that, the night had a damn good grip on the mountain. I asked a passing crew member for the time, stunned to learn I'd been out here for two hours. On cue, a sharp wind kicked up, biting straight through my suit to confirm the fact.

Two hours. Mom and Margaux had to be finished with their commiseration of fury by now—though I wasn't startled to see the shiny Maserati still parked outside the main house as I walked back up the hill. The mix of joy and agony in my chest wasn't a stunner either—not that I planned on examining it beyond that. I wasn't sticking around long.

The first surprise I did get was trudging into the living room and not finding my girlfriend—ex-girlfriend—and my mother cuddled up on the couch together. Only the second half of that dynamic duo remained, waiting with her e-reader perched on one knee, an expectant scowl on her face.

Suddenly, I was sixteen again, jabbing a foot at the rug with hands stabbed in my back pockets, wondering how to explain a broken curfew. Only this time, despite Mom's accusing brows,

I wasn't the only one who'd made a mess here.

"She's already gone up to bed," she explained as I threw an inquisitive glance around. "Actually, I ordered her to go. No way was I letting her drive that zippy sports car back home in the dark—or deal with you again."

"That zippy sports car is a Maserati Coupe," I rejoined. "It can handle the road better than my Sierra. And I think Margaux is used to dealing with the bear by now too—even if she's the one who ambushed me in my own home."

She slammed the reader down on the table. "Nobody ambushed anyone. I invited her up here, you oaf."

I rolled my eyes. As long as I was reverting to sixteen again... "Right. I forgot. Girl time. Because you two have become such great pals over the last couple of weeks."

"Now that you mention it, we have. And you know what I've learned?" She straightened her shoulders and nodded, indicating I was getting the answer whether I wanted it or not. "You're a bigger idiot than I originally thought."

"Of course I am." I gritted a smile. "Sorry. We bears aren't the brightest animals in the forest."

"That is more than enough lip, young man. I'm still your mother, and—don't." She snarled it after pushing to her feet and instantly grimacing, making me lunge forward without thinking. "Do not come near me. Yes, this hurts like hell. And no, it's not easy. But I need to start doing it on my own." She stabbed a finger at my tight glare. "Were you listening at all to what they told us at PT today? That pain is part of the move forward?"

Despite the firestorm tearing across my chest, I nodded. "Yeah. I remember."

"I didn't ask if you remembered. I asked if you'd listened."

I knew better than to throw any "lip" back this time. When she was set on making a point, it was best to get the hell out of her way.

"Michael...you're stuck in the pain."

I waited for more. None came. Screw the part about not wanting to hear her point. It'd be good if I understood it. "What the hell are you—?"

"You're stuck." She stepped closer, pressing a hand to my jaw. "My amazing, courageous boy. I'm sorry, I'm sorry. You're so stuck, and it's so my fault."

I crunched a hard frown. "Are you high on pain meds? I have no idea what you're—"

"I'm lucid," she retorted. "Regrettably. Maybe if I weren't, I'd just shut up. But I can't shut up; not anymore." She brushed fingers through my stubble. "Outside, you may be the awesome lawyer nearing thirty, but inside, you're still my brave little man, standing up against that monster." Tears turned her eyes the color of chardonnay. I loved it when they were happy tears, hated it when sorrow brought them—but which was it this time?

"Mom." The clutch in my voice was unavoidable. "He still is a monster. That's why I have to—"

"I didn't tell you enough." Her words were vehement but shaky. "Not nearly enough...how proud I was of you."

"What?" I shook my head, baring my puzzlement. "Of course you did. All the time—"

"No. No, I didn't. Not when I should have. Not when you were actually standing off against him, taking his ridicule, trembling from head to toe. And I—I said nothing." The creases in her face, usually only evident when she laughed hard or smiled huge, turned into crevices of grief. "I said nothing...and

I should have."

"Because you were scared of him." I braced her shoulders, digging fingers in, making her feel my understanding. "I know, okay? I know."

She looked up and framed my face with both hands. "I wasn't scared because of that asshole, bear. I was terrified... because of you."

"Me?" I dropped my hands. An iceberg crashed atop the fire in my chest. "What the fuck?"

"Yes. Because of the reckless places your fear took you to. The anger, the fire, all the taunts you kept up..." She spurted a teary laugh. "God, Michael. You really were just like a baby bear, poking the grizzly who was ten times bigger and twenty times stronger, but you never cared. You just kept going at the bastard, you valiant little fool."

The ice and the fire collided. A spume of outrage erupted. "Fool? He might have killed you."

"He might have killed you!" Physical pain had nothing to do with the new contortion on her features—or her shove at my chest. "Do you know what it was like for me to cower there and watch you? Can you fathom how badly I wrestled between cheering you on and holding you back? If I tried the first, it would send Declan and his belt harder at you—but if the last, your pride would've propelled you right back into his path." She shoved aside tears with her palms. "If I did anything, any goddamn thing, I risked that monster getting mad enough to go harder at you—to hurt you for good."

"All right," I countered, "I get that. But I'm not that stupid kid anymore."

"Truly?" She rocked back, shocking me by keeping her balance. "Because I could swear that's who I've been dealing with for the last three weeks."

"Because I'm the only one who's actually thinking about this situation?"

"Thinking?" She folded her arms. "Oh no, son. You're reacting, not thinking—and it's paralyzing you fast. It's trapping you in a place of nothing but fear, and it's only a matter of time before that fear manifests into something worse—something that will turn you into a person you don't recognize." She sucked in air through quivering lips. Her hazel eyes turned deep brown, giving away her sorrow. She didn't relent the look, despite my derisive huff. "Don't take my word for it, then. You want evidence? Look no further than your uncle."

The iceberg inside me shattered. Its shards fanned to every nerve ending in my body. "I am nothing like that man."

She dragged in another tormented breath. "Not yet."

I stumbled backward. My lungs searched for the instruction manual on breathing and never found it. Bitterness, bile, and chaos ripped the thing to shreds.

Pain is part of the move forward.

If that was her point, she'd sure as fuck made it. This was pain—though I sure as hell couldn't determine the moving forward part yet. Had a good idea about how to get the proverbial ball rolling though.

Wordlessly, I spun toward the stairs. In five minutes, I'd have enough personal shit thrown into a bag for a few nights. I'd go into town and crash at one of the B&Bs tonight and then hit up Ross or Deacon for a pillow on their couch until Mom and I had cooled off. With Declan still MIA, I wouldn't be able to sleep if I was more than a few miles from the farm. Wasn't like I had any other place to consider right now. So much was up in the fucking air.

Who the hell was I kidding? Nothing was up in the air. It was all Pottery Barn after the San Andreas Fault hiccupped, broken to the point that I didn't know what fit with what.

Was this it?

This confused rage...the aloneness...was this the first step in transforming from myself into Declan? Was I simply damned to walk that dark path, no matter how violently I'd fought to stick to the light?

Mom didn't come after me. It was definitely for the best. As I stomped up the stairs, I heard her rummaging across the coffee table for her iPod. We each had our own methods of cooling off and blocking any more of the other's advice.

Twenty minutes later, I was no closer to being the packed-up, pissed-off, misunderstood Bruce Banner that I'd cast myself into. Fuck, I hadn't even made it back to my room, thanks to a stop in the bathroom to retrieve my toiletries.

The bathroom, where the scent of Margaux's hair and skin and soap consumed every breath I took.

Where I was still staring at her hairbrush, left behind on the counter...and her clothes, tossed aside on the floor.

Beautiful princess.

God, I miss slipping across all your shit.

Where I lifted my gaze inside the shower, at the corner that brought back every hot memory of what we'd done there three months ago. Of how I'd spread her wide, fucked her hard, and fallen deeper in love with her. We'd gone to the meadow that afternoon, where we'd screwed beneath the sun and between the flowers...and I'd lost my soul to her as well as my heart.

I'd never been the same since.

I never would be again.

Margaux Corina Asher had turned me into a different man. Had, through the sheer force of her passion, honesty, and fearlessness, turned me into a better person. A better person— not the beginning of Declan Pearson's heir apparent.

I had to believe it. I had no other choice. I'd succumb to a fucking lobotomy before becoming even a dim facsimile of that heartless prick.

The resolve did nothing to move me. Imagine that. My worst nightmare handed over on a goddamn platter by my own mother, and now I could only stand and stare into a shower, toothbrush held like a shiv to hold off the mind fuck for just another minute.

I had to get out of here. Now.

But fate wasn't done with its fun little detours for the night.

I left the bathroom—and instead of turning left, toward my room, I was compelled to the right...toward the closed door of the guest room.

Toward the woman behind it.

Toward the presence my confusion needed. The safe place for my soul. The only one on this planet who'd speak it all to me straight—with a chaser of her brutal, beautiful love.

By the time I stood in front of the portal, I yearned to bash the fucker down. A deep breath and a clenched jaw later, I turned the knob gently instead.

I really should've knocked—but so much about that felt wrong after sharing nearly every aspect of my life with her for the last three months.

Nearly every aspect.

For the last three months—minus three weeks.

Three weeks that vanished as soon as I stepped closer to

the bed.

The act of simply gazing at her... I had no idea how thoroughly I'd taken this small privilege for granted. I ached with thanks for it now, taking in the slopes of her body beneath the blanket, the rise and fall of her shoulders, the brilliant fan of her hair against the pillow. Before I could control it, my hand rose, drawn to those white-gold strands...

An inch before I touched down, she rolled over, onto her back. Blinked up at me with the inquisitiveness of a napping kitten.

"Hey."

Her voice didn't have a note of anger in it. Not even surprise. But her uncertainty, serrating the edges of the word, made my jaw tighten. She sounded that way—again—because of me.

"Hey." The sandpaper in my own voice was impossible to mask. It made her prop on her elbows, gazing more intensely. She was wearing one of my old Ron Jon T-shirts, an observation that stirred every ember of possessive lust in my blood. I couldn't help wondering what she wore—or didn't—besides the shirt.

Not the time. Not the place. Getting horizontal with her right now would release the fucking Kraken of mixed signals—and right now, we had enough monsters crowding the roster.

"Are you all right?"

I didn't answer. Just returned to the sixteen-year-old stance, hands in my pockets, one foot jabbing the carpet. But I sure as hell didn't feel sixteen now. I was suddenly old, tired, frustrated.

"Look...your mom made me stay, okay? I was emotional earlier"—she winced as if not believing she'd said it—"and it was dark. If you're that uncomfortable about this, I'll get up and—"

"Stop." I beat a fist against the bedpost. "Stop it, goddamnit." The tension of the day—fuck it, of the last three weeks—piled into my lungs, making them pump. My throat constricted around my gritted words. "I'm not a monster."

She inhaled deeply. "I didn't say you—"

"I'm not a monster." Repeating it didn't help. I spread my hand, gripping the post instead, letting myself sink to the mattress near her feet. Margaux pushed the comforter back in order to crawl over and reach for my other hand. "I know. I know."

Don't look at her. Don't look at her.

Like that helped. Throwing my gaze to the floor was just as useless. Hurray for peripheral vision, making me all too aware of her bare thighs peeking out from the T-shirt. My body, still clad in most of my work clothes, shivered as if I was just as barely dressed—except my cock, which jumped straight into hot-poker mode.

Margaux slid a little closer. Wrapped her other hand around mine.

Fucking. Awesome.

The grim thought shook me to my core. I attempted to inhale—like an alcoholic forced to hold a bottle of Stoli.

"Maybe...that's the problem," I finally uttered. "Maybe I do have to be a monster. Be like them to protect you from them."

"Michael." It was a scream disguised as a rasp. She dug her grip into my arm, nails almost ripping my shirt. I twisted, praying for the tear. The heat of her was too damn good, the force of her too damn amazing, the strength of her too damn impossible to resist. I pulled it into my soul, greedily wrapping it around my will and shoring up my resolve.

"I'll do it," I grated. "If that's what it takes. I'll do it, princess, and I won't be one fucking speck of sorry." I seized her wrist, possessing her flesh exactly as she possessed my soul. "So help me God, I'll let Satan himself crawl between my thighs if it means keeping you safe."

"Michael." It crumbled to a whisper as she crawled up, curling against me. "Don't do this. Please don't do this."

I lifted her fingers to my lips. The tips were cold. Her body shuddered in the circle of my arms. I folded her in, tighter... tighter.

Not tight enough.

"If anything ever happened to you—"

"You won't let it." She caressed her other hand up my nose, over my eyebrows, into my hair. "But you don't have to do it alone." Lifted her face to kiss the underside of my jaw. "You're not alone, Michael."

My breathing shook. My grip tremored. Everything she touched turned to fire, torching the walls of my resistance. How the hell had I come in here with half a prayer of fighting this? How the hell had I even wanted to? "Princess," I whispered. "My beautiful, stunning princess."

"Damn straight." She yanked on my scalp, forcing my gaze down to her face. The corners of her silken mouth were already turned up, as if she knew exactly what the expression did to my self-control—what was left of it. "Yours," she murmured. "Which means nobody gets near your thighs except me—even that bastard Satan."

"Fuck."

White flag or rally cry—and did it matter, when the

battlefield of my will was totally razed? Did anything matter beyond the ecstasy of taking her mouth beneath mine, the bliss of pulling her body closer, the joy of racing a hand beneath the shirt to her thigh, her waist, her breasts, even her perfect collarbone? Once I reached her neck, did anything in the world compare to pressing in on her jaw, forcing her wider for the invasion of my lips and tongue?

Was there a world left to give a shit about beyond this? Or had we just burned every inch of it away with the force of this kiss alone?

When we tore apart, it was only to get in more breath—the physical support for fulfilling what our spirits, hearts, and souls demanded. Her throaty sighs were my libido's symphony, drowning all doubt about this choice. For now, for just this one last time, I'd be her hero instead of her heartbreak, her desire instead of her disappointment, her fantasy instead of her failure.

Yes...

The resolution made it easy to fall backward beneath her push and then let her straddle me with her lush thighs. I glided up with both hands, turning them into Vs for the valleys between her torso and legs while watching silvery moon fingers sneak through the window and shamelessly caresses her body. Their light soon became an open invitation to join in.

Who the hell was I to argue with the moon?

"Oh, God!" Margaux husked as I trailed both hands in and then up. Beneath the shirt once more, I traced her waist and ribs before working my hands over the erect buds of her breasts.

Damn. Three weeks, and unbelievably, it felt like the first time I'd ever stroked her like this...an impression she seemed to share, if her sexy-as-fuck undulations were any indication. I marveled at the weight of her mounds, the density of the flesh beneath her creamy skin, the way her nipples hardened like diamonds beneath my fingers. Her lips parted, showing me the bared teeth that perfectly matched the feline glow of her eyes.

"Wicked little wildcat." I growled it while pinching her points, savoring how they stiffened even more.

"Shit!" she cried. "Ohhh, hell!"

I paused. Lightened my touch but only a little. "You asking for more or for less, sugar?" Sarcasm aside, reading her was suddenly very interesting. While I'd barely pinched, she'd reacted like I'd just put her in nipple clamps and then torqued the pressure.

The confusion was worth it. She dipped a kiss into me as gentle as a whisper though scratched the top of my chest hard enough to bust my top button free. "Always more," she pleaded against my lips, "if it means you'll stay."

Before she could move away, I bit her lower lip. As her moan vibrated into me, I squeezed her nipples again. The moan became a scream, undetected by anyone but us since I absorbed it with my mouth. Her shriek subsided the moment I let up on her nipples—though that was far from her flag of surrender. With a sharp jerk, she ripped another button off my shirt but wasted no time in letting the exposed flesh go pristine. She clamped her nails in again, scratching so hard that I arched and hissed, choice filthy words exploding between my gritted teeth.

When she let up, I looked down.

Her brand on my chest, five distinct lines of red, affected me like five ropes around my cock as well.

"Little fucking vixen," I grated.

"Huge fucking scoundrel." She grinned—and then popped another button free.

I clamped a hand to the back of her neck. Yanked her down, kissing her brutally. "The scoundrel who worships you."

She trailed her lips down, sinking teeth into my chin. "The vixen who needs you."

I clamped my teeth around the edge of her jaw.

She whined, clawing my chest deeper.

I gripped and yanked her hair.

She bit and licked my neck.

I twisted her breast.

She squeezed my nipple.

I swept the T-shirt over her head.

She jerked at another button, bulleting it across the room, allowing my shirt to fall fully open.

We swore and sighed, tasted and scratched, sucked and scraped, kissed and cussed, until I snarled low and flipped her over, one swoop that pinned her under me, wrists beneath my hands, thighs still cradling mine.

Absence made the heart grow fonder?

Screw fonder.

I craved her. Was starved for her. Thirsted for her like I'd been stumbling through the desert for three weeks and she was the naked nymph in the oasis, cavorting in a lagoon as lush and green and perfect as her gorgeous eyes.

An almost naked nymph.

Another growl curled through me, a mixture of raw lust and tight aggravation, while shoving aside her panties to delve fingers into the core beneath—or, damn it, trying to. How much trouble could a few scraps of satin be? Answer—a hell of a lot, if they got twisted by the friction of two impassioned bodies. I could barely slide one finger past the barrier, let alone the two Margaux always loved.

"Damn it."

"What?" she demanded. "What is it? Oh God, Michael. Please don't stop!"

"Not even if a train hit this place, sweetheart."

I whispered the promise into her neck, shoulder, breasts, and then lower, kissing and nipping down her quivering body, lost to the expensive ice cream taste of her skin again. After licking through the curve of her waist, I finally hit the tight string of her lingerie—and bit to secure it between my teeth. With a grunt, I dragged down hard. Leaned back long enough to fully tear the panties away.

"Much better."

With the garment gone, I pushed her thighs apart. Once more, spread my hands over the junctures between her hips and thighs—though this time, swept my thumbs across her damp curls.

"Michael," she begged. "Ohhhh...yessss."

"Damn." I rubbed deeper despite the skirmish it started between my cock and fly. "Look at this. I've missed this pussy so much. Yeah...just look at all this wet, perfect sweetness." I growled low as she whimpered high, throwing her arms back, wrapping them around the pillow. "Have you been this wet for three weeks, sugar?"

"Michael!" She bucked. "For the love of fucking—"

I chuckled as she choked into silence. "What? No designer deity to call on, sweetheart?"

"None of them can help me. Nobody can...except you. Please!"

"Hmmm." I lifted a teasing smirk. "After you've answered

my question."

"Wh-What question?"

"You mean...you forgot?"

"I—I can't remember my own name right now."

Gently, I parted her labia. The fruity flesh beneath gleamed, soaked in her gorgeous juices. "We were discussing your beautiful cunt. Has it been this wet for three whole weeks?"

She keened as I curled a finger in, teasing the hood of her clit. "Y-Yes. Yes, goddamnit, no thanks to you!"

Victory fired my blood. It had to be wrong, coming at the price of her torment, but I couldn't wrap my head around that. For the first time in nearly a month, everything felt right. Aligned. Complete. "Wait. You haven't played with your pussy at all? No fantasies or vibrators or clamps for a little fun?" At my insistence, she'd kept a lot of her naughty single girl toys. Using them on her had been a hell of a lot of fun from time to time, but I'd never harbored illusions that a passionate creature like her would leave them alone in my absence.

Until now.

Until the moment she hiked back up onto her elbows, piercing me with a gaze full of such sharp green pain, I was locked completely in place.

"Have you?"

My mischief dissolved. I lunged, cupping the back of her head and smashing a kiss to her twisted lips.

"No."

It was the truth if there ever was one. Every time I'd walked into the orchard to take care of business, I'd ended back up at our meadow. With the grass turned brown and the flowers slumbering for the season, I'd clung to the only thing that remained the same since that summer day we'd visited. My raging hard-ons.

I sure as fuck regretted that choice now.

Abstinence could be a hard taskmaster. Nothing like firsthand experience to enforce the lesson, especially as she tore at my fly. My eyes flared, though nothing changed about the determined light in Margaux's. She might not have thought me a monster, but she was resolute about unleashing my inner beast, ramming my zipper down with a harsh rasp. Without skipping a beat, she continued her hand in, wrapping fingers around both my balls.

"What if I don't believe you?" She cupped me, pressing and kneading, yanking primal sounds from deep in my throat. "I know how you like to come, Michael. I know how you need to explode, how hard these balls shake when you do. What if I don't believe you've been denying yourself for three weeks?"

She pushed a couple of fingers into the base of my shaft, and my knees threatened to give out. My thighs burned, battling to hold my body over hers. My ass flexed. Torture was damn near the correct word for this after all.

"Sugar," I groaned. "Shit! Feel me...do it tighter if you have to." *Tighter...please.* "Feel me, swelling at you, pulsing for you... needing you." Maybe the cause required assistance. I locked my elbows and braced my knees, pushing my crotch deeper into her grip. "Do you think this cock has had one goddamn orgasm in the last three weeks?"

As my hardness filled her fingers, her mouth popped open. She clenched her teeth, torn between her pride and libido. I groaned, empathetic to the cause. For a guy who'd just declared he wasn't a monster, every bone, muscle, and blood cell in my body yearned to go completely King Kong on her sweet Fay Wray ass.

"Prove it."

Her challenge, delivered with chin defiantly hiked, sent a new rush of blood between my thighs—and a fresh fire of challenge to my stare. "Gladly." I pushed harder against her, relishing the tremble of her inner thighs against mine. "Name your criterion."

Her gaze glowed like the Northern Lights. I curled up the edges of my mouth.

"Well, nothing beats hands-on analysis." She demonstrated exactly that by lifting my briefs up and then down, freeing my naked flesh for her eager fingers.

"No." I treasured the sight of her hungry gaze as my tip surrendered a spurt of precome. "Nothing really does."

As she spread the milky drop, tracing a vein in my dick, her gaze never left my face. "You're as hot and trembling as a virgin, Mr. Pearson."

I spread my knees, fitting our bodies tighter. "So are you, Miss Asher."

She licked her lips. "Maybe I need...just a little more proof."

"Maybe you need a lot more."

"Such as?"

I could've bantered back. Played with her a little more. Used my cock in a dozen more forms of foreplay, driving us both to the brink of madness—but why? We were already there. Before Declan had brought his chaos to our front door, spending three hours from her was often its own special suffering. And three weeks? I'd often gotten through the days by sheer force of will alone.

Fortitude I no longer had—or wanted to have.

A monster I just couldn't be anymore.

Or maybe...a monster I could no longer ignore.

Fuck.

"Michael! Yes!"

I tensed, struggling to heed the message scrolling across my conscience like a level-red terror alert. This doesn't fix anything. This doesn't fix anything. This doesn't—

The screen went blank.

The world was nothing but static, noise, light, heat.

Intense. So goddamn intense that my head swam, my senses reeled, and my throat went dry—

As my body fucked.

Deep. Plunging into her tight tunnel of fulfillment. Hard. Punishing myself for succumbing to all of it. Brutal. Greedily grabbing every sensation I'd been numbing myself to, pulling them down like the walls of Jericho, letting them crash my psyche to the point that it bled. I siphoned it all back into the rod between my thighs, stabbing her so hard that she bit my chest to keep her screams from being heard into the next county. She grabbed my ass so hard, I was stunned it didn't bleed.

She climaxed around me.

Then again.

I didn't stop. I couldn't.

Deeper. I needed to be deeper. A part of her, branded from the inside out, just as she'd claimed me from the very start. No matter how hard I lunged or how loud the smack of my balls against her ass, it still didn't feel like enough.

I pulled out. Flipped her over with a ruthless toss.

Sweat shone on every inch of her skin, pooling in the hollow of her back. She writhed like an animal in heat, sexy-as-fuck sounds emanating from her throat, her ass rising, readying for my invasion.

"No." I yanked on her ankles, flattening her again. Slicked my hands up to her thighs and spread them apart. "Like this."

I entered her again, impaling her fully, welcomed again by her soaked, gripping channel. With one hand, I pinned her wrists over her head. With the other, I fisted her hair away from her face. Licked along her cheek and neck, sucking up the salt of tears and the musk of sweat. The air smelled of nothing but our joined arousal, primitive and pure. I soaked in the sound of her, the feel of her, the taste of her, the tightness of her.

"Vixen...mine," I growled against her ear.

"Yes," she breathed back.

"Animal...mine."

"Yes. Yes!"

"Cunt...mine."

"Yes!"

"Climax...mine. Now!"

Her body tensed. She grabbed the bedsheet, coiling both hands into it. As the cotton ripped beneath her grip, she screamed into the mattress—

As her sex demanded the explosion of mine.

I poured myself into her, so intent on the mission that my groan was soundless. Wave after orgasmic wave pounded me, squeezing my ass, gripping my thighs, stripping my sanity. When I didn't think I had anymore to give, her body claimed me all over again. Drained every drop. Exacted every tremor. Confiscated every thought.

Dominated my soul.

I kept it that way until long after we fell apart, still breathing hard, bodies pretzeled. Somewhere in that process she turned again so we shared a pillow with foreheads together and breaths mingled.

There, tangled in her softness and breathing in her essence, I added one more whopper to my long list of mistakes since walking in here.

I gave in to the deepest, hardest sleep I'd had in weeks.

★ ★ ★ ★

Sometimes, waking up with every brain cell firing on full was not a good thing.

Especially when every one of them confirmed that Margaux hadn't left for town yet.

Though her bag no longer rested on the dresser and the room only carried traces of her amber perfume, my senses resonated with her nearness. My nerve endings crackled like the old days, when I knew she'd entered the building long before she strutted into the office behind Andrea.

I swung out of bed, trying to gauge the hour by the light through the window. Even from the edge of the bed, I observed the shroud of low clouds over the orchard, meaning it was still early or we were going to have shit weather today. In short, no help there.

I reached for my watch on the nightstand. Six a.m.—not the coolest time to be awake on a Saturday—but I curled a huge smile anyway. I didn't remember taking the watch off, meaning Margaux had. She'd done the same so many times back at home, it had become a routine. Poor thing had been bonked a few too many times with the big Tissot, built for beach workouts and days on the farm, not spooning and cuddling. The sight of it there, perfectly positioned where she knew I'd find it, made me ache for our days in the condo again.

The condo?

I didn't give a fuck about the condo.

I just wanted to return home—any home—with her by my side.

What would our own place be like? Something closer to the water, probably. A little place in Carlsbad or La Jolla, so she could be closer to Claire...

And what the hell kind of crack are you smoking?

Nothing had changed between yesterday and this moment. Not a goddamn thing. Though Doug's team had possibly sighted Declan at the airport last week, my scum-sucking uncle was still missing off the grid at large. That little tidbit wouldn't matter to the Principals, who'd demand payback on their loans in some way, shape, or form. Hell, Menger and his boy toys might be prowling through Julian this minute, stomping the wooden boardwalks between the pie shops and antique stores, thinking they were inconspicuous just because of their scowls.

No. Nothing was different at all. Dialogue echoed in my head courtesy of the party Mom and I had attended at Town Hall over the weekend, celebrating the Triangle Club's annual melodrama run. *"There's still danger aplenty lurking in the forest."*

Not even an hour of I-missed-you sex was going to fix that.

Crazy, catastrophic, mind-blown-off-its-hinges sex.

Memories that had to be forced aside now—and were—as I slinked back into my room and threw on a sweater and jeans.

Memories that returned in a relentless rush as soon as I saw Margaux again.

I'd expected to find her in the kitchen or living room, gazing out of the window in her typical way of easing into the day. So many of those moments, when she stilled her inner dervish long enough to soak in the world instead of contemplating a conquest of it, were my favorites.

I'd get no such moment today.

She was out on the porch swing, coffee cup perched on her curled-up knees, beneath a heavy wool blanket. She wore a pink angora sweater in that funny backward way, so odd it looked cool, but that wasn't what arrested me at first glance. That came in the form of her sleek, French-twisted hair and her to-the-eyelash makeup job, including the perfectly applied berry stain on her lips. Even with the turned-around sweater, she emanated class and polish and perfection.

And detachment.

Decision.

Resignation.

As if she'd woken and performed the exact same mental game I had. Purging all the memories, forcing down all the reality.

Of course she had. Because I hadn't fallen in love with a stupid woman. She was the exact opposite.

She was your equal in about a thousand ways.

And your superior in about a thousand more.

I should have been relieved. After all, she'd done all the hard shit already.

I wanted to lean over the rail and puke into the bushes.

Instead, I shuffled to the empty end of the swing and eased onto it. When she didn't kick me off, I scooted back a little farther. Wrapped one hand around her bundled feet and rubbed gently. "Hey."

She didn't echo the greeting or acknowledge the massage. After half a minute of silence, she finally murmured, "Your mom and Carlo took off a while ago. Grabbed an early breakfast in town."

I almost laughed. "Sure." Early breakfast, my ass. Mom rarely even thought of food before ten—unless she didn't want to be lurking during the most uncomfortable morning after in history.

Margaux sipped her coffee. "I made a full pot. There's plenty left, if you want some."

"No, thanks. Not yet." I plunged again into the stillness as thick as the mist. "You look beautiful."

"Thanks."

"Big plans for the day?"

"Not really." She sipped again. Gazed out toward the barn. "Looking put-together helps me deal better with wanting to fall apart."

I exhaled through my teeth. "Fuck."

"Hmmm. Yeah. That about sums it up." Then, after she sipped again: "Dumb shit."

I grimaced. "Guess I had that coming too."

She flung a side-eye like a wet towel embedded with razors. "What were you expecting? That I'd suddenly become 'that' girl, rewriting today because of what happened last night?" She let out an all-too-quiet sigh, set down her cup, and then folded her arms. "Your cock and your heart are two different things. While I enjoy the commitment of one, nothing between us is going to be right without the commitment of both."

I turned to swipe my hand around her nape. "Every fucking inch of my heart belongs to you."

Her lips tilted up, though she might as well have sobbed. The expression clutched my gut just as violently. Sadness, so deep it transcended tears, poured off her stronger than a nuclear haze. "No. Not every inch—and we both know it."

I snarled. Jerked back to my feet. Shuddered as Mom's words from last night echoed within, adding to the agonizing cloud. *You're reacting, not thinking. It'll only be a matter of time before that fear manifests into something worse...*

Fine, goddamnit. Let the manifesting begin.

"Margaux. Fuck." I slammed both hands to the rail. "I don't know how to do this any other way." Twisted my hands around the damn thing until I trembled, my only defense against a full plummet to my knees. How else could I translate the mess in my mind to her? To communicate that I'd learned no other path than this? Did she think I hadn't explored those other roads? Used compassion, understanding, and the whole teamwork thing with dear ol' Uncle Dec—even against him? Good beats evil, was that it?

But that wasn't it.

Captain America beat the bad guys by understanding them.

Then pretending to the rest of the world that he didn't.

Nobody ever told him it was going to be easy either—especially in a moment like this, when the love of his life rose to her feet with such singular grace she knocked the air out of him as if they'd met for the first time. Yeah, even more than the night she'd shown up half-drunk at his place and dropped her dress, offering herself to him in the sexiest red lingerie he'd ever seen. Even more than the first time she'd confessed her love for him, in the middle of the airport, begging him not to get on a plane and leave her.

Those moments—and all the incredible ones in between—glittered in the depths of her eyes, trembled across both her lips, echoed in every breath that stuttered from her...and coiled in every knot in my gut.

"Until last summer, I didn't know how to do things any other way either." Her shoulders hunched in as she started kneading at her ring. "I didn't know if I had the capacity to even love someone, let alone to show it, to say it. But you—" A hard breath halted the rip in her voice. "You came along and changed all of that, Michael. You helped me. You taught me." She lifted her head, stabbing me with the emerald dagger of her stare. "You...changed me."

I didn't look away. Fuck, did I want to. "Margaux—"

"Don't." She lunged up, tearing at my shoulder. "Don't you dare throw up your love as an excuse now, goddamnit. I changed, Michael. I changed—because of you." She pushed off, curling her arms in, standing away once more. "I love you so much, it hurts. This hurts. It hurt when I opened my heart to you, my secrets to you, and when I chased you across the airport, deciding to fight for you. It hurt in all the scariest ways when I sat in the waiting room at county lockup, praying they'd let you out of that horrible place. It sure as fuck hurt when I got into the car yesterday and hauled my ass up this mountain, knowing I was getting ready to put my soul on the chopping block again—for you. For us."

Her voice shuddered once more. She visibly gritted her teeth, and her throat vibrated with deep, hard swallows.

I...stood there like a nimrod.

My dim consolation rested in watching her breathe, because I couldn't even do that. Her pain was a palpable force on the air, clinging like bitter smoke.

She screwed her shit together faster than me. Pivoted on her heels, storming back into the house only to emerge ten seconds later. Her bag was in one hand, the Maserati's keys in the other.

"What...are you doing?"

"Following orders, Mr. Pearson. Getting the hell out of here. Going home." She took the three steps to move right into my space again. Leaned in and up, her breath fanning my neck, as if to nuzzle against me in her favorite way. My arm rose to keep her close, though my fingers visibly shook—

Before she tore away, choking down a sob.

"Margaux—"

She twisted her wrist free from my grip. "I won't be back again, Michael. Not like this. Not ever again like this."

She didn't turn back to finish it. Just let me watch her shoulders sink and her head fall between them.

"Justify it all you want now. Go ahead and tell yourself how noble you are for saving me. But let me make one thing perfectly clear. If you remain here, Michael Pearson, you'll have saved only yourself. Have fun becoming that monster you talked about—because the biggest part of me is still right in the middle of your chopping block."

CHAPTER SIXTEEN

Margaux

"Hey, Alfred? I'll just leave the Maserati's keys on the entry table, okay?"

Alfred's steps echoed on the marble floor of Kil and Claire's front foyer. Despite the formality of the setting and the man, I'd relaxed a little just by stepping through the door of this place.

God knew, I needed all the help I could get.

"That will be fine, Miss Asher. I'll let Mr. Stone know you returned the car when he comes home tonight. I would've been happy to come into town to pick it up, though. I'm sorry you drove all the way out here."

"It's fine, Alfred. I needed the head time, you know? May even hit the beach on my way back, since I'm already up this way."

"Very well, Miss Asher."

"Tell my brother thanks again for the loan. It's a sweet ride."

"So he tells me, ma'am."

I paused near the front door to take in the ground floor expanse of Claire and Killian's Rancho Santa Fe home—and despite my misery, I smiled. Even though no one was home, there was unmistakable warmth and open invitation here, drawing me in, making me long to stay. The love they had for each other permeated everything in the place. It was so strong that even an outsider felt it when standing inside their front door.

Love. Warmth. Magic.

They had it, and I wanted it.

This wasn't a jealous or petty whim like I once would have had when coveting some trinket or pair of shoes. This was something I'd never experienced in a home before, something deep and devoted and connective. And it was something I craved with Michael. I yearned for people to feel this inside our home.

Our home.

A dream that would never be.

"Fuck." I burned to repeat it a dozen times but bit the inside of my cheek, checking it. What good would it do? For the first time in my life, I'd admitted the longing to create a home with another person—a place where people would come and enjoy spending time with us, where it wasn't all about me. A place where I no longer needed to be the star of the show. I wanted to share the spotlight. With Michael.

The man I still loved so much, it was a physical ache. The man I was still so sure of, I spoke it out loud, still standing there in the foyer.

"Yes."

This was what I wanted. Our home. Our connection. Our love.

Could I wait for it...even for forever?

I left the house, closing the door quietly before meeting Andre in the driveway. My head was heavy and hurting, like I'd been whammed by a sledge hammer. Well, now I knew what I wanted but was so lost on how to get there.

We had to handle the shit with Declan first. Yes, we. I'd start tomorrow morning by calling Killian. Since our little chat in his office, I'd snapped together some conclusions about the homework he'd done regarding Michael's uncle. First, there was no way Kil would drop that shit at mere homework. The man had assigned a whole team to the damn subject by now, I was sure of it. That led to an unnerving number two. No news wasn't often good news. If Kil's people had learned anything useful that would give me an inroad back to the stubborn ass on the mountain, I was sure he would've shared it yesterday. But maybe he knew something. Anything.

If not, then I had to figure out another way to convince Michael that we could get through this. For now, I chose to ignore the memories of how I'd last seen him, with shadows of doubt in his eyes and lines of desperation across his brow.

His gaze of goodbye.

That was the tragic story of us. One step forward, two steps back. I wondered if the pattern had continued for so long, we were more lost now than three months ago—attempting to figure shit out after that first night of amazing sex at his old place.

"You ready to head back home?" Andre's deep voice shook me from my musings. "On second thought, you have that 'I need retail therapy' look."

Shit. The guy knew me so well, it was unnerving. He emphasized the offer with his signature half smile, my favorite expression on him. It was also his look when he wasn't sure about overstepping the line between our business relationship and friendship.

I threw back a glower, unwritten assurance that all was

okay. I needed a friend right now more than a minion. "I'm going to let that one slide—only because I'm too exhausted to kick your scrawny ass today." I knocked my shoulder to his— well, technically, my head—which bumped his massive biceps.

He turned, mocking his self-defense. "Yes, Miss Margaux." He spilled a rich laugh, not bothering to contain it. "Where to, then? Highway 101 in Encinitas? The Forum in Carlsbad? You don't get up to North County that much. Why not make the best of it?"

"Andre." I stopped beside the BMW, looking up at him with purpose. "Will you marry me?"

It was fun, weird, and sad to witness the million and one thoughts running through his mind. He finally opened his mouth to answer, but nothing came out. He was measuring his words so carefully I didn't dare tell him I was kidding.

"Miss Margaux," he finally offered, "I'm flattered, truly— but first there is the issue of Mr. Michael. He is not only one hundred percent in love with you, he is my friend. And you see, there is a code about that."

I bit my inner cheek to force a solemn stare. "Code?"

"A code among men. We don't poach on our brother's territory, you see."

"Oh. Well, yes, I see."

"Secondly, there is the issue of how much I care for you. I would never subject you to a life with me. You truly are a princess, Margaux. You deserve to be treated like one, whether you believe that in here"—he touched a warm finger to my temple—"or in here." He tapped the same finger to my sternum. "It's the truth, girl—but I still cannot marry you. Lastly, and most importantly of all, you can't cook worth a damn. This man needs to eat—and none of that organic, super food, quinoa, grass-fed, wonder-tofu, tastes-like-cardboard crap you call food!"

I burst into giggles. His levity, on top of the wonderful things he'd already said, were what my day needed. Regrettably, it had only worsened my immediate challenge. I was still an emotional basket case, with an epic public meltdown imminent. Knowing Andre, that was why he'd ended his list on that special note. This man was so much wiser than he let on. When my life was fully squared away and I cornered Claire for some stress-free girl time—in short, about ten years from now—I had to talk to her about finding a perfect match for Andre.

But first things first.

My life.

Squared away.

"Okay, big boy. Let's hit the road."

Andre grinned. "Where to?"

"Torrey Pines."

"Golfing? You didn't tell me to schedule a tee time. And since when do you play?"

"Don't be an ass. I mean the beach."

"Excuse me? Who are you, and what have you done with my sweet boss lady?"

I whapped his brawny shoulder. "Pushing it, buddy. I have some serious thinking to do, and since it worked last time..." It had also become a special place for Michael and me, period. I actually liked hiking there now—a little—but would let that be a little surprise to Andre, who already sneaked a peek at the dashboard's temperature readout. Clearly, he was worried about a repeat of the last time he'd dropped me off at the beach route's trailhead, before I'd nearly died hiking back up to the parking lot.

"Stop worrying, you big mother hen. I'll be fine. We can pull over and get a few bottles of water." I scrambled into the car.

"Yes, ma'am," he grumbled while sliding into the driver's seat.

Within minutes, we eased onto I-5, heading south toward La Jolla.

Andre still frowned a little when I got out at the trailhead but loosened up once I pulled a blanket out of the 750i's trunk, took a big swig of water, and then sprayed on some sunscreen. Last but not least, I switched out my heeled boots for easy sneakers.

The hike down to the beach was easy and even invigorating. I spread the blanket on the sand. After kicking off my sneakers, I planted myself in the middle of the square.

At first, I simply watched the waves chase each other onto the shore and then back out toward the ocean. Over and over the cycle repeated, absorbing me into its timeless rhythm. The sound of the water crashing was my favorite part of the beach experience. Droplets of ocean spray carried in on the breeze, misting my face just enough to keep me cool.

Tilting my head back, I let the brilliant light soak into my skin. I visualized myself as a tree, being nourished by the sun's rays, made stronger by the radiance I absorbed. I didn't usually go for the new age bullshit, but I desperately needed some inner peace. I had to find the strength to move forward, develop a game plan that was going to work for Michael and me. Failure wasn't an option. It couldn't be.

Besides, this just felt good. The sun was warm and forceful, literally filling me with new strength as I continued to picture gaining its power. I was a survivor. I was capable. I could hold us up if Michael wasn't willing to. I needed to show him that I wasn't afraid of Declan or the scary-mafia-whatever bastards, and that if we had to, we'd figure a way to beat them at their own game.

But we had to do it together.

Yes.

I pulled up his beautiful face in my mind.

No.

The only memory I could access was his face from this morning. The sorrow of it. The finality of it.

My newfound light crashed into darkness.

I needed to be stronger. I had to be. Why couldn't he see we could conquer anything we set our mind to—any enemy or monster that threatened to tear us apart? Why didn't he believe in us the way I did?

My thoughts commingled like the colors on the old Rubik's Cube I just couldn't master. I needed to compartmentalize in order to see things clearly. But was that the answer I didn't want to face? Had it been staring me down all this time, and finally, there was just no other place to look but dead ahead, right at it?

Michael didn't believe in us the way I did. Was he scared to? Unable to? Was the answer even relevant? Simply put, I loved him more than he loved me.

He wasn't breaking up with me to protect me. He was just...breaking up with me.

Cue the fucking waterworks.

I fell to my side. Curled my knees to my chest. And, like the foolish girl I felt, bawled my eyes out. Ugly sobs. Heaving breaths. A grief I hadn't fully allowed to invade—until now.

I cried until the sun went down—or at least it seemed like that.

Eventually, I realized someone was hovering nearby. No. More than that. Standing at the edge of my blanket, blocking the sun's rays. Well, shit. I didn't want to see or speak to anyone. But because this day wasn't hideous enough, the shadow wasn't changing. Didn't move.

I forced myself to sit up, swiping tears from my cheeks. I had to shield my eyes while looking up, but the glare made it impossible to see the person only three feet in front of me.

Finally, the visitor got a clue and moved to sit on the blanket, right beside me—a little too close, actually. As I scooted by an inch or two, my eyes began to refocus...and a gentle voice reached my ears.

"You look like you could use a friend."

"You—"

My mouth worked, trying to produce words, but everything was strangled in my throat as I took in the woman's sun-streaked hair, dancing green eyes, and warm smile lines— none of which had vanished.

"You—"

"Hello, sweet girl."

"Oh, my God." Was this happening? Was she actually sitting here, the woman who'd only made cameo appearances for most of my life? "C-Caroline. It's really you...right?"

She brushed strands of hair off my face. "Yes, sweetie. It's really me." Her stare... She didn't just look at me. She peered through me, as if needing to read every thought in my head. Normally, I'd think it was creepy. At the very least, irritating as hell. But I only felt...cherished. Special. Completely perfect in her eyes.

A fresh flood of tears burst out.

Caroline drew me into her arms, crooning quiet sounds of comfort and strength. "It's all right, my little star. Sshhh. It's going to be all right."

I burrowed against her shoulder. "How—how did you know I'd be here?"

"I've always known where you were. I've never left you. I just couldn't come near because of—"

"That witch who dabbled at being a mother? Yes, I know what happened, how she turned you out for getting too close to me."

"She's not here anymore. I am—and I always will be. I'll never, ever leave you." Her grasp closed tighter, but her voice grew shakier. "You are the most important thing in my world, my beautiful girl. I knew it—I swore it—from the moment they put you in my arms and I first laid eyes on your beautiful face."

Tears. Breath. Thought. Stopped.

Shock. Amazement. Joy.

Oh.

My.

God.

Now what?

"I—" I pulled back, gawking at her. In so many ways, it was like peering at an older version of myself. "How the hell did I not see it before?"

She laughed. The sound was feminine and cute but flared with snark—just like mine. "Of course you knew, my little Mary." She pressed three fingers to the space over my heart. "Deep in here. Where it mattered the most."

"Holy shit."

I threw myself at her, hugging her so tightly that if a

hurricane hit the beach right now, she wouldn't be ripped from me again. After she joined a lot more tears to mine, I managed to rasp the one word in the world I never imagined speaking with love.

"Mom."

She burst with another sob, the sound that belonged to dammed-up emotions finally granted freedom. "I've waited twenty-seven years to hear that, honey. And every second was worth it."

CHAPTER SEVENTEEN

Michael

"Dude. This is amazing."

I couldn't help but laugh. "Sorry," I explained, cocking a brow at Killian, "I just don't think I've ever heard you say dude."

"Surfer Jesus has to represent sometimes." He finished it with a grin, still circling his stare around the small underground cavern I'd led him to. Watery patterns danced across his face courtesy of the LED lights Carlo had mounted to the walls, though they were the only signs of recent technology down here. On the other lip of the spring, about thirty feet away, a grotto was consumed by an electric pump that would've been at home during the days of Reaganomics and *Flashdance*.

"What does surfer Jesus think about all this?" I asked.

"He's impressed," Kil returned. "There's workable infrastructure here. I think we can access the spring with very little impact to the orchard." His face tightened as he went on with noticeable care, "The only thing that might have to be relocated...is the main house."

I almost chuckled again. "Go ahead. You can breathe. Mom and I don't have fond attachments to the building itself." *Not with the ghost of Declan lurking in nearly every room.* "Razing it to the ground and starting something new might even be therapeutic."

He nodded, picking up my subtext with his famous sixth sense. "You'll have the money to erect a castle after we're done with this deal."

"Mom's not the castle type."

He worked his jaw back and forth as if tempted to spin that comment—toward the subject of a certain princess, perhaps? I whipped back a searing glare, sending a silent message of my own with it. *Don't go there, Stone.*

Wisely, he rolled his shoulders. Wiser still, he snapped back to business mode. "I'd like to send out a survey team next, along with an environmental engineering crew. They'll measure everything out, take a bunch of soil samples, examine the farm's layout again, that sort of shit."

I frowned. "Is all that necessary at this point?"

"In this case, it is. I predict things are going to move quickly and you want SGC to broker a deal that'll make everyone happy, including your neighbors. That means working smarter, not harder."

I smiled and nodded to mask my jolt of realization. *Wow. Shit was getting real.*

"Here's the number for my buddy, Fletcher Ford." He pulled a business card out of his pocket and extended it. "He owns FF Engineering and will personally supervise the survey as a favor to me."

My smile grew. "Yeah. I remember meeting him at your wedding. Good guy." I clapped his shoulder. "Thanks for all this, Kil."

One side of his mouth lifted in slow sarcasm. "Aren't you glad you didn't beat the shit out of me last year?"

I mocked a glare. "Smartass."

"Pretty boy."

"Pretty? What the hell?"

"Hmmm. Good point. Normally, you are much prettier."

His tone hinted at enough sobriety to yank me back in the same direction. "Sleep hasn't been abundant lately. Managing a lot of the shit around here and then up and down most nights with Mom..." I shrugged, knowing the rest would fill itself in.

Killian did that—and then some. Damn it.

"Fairly sure those aren't the only reasons, man."

I leaned against the wall, glad I hadn't fully surrendered the glare. The guy was as smooth as his custom leather jacket. Though the rest of his attire—beat-up cargo pants, a faded Henley, and shit-kickers—conveyed a badass vibe, I wasn't intimidated. "That's not a subject we're tromping to, Kil. I invited you up here for advice about our options for rights on the spring. You knew the boundaries coming in."

He narrowed a contemplative gaze. "Boundaries? You used your mom's pie as bribery, dude."

"It got you here, didn't it?"

He found a sizable boulder and straddled it. "Agreed." Angled a smirk up at me. "As you know, I do like bending boundaries."

My shoulders tensed. Screw it—everything else did too. "Fuck."

"Oh, come on." He planted his elbows to his knees and threaded his fingers. "Did you really think you'd get out of this without the get-your-head-out-of-your-ass speech?"

I turned my back on him, ground a fist against the stone wall, welcoming the distraction of the pain. "Too good to hope for, huh?"

"Pretty much."

"God damn it."

His answering pause was not encouraging. "Stop kicking at the ground like a twelve-year-old. Your game's already transparent, man."

"Who says I've got a game?"

"The guy who dabbles in playing them for a living."

Bastard had a point.

I glowered over my shoulder. "All right, oh great and wise enigma. What is my game?"

He squared his shoulders while sliding his fingers atop his thighs. "It's called your-head's-up-your-ass, remember? Like that one we played as kids, where everyone gets to pull the little plastic body parts out of the electric holes, only you're going to need something bigger than those tweezers."

"Such as?"

"My boot."

I pivoted, baring a challenging grin. "Little hint? That'll probably set off the buzzer. Sorry, you lose."

"Not if I kick so hard your skull pops out your dick."

He let that one plummet right into silence. Long, unnerving gobs of it.

"Shit," I finally muttered.

"Something like that."

A hard push off the wall sent me pacing across the packed dirt. "I'm not going to do this, goddamnit."

Kil rose as well. "The fuck you aren't."

"Okay, listen—"

"No." He arrowed a finger back to the boulder. "This time, you'll listen." He cocked his head, flinging our imaginary ball back to my end of the court. "Unless you're not serious about loving Margaux...about wanting to protect her?"

I wheeled around. "Fuck you."

"That's not happening either." His outstretched hand didn't falter. "Sit the hell down."

I openly snarled.

Then reluctantly sat.

Killian lowered his hand with solemnity that made my teeth grind. Why the hell was he evoking an emo-goth video? The fucker wasn't the one now contemplating barbed wire atop his property's border fence or waiting for a whacked-out band of organized-crime thugs to break in and shoot up his home in the name of Declan Pearson's unpaid gambling debts.

And why the hell are you so pissed about it, wuss? You're the one who invited him up here. Did you expect he'd show without an agenda of his own for the meeting, dictated by Claire, if not Margaux herself?

No. Not Margaux. Definitely not Margaux.

I won't be back again, Michael. Not like this. Not ever again like this.

Or, for that matter, in any other way.

She hadn't said it, but she hadn't needed to. Her tearless sorrow, there in the mist, had conveyed the message clearly enough—and her ensuing eight days of radio silence had congealed the message into reality. There hadn't been a call, email, or text, not even to Mom's phone. Yeah, I'd spied again. No, I didn't regret it.

And, yeah, here I sat, maybe a little baffled by it. A little bit more ticked off.

A thousand more kinds of scared.

Why? She was back in the city, and she was safe. I knew that much, thanks to Doug's regular reports. That was the goddamn end of that.

So why the hell did it feel like just the beginning—especially as Killian strode to stand in front of me, feet spread, hands deep in his pockets?

"For the record, both Claire and Margaux think I'm at the LA Auto Show today."

Time for a double-take. "Why?"

"Because I'm about to force some major reality down your throat—along with a few other tasty morsels of ugliness. Because of that, I'm only going to say it all once—and you'll never speak of it outside this cave again. Got that, dude?"

I frowned.."Yeah."

For a long moment, he didn't speak again. My face tightened. Why did I expect spooky music to pour from the walls before Kil transformed into an eight-foot giant with a beard like a tumbleweed? *You're a wizard, Michael...*

Killian didn't help the impression by tossing up his head and then staring at the ceiling.

"Okay, dude," I finally bit out. "What the hell?"

"Sorry." He grunted and then sniffed, lowering a look of introspection. "I was reaching for a word to better describe your paranoia, but it's hopeless. Pearson, you're paranoid."

"That's the classified information I'm supposed to take to my grave?"

"That was an appetizer."

I rolled my eyes. "Buttering me up to get the boot all the way in?"

"Please. I can do that part by myself." He rocked back on his heels. "But you ever think that it takes one to know one?"

He was sure as hell determined to milk the double-takes out of me. "Huh?"

He paused again. Pivoted with enough precision to

make good in a military parade, and began pacing with equal deliberation. I watched with interest. I'd seen a lot of versions of the Kil Stone pace, but this one was different. It had an end game.

"So...welcome to Club Paranoia."

"Thanks. I think." I studied him again. "You been president of this outfit for long?"

He stopped. Linked hands behind his back. "Oh, I'm not president. Too obvious."

"So you're the CIA?"

A smile lifted one side of his chiseled jaw. "Sneakier. More like coordinating the SEALs."

I could respect that. But was still confused. "Where are you going with this?"

"As you might remember, you're not the only one with evil bats in the family belfry."

"Whoa." I let him see my rocketing brows. "Of course." But not really. Of all the subjects I'd expected Kil to broach, Trey didn't remotely make the list. The asshole's name topped even religion and politics when it came to taboo subjects when hanging with the man. The oldest of the four Stone family heirs was the rotten fruit on their family tree, the sphincter who'd been responsible for exposing a family secret so destructive, Killian had pulled a Howard Hughes on the world for six months last year.

More recently—and even worse—Trey had attempted to blackmail Margaux for her own cut of the Stone fortune. When I'd discovered he was in league with Andrea Asher, the person responsible for fucking up Margaux's head the most, I'd worked with Kil to report their deceit to the FBI. But as the saying went, good deeds didn't go unpunished. Before the Feds could close in on Trey and Andrea, the pair fled the country, where, as best I knew, they remained—and, as much as I cared, could stay. Regrettably, Kil had a bigger stake than I in hauling them back to the States to face justice—as he confirmed the next second.

"You're a smart guy, Pearson. Do the math. You think I'd be satisfied with the spooks having all the fun of locating my brother and his sweet lady love?"

I snorted. "Just point when you want me to laugh at all that."

"Better indulge now," he advised.

I leaned forward. "Why?"

"Because my boys are damn good at what they do—which means I had no trouble redeploying them to a new assignment two weeks ago."

Shock tumbled through my gut like a knot of barbed wire. "Declan Pearson."

"Like I said...smart guy."

Acid started eating at the wire inside. I didn't waste time asking how he even knew about the mess with Dec. It didn't matter and was actually a relief. Perhaps he'd been able to give Margaux some comfort and advice about it over the last month. For that, I was thankful. Killian's discretion was better than a priest's.

But for this...

I had no idea how to feel.

No answers came. Only a slew of new questions.

I scrubbed a hand down my face. "Why the hell did you waste money on watching that douche? And how long has this been going on?" More critically, had Declan caught on to the tail by Kil's ninja boys? Was that why he hadn't shown at the farm?

Killian's spine stiffened so much, he gained at least an inch in height. "I didn't get to be one of the world's most successful son of a bitches by wasting my money, Michael... especially not on scum like your uncle. But know this"—his eyes narrowed, and his jaw hardened—"I'll go bankrupt in a heartbeat if it means defending the people I love and ensuring their happiness. Couldn't do much about the latter when you shattered my sister's heart, but I sure as hell could tackle the security issue with a waste of DNA like Declan."

"Which is still an issue." I refused to let him sway me from the decision I'd made about Margaux. "Declan's still alive and well and ready to cause havoc somewhere, I'm sure of it. If he wasn't, Mom and I would've been informed as next of kin."

I didn't expect the slight incline of his head, giving wordless respect for my conviction—but that surprise was kicked to my rearview after he spoke again. "Well, you haven't been informed...yet."

I pushed up, hands on thighs, the barbed wire in my gut slicing to my nerve endings. "What the hell?"

His mouth quirked. "Let's just say the Principals aren't the memento book sort."

"Shit," I muttered. "So you know about them too?"

"Impossible not to, under the circumstances."

My reaction to that was a weird mesh. Part of me abhorred the confirmation that Dec was still in bed with those bastards. It had been easier to hope he'd just gone to ground on his own, staying away from the farm so they wouldn't track him there. The other half seized at the crazy clue Kil had just dropped...

"What...circumstances?"

His answering stare was like diamonds glittering on coal.

"My guys picked up the asshole's trail about ten days ago. Found him poolside at the Belmond Copacabana, in Rio."

Screw the nerve endings. Shock went straight for the center of my chest. "What the hell?"

"He was there with a couple of the Principals' big ponies, burning through blow and babes like the world was ending." He lifted both hands. "Whoa there, tiger. Breathe. The story's not done."

"I sure as fuck hope not." The growl calmed me enough to keep my ass planted.

"My guys were just as shocked," Kil went on. "They assumed Declan had signed on totally with the dark side and was being set up to run an operation in Cidade Maravilhosa for the organization."

"And?"

"Well, a setup was the idea."

"Meaning what?"

"On their third night there, Declan met on a couple of reps from one of the biggest cartels in the city. The face-to-face took place on a yacht, with full suits, champagne toasts, and shit. My guys assumed it was a deal-sealer on an alliance with the cartel and the Principals—until the yacht returned a full two hours later, and only the fancy boys from the cartel disembarked."

My eyes flared as my jaw dropped. "Huh?"

Kil kicked up a brow, his version of *that's not all, kids.* "After the crew cleaned up and left, one of my guys sneaked aboard the vessel for the full scoop—but there wasn't one."

"At all?" I pressed.

"Not even a stray drop of bubbly," he countered, "let alone any weapons, signs of a struggle, or a thread of evidence that Declan had been aboard." He hitched the brow again. "But while my first guy searched the yacht, his buddy found the marina's trash bins. Surprise, surprise—there was a wiped diving knife stashed in one of the bags on top, along with two pairs of bloodied work gloves." He paused, hands behind his back again. "Just a guess, but I think the sharks off the coast of Brazil were happy campers that night."

For the first time, I was glad my ass was still parked on the rock. Even so, the strength drained from my legs as all the air rushed from my lungs—and a weight lifted from my conscience that was damn near a religious experience. As I looked back up, the cavern tilted in my vision. And I'd always thought dizzy with relief was just a stupid expression.

"Shit."

I blurted it on a laugh. Was it really all over? Here, in the beauty of the cave Declan had fought such ugly battles for... Was this the moment I'd actually get to finally spit on his memory and accept my final justice?

It was eerie.

And poetic.

And so fucking cool.

"I don't know what to say." I looked up, hoping Kil would see that glaring truth in me. Thanking him seemed like taking a bite from an elephant—meaningless and stupid. "I just thought—"

"You were in this alone because you've never known things any other way?" One side of his mouth kicked up, confident he'd bulls-eyed that one. "At the risk of sounding redundant, takes one to know one, man."

I leaned over, letting my head fall while trying to wrap logic around that. Since Killian had finally done right by Claire, I had no problems with the guy, but seeing parallels between his life and mine was like staring at one of those eye-trick paintings they sold on the boardwalk and never getting the bigger picture.

"So what now?"

He angled his head—eyes narrowed the same way as ten minutes ago, when wondering how to spin my castle comment. "You remember the part about me promising to pull your head from your ass?"

"Fuck."

He growled loud. "Sit the hell back down."

I took another defiant stomp from the boulder. "Why? To have you make a point that still isn't valid?"

"Cut the fuckery, dickwad," Kil snarled. "You think I didn't see this mass of crap coming from you either? That I didn't know what a hardhead you'd be even after learning your uncle's black heart has been ground into shark loaves?" He whipped up a hand, Sermon Jesus style. "I can already write this script for you. It goes something along the lines of, 'Damn it, Kil. This doesn't change a thing. That ship has sailed. Margaux Asher has cut me free and she's all the better for it.'"

I closed my jaw with an audible whump. "And what if she is?"

While lowering his hand, he turned it into a fist. "You know, I'd crack you across the face right now, Pearson, but I'm enjoying the sight of that chicken beak sprouting from your pretty nose."

"Excuse the hell out of me?"

He leaned over with unblinking accusation. "Go ahead, man. Keep making this about her welfare, her best interests, the fear you have of fucking up her life, but you're not fooling the original chicken-shit-for-brains on this."

I reared back. "You have no goddamn idea what you're talking ab—"

"Shut up. I'm not finished." His glare turned darker. "Not by a long shot."

As comprehension hit, my own stare flared. Was the weirdness on his face...shame?

"You're the only person I've ever told this to—and so we're clear, this shit will go to your grave with you."

Damn.

I sat up straighter, unsure whether to be honored, freaked, or both. "You haven't even told Claire?"

"Not yet." His shoulders developed a full hunch from tension. "I will, just not...now. This isn't the kind of thing divulged over wine and dinner."

Understanding struck again, this time square in my balls. "Holy fuck. You and Margaux did get horizontal, didn't you?"

"What?" He whirled. "No! Christ."

I pushed out a heavy breath. "Thank fuck."

He turned. Resumed the pacing thing. This gait, I recognized. It belonged to the Killian Stone of the family's prime scandal days, a guy resolved to meet every crisis head-on, march through the crucible, and emerge on the other side stronger for it.

What the hell was he about to tell me that met such criteria?

"Last year, when I vanished from the grid, I existed in some low places, mentally and physically."

I leveled a questioning stare. "So? We'd all suspected as much."

"I missed Claire...like the fucking sun. That was why I kept moving. Too long in one place, and I'd begin to think about what an ass I'd been, what a failure the world had painted me to be...how I thought I'd failed her."

"'The world'?" I snorted. "You mean the three-point-five percent of the population who gave a damn about your real birthright? The herd of sheep led by the 'financial experts' who take consulting gigs with news media just to write off their facelifts and bad toupees?"

Before I finished, he'd pivoted around, arms folded, a cocky smirk spreading his lips. "Funny how small it all seems now, right?"

So this was what the view looked like—from the corner one had just painted themselves into. "Do you have a real point?"

He turned and restarted the methodical pacing. "I stayed on the move. Couldn't stay in one place for too long. If I kept moving, nothing would...hurt. Didn't have a rhyme or reason, just shifted to the places where it became easiest to lop off more pieces of myself and leave them behind." He stopped. The hunch of his shoulders got bigger. "By the time I hit the other side of Texas, I wasn't sure who the guy in the mirror was anymore—not that I was peering at too many mirrors by then. I just...couldn't figure it out. Who the fuck had I become? The only answer that made any sense was the face I couldn't forget, mirrors or no."

I nodded in quiet understanding. "Claire's."

"She knew...everything," he confirmed. "You know that, right? All of it, all the secrets about me. Even before Trey took them public, she knew them and she didn't care. She knew me, loved me, for me." He lifted his head, illuminating the new torment across his features. "Then I left her."

For a long moment, I studied that prominent profile.

Amazing. Even in the midst of a self-flogging, Killian Stone was the picture of composed command. I wondered if the guy had ever lost his shit, even in front of Claire.

Finally, I asked, "Why?" Asked, not accused. I was sincerely curious about what had driven him to vanish from society for half a year.

His reply was simplicity and complexity in one. "I was lost," he explained. "He was lost. At least I thought so. The man Claire Montgomery had fallen in love with, everything I assumed she valued in him, was stripped away after Trey worked his magic with my reputation. Once I ran off after that bar fight, I was stupid enough to think I'd embarked on some romantic vision quest, out to find the man I really was..."

"And you learned Yoda was actually just a Muppet?"

We shared a short laugh.

A very short laugh.

"Trouble is, it took me four months to realize it," he uttered. "And when I did, the need for her—to see her, to hear her—hit me like one of the trucks parked outside the Texas burger dive I sat in." His face contorted harder. "Like she was the key...back to me."

I didn't say anything. Talking got difficult when a guy felt like someone had pried open his head, dug out his most terrifying thought, and then let that oh-so-awesome freak flag fly.

"One of the drivers lent me his phone. I couldn't punch in her number fast enough."

My heavy swallow matched his. "But she didn't pick up?"

"Oh, she picked up."

"And?"

"And I couldn't say a fucking word." He slowly shook his

head. "From the moment she uttered her greeting, it was—well, it was hell. She had no idea it was me on the line, and I still heard it all in her voice...the pain she'd been through...the battles she'd waged to get through the days we'd been apart. Until then, I had no concept of what I'd done to her. She's such a rock, you know?"

I didn't disguise my disappointment. "Rocks break."

He smacked a hand on the wall. "They also survive."

"A lot of times, after breaking."

"Not a lesson I didn't learn, my friend—the hard way. I turned to dust because I'd done the same to her. I had no clue what to do for her—or for me, at that point. I couldn't speak."

"Not one word?" I fired back. "As in, letting her know you were okay and not balls-up in a gutter somewhere? Telling her you missed her? That you still loved her?"

"I was a moron."

"Damn right you were."

"Selfish."

"Still no argument."

He cocked his head, exposing his face fully to me again. "That wasn't even the end of it."

Surprising, how his confession wasn't a surprise. I lifted a black stare, the same one I used on Keir when he dropped in a workout surprise of fifty more soft-sand burpees. "Shit."

He coiled and uncoiled his fists. "After I gave the driver back his phone...I asked if he knew where I could get a gun fast."

I shot back to my feet. "What the fuck for?"

He gazed back out over the water. Other than that, he was as unreadable as the walls around us.

"Killian?"

More of the human stone wall impersonation. The harsh jerk of his shoulders didn't herald unicorns and pixie dust either. "As I said, I was in a bad place."

"You don't fucking say." I wasn't bound to the granite-for-blood thing, and thank God. I stomped from one end of the little shore to the other. "How much of a bad place?"

"I'm still here, aren't I? I got as far as buying the thing, making off to the bathroom, and lifting the barrel to my mouth—and then stopped cold, trying to remember if I'd ever read anything about the proper angle for blowing one's brains out."

"Christ fucking wept."

"Now you understand why I didn't tell anyone I'd returned to San Diego and was living on the yacht." His eyes raced with determined shadows. "I refused to be away from her any longer but couldn't be near her either. Not in that fucked-up state."

"I take it you found a good shrink too?"

A smile floated across his lips. "I saw Doc Straten before even moving my shit aboard the Queen."

"And he was the one who encouraged you to paint."

"Smart young bucko." His smirk widened before totally fading again, committed once more to his audition for gargoyle status. He did prove his feet still worked, turning toward me once more. "That hour, alone in that bathroom with that gun, was the most selfish thing I've ever done in my life, Michael."

I stopped and pounded a stare into him. "Don't think I'll deny you that one, either, man."

He took another step. Raised his chin and folded his arms as if he moved through water, graceful but resolute. "So when are you going to pull the gun out of your mouth?"

Now I was the frozen one. A thousand daggers of ice in

one's bloodstream usually does that. After a breath finally made its way to my lungs, I blinked in harsh disbelief.

Idiot.

How the hell hadn't I seen that coming from a hundred miles away?

The answer hit with furious clarity.

"You're pushing apples and oranges," I seethed. "Freud-talking your cash-out from humanity doesn't erase the fact that you did it or the agony you caused. It sure as hell doesn't qualify you to read the roadmap in my head."

He cocked an eyebrow. "Didn't know that shit was such a state secret."

I stabbed a figure between his chest and mine. "We aren't the same, Killian. This isn't the same!"

"Hmmm." He rolled his head a couple of times, a deceptive ode to relaxation. As he fastened his stare to me once more, nothing about him was remotely relaxed. "I'm not sure whether to call bullshit on your ass now"—in one lunge he pinned me against the rock, forearm caging my sternum—"or maybe now. Yeah, this is better."

I growled and shoved back. Kil pressed in harder, backing up the motion with a glare dark as coal, snorting like a damn rhino.

"Fucking hell!"

"Took the words right out of my mouth." He bared his teeth—the rhino turned black adder. "That's a good thing, considering I'd get myself all riled up and want to turn this into a true choke hold." He cocked his head, looming closer. "Not that it won't be out of the question, once I consider the state you left my sister in."

I relented on the escape effort, though not without a deep

snarl. My lungs stretched for air, heaving my body beneath his clutch. Jackhole. He knew what a mention of Margaux would do to me. "You think I enjoyed any part of what I did?" I countered. "Any part of those decisions? Any second of hurting her like that?"

His glare turned incredulous. "That's what you're calling it, eh? Hurting her? Awww. So noble, so tragic. Poor, poor Saint Pearson. You had to hurt her to save her, yeah?" He nodded, seeming to reach a secret satisfaction. "No wonder you're sleeping for shit. And I'm really fucking glad."

I grimaced as if hit by a toxic stench. "Margaux is strong."

"Just like Claire was?" he countered. "Like a rock, right?"

"I'll be a blip on her radar in a month!"

He released me with a brutal shove. Laughed without a shred of mirth. "Holy hell. That bubble of delusion you're living in must be such fun, Pearson. But hey, you're right on target, calling out my bad in comparing my fuck-up to yours. I got that all wrong, considering I slept next to hobos with a better grip on reality than you."

"Shut up." The words were weary and angry and frustrated, perfect accelerants for the rage that finally exploded, driving me away from the wall. "Shut up, okay?"

"Not a problem." He spun toward the passage that led back out to the orchard. "Mustn't dent the bubble, after all." Stopped short to swing the side of a fist into the tunnel's support frame. "Man, I was a moron...thinking you were made of tougher stuff. That supporting Claire through all my bullshit would help you save Margaux from yours."

He'd barely uttered the words, but the cavern's ventilation picked them up, blasting them back through the air. Not that he needed the architectural help—after speaking the words that delivered my second paralysis of the night.

Save.

Margaux.

"Save Margaux." I'd said it so many times over the last month. As a vow, as a credo, as a promise, as a fucking plea to any higher power willing to listen—but never like this. The words crawled from my gut like a question, tearing past every conviction I'd had since deciding to let her go, in those bleak hours in the UCSD waiting room. I'd never known terror like the slime that crawled over me that day. As my exhaustion had progressed, the memories of Mom received nerve-shaking overlays. I began to see Margaux's face and body covered in bruises and blood instead. When Margaux finally appeared in the waiting room, I'd been petrified to look. Was she real...or a wraith?

It was the worst moment of my life. But it had given me the courage to make that clean break. Snap her off, set her free...keep her safe.

I'd clung to that feeling just to keep going. Remembering the fear meant keeping alert, staying alive...staying sane.

Remembering the fear.

Welcoming the fear.

"Holy. Shit." Both words choked up from my gut.

It's paralyzing you, Michael...trapping you...

"Holy. Shit." It needed to be repeated.

Mom was right. And fuck me, Killian was right. I was so addicted to fear, I'd woven a damn superhero suit out of it—*to keep everyone safe.*

You fucking fraud.

The suit wasn't to keep everyone safe. It was to keep everyone out.

Even myself.

Now, I was trapped inside the thing—even with the knowledge of Declan's carcass at the bottom of the Atlantic—with the zipper glued shut.

"Killian!"

He scuffed to a stop outside the tunnel's entrance. Said nothing as I caught up, though his face reflected something new. I prayed like hell that it was hope.

"Did you drive the Aston Martin up?"

He cracked half a grin. "Knowing I was going to get in some mountain hairpins? What do you think?"

I smiled back. It was damn awesome to be feeling the vibe behind it again. "Can I talk you into pushing the RPMs higher back to the city? With a guest passenger?" Though the car came damn close, I wished it was a space-age transporter. Every cell of my body threatened to explode with the need to crush my princess in my arms again.

Kil split a blinding grin of his own. "That is entirely possible, my friend."

A sensation surged me, strange but welcome. It took a couple of seconds to recognize it. Exhilaration. Despite that, as we walked back to the main house, the suit of fear tightened again. "Shit. What if she refuses to talk to me? What if I'm too late?"

Kil grunted and punched my shoulder. "You want to give my sister more credit than that?"

"What the hell does that—?"

"Pack a bag, dumb shit. You're not too late." He slanted a knowing glance. "Just one helpful hint, if I may?"

"Yeah. Of course."

"Keep your head out of your ass this time, yeah?"

★ ★ ★ ★

"What's going on?"

Mom appeared in the doorway to my room, obviously startled by the way Kil and I had barreled into the house. Poor woman probably hadn't heard that much pounding on the stairs since I was eight, dragging in my friends from our superhero skirmishes in the orchard to demand an afternoon snack.

I looked up, bolting my stare to hers, not even trying to hide the swell of feeling that overtook me. Instantly, her eyes bulged.

"Michael."

Air burst off my lips. A laugh? A sob? No. Neither. The moment surpassed those boundaries. It was too damn surreal. Too damn good.

"Mom."

"Michael?"

Just like that, a grin split my lips. "Dec is dead."

She plunked onto the bed. Her hands shook in her lap. "Wh-What?"

"It's true." Killian inserted it as if he knew she needed the outside confirmation.

"Oh, my God." Her face twisted on a sob as she rose again, crushing me with a hug. "Oh, thank God."

I returned the ferocity of her hold until my shoulder was soaked with her tears—the best puddle I'd ever wear in my life. I was still smiling as she finally pulled back, though a new frown crumpled her features.

"So...where are you going?" She scowled at my bag.

"Kil's driving me back to the city," I explained. "He's got

his Aston Martin, so we'll fly." Right now, that was exactly the intention. "I'll come back for the truck this weekend and to check on you."

Her excited smile formed at last. "And it won't be Killian driving you?"

I leaned and kissed her cheek. "That's the idea, mama bear."

She let out a squee and then hauled me into another stranglehold. "Holy shit! At last!"

I chuckled. "Guess I'll bring a big bar of soap with me too."

"Pssshhh. Just go get our girl. Shoo, both of you."

I didn't need to be told twice.

★ ★ ★ ★

By the time Kil dropped me at the El Cortez, the setting sun danced with dramatic clouds across the downtown skyline. I thanked him—well, tried to—and then took a moment to look around before entering the building. The gold and gray twilight washed over the neighborhood, turning the pavement and walls and windows into something ethereal. The transition between day and night was one of Margaux's favorite times of the day, when she could simply stop and be. I wondered if that was how I'd find her...and if we'd be able to borrow some of Mother Nature's alchemy for ourselves.

Just one magic moment. Please.

I yearned for it so badly, I stopped and prayed for it.

As the elevator took me higher, my pulse pounded my body like artillery tests from Pendleton, shaking every foundation until the roots of my teeth rattled. My sweaty palm slipped on my duffel's strap as I readjusted it against my shoulder. The ding at the fifteenth floor jolted me like rifle fire.

"Man up, candy ass." I channeled the determination into every stride toward the condo door. I didn't dare think of it as our condo door again, though I went ahead and grabbed the proverbial bull by fishing out my key and testing it in the lock.

It still fit.

The door clicked open.

My chest turned into a nuclear test range.

I wasn't sure what to expect when I walked in—or that she'd even be home. It had just felt right to come here. At this time of night, we were usually on the couch making fun of the trashy TV gossip shows or on the patio having dinner and trading sarcasm—mental stimulation usually ending in fun of other kinds.

Right now, I just hoped she wouldn't toss my ass back out into the hall.

Music. An alt-rock station.

I kicked up half a grin. No surprise there. Our debates about the merits of Led Zeppelin versus Coldplay were a running joke in our relationship. Or had been.

Two factors turned this particular discovery into a surprise. One, the Coldplay tune was coming from the kitchen. Two, Margaux was singing along to it. And she wasn't alone.

I stopped short after the air itself delivered surprise number three.

It smelled like cookies. Actual, baked-in-the-oven, non-burned, tons-of-butter-and-other-crap cookies.

I dropped my bag as quietly as I could. Just as carefully, stepped around the corner.

After that, silence wasn't such a problem. If asked to issue even a word, I would've been a dumbstruck fool.

The woman of my dreams had never taken my breath away more. Her hair was pulled in a high poof of a ponytail over her makeup-less face, which was smudged with flour. A streak of red frosting trailed down her neck, and I instantly imagined licking it off.

Are you even considering the concept of letting your dick lead on this one, fuck brain?

There were some pressing priorities on top of that anyhow—like the thousand questions about who stood next to her. I'd stared at the truth for at least a minute and still hardly believed it. She was really here, the woman so elusive I'd almost thought her a ghost if not for the photos Margaux had kept pristine as a shrine. Though she was almost twenty years older, hardly anything had changed about the structured beauty of her features.

Caroline.

What the hell?

It wasn't even the most stunning revelation. Staring at her now, sharing a laugh with my girl as she iced a star-shaped sugar cookie, the truth hit like a damn nuclear holocaust.

"Well, hello there." The woman's resemblance to Margaux was even more stunning as she looked up, smiling as if I'd just returned from fetching them some more flour.

Margaux tossed Caroline a puzzled glance before her periphery snagged on me. "Holy shit." A knife full of frosting dropped from her hand, streaking her apron and the floor with red. I swallowed, hoping the murder scene palette wasn't a harbinger of things to come.

I finally managed coherency. "Hey."

Margaux wiped her hands on the apron, smearing the red shit even more but hardly noticing. Her gaze crashed into mine, glistening and tremoring though she clenched the tears back, ordering them not to spill over onto her face. Her breathtaking, soul-stealing, torment-filled face.

"Hey." She barely rasped it. I watched her start to unspool the mental caution tape, her expression switching from cookie-making joy to monster confrontation. I hated that look. I hated myself for being the cause of it—but law school gave no pointers on conveying the right demeanor for this one. So I stood there like a goddamn slab, hoping my remorse blasted through the rips in my gut.

"Michael." Thank fuck for the third wheel in the room, proving to be the savior of the moment. "I'm so glad we finally get to meet," Caroline said while seizing me in a full hug. Her warm grip was so much like Mom's, I forgot to be stunned. "I'm Violet. Mary's mother."

That did it. My confusion was officially validated. "But...I..."

She smirked back at Margaux. "Eloquent, isn't he?"

I ignored Margaux's answering eye roll. "Your name's supposed to be Caroline."

"Ahhhh." She pulled her hands up beneath her chin. "There's the tiger on your tongue. Caroline was the name Andrea made me take when I lived with her and Mary." As she looked to Margaux, I recognized I wasn't the only one in the place battling regrets. "A legally binding contract was the only way she'd let me be near Mary at all. I signed it in desperation when Mary was four days old, never comprehending Andrea would consider throwing me out."

Her voice cracked as she relayed the story, the pain tangibly mixing with the butter and sugar aromas in the air.

Margaux wrapped both hands around her mother's.

"Ancient history now, Mom."

The smile she gave the woman turned me back into a block of clay. I'd never seen such a look on her face before. A new light infused her skin and glowed from her eyes, reminding me of angelic maidens in illuminated manuscripts from the obligatory museums in Europe.

Great. Now I was a star-struck poet—who still stood like a speechless lump. Her joy from reuniting with Caroline—Violet—was clear as sunlight on the bay. Maybe she'd come to the conclusion that I was actually useless weight in her life, best cut free forever.

If that was the case, it was best to find out now. God damn it.

"I'm honored to meet you, Violet," I forced out. "And from the bottom of my heart to yours, thank you for having the courage to come forward."

I wanted to say more but was suddenly edgy. Hopefully, the soft smile I directed at Margaux was my megaphone. *Most of all, thank you for making her so happy.*

When the older woman smiled, I knew at least part of the message had gotten through. "Please, call me Caroline if that's more comfortable for you. It's my middle name anyhow." Her sparkle faded by a degree as she added, "As for my courage? Well, that should have happened sooner. When I think of how Andrea's pettiness kept me leashed—"

"Okay, stop." Margaux locked both smudged hands on her blue jeans-covered hips. "Wallowing is for swine. And we'll let the authorities deal with Andrea Asher. She's not worth another second of our energy."

I cast a meaningful glance at the cookies. "Especially when there's important other work going on."

Caroline laughed. Her energy was a little less intense than Margaux's, imparting a peaceful happiness to the air. "This sweet girl is helping me fill baskets for the Children's Hospital bake sale. We do it every year at the Seaport Village holiday kick-off festival. It's a lot of fun. You two should come!"

I averted my gaze. From the rustle of her apron, I judged Margaux had done the same, betraying the sync of our thoughts. The last time we'd ventured over to the Village, truths had been shared, passions exchanged, unforgettable moments created. Just thinking about it eased the weight on my chest. Those had been some dark times, but we'd made it through. Did I dare hope that such a light would shine for us again?

"I think it might rain tonight." Margaux's nervous murmur disrupted the silence. "I'd better go cover up the chaises and barbecue."

"I'll help." I fell into step behind her, not leaving her time to protest. If she wanted me out of here, now was her opportunity to let me know—and I didn't doubt she'd use it.

We'd stepped all the way out to the patio before she turned again.

Correction. Spun.

Shit.

I braced myself for the princess seethe but was broadsided by her quiet grief instead. She waged an intense battle against her tears, nose crinkling and lips twisting. "Just shoot it to me straight, Pearson."

The mandate, I should have anticipated. Knife through the bullshit... There was my perfect princess.

"Well?" She braced hands to her hips. "What can I do to really help you, Michael? Did you come back to grab more clothes? Pack up your shit for good? You weren't just passing through, that's for damn sure."

I dragged in a deep breath. *Calm. Calm. Calm.*

"You're right." Damn it. In this case, calm also meant cagey. I refused to get in her face like a shoe salesman on commission, demanding she buy my plea for redemption if she'd already cut up her card for my store. "As a matter of fact, Killian dropped me off."

That got rid of the tears. She flashed a trio of stunned blinks. "The hell how? Or why?"

"Because I wanted to get back here as soon as possible, and he was the one at the farm with the Aston Martin."

"The farm? No. He went to the car show in LA."

"He told you and Claire that." I dared half a step more toward her, thankful my news had mystified her too much to notice. "He came clean to Claire when we were driving back in."

"And she forgave him?"

"When she found out why he kept the trip a secret? Yes."

She tilted her head, training her wary cat's gaze on me. "Why'd he keep it a secret?"

"Because he might not have been successful in his mission."

"His what?"

"You heard me. He had a mission. I was part of it."

"A mission to do what?"

I leaned a hand against the barbecue. The move didn't box her in completely, but she'd have to scramble backward over one of the chaises to escape me at this point.

Dear God, don't let her want to escape me.

"To yank my head out of my ass."

Her face crumpled with new emotion. The look didn't disclose anything about whether she'd longed or dreaded to hear that. Her heavy swallow didn't help either.

"So...was he successful?"

What the hell was the right reply for that? A dorky nod? Oh, that's smooth, dweeb. A tentative yes, blurted like one of the drops that began falling from the clouds, splatted into nothing between us when done? Because she'll find that so much more appealing? Or trust it at all? Like that was happening. She had no reason to trust any testimony I gave, declaration I swore, or promise I vowed.

She had no reason...so I had only one option.

Show her.

It was the only option that made sense—and the only one that terrified the marrow from my bones.

Show her.

I dared another step toward her. Lifted a hand to her cheek. She was so goddamn beautiful. Her eyes, alive with green fire. Her chin, set with such pride. Her sweet little smile, filled with such hope.

Her strength, pulling me through the fear.

And down, down, down...to kiss her with the force of my love.

Her mewl harmonized with my groan, just before she wrapped her hands around my neck...and she opened all the way for me.

I plunged harder, pouring myself into her, silently begging her to feel the sorrow of my contrition...the depth of how she completed me. When I urged her body against mine, fitting the centers of our bodies tighter, the pulse of her desire came alive...and ignited mine. A tremor claimed every inch of her...

and then me too. I never wanted to rip myself away from her—ever. Even the spare inch I allowed, necessary for us to catch our breaths, now seemed like the goddamn Grand Canyon.

"Sugar." I claimed her upper lip with the rasp. "Princess." The lower. "Margaux. Margaux. I've been such an ass."

Her laugh washed over my mouth. She bit both my lips before whispering, "I know."

"And I'm not sure how to do this."

"I know."

"And I'm so fucking scared."

She brushed the barest kiss across my lips. Pulled my head down so she could continue up my nose and over both my eyebrows. "I know that too."

I rolled my head, unashamed about pleading for more of her kisses. At the same time, I yanked the tie out of her hair to let the thick golden waves fall over my hands. Some of it was damp now as the rain fell heavier. The pungent clarity of it on the streets below swirled with the lavender of her shampoo, walloping me with homesickness, though our living room was only a few feet away.

Ours?

On a surge of determination, I pulled so our foreheads aligned. "I swear I won't live in fear any longer. I swear, Margaux, with every thought I have and breath I take, I'll live every day for us."

She lifted her face and kissed me again. It was long and deep and rain-drenched, ending when she pulled back to stare at me. Adoration and joy flooded her face, in a look I hadn't seen on her face in—

Ever.

"I swear the same. All of it, Michael, with all of my heart

and every ounce of my love."

My senses burst like the sky over our heads. As a fat raindrop plopped to her cheek, I swiped it away with my thumb...only the water wasn't completely chilled. Warmth came away on my finger too. I leaned in, fervently nipping at her skin, treasuring every drop of her sweet, joyous tears.

"I love you, Margaux Corina."

"I love you, Michael Adam."

As we locked that up with a passionate dance of tongues and exchange of moans, Mother Nature decided to unzip the sky. Within seconds, we were as drenched as if we'd taken a dip in the patio fountain.

We laughed together, turning up our faces into the rain... accepting heaven's sanction on this new voyage of our love. Oh, the little boat with all the baggage was still there, but now it floated on the waves instead of floundering.

Margaux finally stepped back toward the door. "Come on, Captain America. You're drenched."

"And you're not?"

She flashed a coy smile. "You like it when I'm drenched."

I returned her tug with one of my own. As long as I was moving past the fear...

"There's actually one more thing I want to discuss." Another yank brought her to stand completely in front of me. I caught her other hand and held on tight—as I dropped to one knee on the drenched patio deck. "For the record, I requested a sunset, a coconut breeze, and a couple dozen doves for this."

Margaux tossed her head back on a full laugh. When she gazed back down at me, the sunburst of her smile sucked out my breath. "This is perfect," she whispered. "And you are my magic."

CHAPTER EIGHTEEN

Margaux

"Cards Against what?" I'd never heard of this game, but Claire smiled like a Cheshire cat as she pulled a couple of long boxes from her gigantic purse, clunking them onto the coffee table in front of Talia's big leather couch. There were a bunch of us here from SGC, invited over by the cute little brunette for a girls' night we'd all needed for a while.

"Cards Against Humanity," Claire replied.

I scowled. "Sounds like an emo rock band."

Taylor from the sales team giggled as she sat down on a floor pillow. Taylor had been my go-to girl for mindless partying during some of the rockier days with Michael. We'd woken up on my couch together a few times after nights I could barely remember. Thank God she was a woman who knew how to tell reporters no.

"It's a total blast," she chimed in.

"Hmmm." I watched Claire shuffle a thick deck of cards. "What do I win?"

Taylor mock-glared. "How do you know you're going to win?"

"Pssshhh. Losing isn't in my DNA. Deal me some cards, tell me how to play, and then prepare to lose."

"Ooooo, what's all this?" Claire made little claps as

Talia lowered a round tray filled with tequila shots. The tray also supported salt shakers and a colorfully painted clay dish holding lime wedges.

"These are shots, brain surgeon. Have you really been off the bar scene that long?" My sister was so easy to tease I couldn't pass up the chance.

"Rhetorical question, *princessa*," she shot back, handing me a small glass while keeping one for herself.

"What are we toasting to?" I tossed salt on the back of my fist.

"How about Talia's new promotion?" Claire suggested.

"How about Talia's new bosses?"

We all cooed in approval at Taylor's upgrading of the toast by a certain pair of hot, sexy water polo players—who happened to be Killian's fellow SGC board members and special consultants to Talia's newest marketing assignment, the worldwide marketing rollout for Stone Global's cosmetics lines. Fletcher Ford and Drake Newland were a hot-blooded sandwich a lot of women dreamed of filling.

"Mmmm. Better." I purred the agreement while licking the salt off my hand.

"Aaahhh!" Talia laughed—sort of—while reentering the room with a bowl of fresh pita bread and hummus. "Both of you stop, before you even get started."

"Oh, don't turn shy on us already, girl." I tilted my head and threw a stare conveying how serious I was about the advice. "And especially not with them. The sweet and demure thing is like shark chum to Fletch and Drake."

"Huh?" Talia blinked, genuinely confused. Damn it if the innocence didn't make her Eastern European beauty that much more appealing.

"Oh, Lord." I shook my head before sucking into a lime and then tossing back a shot. "Help her. No, really. Divine help. She needs it now." Truly, the girl was dusted.

"Margaux." Claire Bear leaned in to the rescue.

"What?"

"Stop."

"Seriously?" I swung a glare at her, blinking to correct the double image back into one. Whoa. What the hell? Tequila and I were normally better amigos than this. "You know I'm right," I went on anyway. "Those two can smell fear. They feed on it. It's like a special perfume they're attracted to. Really attracted."

Conviction fortified my tone. I'd seen Fletch and Drake in action before I started dating Michael—and at one time, had considered that game for myself—not that I would air that laundry to this crowd. If that pair were eyeing Talia that way, I was worried. Those two sex machines would eat a girl like Talia for breakfast and then move on to a new conquest by lunch.

"Why do you know so much about those guys anyway?" Taylor chimed in.

"Oh, God." Claire dropped her head to her hands. "Please don't tell me you slept with them."

"Slept with—" Talia, again with the cluelessness. "Them?"

"Yes, them." I cocked my head sharply. "Are you the last human being on the planet?"

"What's that supposed to mean?" Apparently, defensive followed clueless—deserved, I supposed, after my tough-love segue, which was a tiny nibble compared to how Fletch and Drake would sink their teeth into her. Literal translation intended.

"Damn," I muttered. "I just thought everyone knew about

those sexy bastards."

Talia looked five shades of butt hurt. "Apparently not."

"They are best friends."

"So?" Taylor jumped in, diffusing the air of confrontation surrounding my exchange with Talia.

Okay... How to be as obvious as possible without being crass? "They share...everything," I finally stated.

"So?" Talia countered. "Most friends do."

Hell. Had she really been raised in a barn somewhere? "No." I dipped my head in emphasis. "Ev-er-y-thing."

"Ohhhhh!" Taylor sing-songed.

"Oh." Talia went white.

"I think the light's finally coming on," Claire inserted.

Taylor giggled but interrupted herself by whipping a stare at Talia. "Oh shit, girl! Aren't you going to Vegas with them for the cosmetics launch?"

"Y-Yes."

"Now don't sound like you're headed for the stockade." Claire, being her highly perceptive self, patted Talia's leg in comfort. "I'm sure they'll keep it professional, hon...if that's what you want."

"Is that what you want?" I, on the other hand, didn't have to worry about the perceptive thing.

Talia moaned. "God. That's the problem! I don't know what I want!" She exploded to her feet and started pacing. "I know exactly what I want regarding my career, but when those two are near me..." She stopped, exhaling hard. "Shit. They're so...overwhelming...and they're not even trying!" We all giggled, but she downed another shot without hesitation. "I'll be toast if they turn it on, I can tell. But really...I don't think they have any interest in me like that though, so it shouldn't be an issue."

As she plunked onto the other floor pillow, she waved her hand as if batting away a pesky fly.

I traded a fast glance with Claire, bugging my gaze in a wordless command. Say something. Damn, damn, damn. The poor girl had no idea what she was up against.

Claire swiveled and grabbed Talia's knee. "Ohhhhh, sweet, sweet one. How long have you been single?"

Talia frowned. "Little over a year. Why?"

"And you're still letting that asshole do a number on you?"

Silence handcuffed the room for a moment. Everyone had suspected Gavin, Talia's ex, of being physically abusive with her, but she'd never offered any details. Her ashen face filled in those blanks.

"Wh-Why? What do you mean?"

Claire psshhed. "Any living, breathing person who gets within fifty feet of the three of you can see what's going on. You're the only one late to the party, girl."

Talia's brown eyes widened. "Really?"

"Really." We all answered her in a chorus—before bursting into giggles.

Fuck, yes. I instantly felt ten pounds lighter. It was so great to be with these women. So much had happened in the last few months, I'd forgotten how good a simple girls' night could be—freedom to just have fun without heavy emotions or dangerous situations over the horizon. I was grateful to be happy and content in the company of my girls.

All that—and tequila.

We toasted Talia's new job and found two more excuses for shots—Claire's new Prada bag and the newly single status of our favorite Armani underwear model, I think—before taking a break from the Patrón for a while, thank God.

Wow. I was so off my game. My stomach had protested the first shot before it hit my bloodstream. With the second, I intentionally spilled a bunch down my chin in order not to drink it all. On the third and hopefully last, I simply left a good portion in the shot glass. Hell. Either I was coming down with a stomach bug or my shooter days were well behind me. Michael and I only drank here and there, keeping it to an occasional beer or a wine with dinner, completely proven by my poor showing around the old cactus cooler tonight. Consolation? Claire actually looked a shade greener than me.

Talia was really the hostess with the mostest, coming back out with hot dishes for us to snack on. Food usually settled my stomach in no time, so I made myself a little plate. Claire joined me, a perfect partner for hovering over the hummus.

She moaned around a bite. "Shit, this is good."

"Talia makes it herself," I replied. "It's the creamiest hummus I've ever eaten."

"I'll have to get the recipe from her." Claire piled another spoonful onto her plate and grabbed some pita bread.

"Good plan. I'll bet Caroline would love th—" Against my restraint, a little belch broke free. "Oh, God. Sorry. That tequila is not sitting well with me tonight."

"Tell me about it," Claire commiserated. "I'm hoping this will soak it up. I must be fighting something. I haven't been myself for a couple of days."

"Gee, thanks." I narrowed my eyes.

She frowned. "For what?"

"You're the culprit who gave it to me at the office. I felt like yuck today too."

She patted my hand. "Oh, Mare! I hope not. I'd feel awful."

I rolled my eyes. "It happens, okay? Just don't share the

PMS, and we'll be fine."

"I'm working on ending the PMS...at least for nine months."

I smiled and hugged her. "Really?"

She pulled back, keeping our hands entwined. "Let's not jinx it by talking about it. Besides, I want to know how it's going with Caroline."

"It's pretty amazing. But I'm trying to go slow, you know? Hey...that rhymes." We chuckled again. I twisted to bump her shoulder. "Seriously, it's weird. But great. And weird. I have so many questions, but I don't want to scare her off or make her feel bad. But, God, all these things I want answers to, you know? Does that make sense?"

"Perfect sense." Her smile was radiant, sharing in my happiness, until it was washed away by a sudden look of alarm. As the color drained from her face, she murmured, "Sweetie, can you excuse me? I'm going to hit the ladies' room, but I really want to talk about this more." She held a hand against her stomach like she truly might be sick.

"Bear...you okay?"

"Think so," she answered. "Hold that thought, okay?"

"Sure. I'll be right here."

I watched my sister totter off in her ridiculously high heels, slinging a gigantic purse. Some things would never change, no matter what. Claire and her bags and heels would be the top of that list. I loved her more than words and didn't want to even think of life without her. It was amazing. A couple of years ago, I'd never thought of myself as capable of real love. These days, my inner circle of it grew more every day.

Crazy. Now I actually had a mother there too. Caroline and I were getting to know each other more every day but setting an easy pace. We had a lot of time to make up for, and neither of us saw the need to cram it into a few weeks, though it was hard not to go faster. We'd quickly discovered we were a lot alike—although she had the patience of a saint, a gift I'd never really mastered. When I pointed out my shortcomings, she reacted like a real mom, promising to help me work on it.

As for the woman who'd phoned in the part? Interesting shit, indeed. The FBI had contacted me on two separate occasions regarding Andrea, continuing to think she'd reach out to me in a desperate plea for help in one way or another, most likely for money. Her trail had run cold a few weeks ago, somewhere in Barbados, but they maintained she and Trey were still together, taking advantage of people with high-end business scams. It was never anything huge or flashy, just enough to keep them living in luxury before they'd cut and run again. They'd both racked up serious rap sheets. When they were caught, years behind bars were their destiny, no matter how fancy the attorney.

I always tried to be cooperative but repeatedly told the Feds that I wanted nothing to do with that woman. Even if she did contact me, I wouldn't be rearranging my schedule for a heart-to-heart with her.

Other priorities took precedence tonight.

Most immediately, my need to pee.

I rose and found Talia, asking if I could use the restroom off her bedroom. Claire was taking forever in the one off the living room, but I didn't want to be rude and tromp through Talia's private space.

Talia told me where to find the light switch for her master bath. I grabbed my purse and headed that direction, shuffling for my phone on the way to check the time. Man oh man, I didn't feel good. As much as I wanted to stay at the party, I wondered how early was too early for a graceful exit.

On its way into my purse, my hand hit something, sending out a distinct crinkle. The little bag from my drug store purchase this afternoon.

I huffed. Dismissed the idea that my new bout with the flu had anything to do with what the contents of that package were going to tell me. For chrissake, my period was only two days late. Just to prove it, I yanked out the damn box once I'd locked the door. No time like the present, right? Every test maker bragged that a girl could now pee on the stick any time.

The box itself was marked in curly purple birthday cake letters. Why did female product makers think it necessary to evoke frosting-style Barbie at the most awkward moments of a woman's life? The tequila boosted my courage yet again, for which I was oddly—and unnecessarily—grateful. I had nothing to worry about, and now was the time to get this shit out of my mind.

I opened the box to take out the test, only to find it encased inside a smaller box. Inside that was a fucking plastic wrapper. Christ, was this the Fort Knox pregnancy test?

Finally, it was go time.

Literally.

I dropped trou, followed the instructions to the letter, and then balanced the stick on the edge of the vanity. Set my phone timer for five minutes and then kicked back and waited. Annnnd waited. Shit, how long was five minutes?

I checked my email and then peered at the test. One solid line definitely appeared in the window...with the shadow of a second line starting to show beside it. Wait. What? A second line? No. It had to be a trick of the trendy lighting in Talia's bathroom, a shadow from the edge of the test window.

I distracted myself with text messages next. Looked like I had a prescription to pick up at the pharmacy—look who needs more birth control pills, said fate with an evil laugh—and my new favorite author was releasing a book on Tuesday. Other than that, I'd seen everything already.

I looked at the test again.

Shit.

That was definitely not a shadow.

That was a motherfucking second line.

I fell to the closed toilet seat with a thunk. Twisted my pinkie ring hard enough to damn near tear off flesh. No sound fell from my stunned lips. My brain could only summon one word as it was.

Shit.

Shit.

Shit!

This was not part of the plans Michael and I had discussed. Sure, we'd been humping like bunnies—duh—but we'd only started playing with wedding ideas, let alone set a date. Since he'd put the ugliness of Declan aside, we'd been able to settle into a life resembling normalcy.

So much for normal.

I slapped one hand over the other, ordering their shaking to stop. Didn't work so much on my thoughts. A baby. What the hell was I going to do with a baby? How had this happened? And would I ever stop asking myself such dumbass questions?

I was on the pill. Foolproof.

Well, almost.

Sort of.

When you didn't let a thousand and one other things

distract you from taking it on time.

Mother. Fucker.

I threw away the three cubic yards of trash from the test packaging but not the test itself. Hit by weird sentiment or some strange shit like that, I wiped and wrapped the test and then stashed it in my purse.

While washing my hands, I gave myself a once-over in the mirror. I didn't look different. I didn't feel different. I felt completely the same, except for the stomach bug really hitting me hard now.

Oh...damn. It wasn't a stomach bug now, was it?

Son of a bitch.

I walked back out to the living room, fighting for an air of snarky nonchalance—though I doubted anyone was taking notice anymore. Talia and Taylor buzzed around Claire, who'd returned to the sofa with an ear-to-ear grin.

"What's going on over here?"

If it were possible, Claire's smile widened. "How would you feel about being an aunt?" She thrust a pregnancy test, not much different from the one in my purse, into my hand.

I just stared. Probably a little longer that I should've, judging by the giggles and jubilance that faded into tenuous silence. Clearly, the three of them wondered why I was gawking at Claire's stick as if it was a ticking time bomb.

"You okay?" Taylor broke the pause, turning her stare into full-bore scrutiny. "You don't look great, woman."

I directed my response at Claire. "Pretty funny you should ask me this again."

"Why?"

As Claire queried, I unzipped my purse and pulled out the test. "How would you feel about being an aunt?"

Everyone's eyes went nickel-sized, though Claire did the moment one better. Like a little bolt of lightning, she leaped into my arms. "Oh, my God! Are you serious? Were you and Michael planning this too? Are you happy? Oh, tell me you are!"

"Fuck, woman. Stop talking for one second so I can get a word in." I squeezed her a little before backing up. We exchanged tests so we each had our own again. "I—I don't know what I am. And, no, this wasn't planned, so more than anything, I'm a little shocked. Maybe more than a little."

"So you were using...protection?" Talia's face was a hopeful smile of tact.

"Of course," I volleyed. "I've been on the pill, but with everything that's been going on"—a circular wave of a hand indicated my version of everything—"I guess I missed a few here and there." Which had added up to a stunning here and here. "I don't even have to ask how you're feeling," I continued to Claire with a smile, "and let me be the first to say how happy I am for you, sister. You two have wanted this more than anything. Killian's going to be over the moon."

"He is, isn't he?" Tears filled her eyes and spilled down her cheeks. "He really is." She pulled in a deep breath. "I just hope this one...sticks. We didn't wait that long after the—" Pressed a hand over her mouth. "I just can't take another—"

"Hush," I ordered. "Don't even go there. Do not do this to yourself. You know what the doctors said. That all just wasn't meant to be. This is a new beginning—so you be happy and celebrate the life you created. One step at a time. And this time...I guess we're doing it together. Okay?"

"Okay." A huge smile spread across her lips.

"Okay." No smile for me. Crap. My brain scrambled to

process the enormity of it—and couldn't.

"Oh, my God!" Claire popped around in her seat, channeling the vibe of a jumping bean. "I need to tell him. Kil's going to go nuts. But, ohhhh, shit, he's going to be so mad I drank tonight."

"Then don't tell him."

She arched a brow. "Because you're not going to tell Michael?"

I was glad for the chance to glower rather than trying to fake elation. "Neither of us knew. We can't be crazy and blame ourselves for everything. I hear plenty of that comes after the bambinos actually get here. Shit. Did I just say that?"

She laughed a little but preened too—because she was right. With her Claire Stone sixth sense, she saw that guilt had nudged even me. Shit. Had I done any harm by chugging those shots? Logic took over, thank God, telling me women did way worse things before knowing they were pregnant and then carried perfectly healthy babies to term.

Claire rose. "If you girls don't mind, I'm going to head home. I really want to see my husband all of a sudden. I think we have some celebrating to do."

"Gee, you think?" Talia smirked while hurrying to the bedroom for Claire's coat. She had mine in hand too and offered, "Wasn't sure if you'd be staying or not."

We said our goodbyes to Claire—and I coerced a promise from her that she'd text when she got home, even though Alfred was behind the wheel tonight, at Kil's insistence. We also promised to touch base tomorrow and perhaps arrange a double date with the guys. Now that Michael and Killian were practically in business together around the new plans for the spring at Pearson's, we'd been spending more time as a foursome.

"I think I'll head out too," I told Talia. "Just need to text Andre for a pick-up."

"He's right out front, honey," Claire called over her shoulder. "I'll tell him you're on your way."

"Thank you," I returned, adding an exaggerated smooch sound. "And Claire?"

"Yeah?"

"Congratulations, sister mine. I love you."

"Congratulations to you, Mare-Bear. And I love you more."

"I think that's impossible," I mumbled to myself. Seeing her so happy made me completely overjoyed. I wished I could be a fly on the wall when she told Killian the good news. The miscarriage had devastated them both, but they'd clearly given it another go as soon as they could. I sincerely prayed for their new chance. Hopefully, she'd have no complications—and in nine months, we'd both be holding new babies in our arms.

A baby.

My baby.

The thought took my breath away. Ohhhh, fuck. I wasn't ready to be a mother! I barely had my own head on straight!

What would Michael say? I anticipated his tension, maybe even anger. He'd just started to hit a groove at Aequitas and had even mentioned moving into a place somewhere together closer to the ocean, after the wedding.

The wedding. Oh, God.

Would he want that bullshit with me at all now? Being a father would be such a burden already, if he even embraced it. He was so great with kids—I'd seen that much at Kil and Claire's wedding. He'd also been forced to grow up fast and be the man of the family after his dad's death. What if he didn't want all this? Could I go through with an abortion?

My stomach lurched, answering that quickly enough. I couldn't bring myself to do that. The new life inside me had already caused huge changes. Of course, it was a living thing. I'd just have to raise it on my own.

"Hey." Talia held out my jacket while I slipped my arms in. "Are you okay?"

"Yeah." I blurted it so fast, my lie was instantly exposed. "I will be okay," I amended. "Just a little freaked-out. Michael and I weren't planning this like Kil and Claire, so it's different."

Talia yanked me into a hug. "He's going to be thrilled. You'll see."

"You think so?"

"I know so. He adores you, Margaux. The way he looks at you whenever you walk into a room?" Her eyes rolled back, communicating a swoon. "It's all I can hope for when I finally find someone."

I lifted a knowing smile. "Or two someones?"

She ignored the bait. "You're a very lucky woman. Michael will be so happy. Trust me. I know about these things."

She knew about these things?

As she gave me one more hug before seeing me off, I resisted the urge to point out that her knowledge about Fletch and Drake was still a chasm I worried about. Maybe I'd have to sit down and chat with those guys before the three of them left for Vegas.

Not a concern for now.

I shivered on the way to the car. The nighttime temperature had dropped considerably, so I was thankful Andre waited nearly right outside the doorstep, with the car already running.

"Damn, it's gotten cold tonight." I hustled into the 750i. Andre had also turned on the seat heaters, so it was nice and toasty once he shut the door.

"You called it quits early," he remarked as he climbed in. "The girls' night out isn't what it used to be?"

"We...had an unexpected turn of events."

"I see."

The curiosity in his tone was glaring, and I really wanted to tell him the news, but not before Michael. We'd let Andre in on the excitement when deciding, together, that it was time. Some people waited until they were further along to announce, and maybe that would be our plan.

God, another decision. There seemed so many now. I let out a heavy sigh and dropped my head back against the seat.

Once home, I went straight up to our room, where I heard Michael watching TV.

"Hey," he greeted, muting the volume and then sitting up. Despite the continued churn in my belly, I could appreciate the delicious sight of him, shirtless and chiseled in a pair of low-slung navy sweat pants. I was a damn lucky girl.

I desperately hoped he felt the same way in a few minutes.

"Hey." I averted my eyes, dropping my purse—imagining a diaper bag plopping down next to it.

Oh, my fucking God.

"How was girls' night? You're home much earlier than I expected." I felt the intensity of his scrutiny. "Everything okay?"

"Yeah, yeah. Everything is great. I'm—I'm just not feeling well." I hurried into the closet to change into pajamas. "Actually, Claire and I have the same thing."

"Well, you work in the same office. Maybe it's in the

water."

"Ha-ha."

I overlaid it with grim weariness. Contrary to that ridiculous old wives' tale, this definitely hadn't come from drinking the SGC water.

CHAPTER NINETEEN

Michael

Ha-ha?

Never, in the nearly two years I'd known the woman, had she let anyone out of a smartass comment with something like ha-ha.

I sat up straighter, punching the remote to turn off the football stats show. For a long second, just listened to her rustling in the closet. Her movements were slow, almost hesitant. "You sure everything's fine? Did you and Claire have a tiff or something?"

She giggled. It sounded maniacal. "No."

"Can I get you something? Ibuprofen? Some crackers?"

"No." Softer this time. And weirder.

"Is it just your time of the month?"

The crazed giggle again. "Ha! No."

Well, that did it. I swung off the bed, tossed aside the remote, and marched to her closet—

Where I froze in the doorway.

She wasn't standing in front of her drawers, as I'd expected. I found her crumpled on the floor in her panties and a T-shirt that read *Wake the Princess at Your Own Peril.* Her hands were balled against her thighs, her sleep shorts twisted between them. Tension dragged visibly on her shoulders and defined her spine. With her back to me, I couldn't see her face—nor was sure I wanted to, if the apprehension in my gut was an accurate predictor.

This really wasn't a typical girls' snit. Not PMS either. And sure as hell more than a little bug she'd picked up at work.

A thousand what-ifs rained on me like locusts. What was I missing? Or was this yet another squall threatening to capsize our boat again, something I couldn't figure out yet?

"Margaux."

She jerked and gasped as if I'd materialized from thin air. "Damn it," she snapped. "What?" But in doing so, gave me a fast enough glimpse of her face to spur me to motion.

"Margaux." I fell to my own knees in front of her. "Sweetheart." I pushed thumbs against her jaw, lifting her anguished face, running fingers over its distraught creases. "What is it?"

"I—" She twisted her face to the side, eyes jamming closed. "I don't know how to—"

"How to what?" I spread my fingers, framing her face urgently. "Christ, baby. You're scaring me. Did I do something?"

She spurted out a laugh, once more pitched with hysteria. "Did you do something? Hmmm. That's a fun way of saying it."

"What? Tell me so I can undo it."

She snickered—another crazy burst after this, and I'd just chalk up everything tonight to tequila shots that had gone too far—and shook her head. "Nope. Sorry. No Undo key on this one, buddy."

I dropped my hands. "Okay. Not going to guess at this one anymore. I give up."

"Might be the best idea, stud—because you knocked me up."

Not too much tequila.

The absurdity of the thought, along with the wallop of her words, knocked me onto my ass. Another giggle spilled from her, but this time I didn't mind. Not one damn bit. On the other hand, there could've been nails under my ass that I didn't mind either. I couldn't feel a fucking thing beyond the roaring in my ears, the tumult in my blood—

The jubilation in my soul.

I lifted my stare back to her, speechless with wonder, wild with joy. As thoroughly as she'd awakened my heart when walking into the room, she was a goddamn defibrillator on me now.

"Are...you sure?"

She peered at me from beneath her lashes. "Are you happy?"

"You're not answering my question."

"You're not answering mine." She tangled her shorts tighter. "Are you happy, Michael? Damn it, it wasn't like I did this on purpose, okay? Accidents happen, and—"

I silenced her by surging forward, smashing my mouth over hers, and holding as much of my sudden anger back from it as I could. "That phrase isn't to be spoken again," I ordered, "until our little girl spills her milk for the first time."

A tentative smirk teased her lips. "Little girl? You sure about that, stud?"

I meshed our lips together, softer on her now, working the tip of my tongue between the warm cushions of her lips. "A little girl," I whispered, "with huge green eyes, bright-blond braids, and an imp's smile of mischief."

She twined fingers into my hair. "And her daddy wrapped around her finger?"

"Surely." I grinned. "Because she'll know she wasn't an accident." I pressed her back until we were sprawled on the floor, there between her highest heels and her glitziest gowns, the sparkles of the princess I'd fallen inexorably, irreversibly in love with...to depths I could never even imagine until now. "She'll know she was brought into the world because her daddy couldn't get enough of her mommy...and that he never will."

She sighed, curling a leg higher on my waist as I dipped a hand lower...beneath her sexy little panties. Her pussy was an oven, welcoming my fingers with dripping tightness, sparking my desire to the same level as my adoration.

"Just like she'll never get enough of him. Ohhh!" She let out the little squeal as I impatiently twisted the scrap of lace, finally tearing it away. Able to touch her without barriers, I groaned from the ecstasy of thrusting another finger into her wet passage.

I needed to claim her. Tonight more than any other.

"I love you so much, princess." I nipped and licked into the curve of her neck, along the gorgeous line of her jaw. "Will you let me show you how much? With every inch of my body?"

With her head thrown back, her reply was the most arousing rasp I'd ever heard. "Yes. Oh, yes."

She hooked a toe into the back of my sweats and yanked down hard. Goddamn, I loved her toes. And her fingers. And her lips. And her—

No more list-making. No more thoughts at all, swept away in the two seconds my cock kissed the air before sliding up into her wet, tight heat.

We rolled into a rhythm that let us gaze and kiss, smile and adore, connect and complete as our orgasms built like embers into fire.

It was perfect.

It was also kind of crazy.

An hour ago, I was a guy relaxing after work with the sports shows. Now, life was completely different in the most amazing ways, like the universe had waved a magic wand while I wasn't looking.

And wasn't that the key to magic?

It wasn't moments orchestrated into being. It was the surprise that came from surrendering, believing...

Loving.

And God, did I love this woman. The forgiveness she'd given my soul. The completion she'd given my life. The future I beheld in her eyes. The child she carried in her womb.

The heart she held in her hands.

Yeah. Magic.

The...Beginning

Continue Secrets of Stone with Book Five

No Lucky Number

Available Now
Keep reading for an excerpt!

NO LUCKY NUMBER

BOOK FIVE IN THE
SECRETS OF STONE SERIES

CHAPTER ONE

My rolling luggage beat a steady *click-click-click* on the pavement breaks as I walked up to the VIP security checkpoint at the terminal of San Diego's Lindbergh Field. I knew this trip would be a turning point in my career, but a funny feeling nagged at the back of my mind, predicting it would be more than just that.

I'd been feeling stagnant for a while, wanting so desperately to move forward though continuing to be anchored in the same place. This trip, while only a few days, was the change I needed. Our cosmetics line at Stone Global Corp. was finally ready to take flight. Consequently, so were we—to launch the new line and all its products at Cosmetics Con, the internationally attended trade show that took place each year in the City of Sin. What better place to get out of a funk than nonstop Las Vegas?

The team, consisting of Drake Newland, Fletcher Ford, and me, was taking SGC's corporate jet from San Diego to Las Vegas. A thirty-five-minute flight would put us right in the middle of the bright lights of the neon Strip in the Mohave Desert. I'd been to Vegas a few times before with my family— Auntie Maisie's fondness for dollar slots was the stuff of in-jokes for us all—but I had a feeling this trip would be very different from hanging out with my parents, siblings, three uncles, three aunts, five cousins, and a baker's dozen of nieces and nephews.

That premonition didn't have a thing to do with my travel mates.

Okay, maybe a *little* something.

Drake Newland.

Fletcher Ford.

Oh, God.

It was all Claire's and Margaux's fault. They were the ones responsible for the anxiety practically eating me alive. We'd had a girls' night last week at my place, and once they learned I was taking this trip with Drake and Fletcher, the taunting advice and playful jabs had begun in full. They'd teased me with all the love in their hearts, but I still couldn't erase their words from my frontal lobe.

Those two can smell a girl like you coming a mile away. That was the only G-rated dig I could recall. By the end of the night and after a good amount of Patrón, I had been getting advice on what lingerie to pack—and *not* to pack. I was certain my usually olive-colored skin had gone three shades of rose after that one, but Claire and Margaux were good at doing that to me on a regular basis. I hadn't been sure if they had been truly serious or just trying to see how crimson they'd been able to make me.

"Good morning, Miss Perizkova. You look lovely today."

I glanced up at the uniformed steward who appeared just

as I cleared security, not quite sure how to react.

"Stop flirting with my girl, Martinez."

As the man chuckled, heat crept across my cheeks. Fletcher Ford appeared by my side, swiping my rolling bag before it left the TSA belt. The SGC board member, innovator, and creative taskmaster—not to mention dead-on Justin Timberlake lookalike—who'd helped start up this new wing of the company fell into step with me while we headed toward our flight.

"Mr. Ford." I tried to give his physique, perfectly fitted in Armani today, as discreet a once-over as I could. "Good day."

"Well, it's a good day *now*," he murmured in return.

Time for a new subject. Pronto.

"I can handle my own bag, thank you."

I snatched at my roller.

He moved the luggage just out of my reach. "Darling, I'm sure you can handle a lot of things for yourself, but would it kill you to allow me to be a gentleman now and then? Come on. Let all of my mama's hard work do some good." He laid on the killer smile that had earned him the devil's own reputation.

My resistance turned to dust. "Where's Drake? Err, I mean Mr. Newland?"

And I'd asked that...why? The two men made me almost speechless when I was with them one-on-one. When they were together, which was damn near all the time these days, I became a bumbling fool. I should've been grateful for the reprieve.

Fletcher smiled again—though this time a bit of sadness seemed to flicker in his blue eyes. "What's wrong? You don't like *just* me?"

"That's not what I meant at all." Now I felt like an idiot.

"Really, I didn't—"

He put me out of my rambling misery with a steady hand on my forearm. "Easy, Tolly. I was just yanking your pretty chain."

"Why do you call me that?"

"What? Tolly? It's your name, isn't it? Talia?" He said my full name more dramatically—before adding that damn grin again.

Thankfully, we were nearing the plane and I could get away from the uneasiness of having to worry about witty chit-chat. While we were interacting professionally, I could hold my own, but this personal stuff was so far out of my league. I was never really good at it with normal guys, let alone a smooth, gorgeous god like him.

He opened the door to the tarmac, and the San Diego sunshine instantly warmed me. A grin spread across my lips. We were having one of the mildest winters I could remember, and it was wonderful. I really loved living in Southern California.

"Of course," I finally answered him. "I've just never been called anything but Talia."

"Maybe it's time for things to change then, hmmm?" He nodded toward Stone Global's private jet, sleek and white, waiting across the pavement. "And there's the *other* subject of your wonderment—already getting on board the plane, I see."

I followed his line of vision to the top of the jet's entry stairs, where Drake Newland was ducking his tall frame to fit into the doorway. His short hair was spiked in its usual perfect fashion, his tight, muscular body molded into his custom-fit, button-down dress shirt.

Not that I noticed the fit of his clothes.

Okay, I noticed. But it was hard not to—with either of

these men. They were tall, handsome, and very well-defined. I'd been working with them on the development of the cosmetics line at SGC for many long months, over many long hours. I would have had to have been dead not to notice their jaw-dropping physical appeal.

And their flirtatiousness.

Oh, yeah. That.

As in, *flirtatiousness. All the time.*

In the beginning, I'd told myself they simply behaved that way around all females, until Claire and Margaux insisted that wasn't the case. It hadn't been long before Taylor Matthews, my girlfriend from the sales department, had added her own agreement to that theory. After that, I'd begun to watch Drake and Fletcher a little more closely. For research purposes only, of course.

And what had that research told me?

At the moment, the only female I could pinpoint their pulling out all the blatant charm and urbane behavior around for...was me.

So what did I want to do with that recognition?

I had no idea.

The truth of it thrilled me.

But really, it terrified me.

This story continues in
No Lucky Number: *Secrets of Stone Book Five!*

ALSO BY ANGEL PAYNE

Secrets of Stone Series:
No Prince Charming
No More Masquerade
No Perfect Princess
No Magic Moment
No Lucky Number
No Simple Sacrifice
No Broken Bond
No White Knight

Honor Bound:
Saved
Cuffed
Seduced
Wild
Wet
Hot
Masked
Mastered
Conquered (Coming Soon)
Ruled (Coming Soon)

The Bolt Saga:
Bolt (Summer 2018)
Ignite (Summer 2018)
Pulse (Summer 2018)
Fuse
Surge
Light

**For a full list of Angel's other titles,
visit her at angelpayne.com**

ABOUT ANGEL PAYNE

USA Today bestselling romance author Angel Payne loves to focus on high-heat romance starring memorable alpha men and the women who love them. She has numerous book series to her credit, including the Suited for Sin series, the Cimarron Saga, the Temptation Court series, the Secrets of Stone series, the Lords of Sin historicals, and the popular Honor Bound series, as well as several standalone titles.

Angel is a native Southern Californian, leading to her love of being in the outdoors, where she often reads and writes. She still lives in Southern California with her soul-mate husband and beautiful daughter, to whom she is a proud cosplay/culture con mom. Her passions also include whisky tasting, shoe shopping, and travel.

Visit her here:
angelpayne.com

ABOUT VICTORIA BLUE

International bestselling author Victoria Blue lives in her own portion of the galaxy known as Southern California. There, she finds the love and life–sustaining power of one amazing sun, two unique and awe-inspiring planets, and four indifferent yet comforting moons. Life is fantastic and challenging and every day brings new adventures to be discovered. She looks forward to seeing what's next!

Visit her here:
victoriablue.com